THE HEAT OF PASSION

"You ought to head back East," Lucas declared, steeling himself against the agonizing thought of never seeing her again. "You're a woman trying to do a man's job, and you're a woman alone in a country where no female is safe without a man."

"I can see you're just another one of those men who think females are good for nothing but cooking, cleaning, and having babies," Carrie said furiously. "I suppose it's a waste of your precious time to even talk to a female, especially one from back East."

"Ma'am, I never said time spent with you was wasted." There was a light in his eyes that sent a thrill through her whole body; it seemed to be equally divided between pleasure and apprehension.

Without warning, Lucas took her by the arms and kissed her soundly on the lips. Then, thinking better of it, he took her in his arms and kissed her in a way Carrie didn't know a woman *could* be kissed.

There was nothing gentlemanlike about this kiss; it was rough, demanding, and completely devastating, and his hard, muscled body pressed against the length of her merely added fuel to a fire that blazed out of control before Carrie even knew what had started it....

Leigh Greenwood

Colorado Bride

LOVE SPELL NEW YORK CITY

LOVE SPELL®

June 2006

Published by

Dorchester Publishing Co., Inc.
200 Madison Avenue
New York, NY 10016

ISBN 0-505-52655-7

The name "Love Spell" and its logo are trademarks of Dorchester Publishing Co., Inc.

Printed in the United States of America.

Visit us on the web at www.dorchesterpub.com.

Chapter 1

Green Run Pass, Colorado, 1868

Carrie Simpson took several slow breaths, forcing herself to inhale deeply to steady her nerves. It was absolutely essential that no one see the doubt at the back of her eyes or suspect the churning fear that had turned her insides to mush. Her whole future hung on what would happen in the next few minutes, and she was determined that neither her uncertainty nor female frailty would rob her of this chance to create a new life for herself. So closing her eyes long enough to direct a brief prayer to heaven, Carrie gathered up her skirts, took a firm grip on the door to steady herself, and stepped down out of the stagecoach into the full glare of the Colorado sun.

The brilliance of the midday sun blinded Carrie to her surroundings, and she was relieved that for a few extra moments she could postpone the announcement that she had come to dismiss the present manager and take over the running of the Green Run Pass Stagecoach Station herself. This was going to be her home. She had come to stay.

A coarse, booming voice bellowed a welcome from the station house, and Carrie looked up to see a monster of a man roll out of the door and down the steps, his bulging bloodshot eyes savoring the picture of feminine loveliness she presented. Her courage nearly deserted her on the spot. Baca Riggins was a bear of a man, standing over six feet four and weighing close to four hundred pounds, much of it fat, and he looked as though he hadn't changed his clothes or taken a bath in weeks.

It had been difficult enough to leave her family home in Virginia and travel to St. Louis by herself without having to face Baca Riggins alone. She was terrified. And the memory of what the passengers had said of the man's character during the last miserable leg of the journey did nothing to bolster her courage. Her first impulse was to turn around and go back to St. Louis, but she had to stay; she had nowhere else to go.

"Grub's on the table," Baca informed the disembarking passengers with a morose growl. "Help yourself."

"Last time I tried to choke down some of the stuff you serve up, I had a bellyache for a week," complained Bap Turner from his seat in the driver's box.

"Nobody's forcing you to eat," growled Baca, indifferent as to whether anybody ate or not; his eyes were on Carrie.

"You might have a care for the passengers," Bap continued, feeling braver in the driver's box than he would have on the ground. "They didn't know they had to eat enough for two meals at breakfast."

"Then you should have told them. I'm shorthanded today so you're going to have to fetch out your own team. You'd better hustle if you want to keep to your schedule."

"What's wrong with Buck doing it, or you? It's what you're paid for."

"Buck's laid up with a cold, and I've got to see to this here little lady. Do it yourself or drive them horses another sixty miles. It makes no difference to me. Course you could ask Lucas to give you a hand," he said over his shoulder as he turned his attention to Carrie. "He ain't never doing nothing half the time."

Involuntarily Carrie's eyes turned in the direction Baca had indicated and she saw a man seated under a tree, his chair leaned back against the trunk, his feet hooked into the bottom rung, and his hat pulled down over his eyes. He seemed to be dozing and completely unaware of their

6

presence.

"Looks like I'd have to wake him up first," Bap said as he dismounted from the box with a string of pungent curses. "One of these days, somebody's going to throw you out on your ass, Baca, and it won't be none too soon for me." Baca turned a threatening gaze on the little man.

"You aiming to try?" he asked, bringing his bulk close enough to Bap to emphasize the difference in their size.

"I just drive this dangblasted stage, but Duncan Bickett ain't the kind of man to put up with you running one of his stations like this for long. This place looks worse than a squatter's shanty." Carrie guessed the buildings had been painted at one time, but the whitewash had pealed off by now; the yard was unkept and the windows were thick with dust. She shuddered to think what the inside must look like.

"I like it here," Baca said, unmoved by Bap's censure. "And when I like a place, I stay."

Carrie listened to this exchange with a sinking heart. Her first look at the sullen, bad-tempered station manager had warned her he wouldn't take his dismissal meekly. Now she suspected he'd fight, and she had to face him without Robert at her side. She had to do it all by herself. Carrie cleared her throat.

"Excuse me," she said, speaking as calmly as she could. "Are you Mr. Riggins?" Baca turned around slowly, like a big grizzly, cautious but secure in the knowledge that he was too powerful for anyone to be a danger to him; the frown lifted from his unshaven face.

"Yeah. You better hurry inside if you expect to get anything to eat, little woman," he said, coming as close as he ever did to smiling. "No matter what Bap here says, folks'll eat up every scrap of that food."

"That's because there's never enough for more than two or three people," Bap said irritably as he started to lead away the team he had just unhitched.

"You want to change that team, or are you going to bicker all afternoon?" Carrie turned in surprise at the sound of a wonderfully resonant bass voice. The man they had called

7

Lucas was no longer under the tree. He had brought up a fresh team, and now he was just standing there, negligently resting his weight on one hip, waiting. One look at this impassive stranger, and all of Carrie's carefully rehearsed words went straight out of her head.

Though Lucas lacked less than two inches of being as tall as Baca, at one hundred and ninety-five pounds he should have looked almost puny next to a behemoth like Baca, but it was immediately apparent there was nothing insignificant about this man. His worn Levi's clung tightly to well-muscled legs and thighs, his belt was cinched in tight over a flat stomach, but his shirt, open at the throat to expose a thin cover of brown hair on his chest, hung loose, giving his broad, heavily muscled shoulders room to move freely. His battered hat was still pulled down over most of his face, but Carrie could see a firm jaw and thin lips in a tanned face. He gave the impression of quiet, almost insolent power, an impression that was heightened by the lazy impudence of his voice.

There was something about his presence that Carrie found reassuring. It didn't matter that she had never seen him before or that he could have been one of the outlaws her father had warned her about when she told him of her decision to go west. She felt less alone than she had at any time since leaving St. Louis, and from what she had seen of Baca Riggins, the presence of any stranger who was not actively hostile was a blessing not to be spurned needlessly.

"I'm coming," Bap said, disgust apparent in his voice. "I don't have time to talk anyway. What little food Baca does set out is greasy and tasteless, and the passengers will be back out in five minutes, hungry and anxious as hell to get to the next station." He handed the reins of the used-up team to Lucas and started to back the new team into position.

Even though she couldn't see his eyes, Carrie had the eerie feeling this strange man was watching her, and that unnerved her. She didn't know why she should notice him any more than the dozens of other strange men she had encountered in the last week. At least he wasn't openly staring at her, and

8

nearly everybody else had. She was petite, barely over five feet, and the rigors of the trip had reduced her to a wraith, but Carrie Simpson was a beautiful woman, and her appearance had caused a sensation at every stop since leaving St. Louis.

Carrie's wardrobe was exceptional by Western standards. Even though her family had suffered financially in the recent war, and in spite of the privations of the trip, which had been far greater than she expected, she had continued to dress with all the care and richness she had at home. Her dress, which rustled pleasantly when she moved, was made of a stiff green plaid taffeta with a billowed-out skirt supported by the crinoline she wore underneath. Her naturally slim waist was encased in a corset which lifted her bosom and thrust it forward in a most provocative manner. Her rich, chestnut brown hair was parted in the middle, gathered into a chignon, and held in place by several ivory combs. Her bonnet was decorated with flowers and bows inside the brim and tied under her chin with a wide green ribbon. Because of the dimensions of her skirts, she had been allowed the entire side of the stagecoach for most of her journey while the male passengers squeezed into the seat opposite her, their discomfort allayed by the pleasure of looking at her.

She was the kind of woman that usually caused men to scramble to their feet, to open doors for her, to help her down from carriages, to give her most anything she wanted, but this Lucas person didn't act like she was anything out of the ordinary, and that piqued her vanity. She didn't want Baca to admire her, and she was relieved when his spat with Rap caused him to turn his leering gaze away from her, but even though she ordinarily condemned staring as unpardonably rude, she was irritated that this Lucas person hadn't even looked at her. He probably couldn't tell her from any other female in the world.

Carrie struggled to get her mind back on Baca Riggins. She was going to have to stop letting her thoughts wander or she'd never fire this man. And she had to do it now! Every minute she waited just made it harder. It also showed her up for a coward, and Carrie had never been able to abide cowardice in anyone, particularly herself. Things that had to be faced should be faced promptly and squarely. It was easier and quicker that way.

"Mr. Riggins," Carrie began, desperate to get the words out before her courage failed, "I'm Carrie Simpson, Mrs. Robert Simpson, and I have a letter from the Overland Stage Company authorizing me to assume the running of this station in my husband's name."

The three men stopped in their tracks, all three gazes riveted on Carrie. Suddenly, here in the dust and the squalor and the heat, she felt that none of her finery mattered, that she looked ridiculous, a figure of fun. She had no way of knowing that at least two of the men disagreed with her. Her rich clothes and creamy white skin might have seemed out of place on this rough stage road through the wilds of Colorado, but her golden-brown eyes and vibrant beauty would have been welcome anywhere.

Looking into the angry, red eyes of Baca Riggins, Carrie knew her appearance would have no softening effect on him; he wasn't going to quietly accept his dismissal and go away.

"I must not have heard you right," Baca growled, his voice alive with menace.

"I said I have come to take over the station in my husband's name," Carrie repeated. "We should have arrived earlier, but Mr. Simpson was laid up with a serious illness and then had to wait for some equipment, so I decided to come ahead. I have a letter from the company headquarters in Denver. Actually you were dismissed as of three days ago." Even though Baca's face was black as thunder, Carrie felt much better now that the news was out.

"Let me see that letter," demanded Bap. He didn't even take the time to hand the reins to Lucas, just dropped them in the dust. He scanned the letter quickly and then let out a whoop. "It's about time. I said you'd get fired, you mangy cuss. Now maybe we can get something decent to eat around here."

"Nobody's going to fire me," Baca roared. "Not Duncan or

anybody else."

"But you've already been fired, Mr. Riggins, and you've been replaced by my husband."

"I don't see no husband," Baca said, his expression more threatening than ever.

"Nevertheless, I have one, and he will be here within a day or two. Please be so kind as to gather up all your personal belongings immediately. If you have nowhere to stay tonight, you may sleep over at the station, but I would prefer that you be gone by tomorrow."

"I ain't leaving tomorrow or any other day."

"But you must. I have a letter—"

"No letter can throw me off this place, and a little bitty thing like you can't do it neither."

"You might as well go now, Baca," Bap advised, making no attempt to conceal his happiness over the news. "You heard her say her husband would be here in a day or two. You'll have to go then for sure. Wait till the rest of the boys hear this. They've been begging Duncan to get rid of you ever since you took over as a temporary."

"I ain't temporary, and I ain't leaving. Not for no Mr. Simpson, and not for his woman." Carrie could almost feel a tangible threat in Baca's gaze.

"You got no choice," Bap said. "That letter gives her husband your job."

"I don't believe it." Baca tore the letter from Carrie's grasp. It took him a little while to puzzle his way through all the words, but by the time he had finished, he no longer doubted he was out of a job, and blind rage shook his huge frame. With a roar that was more animal than human, he tore the letter into fragments and trampled them into the dust of the yard. The passengers, having eaten what food Baca had provided, were attracted by the commotion and began leaving the station.

"Now you ain't got no letter saying nothing, lady," Baca said, the threat of violence in his voice, "so you get on that stage and go back to where you came from. And you can tell your husband to save himself the trouble to coming out here.

I ain't leaving for you, and I ain't leaving for him neither."

For a moment Carrie was tempted to take his advice. Nothing about this trip had turned out the way she had planned. She didn't have to look around to see the grime, the lonely isolation of the station, or to guess the foreign nature of the life she would lead here. Sitting in her comfortable home in Virginia, the trip west hadn't seemed like much of a risk. She had assumed that things would be very different, but she had expected to have Robert at her side to depend on. Now here she was, alone and facing a man who was determined to defy her. Why didn't she use her common sense and go home?

Carried didn't know why, but she found herself looking to the man called Lucas, and she encountered a questioning, measuring look in his eyes that caused her to turn away angrily. She at least had the satisfaction of knowing he was now really looking at her out of his silver-gray eyes, but his quizzical, almost mocking, glance proved an unwelcome shock to her pride, and her wavering resolve immediately stiffened.

All her life she had made her own decisions, all her life she had been out of step with her family, and all her life she had promised herself that someday she would find a place where she would not be judged by the standards set by previous generations of a virtually closed community. Well, now she was in Colorado, about as far away from Virginia as she could get. And as far as she could tell, it was totally different from any kind of society she knew. This was her chance to begin anew, and if she let this contemptible excuse for a man drive her away now, she would never have any place she could call her own. Nor did she intend to allow this man called Lucas to continue to laugh at her.

"That was only a copy of the letter," Carrie informed Baca, pleased to have outguessed him. "I have kept the original locked safely in my trunks. No, Mr. Riggins," she said, sounding as confident as she could with her blood running cold with fear, "it is you who will have to leave, and I have decided it would be best if you did so immediately. I'm sorry I can't permit you to stay the night, but I don't think it would be wise."

"Can't permit me to stay!" Baca roared in a gobbling rage. "Look, lady, nobody tells Baca Riggins to get out."

"The letter says you've got to go," Bap insisted.

"Who's going to make me? You with your guns?"

"It will not be necessary for Mr. Turner to employ his guns," Carrie said, starting past the curious passengers who had gathered around to listen. "If necessary, I shall throw your things into the yard myself." Baca blocked her path.

"You'd better get back on that stage and forget you ever came to Green Run Station. You come back with your husband, and you're going to leave a widow woman. Now I don't like to have to tell people something more than once, so you just turn around right now."

"Move out of my way, Mr. Riggins," Carrie said, mad enough now to have no trouble keeping her voice steady. "Mr. Turner is not the only one who can use a pistol." She reached inside her purse and pulled out a small derringer. "I would hate to be required to use this, but I will not hesitate."

Baca looked at the small pistol and broke into a shout of laughter. "I ain't afraid of no pistol, especially in the hands of a woman."

"A bullet makes the same kind of hole whether the gun is fired by a man or a woman," Carrie warned him.

"It would if you had the guts to fire it or if you could hit what you aimed at. Now git on that stage before I put you on it."

"As I've already told you, Mr. Riggins, you have been fired, and I want you off this place within the hour. You've allowed this situation to degenerate into a hog wallow. I'm surprised the passengers have the courage to taste your food after getting a look, and a whiff I might add, of your person."

Baca moved toward Carrie with a virulent curse, but just as she squeezed the trigger, Bap rushed to throw himself in Baca's path. In so doing, he brushed Carrie, throwing off her aim, and the bullet went through the fleshy part of Baca's hamlike shoulder rather than his heart where Carrie had aimed. Baca paused a split second, unfazed by the bullet

13

wound but amazed that Carrie would actually have the courage to fire at him, then he rushed in with a roar. He plowed into Bap before he could draw his gun; then Baca threw that unfortunate man at least twenty feet before he hit the ground so hard the breath was knocked completely out of him. He slapped the pistol from Carrie's hand and shook her like a rag doll.

"I told you to git on that stage," he shouted, "and when I say something, I mean it." Carrie struggled to break free, but she knew it was hopeless. Instinctively she looked for the man called Lucas, but Baca had her in an iron grip, and she couldn't turn her head more than a few inches either way. There was no one else to help her. Bap was out cold, and the passengers stood staring at Baca, too frightened of the huge man to move.

Anger such as Carrie had never known flooded over her, and she forgot to be afraid. She kicked at Baca's groin with all her strength, and the sound of an agonized moan just before he released her let her know she had found her target. Then before he could straighten up, she slapped him cross the face as hard as she could, leaving a bright red impression on his cheek. With a vicious curse, Baca drew back a fist, prepared to smash it into Carrie's face. Knowing a blow from Baca's fist would probably break most of the bones in her face, Carrie dropped to her knees.

"Touch that lady again, and I'll kill you." The words were spoken quietly and in a slow Texas drawl, but there was something in Lucas's voice that made Baca's body freeze.

"This ain't none of your concern, Lucas," Baca hissed, crazy with rage. "It's between me and this woman."

"Not after you laid a hand on her. No man mishandles a lady, or stands around and lets anyone do it." One of the male passengers, spurred on by the contempt in Lucas's voice, helped Carrie to her feet. Another came to life and helped her brush the dust from her clothes.

"I'm warning you, Lucas, stay out of this. You ain't got no business here anyway. Why don't you take this here woman back to where she comes from if you're so particular about her?"

"The lady told you what to do." The lazy insolence of Lucas's drawl was like a whip laid across the open wound in Baca's pride.

"And I ain't doing it," he roared, whirling around to face Lucas. "There ain't nobody can make me, not without a gun in their hand." Lucas patiently unbuckled his gun belt and handed it to Bap, who had just gotten to his feet.

"I can."

Just two words, but for Carrie they were more than sufficient.

"There ain't going to be enough of you left for one of your horses to find when I get through," Baca promised, a red light of triumph glowing in his evil eyes.

"Don't, Mr. Lucas," Carrie begged, certain no one could stand up under Baca Riggins's attack. "I think it will be best for me to leave now and return with my husband and Mr. Bickett."

"There's no reason for you to be put to that much trouble."

"But this isn't your fight."

"It is now."

Carrie hardly knew what to say. She knew if she left now she would never return, but she didn't know how she could make Riggins leave, not without killing him. And although she had been willing to shoot in self-defense, she couldn't shoot a man with the intention of killing him.

"Come on, Baca, or pack up," Lucas taunted him.

His relaxed and confident posture was an affront to Riggins's pride, and the huge man charged his opponent with a roar. Carrie wanted to close her eyes, afraid of what she would see, but she kept them open, and like everyone else in the stage yard that afternoon, she was stunned by what followed. In a short, vicious fight which would soon become a legend in Colorado, Lucas brought the lumbering behemoth to his knees without ever receiving a blow himself. "Apologize to Mrs. Simpson," Lucas ordered as Baca gathered his shaky legs under him.

"I'll see you in Hell first."

"Really, Mr. Lucas, it's not necessary—" Carrie began then stopped abruptly. Lucas had hit Baca in the stomach hard enough to double him up. Then getting behind him, he gave him a push with his foot that sent him forward at a stumbling run, aimed directly at the watering trough. Baca pulled himself up enough to veer to the right, but Lucas caught him by the nape of the neck and the seat of the pants and plunged him bodily into the large basin. Then he reached in and pulled Baca's head out of the water by the hair.

"I asked you to apologize." When Baca continued to blubber angrily, Lucas shoved his head underwater and held it there. Several seconds went by and the assembled spectators watched apprehensively as Baca's body thrashed about in the trough with increasingly frantic movements. Just when Carrie was sure Baca would drown, Lucas lifted his head from the water.

"You ready to apologize?" Baca started to mutter something that could be taken for an apology.

"Please let him up," Carrie begged. "I'm sure he won't bother me again." Lucas looked at Carrie as if he didn't quite believe his ears, but he stepped away from the trough. Baca climbed out, stumbling as his unsteady legs tried to hold him up, water cascading down into the dust and turning it into thick mud.

"Empty this trough and fill it again," Lucas said to Cody, the cook, who had watched the fight from the station porch. "It's not fit for the horses to use anymore."

"Are you crazy?" Cody stammered. "Do you know how big that trough is?"

"Empty it or swim in it," Lucas said, and after a moment's hesitation, Cody picked up a bucket and started bailing water.

"Buck, get down here," Lucas called toward the station. When no one appeared, he took his gun belt from Bap and calmly shot out one of the second-floor windows. Immediately they could hear the scrambling of feet from inside the house and a young man, as unkept as Baca and as thin as he

16

was fat, stumbled out onto the porch.

"Thought you might hear that. Pitch Baca's gear out for him. He's in a hurry to leave." Buck looked at Baca, still dripping water and barely able to stand, and at Cody, glumly bailing water from the tank, and decided to do what he was told.

"They won't give you any more trouble, ma'am," Lucas said almost nonchalantly to Carrie. Then he buckled his gun belt around his waist, tied his guns down with strips of rawhide, and turned toward his chair under the tree.

"Mr. Lucas," Carrie called after him. "I must thank you for your intervention. I hadn't expected to receive a warm welcome, but neither did I anticipate such a reception as this. Then it was too late to turn around and wait for my husband."

"You should have."

"Possibly," replied Carrie, irked by his brusk reply, "but I am not in the habit of running from trouble. Nevertheless, Mr. Lucas, I want to thank you."

"Barrow."

"What?" she asked, bewildered.

"Barrow. My name's Barrow."

Chapter 2

"But Mr. Riggins called you—"

"First name's Lucas."

"Oh," Carrie replied, now thoroughly irritated by his attitude. "Thank you, Mr. Barrow, *Mr. Lucas Barrow*," she emphasized. "You've done me a very great service."

But Lucas was already moving with an unhurried stride toward his chair under the tree. "Think nothing of it, ma'am," he said, tugging at the brim of his hat in a salutation before sitting down and leaning back in his chair the way he was when Carrie had first seen him.

Carrie didn't know whether to make a second effort to voice her gratitude or to turn on her heel, march off to the station, and forget him. She had been favorably impressed when she'd first seen him and she was enormously thankful he had disposed of Baca for her, but that was canceled out by the abrupt, almost rude, way he had rebuffed her attempt to express her gratitude. She knew nothing about him, or any other man of the West for that matter, but she assumed good manners were pretty much the same everywhere. If that was so, Mr. Lucas Barrow was just as rude as he was disturbingly attractive.

Yet as the passengers began to climb back into the stagecoach, Carrie conceded she could take Lucas's rudeness better than Baca's murderous hatred. An angry shout from the ex-station manager drew her attention to where Buck had just tossed a suitcase into the yard; it had broken open when it struck the hard, packed ground and spilled Baca's clothes into the dust. After a short altercation, Buck began to pick up the clothes while Baca headed for the barn. Carrie decided she would stay where she was until Baca left.

"This is the last of your luggage, ma'am," Bap said, handing Carrie a battered suitcase from the roof of the stage. "I'd offer to stay and help you take it up to the cabin, but I'm already behind schedule."

"That's all right. Maybe I can get Buck or Cody to carry them up for me."

Bap looked as if he was about to make an objection, but he changed his mind. "You sure you're going to be okay by yourself?" he asked instead. "I could take you back to Denver, and you could wait for your husband there."

"No, I'd rather stay."

"I don't feel right leaving you here by yourself."

"I'm sure there'll be nothing to worry about once Mr. Riggins is gone. Besides, there's always Mr. Barrow."

"I suppose so," Bap muttered, clearly dissatisfied with the way things were being left. "He seems like a dependable sort, he wrangles horses for the stage line, but he's only been here a couple of weeks. Nobody knows much about him."

"I'm sure I'll be quite safe. Now you'd better get started. Won't you get into trouble if you're late?"

"Naw. There's so many things that can go wrong, nobody except the home office expects you to be on time, and they're too far away to know anything about it."

"Just the same, you'd better be going."

"I'll be back in a couple of days to check on you. I wouldn't want anything to cause you to leave and Baca to come back. I'm looking forward to sampling some of your cooking."

"I'll see you get a first-rate meal," Carrie promised and waved a cheerful good-bye. But when she turned back to the station and saw Baca leading three saddled horses from the barn, she felt anything but cheerful. Cody and Buck tied bedrolls to their saddles, then all three riders mounted and rode toward where Carrie still stood in the yard.

"My orders said nothing about replacing you, Mr. Cody,

19

or you, Buck. You still have jobs here if you want them. In fact, I will need your help to run the station."

"What kind of man would I be if I was to stay here?" Cody demanded, glaring at Carrie out of vacant, pale blue eyes. "I ain't working for no woman."

"Me neither," added Buck. "And you won't find nobody else around here anxious to work for you."

"Won't be no need," Baca threatened. "She won't be here long."

"My husband and I intend to make this our home, Mr. Riggins."

"Don't make no difference what you intend. You ain't heard the last of me. Nobody pushes Baca Riggins out of any place he wants to stay."

"I think you'd better go, Mr. Riggins, and take your friends with you. But let me give you a piece of advice before you go. No one pushes *me* out of any place I mean to stay either. I have a right to be here, I am here, and I intend to stay. If you value your good health, you won't come back."

"Why you . . ." Baca's eyes cut nervously to where Lucas still sat under the tree. He hadn't moved, but the very intensity of his stillness signified his alertness. "I'll be back," Baca blustered, almost more for the benefit of his friends than Carrie. "This is my station, and I mean to keep it." He spurred his horse forward, the others following quickly and Carrie had to move swiftly to avoid being showered with the dirt thrown up by their mounts' flying hooves. In a very short time the three men had disappeared down the trail, and Carrie was alone.

Carrie wasn't sure what to do first, but she knew she couldn't give way to the feeling of despondency that was creeping through her body like oil through a wick. She couldn't be sure until she looked at the schedule, but she was certain there was another stage coming through sometime before night. That meant a hot meal had to be ready when it arrived, and she was the only one present to cook it. She certainly didn't expect the sleepy cowboy under the tree to help, even if he could, which she doubted. With a weary sigh, she bent over to pick up one of the smaller suitcases. When she stood up again, she noticed an exceptionally tall young woman approaching from the direction of the manager's cabin; she was a big-boned girl, generous of flesh, and rather plain but of a cheerful and open countenance. Carrie put her suitcase down again and waited, surprise and a feeling of relief flooding over her. At least she wasn't alone.

"I'll be asking your pardon for not offering to help you in that ruckus with Mr. Riggins," the girl said in a heavy Irish accent, "but I thought for certain he meant to kill you, and I didn't want him killing me too before he got the chance to cool down. Whatever did you do to make him leave? And what is a fancy-dressed woman like you doing in a place like this by yourself?"

"I'm Carrie Simpson. My husband is the new station manager, and I've come ahead. As for the clothes," she added with a blush, "they're all I have."

"I best be asking your pardon again," the girl said, blushing rosily herself. "Pay no attention to me spiteful words. It just be jealousy that I don't look like you, though I know there be no clothes this side of heaven that could turn a peahen like me into a beautiful lady like you."

"Thank you," Carrie replied, feeling more embarrassed than ever. "And you don't have to apologize for not having the courage to face Mr. Riggins. If I had known about him, I doubt I'd have gotten off the stage."

"For sure you would. Some people just naturally step up to the line when there's trouble, and you be one of them."

"The courage of desperation," Carrie said with an embarrassed laugh.

" 'Tis possible, but I doubt it. Anyhow, I'm glad you're here. Now maybe I'll be getting something to eat without being afraid of what those wicked creatures had a mind to do if only they weren't so scared of Mr. Barrow. Ah, I be forgetting me manners. I'm Katie O'Malley, and you can tell from me accent I've only just come from Ireland."

"How long have you been here?" Carrie asked, skipping over the mention of Lucas, but making a mental note to get

21

back to it as soon as possible.

"I be waiting for me husband-to-be to come for me. I'm wondering whether he has got himself held up or if I got the date wrong. I have been here six days already, and I can tell you I was hard set to get through six days of Baca Riggins. Besides," she said, gathering in a little slack in the waist of her dress, "I'm naturally plump, and if I don't start getting something to eat, I'll soon be a withered twig like you."

"Come on inside," Carrie said. "I've got to find something for dinner. I'm sure I can find something for you, too." Carrie picked up her suitcase and started toward the station.

"I'll be there afore ye," Katie said. "I'm nigh unto starving. I been staying in the cabin up the road, that's your cabin by the by, because I couldn't trust that Mr. Riggins and his friends not to go getting ideas in the middle of the night."

"Didn't they offer to feed you?"

"For certain they did, anytime I was hungry enough to come down to the station, but I couldn't eat much, not after the first mouthful, and I was frightful of being in the room alone with those three. No matter, I would watch for the stage and hurry down while the passengers were here."

"But that's awful."

"I've no doubt, but 'twas safer."

They had reached the steps and Carrie stood staring at the dilapidated station.

"I might as well warn you. Most likely you never saw anything like the inside of this place, so don't be overset. Though it'll be small blame if ye are. 'Tis enough to make your stomach turn."

They stepped inside and Carrie stared about her in shock. The dishes from the previous meal were still on the table, but more dirty plates were stacked on a table against the wall, several pots covered with the leavings of what had been cooked in them were piled against a corner of the stove, and the cabinet doors stood ajar, their contents haphazardly left open to the ravages of flies and spoilage. The room itself hadn't been cleaned in months and every surface was caked with grease. Carrie had no idea how she was going to get everything cleaned in time to get dinner ready.

"Here, let me lend you a hand," Katie offered.

"No," Carrie said with sudden resolution, "this is my job, and I have to do it myself."

"Then you'd best be changing your dress, or you'll never wear it again. There be rooms in the back, probably as filthy as this, but you'll have some privacy." Carrie found two rooms, both incredibly grimy, but she made herself ignore the debris for the time being. First things first, and the first thing she had to do was to get dinner ready for the passengers she was expecting.

"There be a stage coming through at half past six," Katie announced as Carrie came back into the dining room. "I'm thinking that leaves us something over five hours to get this place looking decent." She had already found a big pot, filled it with water, and put it on to boil.

"I told you I could do this myself," Carrie said, slightly irritated that Katie had started without her permission. She had thrust herself into this job and it was her responsibility to see that it was done.

"Ye can't be doing it all yourself and ye know it," Katie stated, never pausing as she scraped several pots and threw their cold, congealed contents out the back door. "Besides, I'm so starved for female company I probably won't leave your side more than a minute before Brian comes for me. And I can't stand about doing nothing while you work yourself to death. Me mother brought me up to hard work, but she also brought me up to share. It makes the work go that much faster for a little company, some lighthearted gossip, and a wee bit of laughter."

"It certainly does," agreed Carrie, her momentary pique gone. She started to stack the plates on the table. "And from the looks of this place, it's going to have to go mighty fast if we're to have dinner ready by six-thirty. You start washing the dishes and I'll see if I can remove enough grease from this table for us to sit down and have a bite to eat. I didn't have any lunch, and I'm hungry too."

But it was nearly two hours later before they could sit

down to eat. They washed every dish in the station, scrubbed every surface until it shone, and scraped the stove clean of all the baked-on food that hadn't already turned to charcoal. They still had to clean out the cabinets and the storage closet, make an inventory so Carrie would know what staples she needed to order, scrub down the walls and floors, replace the curtains, and clean the windows, but the pots were soaking in hot soapy water and she had found enough food to be able to plan a good, nourishing dinner.

"How long do you intend to wait?" Carrie asked once the edge was off their hunger.

"What for?"

"For your fiancé. You said it had already been a week. Suppose something has happened to him and he can't come?"

"Happen I'll find myself a job then. I'm young, strong, and I can work."

"Don't you want to go back home?"

"I lack the money. Brian paid me passage, but I wouldn't go back if I could. I cooked and cleaned for a passel of men long enough. I made up me mind the next man I done for would be me husband, or I'd do for no one." It sounded so much like Carrie's own situation she experienced a strong surge of sympathy.

"Do you have any family?"

"Do I ever. Eight years it is I've cooked and cleaned for me father and six brothers since me mother died. Still things weren't too bad until the oldest brought home a wife. Hadn't but one look passed between the two of us, and I knew we could never live under the same roof without making everybody's life a misery. I'm thinking we'd have killed each other before long. Anyway when Brian Kelly wrote his ma asking her to pick him out a wife and she asked me, I jumped at the chance. To be sure when he was home, Brian used to be swayed by temptation too often to suit me, but I always say any ship in a storm is better than getting bashed to death on the rocks."

Carrie thought of her own decision to take on the management of the station and felt she had come to much the same conclusion.

"After a time of being tossed about on that wee bit of a ship, I was sorry I hadn't settled on somebody closer to home, but ever since I got to these hills, I've felt right at home."

"These are the Rocky *Mountains*," Carrie informed her.

"To be sure they are a little big, but I'm game to tackle anything as long as it carries no gun."

The conversation stopped abruptly at the sound of footsteps on the porch. Carrie's first thought was that Baca Riggins had come back, but when the door swung open, she found herself staring up into the unnervingly handsome face of Lucas Barrow. Kate had only seen him next to Baca Riggins, so she was stunned to discover just how tall six feet two looked when you were sitting down staring up at it. He was a slim, powerfully built man, but his presence seemed to fill the room and make him seem even more imposing. Despite herself, Carrie felt her breath catch and her pulse quicken; the mere presence of this man charged the air with energy even though he moved slowly and used fewer words than anybody she'd ever known. The channels of her mind were immediately clogged with questions, but they were overridden by the force of his physical presence. It was like an electrical shock, and Carrie found herself staring up at him with wide eyes and a slack jaw.

"You mean to leave those trunks in the yard?"

Carrie continued to stare at him, her mind making only a feeble attempt to deal with anything as unimportant as words.

"Of course she doesn't," Katie answered for her, "but you can't expect her to go hauling those heavy things over to the cabin by herself."

"My t-trunks," stammered Carrie, pulling her disordered wits together. "No, I don't mean for them to remain in the yard. To tell you the truth, we were so busy here I forgot all about them, but I suppose they should be brought in before the next stage arrives." Why did she feel so foolish? And she was talking exactly like one of her silly sisters-in-law.

"Take them up to the cabin," Katie told Lucas before turning to Carrie. "You can't stay here until we've scrubbed those rooms from top to bottom."

"I don't want to run you out."

"You won't. There's two rooms. Besides, it's yours anyway."

"Which will it be?" Lucas asked, breaking in on their exchange.

"Take them up to the cabin, please," Carrie said, happy to accept Katie's advice until she could refocus her distracted wits. She ought to concentrate on what she was saying and not pay attention to his eyes, but she had never seen eyes that shone with such brilliant intensity.

"I don't work for the station," Lucas stated flatly.

"I'm sorry. I just assumed . . ." Carrie searched her dazed mind for words.

"But I'll take your trunks up to the cabin. You'd never get them up there yourself, not if you were to put both of you in harness."

"Thank you," Carrie said rather coolly. Once again she was becoming irked by his attitude, and that helped her to gather her wits and determine to put him in his place if it was the last thing she did. "Naturally I'll pay you for your trouble . . ."

"No you won't."

"I beg your pardon?"

"I don't take money from women."

"Why not? It spends the same as from men." Really, he was ruder than she had thought.

"I'm sure it does, but I still won't take it."

"Don't let it fret you," Katie advised Carrie. "Half the men out here treat a woman like she was dirt, and the other half like she was some kind of angel. Be glad he's one of the angel kind." Carrie decided this wasn't the time to go into it, but she intended to let them both know that Lucas's behavior bore no resemblance to her idea of angel-like veneration. She felt more like an errant child or a plain nuisance.

"You ought to go back to Denver," Lucas said.

"What?" Carrie asked angrily. His effrontery had now

gone well beyond rudeness, and she informed him, "I have a job here."

"You ought to leave on the next stage."

"I assure you I intend to stay. My husband—"

"Come back when your husband is with you. This is no place for a woman alone. I can't always be around to help you, and Baca Riggins isn't the only one of his kind. There are any number of men who'll take advantage of a female if given the chance."

"Thank you for your concern and your warning," Carrie said, unbending slightly, "but I mean to stay. I can take care of myself."

"Do you have any guns besides that toy pistol?"

"As a matter of fact, I do."

"Do you know how to use them?"

"Yes."

"Can you hit anything?"

It would serve him right if she used her pistol on him. At least then he wouldn't have to ask any more impertinent questions. "Mr. Barrow, I appreciate your anxiety, I really do, but I resent this interrogation. I don't mean to sound rude or ungrateful, but my welfare is none of your business. I have a position here and work to do, and I mean to do it. I won't be run off by the likes of Baca Riggins or by your warnings. If you are going to carry those trunks up to the cabin, I would appreciate it if you would do it now. It'll be some time before I am finished here, but I'd feel more comfortable knowing everything I owned wasn't sitting in the middle of the road."

"Where do you want them?" Lucas asked, Carrie's stern reproof having no visible effect on him.

"The bedroom on the left," Katie said. "I'm staying in the other one."

"And I've got a suitcase in the back room as well," Carrie told him. Lucas disappeared into the rear of the station, reappeared moments later with the suitcase, and marched out the front door, all without uttering another word.

"Who *is* that man?" Carrie demanded, hardly able to decide whether she wanted to be angry with him or be tempted by his tremendous physical appeal. "I never met anyone like him in my whole life. You'd think he hated women and was charged for each word he spoke."

"You'll be mistaken if you're thinking I know anything about him. He was here afore me. He keeps to himself, and everybody leaves him alone. Seems to me he's supposed to provide horses for the station, but he never appears to work very hard. He's always around whenever anybody rides up. You'd think he was a welcoming committee except he hardly ever speaks. He's said more words to you than I've heard him say since I've been here."

"I was going to ask him if he would be willing to work for me until I could find the time to go into Fort Malone and hire someone, but the way he stared at me when I offered to pay him, I was sure he'd refuse."

"Could be he would, but ye can never tell what a man like him is going to do. He's taken a liking to you, though, so he just might do it."

"Taken a liking to me!" Carrie exclaimed. "You must be mistaken. I've never been spoken to in that manner by any-one in my life, not even the Yankees who came through our place at the end of the war."

"I know nothing about any Yankees, but he's never said a word to me even though I will take an oath he's been watching out for me all along."

"He gives me the same feeling," Carrie said. "The whole time he was under that tree I felt like his eyes were staring at me. Yet he had that hat pulled down over his face so far I couldn't see his nose."

"He has the appearance of being a strange man, but I think I like him."

"I'm not sure I do, but that's neither here nor there," Carrie said, getting to her feet. "We've got a dinner to fix and there's still more cleaning to do. I'll be most grateful if Mr. Barrow will agree to help me at least temporarily, but if he doesn't learn to speak and behave properly around women, he can eat his dinner in the barn. I'm not sure but what his horse has better manners anyway."

But Carrie was certain Lucas was no man to be ignored, and regardless of how he treated her, she was sure she didn't want him to ignore her.

Lucas climbed down from the wagon and began to unload the trunks. To the women who periodically glanced out at him from the kitchen window, he seemed to be moving with maddening deliberateness, but his mind was racing. He had not expected the arrival of Carrie Simpson or been prepared for the impact she made on him, and he was still trying to get his feelings under control. And to make matters worse, if they could be made worse at this point, her arrival threatened to seriously disrupt his plans.

There was no place in his life for a woman, especially not the kind who looked like something out of a dream and smelled of lace curtains and spicy apple pies. He just didn't have time for that now. One day soon the Overland Stage Company would be his, his uncle was already dying, and it would take every minute he had for the next several years to keep it from being swallowed up by the railroads coming west. He had spent every waking hour for the last twenty years working for his uncle, the last five studying how to take advantage of the railroads, and he couldn't afford to lose it all for lack of attention.

He was also in the middle of a dangerous undertaking. If this gang that had stolen the gold shipment off his stage even suspected who he was or why he was at Green Run Pass, they would try to kill him. They had already shown that nothing was going to stand in their way, especially nothing as easy as killing. They were well organized and operated smoothly, and it had taken all his time to make the little progress he had these last two weeks. It was difficult enough to maintain his act of the laconic wrangler when he would keep his mind on the job full time. If things started to fall apart, it would be virtually impossible to save his own skin and worry about a woman as well. Two women, he reminded himself, but for

29

some reason he'd never worried about it until Carrie stepped down from the stage.

It had been his uncle's lifelong boast that nobody ever took anything off his stages unless they cleared it with him first, but someone had taken that gold shipment, and Lucas was certain they had plans to take several more. It was essential that he discover who was selling information about their cargo, stop the thieves, and recover the lost gold. The loss of one shipment wouldn't damage his business, but it would hurt his pride, and Lucas Barrow had pride if he had nothing else.

He'd have to see about getting that woman out of here. And the Irish girl, too. He couldn't imagine why Carrie's husband had sent her ahead of him. Any Westerner knew women ought never to travel alone, and certainly not a woman who looked like Carrie Simpson. That wasn't asking for trouble, it was the same as getting down on your knees and begging for it. He'd have to talk to Simpson and try to convince him to send his wife back to Denver, or at least to Fort Malone. She couldn't stay here, not with the Staples gang in the vicinity. Jason Staples was known to be hard on men and women alike, but he had a well-known weakness for a pretty woman. In fact, if Lucas had been the type, he would have baited a trap with just such a woman as Carrie. But that wasn't his way, and he would never have used any woman in that manner, certainly not one like Carrie.

He couldn't understand why she kept nagging at his mind. She was a married woman, and Lucas had never allowed himself to even think of messing around with another man's wife. You could kill a man for that, not that he was afraid of Robert Simpson, it was just that he held to a very strict code of behavior. God only knows, if she'd been his woman, he'd have been tempted to kill any man who even looked at her hard.

He had to stop thinking like this. He was getting himself all worked up over nothing. Carrie Simpson didn't even like him. She probably wouldn't like any man of the West. The way she dismissed him smacked of old-fashioned Eastern society, snooty women and stuffy men, all complacent in the security of well-organized towns with a tradition of orderliness and a police force to see it was maintained. She'd never survive out here where there were few rules and those had to be enforced with fists or guns. It was for damned certain Jason Staples wouldn't fade away into the night just because she looked down her pert little nose at him. And there was nothing about her golden brown eyes or pursed mouth to discourage a man either. Oh, they could look daggers at you and say awful words, but her lips were meant to be kissed, and her eyes seemed to be issuing the invitation.

She was such a dainty little thing, she didn't even come to his shoulder, it was hard to see how she could stand up to anybody, although he had been right impressed with the way she squared off against Baca Riggins. Of course, she would have had to leave on that stage if he hadn't intervened, but he was certain she would have come back. With her husband! He had to try harder to remember her husband. Maybe then he could get over the feeling of wanting to wrap his arms around her and stay close so nothing could happen to her. Maybe when her husband got here, he could get rid of the feeling that if he let her out of his sight for as much as a minute, he would never forgive himself.

He tried to concentrate on the trunks he was moving, but that was no help. Those trunks were important to Carrie, and that made them important to him. He cursed. Maybe it was time to go bronco hunting. He sure needed to bust something.

Chapter 3

"I'm thinking the stage will be here any minute, Mrs. Simpson," Katie said as she checked the gravy and prepared to put the ears of corn into boiling water. "Why don't ye take off your apron and meet them on the porch?"

"I can't leave you to do all the work."

" 'Tis nothing left to do. Faith, once they get the smell of food in their nostrils, 'twill be all ye can do to get out of their way."

"It would make a nice impression, wouldn't it, especially after Mr. Riggins?"

"A wild-eyed mustang would make a good impression after Baca Riggins," Katie declared emphatically. "Besides, men always feel better when they're around a nice-looking woman."

"Do you think I have time to change?" Carrie asked, looking with disfavor at her plain working dress. "And I know my hair is falling down my back."

"For certain there's time, but it wouldn't matter if they were to see you just like you are now. Like I've been telling ye, you'll still be the best thing they've seen in a long time."

Carrie blushed with pleasure as she hurried off to the room at the back of the station. When she emerged ten minutes later she had changed her dress, washed her face, and put her hair up under a cap which was a charming confection of lace and ribbons.

"Ye look fresh as a daisy, ma'am," Katie said. "Nobody

would ever guess you had worked like a galley slave to make this place look decent."

"They will if they remember what it looked like before," Carrie said, pleased but embarrassed by Katie's admiration. Suddenly an unbidden thought sprang into her mind. Would Lucas think she looked fresh as a daisy? Carrie was shocked to the core. She didn't care what Lucas thought. She didn't know a thing about the man, and she didn't much like him either. Well, she hesitated, maybe she *was* vaguely interested. Anybody who looked that attractive had to be just a little bit interesting. She conceded reluctantly that she was curious about him, but not in a serious way. He radiated an undeniable physical attraction and there was an air of mystery about him she found intriguing, but he wasn't at all the kind of man she would have chosen for a husband.

Carrie chuckled to herself. The very idea of Lucas Barrow being married, especially to her, was funny. She could just see him with her family, his luminous silver-gray eyes glowing intently as her sisters-in-law tried to flirt with him and her father tried to discover his opinion of the long-term effects of Reconstruction on the South. But that wasn't half as absurd as trying to picture her in some sod shanty or a mud-and-stick lean-to, cooking venison over an open fire and happily bedding down under the stars, oblivious to the rain, sleet, or freezing cold. No, they had nothing in common, and the sooner she dispelled the mystery that hung about him and put him out of her mind, the better. The rattle of the incoming stagecoach broke Carrie's train of thought and she hurried out on the porch to meet her first customers.

It seemed to Carrie that most of the passengers must have been regular users of the stage. They climbed out grumbling about the dinner they thought awaited them, but the first man no sooner set eyes on Carrie than he knew something was different. He perked up, whispered something to his companion, and hurried up to the station.

"Howdy, ma'am. My name's Lloyd Finlay. Am I indulging in foolish fancy to hope that seeing you on these steps means somebody finally sent Baca Riggins packing?"

"I'm Mrs. Robert Simpson, and Mr. Riggins no longer works for the Overland Stage Company. Beginning today, my husband and I will be managing this station." The man let out a cowboy yell and called to his friend.

"Hurry up, Grady. There just might be something we can eat on the table this time." The passengers wasted no time getting their legs under the table, and in the rush to get everyone served, it was some minutes before Carrie realized the driver had not come in. She stepped out on the porch to call him to his dinner before it got cold and saw Lucas helping him change the team. No one saw Carrie's flush of mortification, but she didn't feel it any less. This was her station, but she had been so busy thinking about food and getting herself prettied up to make a good impression on the passengers, she had entirely forgotten that the real purpose of the station was to provide fresh horses for the stage. That there was no one to change the team because Buck had walked off the job along with Baca and Cody.

She stood there on the porch, miserable, unable to make herself go down to the men and offer an apology, unwilling to go inside and ignore her failure, and undecided about what she was going to do next time. She was bitterly disappointed in herself. By means of a willful deception, she had set herself to take on a man's job, and she had been so concerned with what a woman would naturally think of first—food and cleaning—that she had forgotten all about what a man would think of first—the horses. If she was to do this job well enough to keep it, she was going to have to learn to think like a man as well as a woman.

Lucas led the exhausted team away after helping hitch up the new team, and Carrie made herself wait on the porch until the driver had come close enough to speak to. He didn't look the slightest bit pleased to see her waiting for him instead of Baca Riggins. In fact, from the frown on his face, Carrie wasn't sure he wouldn't have preferred Baca.

"I'm sorry you had to help change the horses, but there's no one here but myself. Mr. Barrow has been kind enough to lend a hand for the time being."

34

"He's good enough for now, but it ain't his line of work," replied Harry Keller.

"I'm sure it isn't, but I expect to have someone for the position in a day or two. Come on inside and eat your dinner before it's all gone."

They had prepared too much food for there to be any danger of that, but Carrie was surprised and pleased to see with what purpose the passengers had attacked their dinner. No one spoke except to ask someone to pass a bowl or platter. Carrie helped Katie refill all the dishes and then stepped back outside to wait for Lucas. She didn't know where he was in the habit of eating his meals, but after all the work he had done for her today, providing him with a dinner was the very least she could do to show her appreciation.

When several minutes had passed and he hadn't appeared in the yard or at the corral, she decided to walk down to the barn. He had stabled and fed the horses and was rubbing them down.

"Come on up to the station when you're finished and have some dinner, Mr. Barrow." Lucas turned to Carrie and for a brief moment she thought she saw something stir in his eyes. Then it was gone and a hard look settled over them. "It's the least I can offer for all the work you've done for me today."

"I've got to take care of the horses. And then the harnesses have to be cleaned."

"Surely that can wait until after you eat."

"The horses can't, and the harnesses are easier to clean before the salt dries on them."

"Okay, but I insist you let me give you dinner whenever you finish. Katie and I will wait to have our meal until after we clean up, so you can sit down with us. And there's always a pot of coffee on the stove. Help yourself at any time."

"Much obliged, Mrs. Simpson. Maybe I will come up and sit a spell. A man can get tired of his own company sometimes, and horses don't always fill the void."

Carrie couldn't help smiling. "I don't think I've ever been told my company was only occasionally preferable to that of a horse, but I suppose I'll hear worse before I've been here very long." This time she was certain she saw something in his eyes. Warmth, interest maybe, but definitely something other than the granite look she had come to expect. She even thought there might have been a slight movement of the muscles in his mouth, but that was probably wishful thinking. After all, she had never met a man who was so impervious to her charm, and she couldn't help but feel piqued that she had had to talk him into having dinner with her rather than eating alone, or worse yet, with a barn full of horses.

"Come on up when you're ready. There'll be plenty left over. And Mr. Barrow, I want to thank you for helping out with the horses. I'm ashamed to admit I never even thought about them. I expect the owners wouldn't be very pleased with me if they knew."

"It's only natural for a woman to think of food first. I expect your husband will take care of the horses when he gets here."

"Of course," Carrie muttered, and headed back to the station.

You ought to eat in your cabin, Lucas told himself. Even if you are a terrible cook, it's safer to eat your own cooking than to be around that women too often. She's married, forbidden territory. Her husband will be here any day now, and he'd have every right to shoot you for what you're thinking.

But Lucas couldn't stop himself from thinking of Carrie's pursed mouth and the upturned nose that gave her the look of a pixie. She was a small woman, too small to be ideal actually, but she had a beautiful face and a perfectly formed body. Lucas ached to put his arms around her slim waist, to rest her head against his chest. He could almost smell the freshness of her scent, that faint smell of lavender that hovered around her. He wanted to reach out and touch her skin, to feel the softness of her, to experience her warmth. He wanted to protect her, to keep her from having to clean up after Baca Riggins.

What kind of man was her husband to send her out here alone? Didn't he know it was dangerous to allow a woman like Carrie to travel without protection? In all fairness to the yet unknown Mr. Simpson, he probably didn't know about Baca Riggins and had expected no trouble, but wouldn't it have been more reasonable for him to come out early and let her wait in comfort in Denver for whatever it was that was so important? He'd have to talk with him when he arrived. This wasn't the kind of thing Lucas felt comfortable doing and he knew it could set trouble between him and Robert Simpson right from the start, but the man obviously knew nothing about the West. Somebody was going to have to explain a few important facts to him in a hurry. He couldn't have Carrie's well-being threatened just because her husband was a tenderfoot. He probably was a very good man and Lucas was certain Carrie loved him very much, but they both had a lot to learn if they wanted to prosper in Colorado.

And he had better get Carrie out of his mind, or he might as well go back to Denver and send someone else to look for Jason Staples. The way things were with him just now, they could probably take the gold right from under his nose and he wouldn't even notice.

"That's the best meal I ever had on a stage line, Mrs. Simpson," Lloyd Finlay said as he got up from the table. "I've been telling Duncan Bickett for years he ought to get some women on the line. There's nothing like a female in the kitchen."

"Thank you."

"Looking forward to meeting Mr. Simpson. Shouldn't have sent you alone ahead. Can't expect a woman to do a man's job, even for a few days."

There was something about Finlay's manner that Carrie had found irritating from the start, but there was no question about the effect of his words on her temper.

"I think you'll find you've greatly underestimated women, Mr. Finlay," Carrie said with a forced smile. "There's a great deal a woman can do beside cook, clean, and have children."

"Now ma'am, you know a woman loses some of her appeal, some of that softness a man likes so much, when she steps out of her proper place."

"And just what are you thinking is her proper place?" demanded Katie, who had stopped serving to listen to the exchange.

"In the home, of course, with her children."

"Unless I'm mistook someway, the place for men like you is in the barn with the rest of the animals," Katie told him, brandishing a large spoon in the air for emphasis.

"I think you'd better change your tune if you expect to eat at this table again," Carrie said with a twinkle. "If Katie doesn't brain you with a pot, I'll fill the seat of your pants with buckshot. Because you see, Mr. Finlay, I can not only cook and clean and have babies, I can shoot and ride and outthink any man I know. Maybe I'll give you a demonstration the next time you come through. Now you have a pleasant journey," Carrie said as she ushered the astonished little man out the door.

Carrie accepted the compliments of the other passengers, all of them cowed into near silence by her exchange with Finlay, and watched as they hurried out to board the stage.

"Everything was mighty good, Mrs. Simpson," Harry Keller said as he left, his dark mood somewhat lightened by the food warming his belly, "but I'll be mighty glad to see Mr. Simpson get here. Finlay's right, you know, no matter how much you don't want to hear it. Running a station like this is no job for a woman. Not even for two women," he added, when Katie glowered at him.

"I'm sorry your team wasn't ready, but it won't happen again, whether my husband is here or not," Carrie assured him, her pride stiffening. "Having just arrived and being shorthanded, some things are bound to be forgotten."

"I suppose so, but a man wouldn't have forgotten the horses," Harry said, refusing to budge.

"Perhaps you're right, but in the future I won't forget them either." Fortunately for Carrie's temper, which was beginning to unravel under the sting of the double load of criticism, Harry decided to leave without saying anything else.

"If it was me, I'd have sent him to eat his dinner with his

precious horses," Katie said angrily. "Maybe then he wouldn't be so persnickety."

"I was sorely tempted," Carrie said, her smile returning, "but he had me over a barrel. I *did* forget he needed a fresh team, so I couldn't come down too hard on him, but I'm going to make sure I never forget anything again."

"Could be Mr. Barrow will take on the handling of the horses for ye."

"I intend to ask him when he comes for supper, but I have a feeling he doesn't think any more of having a woman for a boss than the rest of the men around here. But I mean to show them different."

"I wouldn't be letting that get me upset," Katie said beginning to stack the dirty dishes. "Your husband will be arriving any time now, and no matter what ye do, he'll be the one getting the credit."

"I suppose you're right," Carrie said, a sinking feeling in her stomach. What was Katie going to say when she learned Carrie didn't have a husband? More important, what was Lucas Barrow going to do?

"Could I give you some more potatoes, Mr. Barrow?" Carrie asked. "There're plenty more."

"No ma'am, you can't give me another thing, not if I'm to get out of this chair before morning. I haven't eaten this much at one sitting in ten years."

"After that Cody's cooking, I'm not surprised," Katie said.

"Mine's no better," Lucas said with the first grin Carrie had seen. It made him look younger and so much more appealing Carrie wished he would do it again. "You're making it mighty hard to go back to my own cooking."

"You don't have to. There's no reason why you can't take your meals with us."

"I can't be sponging off the Overland, ma'am. That wouldn't be right."

"That's not what I meant," Carrie replied, a stern look in her eye. "I don't intend to allow anyone to take advantage of

39

the company, but I was planning to offer you the job of stock tender. I need someone for the position and you seemed to know it already. Since you work with horses . . ."

"Thank you, ma'am, but I don't think that's the job for me. I guess you're going to have to go to Fort Malone to find you somebody."

What an obstinate man. He seemed to be willing to do anything he could for her as long as *he* thought of it, but just let *her* mention it first and it just wasn't possible. She had traveled two thousand miles to get away from men like that, so why didn't she just throw him out instead of foolishly wishing he would smile again. "But why won't you take it?"

Because I don't know if I can control myself if I'm around you every day, Lucas said to himself. Seeing you making up to your husband would be more than I could stand, but to Carrie he said, "It would tie me down too much. I've almost finished breaking the horses I have in the corral, and sometimes it takes me a week to round up a new herd. I couldn't leave the station if I were stock tender."

Carrie was stymied. She had hoped Lucas would take the job and that one of her problems would be out of the way. Now, in addition to still having to find a stock tender, she discovered Lucas would be going away soon, and for reasons she didn't fully understand, that made her feel uncomfortable. How could she have come to depend on a man she hardly knew in one day?

"Could you take the job until I get someone else?"

"I couldn't promise to be around all the time. Who knows how long it will take you to find a suitable man who will come out here."

"You mean a man who will work for a woman, don't you?"

"Why would I mean that? You've got a husband coming, don't you?"

Carrie wondered how much longer it would be before she would betray herself. Time and time again she was busy trying to figure out how she was going to run the station by herself, and everyone else was thinking she'd have a husband to help her in a day or two. Naturally that would cause them to reach different conclusions rather frequently, and before long she was bound to say something that would expose her deception. She had to get the station running smoothly, and she'd better do it in a hurry. It wasn't going to be possible to keep up the pretense for more than a few days, two weeks at most, and when she did finally admit the truth, the news would probably find its way to the company office with the speed of lightning. If she hadn't firmly established herself as a capable manager by that time, they would replace her with the first man they found, probably Baca Riggins himself if need be.

"There is one thing you can do for me," Carrie said, trying to hide her irritation but hoping he would see her disappointment.

"Anything I can, ma'am."

If he didn't stop calling her ma'am all the time, as if she were some forty-year-old dowager, she was going to brain him with his empty plate. "What are the most important things that have to be done at this station, until my husband gets here, that is?" she added.

"There's really only two things you have to do at any time. Fix meals for the passengers, and have the teams ready when the stage comes in. There's a schedule on the wall over there so you'll know when they're supposed to get here."

"I've seen it," she replied a little more tartly than she intended, and Lucas's eyes opened wider. "It doesn't seem like a very difficult job to me."

"That part is easy. It's the rest that'll cause you trouble."

"And what's that?"

"Staying here."

"Staying here?" Carrie repeated, completely bewildered. "What do you mean by that?"

"There's all kinds of people who might not want you here. To start with, there's Baca Riggins. He's been put out and that's something his pride won't stand."

"I think I can handle Mr. Riggins."

"Then there's Indians."

"Indians?"

"They'll run off your horses. If they're hungry, they'll eat them. Indians love horse meat."

"Is there anyone else I have to worry about?" Carrie asked with a shudder. She couldn't believe that even an Indian would eat a horse.

"Sure. There's outlaws, renegades, and gunslingers, not to mention drunks, malcontents, and a few men who just don't like to see women anywhere but in the kitchen."

"I've seen several of those already. And if I'm not mistaken, you're one of them as well."

"You've seen the ones who don't care for it but will accept it. I'm talking about the ones who will take it upon themselves to do something about it."

"Are there many?"

"You never can tell. With that kind you almost never know until it's too late."

"I think you're trying to frighten me, Mr. Barrow, and I don't appreciate that."

"No, ma'am, I'm not trying to scare you. I'm trying to tell you it's mighty dangerous for a lone female in this country. Fort Malone doesn't have soldiers anymore. There's only a sheriff who's not paid well enough to give any attention to things that happen this far away. You're on your own here, ma'am."

"Nevertheless, I have every intention of remaining at this station and doing the best job I possibly can. And stop calling me ma'am," Carrie added with a trace of impatience in her voice. "My name is Carrie Simpson."

"All right, Mrs. Simpson, I was just trying to explain why your husband should never have let you come out here alone. I'm sure he didn't know anything about Baca Riggins, but if it hadn't been Baca, it would have been somebody else. My advice to you is to get on the overnight which comes through in a couple of hours and not stop until you get back to Denver. No woman has any business out here alone. She's not equipped for it."

"Thank you for your advice, Mr. Barrow," Carrie said freezingly as she rose to her feet, "but I have every intention of remaining here and of proving to you and everyone else in the Overland Stage Company that I can manage this station just as effectively, no, *more* effectively than any man. If you will agree to help with the horses, I will provide your meals. If not, I'll have to charge you each time you eat with us."

Lucas rose to his feet, undecided as to whether he wanted to curse her stubborn refusal to listen to his warning or admire her spunk. It led to a dead end for him either way, and he'd best get back to his horses. Suddenly he felt safer chasing a dozen men who fought with guns than one small woman armed with nothing but her adorable self. He had lost every encounter so far, and he couldn't see his average improving in the future.

"That seems fair enough, ma'am, and I'll be happy to lend a hand if I'm around."

"Thank you, but don't change your plans to suit me. I'm sure we can manage." The twinkle in Lucas's eyes was unmistakable, and Carrie had the distinct, irritating impression he was laughing at her.

"Sleep well, ma'am, and don't forget to lock up tight. There are bears in these hills that would do a lot for some of that ham you just served me."

"I'll be staying at the cabin, at least for the time being, until I can get this place cleaned out."

"You can't clean anything Baca used. Burn it."

"That's what Katie told me."

"Then you listen to her. She's a sensible girl."

"And I'm not?" Carrie asked, her inflection rising with her eyebrows.

"I didn't say that, ma'am. I would never be so rude." Carrie wished she could bite her tongue. Now how was she going to get out of this gracefully.

"Excuse me. I guess I'm a little sensitive. Everyone I've met today has made a point of telling me I had no business being here by myself, and you keep *ma'aming* me until I feel positively decrepit."

"Sorry, ma—Mrs. Simpson. I didn't mean any disrespect."

"Is there anything wrong with calling me Carrie?"

"You're a married woman."

"I'm still a woman. Women have names, just like men, and they like to be called by them. My name is Carrie. Say it."

"Yes, ma'am, Carrie, ma'am." He was smiling broadly now, and it made her want to forget her irritation.

"Go on, get out of here before I run you off like Baca Riggins."

"Now ma'am, you'll hurt my feelings comparing me to Baca. I might get the impression you don't like me."

"You have no such impression, and you know it. Now stop trying to bait me. Katie and I have to clean up before we can go to bed, and tomorrow comes early."

"Thanks again for the food. It was mighty good. Good night . . . Carrie." Carrie spun around, but the door had already closed behind him.

"I can't think how can you sit and talk with him like that," Katie said. "He makes me uneasy all over. Those eyes seem to look right through you."

"There's nothing about him to worry you."

"Seems like he never spoke to me before, just stared at me like I wasn't there. He seems different around you."

"He's like all the rest of the men out here, cocksure and positive there's nothing a woman can do they can't do better."

"You're not afraid to stay here?"

"Why should I be? You weren't, and you've been here a week already."

"But I don't look like you, ma'am, and there be no need for ye say nice things to spare me feelings. I know what I am. I'm big and healthy, and I'll make some man a good wife, but I'm not the kind of woman men dream about nor pine over. Most of them would look right past me if they happened to see a good horse."

"You're being too rough on yourself. You're a charming person and a wonderful cook, and there're probably dozens of men who would be delighted to marry you if you weren't already engaged."

"If I be," muttered Katie. "I'd sure like to know where Brian's got to."

"I'm sure it's something very unimportant, and he hasn't written because he expected to be able to get here any minute."

"Well, I hope nothing happens to keep your husband away. The sooner he gets here, the safer I'll feel."

"Let's finish cleaning up here and go lock ourselves in for the night. Then we'll be safe from bears and Mr. Barrow's outlaws."

"If you be so hard set on him calling you by your first name, you're going to have to start calling him Lucas." Carrie looked startled. " 'Tis no more than fair," Katie added.

"I suppose it is," Carrie agreed, "but if he's going to be off chasing wild horses all the time, I won't be able to call him anything so it won't matter."

"There's nothing about that man that doesn't matter," Katie stated with conviction. "And it won't make any difference if he's right next to you or a hundred miles away."

Carrie was inclined to agree, but she hoped Lucas wouldn't go so far away as that.

Chapter 4

Carrie closed her bedroom door and allowed her body to sag against its roughly carved panels. She had gotten through the day, just barely, but she wouldn't have made it without Katie O'Malley and Lucas Barrow. What ever made her think she could handle this job on her own? Why hadn't she turned around at St. Louis when she found Robert had died of a fever and gone back home while she still had the money? If she had known what she was up against, she might have, no matter how bleak her future in Smithfield, Virginia, promised to be.

Like Katie, she had cooked and cleaned for her father and brothers after her mother died. As soon as the war was over, her older brother had brought home a lovable wife, a beautiful, charming, *useless* creature who gave him three children in less than four years and then died of childbed fever. Naturally Carrie had stepped in to take care of the children, and naturally she had not complained when David had been too grief-stricken to pay much attention to his young family. Apparently Emilie's family was also weighed down by grief because they, too, made no offer to help care for the children.

Carrie said nothing to anyone, though she said a great deal to her pillow every night before she fell into an exhausted sleep. She waited for the wounds caused by Emilie's death to heal. But when everybody had recovered sufficiently to be able to face the problem, Carrie had been handling it successfully for so long no one saw any need to change anything. Carrie could have stood up to her brother, but her father practically made her caring for his grandchildren a test of family loyalty. On top of that, David's in-laws sang the praises of Carrie's unselfishness so loud and long it would have been a social disgrace to refuse. Carrie resigned herself to being a mother without ever having had a husband and children of her own.

She might still have been in Virginia had not her other brother, Sam, brought home a wife, Lucinda, who showed every inclination to yield to Carrie in everything, especially if it involved work. Carrie knew in due time she would find herself mothering another set of children, and she made up her mind to leave home.

The entire household had been stunned when she announced she was going to marry Robert Simpson and move to Colorado, but ironically it was not her family that made the loudest outcry, at least not at first. Lucinda had broken into hysterical sobs, loudly complaining of Carrie's unparalleled selfishness in leaving her family when they needed her. Next it was David's in-laws' turn to carry the tale of Carrie's disaffection throughout the town, making it seem that their grandchildren were being heartlessly abandoned. Finally, Lucinda announced she was expecting a child, and *her* parents expressed their astonishment that Carrie would consider leaving her sister-in-law at such a time.

At this point, her father and brothers took up the by now very well rehearsed cry, and the result was a terrible argument during which they all said things they didn't mean and would have repented of a few days later, but Carrie decided not to give anybody a chance to apologize. She packed her clothes, gave away everything she didn't intend to take to Colorado, and left the house without waiting to receive anyone's blessing. It had hurt, but Carrie longed for a life and home of her own, and she knew she would never get it in Smithfield.

Hers was an extremely handsome family. Her father had been one of the most admired young men in the state, and her brothers were no less handsome. They were charming, gay, and the best of company. Carrie's mother had always pandered to her father and brothers, and they took it as the natural course of events that Carrie should continue to do the same, and they could never understand why she rebelled. Though not as handsome as her brothers, Carrie knew she was pretty, and had it not been a well-known fact that her father and brothers had neglected their lands, she would have been much sought after. In a state where the economy had been ruined by the Civil War and where the number of young men had been drastically reduced by that bloody conflict, a girl virtually had to bring something to her marriage or resign herself to being an aunt. Carrie's dilemma had been even more acute. In the small town of Smithfield, the only unmarried man to come back home after the war beside her own brothers was Robert Simpson.

Carrie knew Robert Simpson's marriage proposal would be the only escape she would be offered, and even though she felt only a mild liking for him, she agreed to marry him. She had known him all her life and knew he would never take advantage of her as her own family had done. She accepted his offer with the single stipulation that he find a job as far away from Smithfield as possible. She had not expected him to look as far afield as Colorado, but she had not drawn back when he wrote telling her of the position at the Green Run Pass Station and sending money for her journey.

She had traveled to St. Louis with hope in her heart and confidence that she and Robert could build a reasonably happy marriage. Their union would lack the passion she had hoped to find and the ardent adoration her mother had held for her father, but she would be comfortable, and that had to count for something.

Nothing could describe her shock when she reached St.

Louis to be told Robert had died only a few days earlier of a virulent fever then plaguing towns along the Mississippi. She was a little conscience-stricken to find she didn't feel any real sense of loss—the officials all seemed as much struck by her coolness as her beauty—but she never had deceived herself into thinking Robert had been able to engage her heart, and this was no time to punish herself for being unable to shed false tears. She had been given all of Robert's possessions, and it was in going through his papers that she found the letter giving him the position as manager of the station. She decided at once to take it herself. Her only alternative was to go back to Virginia, and she couldn't do that. To return while the feelings of resentment and hostility over her departure were still strong would have guaranteed that she would never be allowed a free moment for the rest of her life. Everyone would consider themselves *obliged* to impose upon her, and she decided death was almost preferable to that.

The decision to take on the stagecoach station had been made on the spur of the moment, and she hadn't worked out how she was going to explain the absence of her husband until she was halfway there. Then it had seemed like a simple matter to keep postponing his arrival until no one really expected him. By then she would have established herself so firmly there would be no question of replacing her.

She had never allowed herself to question her reasoning until some passengers who boarded the stage in Denver began to talk about Baca Riggins. She had given little credence to their stories at first, certain they were trying to scare her, sure it was part of the initiation process all Easterners had to go through when they went west, but after a while it was impossible to ignore the fact that there was universal agreement as to the character of Baca Riggins, and by the time she arrived at Green Run Pass Station, she was in such a state it was all she could do not to get right back on the stage and return to Denver.

Now she had survived her first day, but only with the considerable help of Katie and Lucas, both of whom would soon be leaving. Carrie was realistic enough to realize, and admit, that she couldn't run the station alone, but she had no idea what she was going to do. Katie might leave at any minute, and while Lucas would probably be around awhile longer, he might decide to go after wild horses any minute. Then what would she do?

She had to come up with a plan, she couldn't just keep hoping things would work out in her favor, but she would have to put that off until tomorrow. She intended to try once more to talk Lucas into staying, at least to get him to promise to take care of the horses for a definite length of time, but she was sure she could count on Katie to do the cooking until her Brian came. Actually she could handle the cooking by herself as long as there was someone for the horses, but she couldn't do both. That was simply too much for one person, but she had no idea where to look for a cook or a horse tender. Oh well, that was another thing she could ask Lucas about tomorrow.

She realized she was depending an awful lot on a man who had refused to commit himself to helping her, but somehow Lucas was the kind of person one did depend on. Besides, he had rescued her from Baca Riggins, and he had harnessed the team without being asked. Sure, he had told her he couldn't continue to work for her, but he always seemed to be around when he was needed.

Her curiosity about him was greater than ever, but she realized she had to be very careful if she started asking questions about him. Everyone believed she was married, and they would interpret her interest in a very different manner because of it. Suddenly she was angry that she was caught in such an untenable position, and all through no fault of her own. No, she couldn't say that. She had been only too anxious to marry Robert, and it was her own idea to manage the station the station by herself. No, she was in a tough situation because she didn't want to accept the only solution she could think of and go home; she *had* to have a life of her own, and she was determined to fight for it if she had to. She doubted she would have had the courage to come ahead if she had known what faced her, but she was here now and she intended to stay. Bother Lucas's outlaws, renegades, and drunks. She'd make sure the doors were locked at night and that someone was around during the day, but she was going to stick it out. Thousands of other women had endured a lot worse than this to cross the plains in a covered wagon, and she was just as tough and tenacious as any of them.

From long habit, Carrie woke before dawn. She immediately got up, but when she remembered the first stage didn't come through until after nine o'clock and realized she didn't have to get up for another hour at least, she sank back down with a blissful sigh and snuggled under the covers. It was already late spring, but unlike her native Virginia, May nights could be very cold in Colorado, and the warmth of her bed was deliciously inviting. For a moment she enjoyed a feeling of peace and well-being. Just knowing she was in her own home and didn't have to prepare breakfast for seven people, not to mention get them out of bed and see that the children got dressed, added to her contentment, but gradually she started to recall all the difficulties of her situation at the station, and her feeling of contentment faded. If she didn't solve her problems, she would ultimately be faced with the necessity of going back home or marrying the first man who asked her.

The thought of marriage by itself was unexpected and shocking, but even more unsettling was the discovery that Lucas Barrow's was the first name to pop into her mind. And it didn't take her more than a couple of seconds to realize that next to him, every person she had met since she left home faded into insignificance. Yet the idea of marrying a man like Lucas, much less Lucas himself, was

51

ridiculous. Their backgrounds were so different and they were so unalike it would be absurd to even consider it, not that she was actually *considering* it, it was just a thought that occurred to her, and a stupid one at that, so she immediately dismissed it.

But Carrie was dismayed to find she couldn't dismiss thoughts of Lucas that easily, and she was forced to abandon her bed and start getting dressed before she could get her mind off the strange, enigmatic wrangler. And to think she hadn't even known what a wrangler was yesterday morning; now here she was less than twenty-four hours later mooning over one just like an adolescent schoolgirl. Well, she wasn't mooning exactly, really, she wasn't mooning at all, it was just that the man had been so helpful, even if he did have a poor opinion of women, and there was a sense of mystery about him she found fascinating. One of the men on the stage had told her that people in the West came from many different backgrounds, that they were not always what they seemed, and that they had their own reasons for keeping what they knew to themselves. She was not supposed to be curious, but she couldn't help wondering about Lucas.

She slipped out of bed, wrapped her robe around her, stepped into her slippers, and idly moved about the room, ending up at the window, where she drew back the curtain so she could look out. It was still dark outside, but the sky had become a gray vault above the peaks in the distance. In a few moments the sun would burst over the distant mountains and flood the sky with its cold, clear light. She wondered if Lucas lived in a snug cabin or if he camped out. She had been told that men of the West almost always slept out, partly because they were used to it and partly because it was a lot less trouble, but it took almost no time for her to decide that any amount of trouble was preferable to sleeping outside, especially during the winter or when it rained. And that didn't include other considerations like wild animals and marauding Indians! What kind of man would prefer the outdoors and all its dangers to the comfortable safety of a house? Could such a man ever be brought to live inside, eat at a table, and take regular baths? Carrie realized this was just one more thing she had never taken into consideration, and she wondered how much more she would have to learn before she could begin to feel comfortable in her new home.

Carrie suddenly was aware of movement across the hall and she turned away from the window. She must have sat thinking about Lucas for half an hour if the sun was any measure. She'd better get dressed and down to the station or Katie was going to be there ahead of her. And after yesterday's problems, that would be inexcusable.

They met in the hall.

"Morning," Carrie said with a bright smile. "I wasn't sure you'd be up yet. I was woolgathering, or I'd have been gone and not have waked you."

"I've had to be up with the sun for so long, it's gotten in the way of a habit," Katie said with an ironic smile. "Now that there's no need to be stirring so early, I can't break it."

"You don't have to go up to the station."

"I'm coming up to help start the fires and grind the coffee beans," Katie informed her. "Besides, I like company, and I'm sick of staying in this cabin with no one but me own self to talk to." It was only a short walk from the cabin to the station, but there was frost on the ground and they wrapped up securely.

"I've been thinking," Carrie began. "I'd like to offer you a job cooking for me. You're as good as I am, maybe better, and I need someone who is here all the time, someone I can depend on to get food on the table if I have to deal with some crisis."

"It's an idea I like, ma'am, but what'll I do when me Brian comes?"

Carrie swallowed hard then plunged ahead. "I was thinking that maybe you weren't so sure you wanted to marry Brian, at least not yet."

"Now what would make you say a thing like that?" Katie asked, her expression not giving anything away.

"I'm not sure, I guess it was just an impression I got. Anyway, you said you hadn't seen him in years, and you were never more than friends. I thought if you had a job you wouldn't have to get married right away, you could take your time, get to know him a little better, and make sure. I'm not trying to talk you out of marrying him, you understand, but I was in something of the same position myself, only I didn't have time to consider or even look around to see if there was someone I liked better." There was an awkward silence which Katie did not break. "I know it may be presumptuous, but I need someone to help me, and for the time being at least, you have nowhere to go." Still Katie didn't answer. "Anyway it's an idea. I apologize if I've said something I shouldn't."

"No need, ma'am. You're a woman, and ye understand a woman's plight in ways a man never would. I guess I just never thought much about it. There's never much choice when you come to marry back home, but I can already tell it's different here. I don't rightly know what I mean to do, but I do know there's a sight more men than women. Even a horse of a girl like meself won't have to settle for the first man to show his face."

At least she shouldn't, thought Carrie, remembering she had done exactly that.

"There's not a particle of use pretending I haven't been worried what's keeping Brian and that's naturally set me to wondering—a body can't be in one place for nearly a week with nothing to do and not start to think a bit about things—and I would like to work for you. Even if I fall crazy in love with Brian when I see him, and I can't see why I would do that unless he's changed more than a body has any right to hope, it won't do him a particle of harm to wait a little, at least as long as he made me wait. I'll take your job, ma'am, and I'll start to pack right after we clear off the breakfast dishes."

Carrie had been mulling over in her mind what she thought would be a reasonable wage, but Katie's words drove all thoughts of wages out of her head.

"Pack? Why? Where are you going?"

"To move into the station, of course. You're expecting Mr. Simpson tomorrow, or maybe the day after, and I'd be forever underfoot in a small place like that."

"Oh, that's what you meant. You scared me for a minute." Katie gave her a strange look, and Carrie realized that once again she had forgotten everyone still thought she was married. "I mean, you don't have to move out now, not until he comes. I would be rather lonely by myself. Besides," she added quickly when Katie's expression didn't return completely to normal, "the rooms at the station are a mess. We'll have to scrub them from top to bottom before you could move into one of them. I doubt the beds can be used again."

"No doubt we'll have to boil the sheets and hang the mattresses on the line for a good airing," Katie said, relaxing into her normal cheerful, unquestioning attitude.

"About your salary . . ." Carrie began.

"Don't ye be talking about money just yet. As long as I have a place to sleep and something to eat, I'm content. We can talk about me salary when you're more settled in."

The station was cold and empty, but it was clean and orderly and within minutes they had a fire going and water on for coffee.

"Everything is pretty well started," Carrie said a little while later. "Do you think you can carry on by yourself from here?"

"For certain I can. Fixing breakfast won't be any trouble. Something worrying you?"

"No, but I have to make sure the team is ready when the stage comes in. That's one reason I was so anxious to have you help me. I forgot the change of horses yesterday, and I don't dare forget it again."

"Won't Mr. Barrow be doing that for you?"

55

"I don't know where Mr. Barrow is or what he means to do. In any case, he's made it plain I can't depend on him. Until I can find myself a stock tender, I'm going to have to fork out the teams myself."

"Do you know how?"

"If you mean do I know how to harness a team, yes I do. If you mean have I ever done it for a stage before, no, but it can't be too different. Anyway, I've got time to figure it out."

I'll show that Lucas Barrow I can do without his help, she said to herself as she hurried to the barn. I may not be able to break a wild mustang, but I can harness a team. She could hardly wait to see his face when she had the horses ready before the stage arrived. The thought that he might be sleeping at his cabin and not see her caused her spirits to plunge momentarily, but almost immediately she realized he would be around somewhere. Men like him never let any opportunity pass to display their supposed superiority to women. What was so difficult about harnessing a team? All you had to do was harness each horse before you brought it out of its stall. Children regularly harnessed horses to wagons, plows, and even carriages. Surely she could manage a stagecoach.

But Carrie was in for a shock. There was only one horse in the barn, and one look told her it was an animal of scope and breeding, obviously chosen by someone familiar with horses who could afford to pay for what he wanted. It had to be Lucas's horse, but how could a wrangler afford such an animal? Carrie admitted she had no idea what kind of horses one could find running wild, but she knew enough to know this horse had Morgan blood and he had never been wild.

Wondering about Lucas's horse isn't going to get the team hitched, Carrie scolded herself, and she headed toward the doors at the back of the barn. She was nonplussed to discover that the horses were all held in a corral and there were many more than four. Which four should she choose and how was she going to get a bridle on them? One look at the wild-eyed mustang eyeing her with open distrust told her they weren't going to stand still while she walked up and invited them to put their heads into a collar.

Unknown to Carrie, Lucas had preferred to be close at hand rather than sleep at his cabin; he had spent the night in the barn, and at this very minute he was looking down at her from the loft. He had intended to hitch up the team himself, but when he heard someone enter the barn, he had remained where he was, preferring to see who it was. When he recognized Carrie, he waited to see what she would do. Those horses couldn't be caught without a lasso, and he doubted Carrie knew how to use a rope. He watched as Carrie went up to the corral and stood for a time studying the horses. To his surprise, she entered the corral without a halter. As he expected, none of the horses would allow her to come close, but Carrie continued to move among them, and it took Lucas only a minute to realize she was making the horses move about so she could pick out the ones she intended to use in the team. Intrigued, he sat down on the hay, waiting to see what she would do next.

After a few minutes Carrie left the corral and disappeared around the side of the barn. In a moment, she reappeared dragging a bale of hay. She stood it on end near the opening of the corral and went for another. Soon she had a line of bales on one side leading from the corral to the barn. The light of understanding gleamed in Lucas's eye as he figured out what she was doing. In a little while, she had set up a second row of bales and she had a chute from the corral to the barn. Carrie went inside, filled four troughs with oats, then returned to the corral. She took down the top bar and pulled back the second bar until she had a small opening. Then moving carefully among the horses, she cut out one of her choice and herded it toward the chute. When it was directly opposite the opening to the chute, Carrie threw up her arms and yelled at the same time. The nervous horse darted through the opening and into the barn.

"Well, I'll be damned," Lucas thought to himself, a reluctant smile of admiration transforming his face. "That woman may be a tenderfoot, but she's got a head on her shoulders." It wasn't long before Carrie had chosen her team, and it included only one horse Lucas would not have chosen himself.

Being very careful not to upset the animals, Carrie moved into the stall with each horse, petting and talking to them as she slipped the halters over their heads. The horses didn't like the halter and tossed their heads obstinately, but they wanted the oats and they were too familiar with the halter to object for very long. Once all four horses were haltered and hitched to their stalls, Carrie searched for and found the harnesses. She laid them out on the floor until she was sure she had every piece she needed. Once she started, she wouldn't be able to leave the horses to look for some forgotten strap.

It wasn't easy for one person to harness four horses into a team, but Carrie had the good sense to find nose bags, which she filled with more oats, and the horses, restless and half-wild as they were, stood relatively still as she put them in the harness. Lucas didn't get too close for fear Carrie might see him, but as far as he could tell she hadn't made any mistakes. He'd check behind her before the stage left the yard, but he had to admit he'd never been so impressed with a woman. He sure hoped her husband turned out to be worthy of her.

A few minutes before Carrie heard the yell of the stage driver heralding his arrival, she stepped back to look at her work. The team stood quietly in the confines of the barn contentedly munching their oats, completely harnessed and ready to go.

"That ought to show that strutting Prometheus," she said with a brilliant smile of satisfaction, then she hurriedly left the barn and returned to the station. A brief stop at a mirror to fix her hair, a brisk shaking of her skirts to get rid of the dust and a few pieces of straw, and then she was standing on the porch to welcome her guests, calm and in control, when the stage pulled into the yard.

"You're right on time," she told the driver, one she didn't know. "The food is still hot, so hurry in before it gets cold."

"Where's my team?" Jerry Blake asked.

"It'll be ready when you're through eating." Everyone settled down to the table except for two men.

"Never have more than coffee in the morning," one said. "I'd rather stretch my legs."

"I think I'll take a walk too," the second man said almost as soon as the door closed behind his friend.

"Don't wander too far," Jerry warned him, talking with his mouth full of flapjacks. "We'll be back on the road as soon as I change horses."

"You won't get through that plate of food in less than fifteen minutes," the passenger joked, pointing to the food mounded in front of Jerry. The man just grinned and dug in again.

"I guess I'd better be seeing to the horses," Jerry said as he got to his feet later, "but I want to tell you this sure beats anything Baca Riggins ever served up. I hope you and that young lady don't plan to go away anytime soon. A man could get used to this kind of food."

"There'll be something just as good every time you come through from now on," Carrie promised him.

"You wait until the passengers hear about you. They'll probably start riding the stage just to get a decent meal every now and then."

"I appreciate your compliments, Mr. Blake, but don't you think you ought to be getting back on the road?"

"You're right, ma'am. If you'll just tell your tender to rustle up that team, I'll be on my way."

"I'm the tender for the time being," Carrie calmly announced, "and the team is already *rustled* up." Two of the

59

passengers stopped eating at that remark. "Just follow me," Carrie said and led the way to the barn.

Lucas had climbed down and inspected the harnesses in Carrie's absence, but he was back in the loft waiting when Carrie opened the barn door and Jerry Blake got an eyeful of the team standing there, quiet as you please, fully harnessed, all munching complacently from their nose bags. His jaw started to sag and it didn't get any better when Carrie calmly removed the nose bags and led the team from the barn toward the waiting stage.

"If you'll unhitch those horses, Mr. Blake, I'll back the team into place." Jerry was a little slow off the mark, but his jaw closed with a snap and he ran to get the horses unhitched from the stage before Carrie got there. "Just tie them to that rail over there," she directed. "I'll unharness them after you're gone." Jerry did as he was told, and Carrie was just backing the team into place when a shotgun went off practically in their ears. Carrie had chosen the wild-eyed mustang as one of the leaders. Until the gunshot, he had responded calmly to the whole procedure. But before the sound of the blast had finished echoing through the hills, he rolled his eyes back in their sockets, threw up his head, and started to buck in the harness. Carrie hung on to his bridle with grim determination and would probably have gotten him under control had there not been two more quick blasts from the unseen guns. That was too much for the nervous team. In unison, they started down the road at a run.

Jerry Blake had his hands full with the used-up team. Only their exhaustion kept them from breaking loose and following the others, but he looked up in time to see Carrie still holding on to the harness of the dun mustang. *She wasn't going to let go!*

Chapter 5

Jerry dropped the reins he was holding and made a dive for Carrie's team, but they were already past him. "Let 'em go!" he shouted, horror of what could happen any second raising the hair on the back of his neck. "They'll kill you!" But Carrie couldn't hear him, and he stood rooted to the spot, watching helplessly as the team reached the road and turned toward the narrow mountain pass at a full gallop.

Lucas had come down from the loft and was watching Carrie from his favorite spot under the tree when the sound of the first gunshot brought him to his feet. He started toward her, but when he heard the two additional shots and saw the horses bolt, he instinctively headed through the trees at a dead run, racing toward the road at an angle he hoped would enable him to intercept the runaway team.

Lucas didn't know how long it took him to reach the road, but he seemed to be moving in slow motion, every second like a lifetime. He could see Carrie hanging on to the leader's bridle, being bounced like a rag doll, and he knew she wouldn't be able to hold on much longer. Ordinarily her weight would have slowed the horses down, but these brutes were accustomed to pulling a stagecoach loaded with up to six people; one tiny female was a burden they hardly noticed, and they were racing at a full gallop. If she lost her grip on the bridle, she could fall under the horses' hooves or down the mountainside into the rock-strewn ravine.

Suddenly Lucas saw he was not going to be able to intercept the wild-eyed dun mustang that was catapulting Carrie down the road as if she were no more than a bothersome fly, and he realized Carrie could die. A horrible vision of her mangled and bleeding body flashed through his mind, and a terrible fear took hold that spurred him to superhuman effort. With one final, agonizing explosion of energy, he threw himself into the air, desperately reaching for the harness of the second horse. Miraculously his fingers closed around the straps on the sweat-flecked gray and he felt the leather bite deep into the flesh of his hands as he was jerked forward along with the galloping horses. Desperately calling upon every reserve of his strength, Lucas fought to reach the gray's halter; only by pulling his head down could he slow the fear-crazed horse.

"Throw your heels forward and dig in," he yelled to Carrie as he seized the gray's bridle. Putting his whole weight on the horse's head, Lucas threw his legs in front of him and dug his heels in to force the gray's head down. The excruciatingly painful jarring on his legs threatened to tear bone from sinew and to wrench his shoulders from their sockets, but he doggedly pitted his straining muscles against those of the powerful animal; it was the only way he could save Carrie.

Try as she might, Carrie could not move her legs, but she followed Lucas's example and put all her weight on the dun's head. The drag on the two horses slowed them down and caused the others to slue around and become entangled in the traces. Within moments the team had come to halt, hopelessly tangled in their own harnesses. In a flash Lucas was at Carrie's side, his white face showing none of his usual lazy unconcern.

"My God, you could have been killed!" he said, prying her paralyzed fingers loose from their hold on the bridle; as part of the same motion, as though it were the natural thing to do, he wrapped Carrie in a crushing embrace.

One bleeding hand pressed her head tightly against his heaving chest, and for a few soul-wrenching seconds, Carrie was conscious of nothing but his racing, pounding heart. "Are you hurt?" Lucas asked, staring intently into her face as though by so doing he could tell if any part of her were injured.

"No," Carrie tried to assure him. "A little jarred perhaps, definitely petrified with fear, but unhurt."

Lucas took a deep breath to calm his pulsating senses. He had not stopped to think when the horses bolted; he had just acted. Gradually he became aware of the way he was holding Carrie and realized he had lost control of his emotions; if he didn't get himself under control before the people running toward them saw what he was doing, they were going to guess far more than he wished anyone to know.

"Are you certain?" he said, releasing her and stepping back.

"I'm fine," Carrie said, trying to convince her legs to support her without his assistance. "Or I will be as soon as I get my breath." She didn't know whether she was more stunned by her close brush with death or the look of near torment she had seen in Lucas's gleaming silver-gray eyes just before he enfolded her in his fierce embrace. She could still feel his arms locked around her, immobilizing her against his hard, sinewy body, and the memory of that moment made her feel as dizzy as if she'd been spinning in circles.

Jerry raced up to them, his breath labored from the exertion of running at top speed. "I thought you were a goner, ma'am," he gasped, admiration making his eyes gleam like water in the bright sun. "I never saw anything so brave in my life."

"Or foolhardy," Lucas said. Reaction had set in, and a look of blazing anger flared in his eyes. "You may be a heroine now, but blind stupid luck is the only reason you're not dead. Why in hell didn't you have the good sense to let go? You could have been killed."

Carrie was too dazed to be angry. Her heart was beating so hard she could hardly breathe, God knows she couldn't think, and she struggled to regain her equilibrium. She hadn't stopped to think when she held on to the horses. At first there didn't seem to be any reason to let go, and then she *couldn't* let go. Everything had happened too fast.

And now Lucas was furious, was actually scolding her as if he cared what happened, and this after he had made it clear she couldn't depend on him. Well, she wouldn't be treated like this, not by him or any other man, and especially not in front of Jerry Blake and a stagecoach full of goggling strangers. The station was her responsibility, these were her customers, and she would not be shouted at by some wrangler as if she were a common female.

"I had to hold on to them, Mr. Barrow, or they would have gotten away. I don't have a replacement team, something I think *you* were supposed to correct. Besides, they could have been injured, and then they wouldn't be any use to me or the company. I don't think the owners would consider that taking proper care of their property."

Carrie's words caused the flames in Lucas's eyes to flare higher and his lips to compress into a thin line. He and Jerry finished untangling the harnesses, and Carrie stepped forward to lead the team back toward the station.

Lucas put a curb rein on his temper. After all, what this woman did was none of his business. It was her husband who ought to be rampaging about, threatening to wring her lovely neck. He kept the team between them, hoping they could somehow block the magnetic force which seemed to pull him to her side.

"The company doesn't expect you to take such a risk on their behalf," Lucas assured her with what Carrie thought was a good deal too much presumption. What did he know about what the company would do? He had probably never even seen the company headquarters, much less talked to one of the owners. And she certainly wasn't going to allow a temporary employee to be the arbitrator of her conduct.

"Nonetheless, all company property is my responsibility and I don't intend to lose any of it." Suddenly, she was amused rather than angered by his look of tightly contained fury. "What would you have had me do, let them run off?" she asked, her goading smile irritating Lucas still further.

Lucas would have given half his inheritance to tell her what he wanted, but he was stymied. As only a wrangler, he couldn't advise her on how to run the station, but neither could he say what he wanted to in front of Jerry; he couldn't say it anyway because she was a married woman, and he felt his bottled-up anger building up steam during the walk back to the station until it boiled over. Striking out like an angry animal, he turned on the two men who had left the breakfast table early, each of whom had a shotgun in hand.

"Are you the fools who fired those shots?" he demanded, unleashing the full force of his considerable fury on them.

"We were just trying out these guns to see which one we liked better," one man explained.

"If you're a fair sample of the kind of settlers coming West, God help the rest of us. Any fool knows not to go firing shotguns around people, and even a *damned* fool knows not to shoot anything around half-wild horses. Put those away before you hurt yourselves, and don't take them out until you're at least a mile from any human target."

"Now look here," said one man, "we're right sorry we caused the little lady any trouble, and I do apologize, but you've got no right to talk to me like—"

Lucas reached the man in three strides. "Give me that shotgun."

"I'll be damned if I will. It's mine and I—" A single, swift movement of Lucas's fist, too rapid for anyone to see, and the man was on the ground. Lucas picked up the dropped shotgun, took out the shells, and broke it down. Then he turned to the second man. "Give me yours." The man handed over his shotgun without hesitation. Lucas emptied it and broke it down too. He put the shells in his pocket and handed the disassembled shotguns to Jerry Blake. "You can give them back whenever they get where they're going. And don't either of you come around here again with a gun unless you want me to use it on you."

The man on the ground picked himself up slowly, rubbing his jaw, anger strong in his face. "You'll hear about this. I'm going to file a complaint against you when I get to Denver, with the company and with the sheriff."

"You can talk to anybody you like," Lucas replied, regaining some of his indifference. "Just don't show your face around here again."

He then helped Jerry hitch up the new team. There was a good deal of muttering among the passengers, but none of them wanted to test Lucas's temper too far, and they boarded the stage without any further trouble.

"Come on. I'll help you unharness the horses," Lucas said to Carrie after the stage pulled out. He started for the barn, and Carrie followed a little behind.

As she calmed down, she realized more clearly what a chance she had taken holding on to the runaway team. It didn't take much imagination to realize she could have been badly trampled, even killed. But she was even more surprised by Lucas's outburst. She had known from the first that any concern he may have had for the horses was overpowered by his worry over her. She had never had any doubt in her mind that he was furious with the men because they had endangered *her* life. This thrilled her, but her response frightened her. She felt as if she wanted to fling caution to the winds, to ask him to put into words all the things she had seen in his eyes and heard in the loud hammering of his heart, but her common sense, her determination to never again allow anyone but herself to control her life, made her lag a safe distance behind.

At least she thought it was safe until she realized she was walking on the same side of the horses as he was, *directly behind him*. That was a bad mistake. She had a close-up view of his lean, sinuous body, and all thought of control was forgotten. She had already admitted the attractiveness of his powerful shoulders and torso, but her judgment was wholly suspended by the riveting effect of his backside; powerful thighs encased in skin-tight jeans, rounded buttocks slowly undulating as he walked, heavily muscled shoulders threatening to burst from his shirt, and tendrils of moist black hair on the nape of his neck all combined to overwhelm her senses.

"Don't you think you were a little too rough on those men?" she made herself say as she closed her eyes against the mesmerizing vision. She would never learn to run this station successfully if one good look at a man's backside could turn her mind to mush. "They certainly can't have much of an opinion of your manners, and they didn't mean any harm."

"I can't think of anything more dangerous out here than a stupid person full of good intentions." He didn't turn back to face her, just tossed his words over his shoulder. "Nor do I give a damn about good manners. Neither would have done you any good if you'd been thrown under their hooves. They'll either kill themselves or someone else."

"You seem to have a pretty low opinion of other people, Mr. Barrow. Is it limited to females, Easterners, or does it apply to everybody?"

"I take people as I find them," Lucas replied. He had brought the horses to a halt and was beginning to strip the harness from their backs. "I don't find them any more stupid in the East than in the West. I certainly don't find women any more stupid than men, but Easterners are used to a very different kind of life, and they have to learn quickly when they come out here, or somebody pays. People like those two won't learn because they're not interested and they're not observant. If they don't settle in some town soon, they'll be dead or broke within the year. Everything out here is half wild, ma'am, the people, the horses, the country. Much of it will never be tamed, so you have to learn to live with it, adapt to its rules. They'll never see that, but you will. You're different."

Carrie's heart beat a little faster. Maybe he didn't think so badly of her after all, even though he clearly considered her as ignorant of the West as the worst neophyte.

"You're smart and you've got guts. You've also got a way with people. Being a woman, and a mighty pretty one at that, is a big help. You'll do fine someday—you'd do okay if you were as plain as that Amazon you've got in the kitchen—but this is the wrong place and the wrong situation."

"What do you mean?" Carrie asked, her friendly feelings toward him evaporating.

Lucas had kept his head down and a horse between them as he stripped the harness off the horses, but now he came around the leader and faced Carrie with a disconcertingly cold gaze. "Two things. You're a woman trying to do a man's job, and you're a woman alone in a country where no female is safe without a man." Carrie began to get angry. "I don't mean to take anything away from what you've done," Lucas continued. "You can turn out a first-rate dinner and the inside of the station is so clean it looks spanking new, but this is the second time a stage has come in and you've had trouble with the horses. You might have been able to handle those two idiots with the shotguns, but you won't be able to handle the saddle bums or renegades that might come through, and that'll end up causing the station no end of trouble."

Carrie was so angry she knew she shouldn't answer him. She knew from experience with her father and brothers that when she was this angry, she always made things worse. But she spoke anyway.

"I was under the impression that I was supposed to take care of them because they were *my* customers riding *my* line, but then maybe I'm mistaken. Suppose you tell me what you think I ought to do, you being so well versed in the ways of the West."

Lucas directed his penetrating glance at her. Carrie's face was innocent of mockery or derision, yet he was certain her heart contained plenty of both. Oh hell, it couldn't be helped. The sooner she went back to her husband, the sooner he could get her out of his mind. Just look at her. She was such a tiny little thing he had an overwhelming urge to wrap her safely in his arms. Her face was tilted up now as she squared off against him, her eyes bright with anger, her lips tightly pursed with determination. No matter, he wanted to kiss them anyway. He wanted to touch her flame-spotted cheeks, caress her rigid shoulders until she relaxed into his embrace. Even here, in the cold thin air of a Colorado mountain morning, he felt himself burning with an inflamed heat, fired with a need to touch her hair, to bury his face in the lavender scent that always hung faintly around her.

But she's married, a strident voice shouted in his head. She has a husband; she's beyond your reach *forever*. Lucas's senses bucked wildly against the constraints they felt coming, but he knew he had to get himself under control or he would do something unforgivable.

"I've already told you what I think you ought to do."

"That was yesterday. I was hoping you had changed your mind since then."

It had changed all right, but it wasn't anything he was going to tell her about, and it wouldn't do him any good if he could. He found himself irresistibly drawn to the tiny sprite of a woman who had more fire in her little finger than most women had in their whole body, a woman who had the courage to take on a man's job in a man's world, to hang on despite setbacks, a woman who faced him without the slightest tendency to swoon over his looks or hang on his sage, male-oriented advice. Staying around her was like sticking his head into a lynx's den. He knew he would be torn to ribbons, but he couldn't stop himself.

"I think you ought to go back to Denver, or wherever it was you left your husband, and head back East," he said, steeling himself against the agonizing thought of never seeing her again. "This country has a way of destroying any beauty not its own, and I'd hate to see you looking like an old woman before your time."

"Thank you for your concern, but I didn't invite your opinion on my person," Carrie told him frigidly.

"It's hard not to think of your *person* when it's right in front of me." Carrie couldn't fail to catch the look that was much more than appreciation of the female form, and she didn't know whether she felt drawn to him or repelled because of it. He had stepped closer, and she felt intimidated. She wanted to step back, but she didn't dare. He might think she was afraid of him, or even worse, that she agreed with him.

"Nevertheless, I would appreciate it if we could keep our relations on a business basis."

"Ma'am, we don't have any relations, and we aren't going to have any business either."

"You call me *ma'am* one more time, and I'm going to brain you," Carrie said, suddenly furious. He was too sure of himself, too certain he had the answer to everything. "I'm a person, a *real* person like you, not some china doll to be put on a shelf and admired when there's nothing more important to do." That wasn't what she'd meant to say, and the changing light in his eye prompted a feeling of panic. Suddenly things were getting on a personal basis, and she didn't want that. "I intend to stay here and be a success," she said, trying to sound as impersonal as she could. "I would appreciate it if you would help me with the horses, but if not, I'll manage to deal with them myself."

"Like you have so far?" So much for her thinking he might have taken a personal interest in her.

"Mr. Barrow, if you're determined to make me dislike you, you can spare yourself any further effort. I thought when you threw Mr. Riggins into the horse trough you were a gentleman, but I see you're just another one of these bigoted males who thinks females are good for nothing but cooking, cleaning, and having babies."

"I never said that was all—"

"No, but your actions have," Carrie declared, ruthlessly interrupting him. "Of course you don't have to help me if you don't want to, but—"

"I've done everything I could to help you from the beginning. Why do you make it sound like I'm personally trying to run you out of Colorado?"

"Because you are."

"All I said was that I can't be around forever, that I have a job of my own to do. That seems to me to be a reasonable statement."

"Now I'm not reasonable," Carrie spurted.

"I never —"

"I suppose it's a waste of your precious time to talk to a female, especially one from the East."

"Ma'am, I never said time spent with you was wasted." That light was back in his eyes, and there was nothing impersonal about it this time. Carrie suddenly felt a thrill go through her whole body; it seemed to be equally divided between pleasure and apprehension. All this man had to do was look at her hard, and he upended her ability to think clearly.

"But you just —"

"I said I wouldn't be around all the time to help you. I never said it would be a waste of my time." Carrie felt disarmed, but irrationally that fired her anger rather than cooled it.

"I see. Women have their place, and as long as I keep to it, I'm worthwhile. But suppose I decide to step outside your proscribed line. Will I become a waste of time then?" An ironic smile chased the severity from Lucas's expression. He came even closer, and to Carrie's shock and dismay, he took her chin in his hand and gently tilted her head up so he could look into her eyes. She had never seen such eyes, so clear and intense; she had never encountered any gaze she felt could penetrate her defenses . . . until now.

"I never saw anybody to beat you for twisting a man's words. Any man who didn't know you might get the notion you were trying to make him mad." Carrie wondered how she could make anyone mad when her mind was in such chaos she didn't know her own thoughts.

"I'm afraid that we women tend to let our emotions color our thinking. And in case you haven't noticed, I am a woman," she said a little hesitantly.

"That's one thing I noticed right off," Lucas stated, dropping his face until it was only a few inches from hers. "I knew the moment you stepped down off that stage you were more woman than I'd ever seen before, a woman a man could feel proud to call his own." *His own*, Carrie thought, quickly recovering from her momentary bemusement. She'd show him Carrie Simpson wasn't going to be owned by anyone. She reached up, pushed his hand away from her chin, and stepped back so she could see him without craning her neck.

"Treating me like the witless other half of some man is a mighty strange way of showing it. No woman wants to feel owned, not even one as silly and helpless as you seem to think I am."

"Ma'am . . ."

"And don't call me ma'am," Carrie nearly screamed. "My name is Carrie. You said it once, and I doubt it would kill you to say it again."

"I hope not, but you never can tell about things like that."

"What *are* you talking about? First you insult me by telling me I ought to go back to Denver before I get myself hurt, then you start to make me feel like you *want* me to leave."

"Ma'am, I mean Carrie ma'am, you sure do make a right spirited attempt to read a man wrong." Furrows of frustration crisscrossed his brow, but Carrie could see the indisputable twinkle in his eye and feel the magnetism radiating from his body. He was laughing at her again, and she struggled to fight off the numbing effect this attraction was having on her ability to resist his blandishments.

"I wasn't aware that your words left any room for interpretation."

"You know, it's silly for you to be getting so angry at a man when he's doing everything he can to help you." He came a step closer, and Carrie moved a step back, but his stride was much longer than hers and he was closer now. "We ought to be friends. I'll help you as much as I can, but I've got my own work to do."

"So you keep telling me, but since you're supposed to be providing the station with extra horses, I would think that you were, in a way at least, working for the company. If that's the case, I don't see why you can't consider helping with the horses part of your job."

"You seem determined to keep at me until you get your way," Lucas said, and the twinkle turned into a smile. "I might as well warn you that I never give in to any female, not even when she's as beautiful as you."

Carrie felt as if she'd received two crushing blows and didn't know which one to respond to first. That Lucas thought she was beautiful was a thrilling disclosure and made her want to sing and dance at the same time, although she knew she did both very badly, but the fact that he had interpreted her need for his help as a poorly disguised attempt to gain her own way, with God-only-knew what further demands he thought she might make, made her so angry she quite forgot the compliment.

"I would find it quite easy to remain angry with you whether you agreed to help me or not," she said with lofty scorn.

Without warning, Lucas took her by the arms and kissed her soundly on the lips. Then thinking better of it, he took her *in* his arms and kissed her in a way Carrie didn't know a woman could be kissed.

Carrie felt as though her lips were touched by fire, a hard and insistent heat that was determined to blaze a path all the way to her heart. There was nothing timid, chaste, or even gentlemanlike about this kiss; it was rough, demanding, and completely devastating, and his hard, muscled body pressed the length of hers merely added fuel to a fire that blazed out of control before Carrie even knew what had started it.

Lucas's lips took hers and without hesitation his tongue

eased its way between her teeth, thrusting, seeking, demanding. She was certain shock and mortification would hold her lifeless in his arms, but she found herself responding to his warmth, her body taut with yearning, her arms tentatively around his neck. Her mind shouted at her to resist, to push him aside, but her body remained helplessly enthralled and it was Lucas who ended the embrace.

"There," Lucas said, his impish grin disguising the fact that he was as thoroughly shaken as she, "now you have a reason to be angry with me." Then he turned, picked up the dropped harnesses, and disappeared into the tack room, slamming the door behind him.

Carrie was immobilized. Her whole body had shut down, even her heart and breathing seemed to have stopped, and she was unable to stir from the spot. Then suddenly she gave a convulsive sob, turned, and ran toward the cabin.

Katie was finishing up the last of the breakfast dishes when Carrie returned to the kitchen sometime later. She poured herself a cup of coffee and almost collapsed into a chair.

"You have the look of a ghost about you, and no wonder," Katie said. "I stepped outside when I heard the shots, and I saw you being carried off like you were a doll in a dog's teeth. Me heart was in me throat, I can tell ye, I was so scared. If it hadn't been for Mr. Barrow, you might have been killed."

"It seems I have still another reason to be grateful to him," Carrie said. The bleak note in her voice did not escape Katie's notice.

" 'Tis mighty useful to have a man like him about," Katie said, watching Carrie out of the corner of her eye. "And mighty agreeable he is to look on too," she added with a giggle. "Had there been any like him back home, 'tis certain I would never have left Ireland. Some girls would do desperate things to get a man like that." Carrie refused to allow her mind to think of Lucas as *her man*, but a tremor arced through her body and she felt betrayed by her own flesh.

"Maybe some girls would," Carrie said, bringing her wary gaze up to meet Katie's, "but I'm not in the habit of pursuing men."

"Oh, you don't count," Katie said blithely. "You're married."

I'm not married and I *do* count, Carrie's body screamed. But her mind warned her that everyone thought she was married and that *they* had decided she should be beyond feeling an attraction to any man other than her husband, and especially a man like Lucas.

"And naturally everybody knows married women lose the urge right quick."

"What *urge?*" demanded Carrie, her thoughts wrenched around by this unexpected statement.

Katie blushed scarlet. "To be perfectly honest, I don't know exactly," she admitted. "I'm not stupid and I have a pretty good notion, of course, it's just that no one ever saw fit to explain things to me. First they said I was too young to know, and then they said I'd be better off not knowing, living in a house full of men like I was." She paused, an arrested look in her eye. "Perhaps you can tell me, ma'am."

"Tell you what?" Carrie asked, panic routing any other emotion.

"Do married women lose the urge for a man? Us young girls didn't see how it could be true, but the older women say that having a baby takes it away."

"I couldn't say," Carrie replied, praying she could think of some way to halt this conversation before she both mortified and exposed herself. "I've only just gotten married, and of course I haven't had a baby."

"I was forgetting that." Katie sighed. "I hope it's not true. It would be such a waste."

Carrie knew she should keep her mouth shut, but she just had to ask, "Why?"

"Because men seem to like it ever so much, even when

they can barely find the energy to stir from their own hearth. It seems a shame for a woman to have something she starts out liking turn into a misery, especially when the menfolks can't seem to get their fill of it." She sank her voice into a conspiratorial whisper. "I heard tell that some men who are quite old make their women's lives a purgatory with their constant demands."

"Do you know anything about Mr. Barrow?" Carrie asked, desperate to change the subject to something less likely to cause her difficulty breathing. She absolutely refused to allow any thoughts of Lucas coupled with *the urge* to cross her mind, but her body was not nearly so squeamish, and she soon found herself squirming restlessly in her chair.

"No more than I've done told you already. He was here when I got here. Not long. I figure, but long enough for everybody to stop paying him much attention. He spends his time with those wild horses of his or sitting under that tree. It's like he's waiting for something, or someone, but he doesn't miss a thing. The first night I was here, they decided I was to stay in the cabin. Seems they were too lazy to keep up two places and no one used it. Anyway, I went to bed early, but I couldn't sleep, too tired from the stagecoach ride I guess, and I was standing near the window, looking at the moon when I caught a movement out of the corner of me eye. I stared hard into the dark, but I didn't see anything for a minute. I had almost decided I was wrong when a man moved out of the shadows and darted quickly down the road to the next clump of trees. It was Buck and he was coming here. I had barred all the doors, but I tell you, ma'am, I was scared. I didn't have a gun or anything else to defend meself with. I ran downstairs and found a knife in the kitchen, a real long butchering knife with a sharp blade. I tiptoed to the front door. I was going to let him think I was upstairs, and get him when he turned his back."

"Weren't you afraid to think of killing a man?"

"To be sure I was a little nervous over it, but I wasn't

76

upset about cutting him up. After all, what he was wanting to do to me wasn't no nice thing."

"No, but to kill a man."

"I wasn't hankering to do it. I just wanted to hurt him enough to let him know I didn't want him sneaking back over the next night. Anyway, he no more than put his foot on the first step when I heard a pistol click. He heard it too because he froze and looked to either side, trying to see in the dark."

" 'Well now, I'll be dad-blasted,' this voice said out of the dark, sort of conversational-like. 'I didn't know Cody walked in his sleep.' It was Mr. Barrow, and he had a gun. Cody just stood there, not moving a muscle. 'I sure hope he turns around and goes back. I'd hate to have to wake him up. I hear tell it's better to put a sleepwalker to sleep forever than to wake him in the middle of one of his perambulations. Addles his brain forever.' Well, you should have seen Cody. He slammed his eyes shut, raised his arms up in the air like he was levitating or something, and turned around and started walking back to the station.

"Guess I'd better tell Baca to lock him in at night for his own good,' Mr. Barrow said loud enough for him to hear. 'He might get lost in the woods and never find his way back. Or a grizzly might get him.' You could see Cody walk a little bit faster every time Mr. Barrow spoke. He was nearly running by the time he reached the station steps.

"You okay, Miss O'Malley?' Mr. Barrow asked real soft-like.

" 'I had me a butchering knife,' I told him. 'I always did want to see what a skunk looked like skinned.'

" 'Same as any other wild animal, Miss O'Malley. They all look pretty much the same.' I never did see him. He just faded into the night, but I knew he was there and I didn't have any trouble sleeping after that. Why do you ask about him?"

"I'm not entirely sure, but he doesn't strike me as the type of man to be a wrangler. When he got mad about me holding on to those horses, he forgot himself and he didn't talk or act the way he had earlier. There's something about that man he's not telling anybody. I don't know what it is, but I'll bet you a new dress he's not what he says he is."

"I don't know about that, but you won't have any use for a new dress. Seems to me like men just don't care about what a woman wears out here."

"They care," Carrie said, remembering Lucas's kiss and the look in his eyes. "They may have a different way of showing it, but they care just the same."

Chapter 6

Katie's story of Lucas's helpfulness did nothing to restore order to Carrie's emotions or still the tumult in her mind. And after she had decided what should be prepared for lunch and helped Katie get the cooking started, she said, "I think I'll set a wash pot on to boil in the back yard and turn out these bedrooms. They can't be used as they are, and we might need to stay over sometime."

"I'll give you a hand if you choose to wait a bit," Katie offered. " 'Twill be me room when your husband gets here, so I ought to be the one to do the cleaning."

"There's no need for you to move out of the cabin, not even after Robert arrives," Carrie said. "We can't use two bedrooms at once."

"Just the same . . ."

"I know what you're going to say, but you're wrong. Now you get on with lunch, and I'll see what I can do with these rooms." But Carrie found that even hard work couldn't keep her unwelcome thoughts at bay. She built a fire under the wash pot, stripped the beds and took down the curtains, put everything in boiling water with strong lye soap, hung the mattresses outside to air, and started scrubbing down the rooms with hot, soapy water, but she still couldn't keep her mind off Lucas.

When Carrie had decided to pretend she was married and tell everyone her husband would be joining her in a few days, she had done it solely to get the position of station manager and prevent the company from dismissing her before she had a chance to prove she could do the job. It never occurred to her that it would also be a bar to any man developing an interest in her. She had been so preoccupied with Robert's death and figuring out how to keep from having to go back to Virginia that she hadn't thought of anything else. It wasn't that she hadn't thought men and women in the West fell in love and married; it was just that she hadn't thought at all.

Now she knew Lucas was interested in her, his kiss told her more than any words ever could, but she also knew he would hold back, might even leave Green Run altogether, because he thought she was married. One of the things she had learned was that most Western men had a solid respect for the institution of marriage, and they would do practically anything rather than tamper with that sanctified relationship.

Carrie wasn't at all sure she wanted Lucas to be interested in her, there was too much about him she didn't know and the idea of falling in love with a stranger with a mysterious past didn't appeal to her—there was too much risk in that—but she was sure she didn't want to drive him away. Setting aside his physical appearance, if you could set aside such a powerful factor as that, he was the most interesting man she had ever met. The very fact that he was mysterious added to his attractiveness, but there was more to it than that. For one thing, he was a gentleman. He had repeatedly come to her rescue without being asked, and he obviously expected no thanks. And Carrie knew the reason he'd slept in the barn was to be closer to her in case anything happened. He hadn't let Baca or the runaway horses hurt her, and those two men with the shotguns wouldn't bring another gun to the station, if they ever dared to come back at all.

She had to grin. What would Emilie and Lucinda have done if they'd been faced with what Carrie had been through in the last few days? A good look at Lucas's piercing eyes would have scandalized their maidenly modesty, and one glance at Baca Riggins would have sent them into a fainting spell. She admitted she had felt a little faint herself when he grabbed her, but she had managed to pull through, with Lucas's help.

But when it came right down to it, she couldn't say what it was about Lucas that captivated her. She might be able to put a name on it when she got to know him better, but all she knew for certain now was that he was the most compelling man she'd ever met.

True, he was handsome. Not handsome like the men you saw in some magazines, but in a rugged way that sort of frightened and thrilled her at the same time. What she remembered about his clothes was not that they were clean or neat but that they were *tight*. She doubted there was a corset in the whole of the South that fitted its wearer's waist any more tightly than Lucas's Levi's fitted his bottom, and she expected his shirt to rip open every time he flexed a muscle. It would take a little time for her to get used to a man walking in high-heeled boots and wearing a flat-crowned black felt hat eighteen hours out of twenty-four, but it took no time at all for her to become captivated by his silver-gray eyes, angular jaw, and flat-planed cheeks. He always looked like he needed a shave and the wisps of curly black hair peeking out from under his collar promised an equally furry chest, but the impact of all his parts came together in his face, in the smiles that could caress her like a soft summer breeze or frowns that could leap from his eyes with the impact of a shotgun blast.

He had a kind of magnetism that attracted the attention of everyone he passed, that drew her to him, that warned her of his presence even before she saw him. To other people it said this was a man to pay attention to; to her it whispered that here was a man she would never forget.

Carrie broke off her daydream. It was all fruitless speculation, all a useless distraction, until she had proved to him she could run this station by herself, that she would not be run off by anyone. Also she had to figure out a way to tell him that she was not, and never had been, married.

Lucas kicked a rock out of his path. As long as he was this worked up over Carrie, he had no business going to the station, not for lunch or anything else. He ought to go after those mustangs now, his bunch was getting down to just a few decent animals, but he knew all the while he was going to stay and have lunch with Carrie. That woman was in his craw and there didn't seem to be any way to get her out. He had thought he was being real smart when he kissed her. He had wanted to make her so mad she would stay far away from him until her husband came. He might have done that, it would serve him right if he had, but that single kiss had also pushed him helplessly over the edge, and there was nothing he could do to right himself.

He could just imagine what his Uncle Max would say if he knew his nephew was getting himself worked up over a woman in the middle of a job. Max Barrow had a tongue that could take the paint off a barn, and he never spared it even though Lucas was his only living relative. Old Max was the oldest boy in a Texas family where thirteen babies died between the first and last children, the only two that lived. Max had left home early and wandered over the West only to come home one day and find his father and brother had been killed in a range war and his sister-in-law dying of a broken heart. Max buried his sister-in-law and then finished up that range war. Afterward he took his nephew and headed west again, and during all those years, he'd never let Lucas forget he had to be tough, that he had to fight his own battles because there was no law in the West to fight them for him. What law there was had its hands full with the Indians and the worst of the outlaws. Everybody else was on their own.

Max had also taught Lucas to take his pleasures where he found them, to never postpone until tomorrow what he should do today, and no matter what else he ever did, not to get tied up to a woman until he was too old to break his own broncos. By Max's reckoning, Lucas had at least twenty more years to go. Lucas had never given much thought to settling down before now, but all at once twenty years seemed like a long time to wait. It wasn't that he would feel particularly old at forty-four—Max was older than that and he could still outride and outdrink men half his age—it was the sudden feeling of loneliness that seemed to discolor all those long years ahead.

For some reason, building the stage company into the biggest line in the West was no longer important enough to devote twenty years of his life to it, any more than finding the men who stole the gold shipment was the only reason he wished to remain at Green Run. Whereas before he used to spend hours trying to approach the problem of stealing a gold shipment as an outlaw would and studying the country so he would know it as well as any native, he now found time weighed heavily on his hands. There was no real need to round up any more mustangs because he could have extra horses sent in from Denver; there was no need to break his neck over the holdup because the shipment was still weeks away; there was no need to hurry back to Denver because, even from his sickbed, Uncle Max could run things without him; there was no reason to worry about expanding the line because he intended to move into railroads as soon as the company was his; there was no reason to eat his meals alone when he could have them with Carrie and Katie; and there was absolutely no reason to try and convince himself Carrie was just another woman when he knew he was lying.

It was hard to believe that the arrival of just one woman, especially one he had never heard of before, was forcing him to rethink just about every major decision in his life. He didn't have the time or the energy for that right now, and it made him mad at himself *and* mad at Carrie that he couldn't control his thoughts and feelings the way he always had before. He didn't want to get tied up with a woman right now, but certainly not a married one who made up her own mind as to what she would and wouldn't do without even consulting him. How was a man to know she wouldn't go off on some harebrained scheme the minute he turned his back? How could he know she was safe when she refused to admit there were limits to what she could do? How could he be the master of his own home when she refused to accept his word for anything?

Lucas worked his way through these arguments and a lot more besides, he even tried giving himself a dressing-down like his uncle would have done, but when he had used up all his energy for argument and exhausted his list of objections, he was left with one unalterable fact: he could not get Carrie Simpson out of his mind. Robert Simpson was going to have to prove himself worthy of her, or he would personally bury his carcass at the bottom of a mine shaft.

Right away Lucas knew he wouldn't do anything like that, but the very fact that he had thought of it scared him half to death. He had to get out of here now, even if it was only for a short time. He would tell her at lunch.

Twelve o'clock came and Carrie had an additional reason to be angry with Lucas—he was late for lunch. She didn't know whether he intended to eat with them or not, he hadn't been thoughtful enough to say, so she had decided she wouldn't set a place for him until he came. She absolutely refused to give him any excuse to think she was looking forward to his company. After the way he had treated her, he was lucky she bothered to feed him at all.

"You can be setting Mr. Barrow's place now, ma'am," Katie said, barely concealing a secret smile. "I see him coming through the trees."

"I might have known he'd wait until I was just about to sit down," Carrie grumbled, but Katie noted that Carrie had his place laid before he reached the door.

Carrie stepped out on the porch to meet him. "There's a bucket of water and a bar of soap around the side of the station." Lucas paused, grinned, and washed up without demur. It was the first time he could remember since he left Denver when it had mattered whether his hands were washed, and it was sort of nice in a way. He was even more impressed when he stepped inside the station. The curtains had been ironed and rehung since that morning and the windows cleaned to allow the bright Colorado sunshine to stream in and make the newly scrubbed table and floor gleam brightly.

"You ladies have just about transformed this place," Lucas said, waiting until Carrie and Katie had seated themselves to take his place at the table. "Poor Baca wouldn't even recognize the place."

"I hope that's not the only difference you see around here," Carrie said.

"No. The food's a lot better. And the scenery has improved too."

"I was not referring to my presence, or Katie's," Carrie retorted, irritated.

"Neither was I," Lucas replied, his expression deadpan. "You've cleaned the windows, and I can see the mountains from here." Carrie's eyes looked daggers at Lucas while Katie tactfully lowered her head.

Carrie had made up her mind to tell both Lucas and Katie that Robert had died and that she was a widow, but Lucas's taunting exasperated her so much she decided to wait until after lunch. He was the most vexing man she had ever met, and she wasn't going to allow him to gloat over her for one minute more than was absolutely necessary. She knew she should never have claimed a husband and that it wasn't going to look very good when she told them she was a widow—she was afraid telling a second lie was going to cause even more trouble before everyone knew all the truth—but she didn't dare tell them the whole truth yet. Being a married woman, even if she had been married for only a short time, conferred a special status on her, and admitting she had never been married at all was going to strip her of that protection.

She watched Lucas during the meal, but he seemed to

be ignoring her, talking to Katie and drawing her out about her family and her home in Ireland. It was all very interesting and Carrie was very fond of Katie, in fact she was quickly coming to like the girl more than any woman she had known, but there was no reason for Lucas to ignore her. *She* had a past, too, and a home he knew nothing about. It might not be as far away and as different as Ireland, but then she guessed he would feel more comfortable in Katie's cottage than in her father's house in Virginia.

"Is your husband coming in on the afternoon stage?" Lucas asked. Carrie hadn't been listening, and Lucas had to repeat his question.

"No, I don't think so. I don't know."

"Which is it?" Lucas asked. "You gave me three separate answers."

"I don't know," Carrie answered. "How could I when I don't know if the shipment he was waiting for has arrived?" This was a perfect time to tell them, but Lucas's question had put her on the defensive and now she was digging herself in deeper and deeper.

"What's he waiting for that's so important?"

"I don't know. He didn't say." Lucas gave her a skeptical look.

"He let you come out here all by yourself, but didn't think you should know what he was waiting for?"

"Robert doesn't *hide* things from me. I suppose he thought it wasn't important. Maybe he just never got around to it. There were so many things to do at the last minute."

"How long would it take him to say he was waiting for a new set of harnesses, or a stage wheel, or a barrel of whiskey?"

"I don't know why he didn't tell me. He just didn't." Carrie was feeling pressured, and she could guess that Lucas could tell something was wrong. His ironic look had slowly changed to one of curiosity. His gaze held her own for so long Carrie was forced to look away. "He'll be here soon," she finished lamely.

"I hope so. You need someone here twenty-four hours a day, not just when a stage comes in."

"I can manage," Carrie insisted.

"For a little while, maybe, but sooner or later you're going to run into trouble when I'm not here to help you. And you've only met the best of the drivers so far. There are a couple of tough cases in that lot." Carrie started to speak, but Lucas forestalled her, the barest trace of a smile in his eyes. "I know what you're about to say. I guess as far as you can see, you have a right to think you can handle this job, but you don't know what you're getting into, you don't know anything about living in the West, and you have no idea what it's like to be here in the winter when snow can drift up to the eaves of the station. I admire your spunk. I don't think I've ever seen any woman who had more pluck and brains than you, but you're out of place here without a man. When your chestnuts really get into the hot part of the fire, you'll need someone to pull them out for you."

Lucas knew his every word made Carrie angrier, and he couldn't help smiling, which was the one thing he shouldn't have done. His air of tolerant amusement infuriated Carrie, and she lost her temper.

"You don't need to say any more, Mr. Barrow," Carrie said, trying to keep her voice from rising. "You have made it abundantly plain, several times in fact, that you don't think that I, or any other woman, can handle this job. You've gotten it into your thoroughly stubborn head that this is a *man's* job, and naturally if it's a *man's* job, no female could possibly manage it. Well, for your information, Mr. Barrow, I am *going* to handle it, and I'm going to handle it without any man's help. I don't really have any choice," she added, sounding a little less defiant. "My husband is dead. He won't be coming this afternoon, or any other afternoon."

The announcement struck her listeners dumb, but for two completely different reasons.

Katie was out of her seat in an instant, kneeling at Carrie's side, her arm around her shoulders. "You poor thing. Why didn't you tell anyone? Faith, you shouldn't have to bear something like this all alone."

"I was afraid they wouldn't let me stay here," Carrie said quite frankly. "With Robert dead, I had no place to go. I *had* to have this job."

"When did it happen? Was it very long ago?" Katie asked.

"No, he died last month in St. Louis. It was some kind of fever, the doctors didn't know much about it, but they couldn't do anything for him. There was an epidemic about, and they had their hands full."

For a few moments Lucas didn't say a word; he was almost totally unaware of the women, totally occupied with his own reaction to the news. He was shocked to realize that not only did he have no regrets that a man had died, he was actually *glad* because that meant Carrie was free. It also meant he couldn't possibly leave her alone. Quick on the heels of that realization came a second that reminded him he *had* to leave her, several times in fact, if he was to find the gold thieves. And now that Carrie had no husband and he didn't have to leave Green Run to keep from disgracing himself and his name, he had no reason not to continue with his job. Almost immediately he began casting about in his mind for someone he could depend on to handle the job and look after the women. He had to smile to himself when he realized he was going down the list of men he knew, automatically eliminating any who weren't old or ugly. He might have to force himself, but he was going to consider everyone. If he couldn't capture Carrie's heart on his own, he didn't deserve to win her.

Lucas nearly choked on his own thoughts, if such a thing was possible. All along he had been thinking he was merely interested in a pretty woman, but already his subconscious had decided he was in love with her. He told himself that was preposterous and that he would deal with it later, that right now he had to find someone who could help Carrie at the station.

"You've got to hire a stock tender right away," Lucas said out loud, as though he had just reached that conclusion.

"I don't need one," Carrie stated, glaring at him from angry eyes. The brute, he didn't have the least sympathy for her bereaved state. All he could think about was hiring a blasted stock tender so he could feel free to go off and do whatever disgraceful thing it was he was dying to do. Well, it had to be disgraceful, didn't it? What man would be in such a fever to do anything entirely respectable?

"You ought to go down to Fort Malone and hire Jake Bemis," Lucas said. "He's the best by far. He's a little hard to get along with sometimes, but you can't beat him for handling stock."

"I told you I don't need anyone," Carrie insisted. "I can do everything myself."

"What will happen when you have to go into Fort Malone to buy supplies? Suppose you have to go as far as Denver to buy harnesses or replacement parts for a stage? Or maybe you're planning on Katie handling the horses as well as the kitchen."

"I could if need be," Katie spoke up loyally.

"No, you couldn't," Carrie said, abruptly reversing herself. "You've got all you can do with the cooking. If you had the cleaning and the horses to do as well, you'd never survive."

"Oh dear," Katie said quite suddenly, "what if me Brian was to come asking after me?"

"Maybe you can talk your Brian into helping with the horses," Lucas suggested, a sly look dancing at the back of his suddenly averted eyes. "I just remembered that Jake is a woman hater. He wouldn't work for you if you paid him twice the sixty dollars a month he's worth."

"What do you mean he wouldn't work for me?" Carrie demanded. "Doesn't he think I know my job well enough to tell him what to do?"

"It's nothing against you in particular," Lucas assured her. "He just won't work for a female. You better see if you can hire old Frank Martin. He's had some trouble

89

with rheumatism, can't straighten up actually and I hear he has trouble keeping off the whiskey, but you might be able to talk him into taking the job if you ask him nicely."

"Do you have the effrontery to suggest that an old, crippled drunk can do the job better than I can?" Carrie asked, her eyes glinting dangerously.

"Not at all," Lucas hastened to reassure her, "but now that you don't have any husband coming to help, and Katie's Brian possibly showing up any minute to take her away, and me going off to hunt mustangs, and you maybe having to go buy supplies, you have no choice but to hire somebody. It's a shame Jake won't take the job. He's really the best choice, but I guess you can get by with old Frank if you don't stay gone more than a few hours and you make sure he's not hiding any whiskey on him."

"Are you implying that I would have to search that old man *bodily* to prevent his secreting whiskey on his person?" Carrie demanded.

"You would if you didn't want him drunk on you half the time."

"I won't have him."

"I can't see that you have any other choice. Jake won't work for you, and there isn't anybody else in Fort Malone who knows the job."

"I'll hire a cowhand from one of the neighboring ranches."

"There's only one ranch within a hundred miles, but it won't do you any good to go looking there. No self-respecting cowhand will take a job that can't be done from horseback. But don't worry. It might take you a little while, but you'll get used to old Frank."

"I refuse to have a drunk work for me. I shall hire your Mr. Bemis."

"He won't come."

"You don't know that yet. I haven't asked him, and even if I do say so myself, I can be rather persuasive." Lucas gave Carrie a look that made her want to slap his face. It was as though he was taking inventory of her charms and found them wanting.

"Naturally I know nothing of your successes back East, but Jake is a very different breed. I doubt even your looks will have much effect on him."

"Why so?" Katie demanded indignantly. "Don't you think Mrs. Simpson is a fine-looking woman?"

"Katie, you shouldn't—"

"I do indeed, Katie, and I've already told her so, but she'll be coming up against a hard case in Jake. There isn't a woman in the world that could talk Jake into working for her."

"We'll just see about that. I'll go into Fort Malone first thing tomorrow morning. I need supplies anyway."

"You'll never get him."

"You just watch."

"Want to make a little wager?"

"I don't gamble," Carrie said rather stuffily.

"Neither do I, in the normal way, but just consider this a friendly wager between friends."

Carrie raised her eyebrows at the word *friends*, but all she said was, "What do you want to bet?"

"How about a kiss?"

"She'll not be doing such a thing as that," Katie exclaimed, scandalized.

"Don't you think that's a little more than *friendly?*"

"You scared?" Lucas asked teasingly.

"No, it's just not in good taste."

"Tasted good to me," he said, and when Carrie blushed, he added, "You *are* afraid."

"No I'm not."

"Then it's a bet?"

"Well . . ." Lucas looked at her with the grin that infuriated her. "Yes," she said with sudden decision. "It's a bet."

"Merciful saints!" Katie exclaimed. "You can't go around kissing people, ma'am, and you a new-turned widow," she protested.

"Don't worry," Carrie assured her horrified friend. "I'd have hired Jake anyway, but this bet is all the encouragement I need to make sure he'll be working for me by tomorrow afternoon." Carrie looked triumphantly at Lucas, thinking she had gotten the last word, but he got up from the table, wished them a cheerful good afternoon, and walked away whistling.

That's when Carrie knew she'd been had.

Chapter 7

"You can't drive to Fort Malone by yourself," Lucas decreed when he found Carrie harnessing a horse to the wagon next morning.

"Of course I can," she replied testily. "Surely you don't expect me to ride on the stage. I could just see the passengers waiting patiently while my order was filled. And of course they wouldn't mind sharing their seats with sacks of flour, sugar, coffee, and I don't know what else."

The sarcasm in her voice didn't improve Lucas's temper, and he answered more sharply than he'd intended. "I'll ride with you." He hadn't meant it to sound like a command, but Carrie had gotten under his skin so badly he couldn't always control his voice when he talked to her.

"No you will not," she stated emphatically. "I don't need you to order supplies, and if I let you go with me to see Mr. Bemis, you'll end up saying the only reason I was able to hire him was because of you."

"Well . . ."

"Well nothing. I can manage this trip without your assistance. And I can hire Jake Bemis without it as well."

"You're determined to throw everything I try to do for you back in my face, aren't you?" Lucas said, feeling his anger rise. He had never taken such an interest in any woman, certainly none had ever taken up so much of his thoughts, and her repeated response had been an effort to prove she had no need of him whatsoever.

"I apologize if that's the way it seems, but every time *I* turn around, you and every other man who so much as opens his mouth around here feels free to tell me what I can and can't do. First, I couldn't do anything until my husband arrived"—she blushed, remembering that lie—"and now I can't do anything without you. I appreciate your help, I really do, but I can't have you standing over me the rest of my life just in case I decide to do something on my own."

"You overrate your charms, Mrs. Simpson. I have no intention of standing over you for the *rest of my life*," a furious Lucas snapped. "I might not even be here by the end of the week." Carrie blushed crimson, anger battling mortification to deepen the color.

"I didn't mean it literally. It's just an expression. I have no desire to have you around for the rest of my life," she responded, recovering somewhat. "I never had a nursemaid before, and I certainly can't see me accepting one now."

"Carrie, *ma'am*, you are a very pretty woman, in fact you're just about the prettiest female I've ever set eyes on, but you'll catch cold if you think every man will fall over his feet to make himself agreeable to you. I'd swear off women forever before I tied myself up like that for the rest of my life." Haughty little filly. Well, he'd show her.

"Mr. Barrow, I have no desire to have you, or anyone else, tie themselves up to me for the rest of my life," Carrie said, determined not to lose her temper again. "This whole conversation has strayed into the realm of the utterly ridiculous, and I suggest we talk of something else before we say things we may find it difficult to forget."

Lucas swallowed hard. He was not used to being called down by a woman; even worse, he was not used to being in the wrong. He had let his concern for her get out of hand; he had allowed her refusal to accept his help to make him angry rather than admiring of her pluck. When, after that, she had made the comment about him being with her for the rest of his life, he panicked and said things he didn't mean.

Boy, it was easy to tell he was no hand with the ladies. An

Eastern woman like her, especially one as pretty as she was, probably had all the local beaux after her, flattering her, saying pretty things, and making her feel like the most wonderful thing God ever created. Well he *did* think she was the most wonderful thing God ever created, even better than his horses or his stage line, but he couldn't tell her that. He would sound like a born fool talking to a woman that way. He'd probably sound like one anyway because he had no experience in saying pretty things. You didn't need many words with the kind of women he was used to. They didn't expect much talk. They didn't have time for it. A tremendous feeling of frustration welled up inside him. How in the world did you go about sweet-talking a woman when she seemed bent and determined on taking the starch out of you?

"Do whatever you please, ma'am," Lucas said, and walked off.

Carrie wanted to say something, anything that would bring him back, but she didn't know how to explain why she had to establish her independence without making him think she didn't want his attention, why she couldn't accept his help unless she absolutely had to, so she turned back to the wagon. It would be better if she got on the road. She had a long trip and a lot to do. It was going to take her the better part of the day as it was, and she couldn't afford to spend her time worrying about Lucas Barrow. He had been taking care of himself for many years, and he would probably continue to do so without her help.

But Carrie's wagon had barely disappeared around the first bend in the road when Katie saw Lucas come riding by from the direction of his cabin. She grinned. She had known all along he was going to see Mrs. Simpson safely to Fort Malone and back. She laughed ruefully to herself. It would never occur to him that he was leaving her here all alone with two stages and goodness knew who else coming in during the day. He had to keep Mrs. Simpson in his sights or he wouldn't be worth shooting. Katie smiled again. That's the way it ought to be. She already knew Carrie and

Lucas were going to fall in love. It was only a question of time before they figured it out for themselves.

Carrie was mad. She had been in town for over four hours and she still hadn't received an answer to her request for an interview with Jake Bemis. She had ordered all the supplies she would need for weeks to come and had made arrangements for everything she couldn't carry in her wagon to be delivered the next day. She had introduced herself to the mayor, the sheriff, and had a visit from the town's ruling matron, and still not one word had come from Bemis. She had finally sent a second message, and she was now marking time in the general store, trying to ignore the curious and admiring looks of its proprietor and the various customers who came in from time to time, while she waited with increasing impatience for a reply.

Finally the last customer paid for his purchase and departed, and Henry Meade, the store owner, was unoccupied. Carrie decided it might be worth her while to see if she could gather a little information about Jake. It looked as though getting him to take her job was going to be more difficult than she planned. He was obviously not interested enough to come see her.

"Could you tell me something about a Mr. Jake Bemis?" Carrie asked, approaching the counter. Carrie was aware of the power of a good-looking woman and she was prepared to use every wile she had to get information out of Mr. Meade.

"Why do you want to know?" Meade asked unhelpfully.

"I need a new stock tender at the station, and he was recommended to me, rather highly as a matter of fact."

"There's nobody around here that's better with horses than Jake when he wants to be."

"What do you mean by that?"

"Jake doesn't work unless he wants to. He gets a little money from an aunt or somebody back East. It's not much, I'm told, but it's enough to keep him out of the cold. Only reason he works is he sometimes gets drunk and then he gambles away his money, or gives it away, and he has to take a job until his next check arrives."

"Then you don't think he's likely to consider my offer?"

"No, ma'am, I don't."

"Would you tell me why?"

"I don't rightly know that I should."

"Look, I'm in urgent need of a stock tender, and I've been told Mr. Bemis is the best. You tell me he doesn't have a job, but you don't think he will take mine. I would like to try and convince him, but I need to know why you don't think he'll take my job."

"Because he just got his check, and he hasn't had time to spend it yet. But that ain't why he wouldn't take your job even if he was broke, which he ain't."

"What could be his objection? The job pays well."

"It ain't the job. It's you." These Westerners are nothing if not direct, thought Carrie, trying hard not to show her frustration.

"But he can't object to me. He doesn't even know me."

"Doesn't have to. He'll know by your name you're a woman, and Jake Bemis is dead set against women. He won't work for them either." So Lucas wasn't just trying to make her mad when he said that Bemis wouldn't work for her. Still, she was certain he had egged her on to make her mad enough to try, and that irritated her as well. She was tired of him trying to take care of her, even when he did it without telling her.

Just then the lad Mr. Meade had sent to deliver the second message to Jake returned.

"Were you able to find him?" Meade asked.

"Sure," the boy replied.

"Well, what did he say?" his employer asked. "This lady can't be waiting all day for his answer."

"He said there weren't no use in his coming to meet you at the general store or anywhere else. He weren't working for no woman, and that was the end of it."

"See, didn't I tell you?" Mr. Meade announced, clearly

pleased to have been proved correct. Carrie got the feeling he was in secret agreement with Jake.

"Was he very disagreeable about it?" Carrie asked, determined not to give up.

"No, not so's you'd notice. But he did say he had got your first message, and there was no use in you sending any more. He wasn't interested in no woman's job, and he wasn't wasting his time talking to people about a job he wasn't going to take."

Sudden anger consumed Carrie. She was damned tired of being treated like a two-headed monster, and a helpless one at that. This drunken woman-hater might never take her job, but he was going to know he was dealing with something other than a shrinking violet.

"Where is Mr. Bemis now?" Carrie asked the boy, her anger under tight control.

"He's over at the bathhouse getting all cleaned up. He's going to the saloon tonight."

"And where is this bathhouse?" Carrie asked sweetly, her smile blinding the boy and Mr. Meade to the glitter in her eyes.

"It ain't no bathhouse for ladies," the boy hastened to inform her.

"I don't want to know for myself," Carrie assured him. "I just want to know so I can recommend it to my workers when they come into town."

"Okay," said the boy. "It's back of the hotel, but it's nothing but a cow shed. Old man Tyler put in some wooden tubs and runs hot water out of a great big copper pot. He keeps a fire going under that pot pretty near all the time, and the water will take the skin off you if you're not careful."

"Thank you," Carrie said, "and here's something for your trouble." The boy was too young to be particularly impressed by Carrie's looks, but he could certainly appreciate the value of the coin in his hand. Carrie grew considerably in his estimation, and he made a mental note to be around the next time she came to town in case she should want him to run some more errands.

Carrie walked slowly, wanting to consider all the possible approaches before she faced Bemis. She probably wouldn't be given a second chance to talk to him, so she wanted to make sure she made the most of what time she had.

The lane behind the hotel was little more than a rubble-strewn alley, but Carrie wasn't about to be stopped now. Her blood was up and nothing but a confrontation would satisfy her. It was easy to find the bathhouse. Even in the relatively warm summer air, the steam escaping from the shed was clearly visible. When she saw an old man enter with a load of wood, all question was removed, but the door was closed when she reached the shed and it took her some moments to decide how best to attract Bemis's attention. After the way he'd already treated her summons, merely knocking on the door didn't seem to be quite forceful enough.

"Mr. Bemis, are you in there?" Carrie called. "This is Mrs. Simpson from the stagecoach station speaking. I would like to speak with you for a few moments, please." Carrie waited for nearly a minute, but there was no answer and no sound from inside. She didn't know whether they were frozen by shock or simply ignoring her again. "Mr. Bemis," she called again, louder this time, "I would like to speak with you. I have gone to some trouble to find you, so I would appreciate it if you could spare me a few minutes." Still there was no answer. This man is rude, Carrie said to herself, actually relieved to have the restriction of polite behavior removed. Now there was no reason why she should continue to be ladylike. She looked about, selected a long, narrow piece of wood, and gave the bathhouse door several good raps. "Mr. Bemis, I will not leave until I have had a word with you, so you might as well come on out." There was no immediate response and she rapped sharply on the door again.

The door opened, finally, and the wizened little old man she had seen carry in the wood stepped out. He looked even worse up close, his body bent, his complexion sallow, and two teeth missing from his head.

"Jake says go away," the little man said scornfully, much like he was shooing chickens. "He already told you he don't want your job. No self-respecting man will work for no woman." For added emphasis, he spat, splattering the ground with a stream of tobacco juice. Carrie stepped forward, being careful to avoid the tobacco juice, and rapped sharply on the door once more.

"Mr. Bemis, I intend to speak with you. If you won't come outside to me, I will have to go inside to you."

"You can't go in there," the little man protested, shocked out of his scornful attitude. "There's men in there in their natural state. It ain't fitting."

"Aren't they in tubs?" Carrie asked.

"Well, yes, but they're still naked."

"As long as I can't see them, it won't matter." She rapped again on the door. "Time's up, Mr. Bemis." There was no response from inside the shed, so Carrie opened the door and stepped into the bathhouse.

For a moment Carrie couldn't see or breathe. The only light in the room came from the glowing embers and occasional flames under the big copper pot of boiling water, but a thick fog of stream made the air virtually impenetrable to the eye. After a moment Carrie's vision adjusted to the dim room and she could make out the heads and shoulders of three men staring at her bug-eyed as they cowered in their wooden barrels.

"I tried to stop her," the wizened old man told them, "but she wouldn't listen."

"Which one of you is Jake Bemis?" Carrie demanded. Two of the men immediately pointed to a third, a crusty-looking man of about thirty-five who sat in his barrel with his hat on and a cigar in his mouth.

"Mr. Bemis, where I come from it's not considered polite to ignore a message, most especially when it's from a lady. You don't have to take any job you don't want, but it's usually common courtesy to say so. I consider your actions cowardly and downright ungentlemanly, and if I weren't a lady I would tell you what I think of men like you." All four men stared at her as if they'd never seen a woman before.

"However, I realize you may not have perfectly understood what I wanted of you, so I'm prepared to forgive your rudeness and start all over again."

"I didn't ask you to forgive me," Jake muttered.

"I shall, nevertheless. The good book says we're to forgive our enemies seven times seventy. Though you're not my enemy, at least not yet, you ought to be worth forgiving at least once." Jake didn't know what to say. Leaving aside the fact this woman was so pretty he couldn't be sure he wasn't dreaming, he'd never seen a female who had the nerve to walk into a bathhouse full of naked men, and then coolly stand around talking about forgiving him just like they were in church. She was the one who ought to be doing the apologizing, but somehow Jake didn't feel she was going to. He stared at her, wondering what she was going to say next.

"I came to offer you a job as stock tender at the Green Run Pass stagecoach station," she said. "Mr. Lucas Barrow recommended you most highly. I fired Baca Riggins, and Cody and Buck left with him." Jake had heard a rumor that some woman had chased Baca off the station, but he hadn't believed it until this tiny mite of a female stormed into the bathhouse to offer him the vacant position. *Now* he could believe it.

"You would, of course, have to see that the horses were properly cared for, the harnesses kept in good repair, and the barn orderly, but you could sleep in the station and take your meals with us in the kitchen. It pays well."

"I ain't taking your job," Jake managed to say at least. "You can save yourself the effort of saying anything more."

"Am I to understand that you are already employed?"

"No, I ain't got no job."

"Are you looking for a job?"

"I suppose so. A man can always use a good job."

"Do you consider the stock tender position a good job?" Jake hated it when people asked questions for which they already had the answer.

"Yeah, but I ain't taking it."

"Could I ask why?" Jake was uneasy now. This woman was taking things too easy. She had looked mighty determined when she came in and she hadn't moved so much as an inch since, but she was talking to him now almost like she was apologizing for taking up his time. He had a feeling he was making a wrong move, but he answered anyway.

"Because you're a woman, and I don't work for no woman."

"But you'd take the job if a man offered it to you."

"Yeah, I suppose so."

"Suppose I could prove to you that I'm just as good as a man?"

"Can't be done," the wizened little man answered for Jake. "Ain't no woman born who's the equal of a man."

"Clearly I'm no man, but suppose I could demonstrate I was no ordinary female?"

"How?"

Carrie opened her purse and took out a small pistol. "Would you let one of these gentlemen shoot the cigar out of your mouth?"

"Hell no," Jake stated emphatically. "I'd be deader'n a doornail."

"Then if I could do it, I'd be better than these three men at least?"

"Yeah, but you can't do it, and I'll be damned if I'll let you try."

"You'd better sit very still, Mr. Bemis, or you will be *damned* quite a bit sooner than you had expected." Jake stared at Carrie, his eyes bugging out of his head. She was aiming the pistol straight at him. The two bathers dived into their tubs, the wizened little man made a leap for the door, and then there was the deafening explosion of a pistol shot.

Jake didn't feel a thing, and he was sure he was dead. He knew he was covered with blood, and his wound would be hurting like sin if he were alive.

"If you will look at your cigar," Carrie directed him as calmly as if nothing had happened, "you will notice I have removed just the end. You may smoke the rest of it tomorrow."

If he could hear her he must still be alive, Jake reasoned, but he was afraid if he moved it would somehow break the spell. Still, his curiosity was greater than his fear, and he looked at the cigar. The end had been neatly shot off. The other bathers ventured to raise their heads, and their goggling eyes threatened to fall on the floor when they saw what Carrie had done.

"Now, I'll expect you at the station before evening," Carrie said, starting to put away her pistol. "Of course, I'll allow you some time to settle your personal affairs, but I need someone on the job immediately."

"I ain't never worked for a woman, and I ain't starting now," Jake stated, still staring at the end of his cigar.

"But you just promised—"

"I did no such thing," Jake insisted.

"Why Mr. Bemis, don't you know it's a sin to lie? With my own ears I heard you say you would take the job if it were offered by a man. These men can verify it. Well, I've just proved myself as good as a man, so you must take the job."

"I don't care what I said," Jake said mulishly, "I won't work for you."

Carrie studied her pistol. "Mr. Bemis, I don't approve of men who make promises and then go back on them. If you go back on your promise, I may feel it necessary to punish you."

"What can you do?" demanded one of the other bathers.

"I could shoot you," Carrie said, turning the pistol in the questioner's direction. The man dived under the water. "But I won't kill you, Mr. Bemis," Carrie said, turning the pistol until it pointed at his heart. "I'll just mark you so everybody will always know you for a cowardly man."

"You can't do any such thing," Jake boasted, then added, "How would you try?"

"I'd shoot your ears off," Carrie told him.

Jake blanched white, but he did not waver. "You're bluffing. Even if you could do it, you wouldn't have the nerve."

"I'll just take the tops off. It wouldn't hurt your hearing a bit, just mark you up a little."

"I still say you're bluffing." Suddenly Carrie elevated her pistol and fired. This time it was Jake who dived into the barrel.

"Look at your hat, Mr. Bemis," Carrie called out.

"I ain't coming out of this barrel."

"Then I'll have to let the water out for you. I think two shots will do." Jake's head slowly came into view. He took off his hat and stared at it. There was a hole through the turned-up brim, just above his ear. He gaped at Carrie, dawning realization telling him this woman meant what she said.

There was a sudden commotion outside, and much to Carrie's astonishment, several people burst into the small shed, the first among them being Lucas Barrow.

Chapter 8

"What in hell is going on in here?" Lucas demanded.

"I was merely offering Mr. Bemis a job," Carrie replied with a self-satisfied smile.

"This old goat told us you were shooting up the place," the sheriff said, indicating the wizened old man.

"I did fire my pistol, but he's exaggerating a bit." Lucas's eyes narrowed suspiciously. "Mr. Bemis wanted proof of my marksmanship before he would accept a job I offered him. Since he was in no condition to step outside, I was compelled to hold my demonstration here."

"She shot the end off my cigar," Jake disclosed, holding up the evidence of his statement in an unsteady hand. "Then, by jasper, she put a hole in my hat right above my ear, said she was going to notch them both if I didn't take the job."

"Now look here, Mrs. Simpson, you can't go forcing people to take jobs when they don't—"

"Mr. Bemis neglected to tell you that we had made a bargain," Carrie said, interrupting the sputtering sheriff in mid-sentence. "He said he would take my job if I proved myself as good as a man. I was supposed to shoot the cigar out of his mouth, but when I did, Mr. Bemis tried to back out of his agreement."

"Is that true, Bemis?" the sheriff asked.

"She tricked me," Jake complained. "Fair trapped me without my knowing what was happening."

"You can ask those gentlemen if you need any further corroboration," Carrie said, indicating the two bathers with a wave of her pistol. The two so indicated took one look at Carrie's pistol and didn't wait to be asked.

"Every word she says is the gospel truth."

"Old Jake was caught fair and square. She's a mean shot with that pistol of hers."

"It wasn't a demanding shot, not at such close range," Carrie admitted modestly.

"I suggest we get out of here and let these men get dressed before they shrivel up like prunes," Lucas said. "Mrs. Simpson needs to be back at the station before the next stage comes through."

"When may I expect you, Mr. Bemis?" Carrie asked, determined not to move until he committed himself in front of all these witnesses.

"I don't rightly know. I got quite a few things that need looking into."

"Such as?" Carrie's tone was not encouraging.

"Personal things," he said, driven to the wall. "I ought to be done in four or five days."

"I think four or five *hours* ought to be sufficient. I'll help you," Carrie offered.

"I don't need no help. You just go back to that station, and I'll be along directly."

"When? I don't want to have to come back after you."

"Never you mind when. I'll be there."

"Give her a time, Jake," the sheriff ordered. "I don't want her back here shooting up the town."

"I'll be there along about midnight," Jake said finally.

"I don't stay up that late. I think nine o'clock would be a good compromise." Bemis started to protest, but a look at Carrie's stern expression changed his mind. He was a reasonable man, and he could see no future in arguing with this woman. She could outshoot and outtalk him, and she had the nerve to do just about anything she put her mind to. That was a bad combination in a man but it was lethal in a woman, and Jake Bemis knew when to tuck his tail between his legs and back away.

"So you're the lady who gave Baca Riggins his walking papers?" the sheriff commented as they walked back toward the center of town.

"Actually Duncan Bickett fired him, but I was the one who presented him with the letter. I should also add that Mr. Barrow's help made it unnecessary for me to employ my pistol."

"And Bickett actually gave you a contract to run that station?" the sheriff asked, unbelieving. "I never heard of a woman station manager, and especially not in that neck of the woods."

"Actually he gave the contract to my husband," Carrie said, furious that she had to perpetuate this piece of fiction, "but he died before we reached Colorado, and I took it up in his name."

"Where did you learn to shoot like that? It's not usual for ladies to handle a shooting iron better than a man."

"I had a father, two brothers, and several uncles, all of whom could shoot a squirrel out of a tree at a hundred yards. Target practice was part of virtually every day of my life. They were actually rather pleased when I turned out to be better with a pistol than any of them."

"Better, did you say?"

"Only with a pistol," Carrie said with an air of guileless innocence that almost made Lucas choke with laughter. "My father said it would be unladylike for me to use a shotgun, and I never had much use for a rifle, not being allowed to go hunting, so a pistol was about all I ever tried. But I always did wonder how I would have done with a rifle."

"I'd give a month's salary to see Duncan's face when he learns what a mess he's got himself into," the sheriff said with a sudden grin.

"Sheriff, I don't regard my presence at the station as a *mess*, as you put it, and I'd appreciate it if you would not go about saying it is. You're welcome to come out any time you please and see for yourself how I'm doing." The sheriff looked taken aback that Carrie would call him down quite so publicly. Carrie accepted his mumbled apologies, but he went away so determined not to miss Duncan's reaction to the news that he decided to tell him himself.

"Well, I must say you've done a good job of setting the town on its ear," Lucas said after they had cleared the edge of town. "Within a matter of hours there won't be a person inside three hundred miles that doesn't know about you, that is if they haven't heard already."

"How? Who'd be interested?"

"There aren't many people in this country, and news travels as fast as a horse can run. Running off Baca Riggins was news. Shooting the end off Jake's cigar was sensational. From now on, they'll want to hear about everything you do."

"And they say women gossip," Carrie remarked.

"I suppose you're determined to stick it out," Lucas said after a long pause. "You won't need to depend on me, now that you've got Jake, that is."

"I never needed to depend on you," Carrie said—she shouldn't have said that, but he deserved it for following her—"but I am grateful for your help. It would have been much more difficult without you."

Lucas's feelings were somewhat mollified, and he stared ahead of him for a time. "I was telling you the truth when I said I couldn't stay around all the time. There are several things I must do that I've been putting off."

"I know, and you mustn't think I don't appreciate your changing your plans, no matter how often we disagree. But now that I have Mr. Bemis, you can go about your business without worrying about me."

"So I can," Lucas said, but Carrie was glad to see he didn't seem to take much pleasure in that knowledge.

They rode for a while in silence, Lucas staring into space before him, Carrie studying the landscape. It was so different from Virginia it was hard to imagine she was in the same country. Ridges ran off in all directions, and valleys opened up before her without warning, some choked with thick growths of aspen and others lush with grass that was waist high, but all around her the gigantic mountains dominated the horizon, thrusting everything else into insignificance. To one who had grown up on a tidal plain as flat as the Kansas prairie, just the sight of the towering peaks, capped with snow and gleaming with blinding brilliance in the sun, filled her with excitement. Everything was so new and unspoiled, so vibrantly alive and full of energy, she couldn't help feeling she was truly starting her life over.

"You've never told me anything about yourself, Mr. Barrow," Carrie said.

"Out here a man takes what he's told and doesn't ask for anything else."

"Not even his name, or where he came from?"

"A lot of people came west to get away from something. Besides, there's nothing in a name except a bunch of letters."

"How odd," Carrie commented. "In the East, your name and where you come from mean everything."

"And how many people found they couldn't live up to their past, or wanted to be something different?"

"Quite a few, I suppose. I guess you could say I'm one of them."

"Sometimes it was a simple mistake. Other times, well, it could be a lot of different things, but there are many reasons why a man might want to start over without having to bear the burden of the past, especially if it's not his own."

"So I shouldn't ask Jake for his references?"

"Out here, nothing counts in a man except the color of his courage and the value of his word."

Carrie doubted it was quite that cut and dried, but she wasn't going to argue with Lucas on his own ground. They continued to wile away the time talking about the countryside and what the new settlers would mean to the state. They both knew they were avoiding questions that would have to be faced sooner or later, but for the time being it was pleasant to enjoy the view and the easy conversation.

Lucas helped Carrie get her supplies inside the station, but he disappeared after that, and it wasn't until he came in for supper that Carrie saw him again. Almost the second they finished, the evening stage arrived and Lucas went off to harness up the team while Carrie welcomed her guests and helped Katie serve the meal.

"It's been a long day," Carrie said when they at last finished up with the dishes. "I wish I could go to bed right now, but I've got to wait up for the new man."

"Why don't ye go on to bed? I can wait for him," Katie offered.

"Don't be absurd. You've been working hard all day, and I know you're about to drop. He's my responsibility, and besides, you don't know what he looks like. I'll just sit here on the porch for a while. It's such a pleasant evening."

"There's some water on for coffee, but don't you go staying up too late," Katie admonished Carrie as she went off toward the cabin.

The night breeze was a little chilly and Carrie wrapped a shawl around her arms and shoulders before settling into one of the chairs on the station porch. The moon was full and the stars shone brightly. They seemed so close Carrie felt she could reach out and touch them. The night was full of sounds that were strange to her ear, but Carrie found them a comfort rather than otherwise. The air was crystal clear and she could see the barn and corral almost as well as in daylight. The stage trail seemed to glisten in the moonlight that bathed everything with a silver sheen. It was a beautiful sight and Carrie didn't think she'd ever seen anything half as exciting at home. There everyone was certain to be indoors after dark. An elk suddenly appeared out of the woods, sniffed the wind, and then began to graze on the grass next to the trail. Abruptly, he looked up and then disappeared into the night. Carrie looked in the direction of his gaze and saw Lucas approaching the porch.

Carrie didn't know until she saw him that she'd been wanting all along to see him.

"Good evening, Carrie ma'am," Lucas said, pausing with one foot resting on the bottom step, his forearms resting on the step rail. "It's a right pretty night."

"Have you come to make sure the wild animals don't get me?"

"I don't know as you have to worry about the ones that walk on four legs. It's the ones that prefer two that'll give you

110

the most trouble."

"So I've noticed," Carrie responded, wondering if he included himself in that group, "but you still don't have to keep me company. You've already used up most of your day following me into town and back, and I would hate to waste any more of your time."

"I don't mind."

"Well, I do," she replied, wondering why his devil-may-care attitude never failed to set her teeth on edge. "I would rather you go back to the barn, or your cabin, or wherever it is you spend the night."

"Mostly here and there, no place special."

"You don't take orders very well, do you, Mr. Barrow? It's a good thing you didn't take that stock job. I'd have had to fire you before the week was out." Lucas grinned broadly.

"I always did like giving orders better than taking them."

"I wish you would drop that idiotic accent," Carrie snapped. "You may not intend to tell me anything about yourself, but I know for certain you're no drifter, you're not uneducated, and I seriously doubt you're a wrangler either."

"Well now, Carrie ma'am, it seems you turned out not to be a married woman. I wonder what else you will turn out not to be?" Carrie was thankful the moonlight didn't illuminate the telltale flush in her cheeks.

"Whatever it is, it's no concern of yours. As you told me earlier, out here it's only honor, courage, and honesty that count."

"But that's just for men, Carrie ma'am. We still like to know where our womenfolk come from."

"Well, you can keep on *liking* to know. I've told you all I'm going to tell you. Now please go away and leave me alone." Carrie wondered for the umpteenth time how Lucas's smile could make her say things she didn't mean.

"I had me a mind to sit a spell in this moonlight. I'm awful fond of moonlight."

"I suppose that short of shooting you, there's nothing I can do to stop you, but I won't put up with being ma'amed to death, and I won't listen to your cowboy drawl. Use it, if you

111

must, for whatever it is you're doing here, but I'll go inside if you don't drop it now."

"Are you always this contrary, ma'am?" Lucas asked, settling into the chair next to Carrie. "I wouldn't be surprised if your father and brothers were relieved to get rid of you."

"My name is Carrie," Carrie enunciated with great clarity, "and if you wish to have me reply to any further remarks, you will use it."

"Okay, Carrie it is," Lucas said, dropping the remaining shreds of his drifter act. "But you've got to call me Lucas. My uncle is Mr. Barrow, and I don't think he's ready to share his name with me just yet."

"So you have an uncle. I had begun to wonder if you might not have come into this world full-grown, clothed, shod, and ready to come to my aid whether I wanted you to or not." Lucas laughed softly at the mockery of her words.

"I had a mother and a father just like everybody else, but they died when I was a little boy. My uncle raised me."

"A mere mortal, huh? What happened?" Carrie asked, her compassion immediately aroused in spite of her sarcasm. Lucas waited a long time to reply, and Carrie began to feel uncomfortable. "You don't have to tell me," she said. "You already said people weren't supposed to ask questions."

"It's not that," Lucas replied. "It's just a hard memory. My grandfather had a ranch in Texas. My uncle Max left years before I was born, but my father stayed and married his childhood sweetheart. Then somehow a range war got started with the Robertson family, and my uncle came home to find our dams busted, our cattle run off, my father and grandfather dead, and my mother dying of a broken heart." Carrie felt a great rush of sympathy, and she was startled and confused when Lucas suddenly started to laugh.

"Those Robertsons didn't know what a fight was until they got Uncle Max mad. Before he was through, they were all dead and their land and cattle were ours. He sold both places, and the herds, and took me back with him. We haven't stopped traveling yet."

"Haven't you ever wanted to go back?" Carrie asked, bewildered that a man could laugh about death.

"What for? There's nothing there for me but bitter memories. Best to forget them. You see, I really am a drifter, not quite the kind you thought, but a drifter nevertheless."

"I see. You just drifted in here, and any day now you're going to drift right back out again." The sound of her words was hard and abrasive, like shards of glacial ice, and she shrank from their meaning.

"Something like that." He turned and faced her. "I never knew you were going to be here."

"Would it have made a difference?" There was such a long pause, Carrie was afraid he wasn't going to answer.

"I would still have had to go."

"I see."

"No you don't."

"I see enough."

"You don't see anything, and I can't tell you now, but one day I will."

"Maybe it won't matter by the time you get around to telling me."

"Does it matter now?"

Carrie didn't want to answer that question, but she knew she must. She also knew she couldn't pretend to him, or herself, any longer. "Yes, I think it does. You've been very kind and thoughtful. It really would have been very difficult without your help."

"To hell with kind and thoughtful!" Lucas suddenly exploded. "You make me sound like some kind of ladies' aid society. Don't you have any blood in your veins? Has all that aristocratic interbreeding back East taken every bit of mettle out of you?"

"Certainly not," Carrie replied with vigor. "But neither has it deprived me of manners."

"So you think it's bad manners for a woman to tell a man he means something to her?"

"I didn't say that," Carrie protested.

"You might as well have. If you think *kind* and *thoughtful* are anything but a mouthful of pabulum, you've never been

113

in love, and I don't understand why you ever married your husband."

"That is none of your concern," snapped Carrie, furious that he could say such a thing about her, and yet at the same time searching for a way to tell him she had never been married and had never been in love.

"Yes it is," Lucas insisted, "because I can tell you your presence means something to me. I doubt you'll take this the way it's meant, but I was never so glad to hear anyone was dead as when I heard about your husband. It was nearly driving me crazy to see you all the time and know I was forbidden to even touch you."

"As I recall, you didn't succeed." Carrie had meant it to be a sharp retort, but to her horrified ears it sounded more like an invitation.

"I know. That's when I knew I had to leave or do something I'd never be able to live down." Carrie knew she shouldn't ask, it was dangerous territory and foreign ground to her, but she couldn't stop her tongue from forming the question.

"Why?" It was such a little word. Surely it couldn't do much harm.

"I've met a lot of women, but never one like you."

"How am I so different?"

"I'm not sure yet, but the minute you stepped off that stage, I knew you were unlike any other woman in the world. I couldn't let Baca Riggins put you back on that stage because I might never find you again."

"And to think I put it down to old-fashioned gallantry when all the while it was nothing but curiosity," Carrie said, trying to keep her trembling limbs still.

"It was both, but don't ask me to say which was stronger."

"And I suppose that kiss was part of your attempt to see just how different I was," she said with an ironic smile.

"No. It was supposed to make you so mad you would stay away from me. I already knew I couldn't stay away by myself."

"Well, you did make me mad."

"But you didn't stay away."

"With you eating at the station and helping with the teams, as well as presenting yourself whenever you liked, it would be impossible not to run into you."

"It'll be impossible for you to stay away from me from now on. I'm going to follow you everywhere you go."

"Is that what you came here for tonight, to tell me I now have a second shadow?"

"No, I came to get a kiss. I liked the first one very much."

"You lost the wager," Carrie told him, her heart pounding so hard it was difficult to keep her voice steady. "Or have you forgotten that?"

"I haven't forgotten a thing you've done since you got here." That statement nearly rocked Carrie off her feet. If it wasn't a declaration, she didn't know anything about men.

"You can't think I go about handing out kisses to everyone who asks." For an answer, Lucas stood up, took her clasped hands into his, and pulled her to her feet.

"Not everyone. Just to me." He was so close her body trembled with excitement.

"Why just you? I don't mean that," she corrected herself quickly. "I mean why you at all?"

"Because you're not indifferent to me either. Look at you now. You're trembling like a leaf."

"I'm cold," Carrie said. Lucas's twisted grin prompted a chuckle and an unwilling truth. "No, I'm not completely indifferent, but I *am* cold." In her agitation Carrie had allowed her shawl to slip off her shoulders. Lucas wrapped it more securely around her then enfolded her in his arms.

"Is that better?"

"Yes."

"And you're not indifferent to me?"

"I never was," she admitted reluctantly. "How could I ignore anyone who could pitch Baca Riggins into the water trough."

"I'm not talking about Baca, or harnessing the horses, or following you to town. I'm not taking about anything I did for you. I'm taking about *me*. Are you indifferent to me?"

"No," Carrie said without hesitation. "Not from the very first." Lucas raised her chin until she had to look into his eyes.

"I knew you weren't, but I wanted to hear you say it."

"How ungallant to force a lady to reveal her innermost feelings," Carrie said, her words barely louder than a whisper.

"It would be much worse if she didn't have any to divulge."

Carrie couldn't think of any answer to that, but it wasn't needed. Lucas bent down until his lips met hers, and kissed her long and tenderly. How like Robert, she thought, and yet how utterly unlike his kisses. Robert's kisses had left her unruffled, thoroughly composed, feeling as though she had just received a compliment. Lucas's lips, while they did no more than seem to taste her lips, left her feeling weak, confused, and assaulted. Suddenly she realized what she felt for Robert was some tepid, pale thing when compared to the emotions that now stirred within her. If a kiss that was hardly more than a brushing of lips could cause such a reaction, what would she do if he kissed her hard like before? And suddenly she realized she wanted him to kiss her again, and to kiss her very hard. She wanted to know everything that had been hidden from her up until now. She wanted to know what it was like to feel so strongly about someone that almost nothing else mattered.

Suddenly she felt Lucas stiffen; then his arms fell away from her, he stepped away, and leaning against one of the porch posts, looked out into the night. Carrie felt stunned. She couldn't imagine why he would reject her so abruptly and without a word. What had she done? Had he changed his mind?

"You better sit back down," he said. "Maybe even go inside." Carrie tried to get her feelings under control. She made no attempt to understand or catalog them, just to corral them so she could get through these next few seconds, or minutes.

"Maybe you shouldn't have kissed me if it was going to be that disappointing," she managed to say. "I guess we Eastern girls just haven't learned to kiss like your Western women."

"It's not that at all," Lucas said, whirling to face her. "I could have kept on kissing you for the rest of the night." Carrie's heart rebounded with such a lurch she spoke before she thought.

"Then why—"

"Someone's coming, probably Jake Bemis, but it won't do to have people see me kissing you. It's bound to lead to somebody getting killed."

Carrie felt she was rapidly losing any understanding of what was happening around her. That Lucas's interest in her could lead to someone being killed was an idea too fantastic to be accepted. He must have meant something else. She tried to gather her sorely tried wits; the rider had come into view, and it was Jake Bemis.

"Evening, ma'am," he said as he pulled his horse to a stop in front of the porch. "I hope I'm not late."

"I'm sure you're right on time. Mr. Barrow has been waiting to show you where to bed down. I'm afraid you'll have to stay in the barn for a while. There's a room for you at the station, but I haven't had time to finish cleaning it yet."

"If it's anywhere Baca Riggins stayed, I'd just as soon sleep in the barn, thank you," Jake said. "Besides, then you won't find me underfoot when it comes time to do the cooking."

"But it's a perfectly good room. I've already washed the bedclothes and scrubbed the floors and walls. I've still got to wash the mattress ticking and fill it with new stuffing."

"You don't worry about no room for me. I'll just make myself comfortable in the tack room. The smell of horse sweat and manure always did make me sleep better." Carrie rather thought it would have made her sick, but she was rapidly learning that not everyone wished to drink from the same cup, and the brew that satisfied some of these Western palates was an odd one indeed.

"That's fine with me. You take him on over, Lucas, and I'll lock up here."

"We'll wait until you're done."

"There's no need. I'll be perfectly safe."

"We'll wait." It was not a statement to be argued with, so

she went inside quickly. She was at the door in a minute, a pot and two cups in her hand. There's some coffee here and it's still hot. I thought you might like some before you went to bed."

"That's mighty thoughtful of you ma'am. I am a mite chilled from the ride."

Carrie stepped back inside and came out in another minute. "And here are some blankets. Keep the extras. You'll need them when it starts to get cold." Then she stepped back inside, took one final look around, and blew out the coal oil lamp. "Breakfast is at seven. If you oversleep, you don't get fed. Now I will say good night to you, gentlemen. I've got a busy day tomorrow."

"That's a handful of woman," Jake commented to Lucas after Carrie was out of hearing distance.

"That she is," Lucas agreed, "and not one to be taken lightly."

"She right nearly scares the pants off me. I was afraid to show up, but I was even more frightened she'd come after me."

"She wouldn't hurt anybody."

"It's okay for you to say that. It wasn't your cigar she shot in half, or your hat she darn near lifted off your head."

"Then I suggest you be at breakfast on time, with your face washed and your hair combed."

"Lord, she's not one of those, is she?"

"There's a wash bucket with soap and water sitting against the station. Even got a towel for drying off with."

Jake groaned. "Leastways I don't have to eat my own cooking," he said, brightening a little. "I hope she's handy with the pots and pans."

"Oh, she doesn't do the cooking. There's another woman to do that."

"If I'd known there was *two* women here, I'd a lit out for Denver as soon as she left town. She never said nothing about no other female."

"You can't back out now," Lucas said, not bothering to hide his broad grin. "If you tried to leave now, she *would* come after you."

"Oh hell," Jake moaned, and spurred his tired horse toward the barn.

Chapter 9

"I'm right pleased you found someone for those horses," Katie said as she broke another egg into the pan. "It's time you stopped having to worry over them."

"I never really did, not with Lucas here."

"Lucas? And just when did Mr. Barrow start being Lucas?" The look in Katie's eye was so much that of the big sister Carrie never had that she burst out laughing.

"Last night on the porch," she replied, mischief dancing in her eyes. Katie's hand paused above the frying pan.

"And what would a young widow like you be doing on the porch last night?" she asked, a stern look in her eye.

"Nothing at all, so you can go back to scrambling those eggs before you scorch them and have to throw them out." With a guilty exclamation, Katie plunged her fork into the eggs and swirled it around vigorously as she dropped bits of bacon into the thickening mixture. "I just got tired of his calling me ma'am, and he wouldn't agree to call me Carrie unless I called him Lucas." Katie's look of disapproval relaxed, but didn't disappear altogether.

"You be careful, ma'am. It won't do for you to be getting too familiar with that Mr. Barrow. Men have a way of taking more than they're offered, and they don't respect a widow any more than if she had never been married."

Carrie didn't know how to reply to that statement so she changed the subject. "The new man I hired came in last night. You'll meet him at breakfast."

"I thought I heard a horse come up. What's he like?"

"I think he's what you call a confirmed bachelor, a lifelong woman hater." Carrie laughed. "At least that's what he likes to think he is, but I suspect there's some good in him. There has to be if he's good with horses, and Lucas says he's the best around."

"Horses are no smarter than people, so don't you be letting that old wives' tale get you into trouble," Katie cautioned, once more neglecting her eggs. "There's been more than one girl brought to grief by that road."

"I think we ought to give him the benefit of the doubt. Maybe your cooking will soften him up a mite."

"I fancy not," Katie said, repugnance inexplicably sounding in her voice.

"But you've never seen him."

"I have now, if you're meaning that shuffling, shiftless scarecrow coming across the yard with Mr. Barrow. I'd not hire him to feed me pigs."

"I don't have pigs, I have horses," Carrie said, "and I want you to be nice to him."

"I'll be making no promises I can't keep," Katie said, unyielding. "I don't like the looks of him, and when I don't trust a body, I say so." Carrie felt a sinking sensation in the pit of her stomach, but she stepped out on the porch to welcome Lucas and Jake with a friendly smile.

"I see you got up on time," she said to Jake.

"It was Lucas here. He pulled the covers off me then threatened to dump a bucket of water over me if I didn't get moving."

"From the looks of you, it'd take more than a bucket to make any difference a body could notice," Katie volunteered. She had followed Carrie onto the porch and was glowering at Jake's disheveled appearance over Carrie's shoulder.

"There's a bucket next to the porch with soap and towels," Carrie told Jake. "Breakfast will be on the table before you can finish washing up."

"You mean I have to wash before I can eat?" Jake asked Carrie.

"You do if you're thinking to sit down to my table," Katie informed him obstinately. It was obvious to everyone she had taken an instant dislike to Jake, and it wasn't going to be easy to persuade her to change her mind.

"Here's your coffee pot," Jake said. "I suppose I should have cleaned it."

"That's okay," Carrie replied.

"To be sure it's not," Katie declared angrily as she took the pot and cups from Carrie. "If he can drink all that coffee, he can clean up after himself," she announced, and stalked back into the station.

"If you like, we could have a pot for you each evening," Carrie offered.

"That's mighty nice of you, ma'am, but I usually have a swallow of whiskey to keep me warm." Carrie was about to step through the door, but she was back on the porch in an instant.

"Let's get one thing straight, Mr. Bemis. I will not tolerate drinking while you work for me. What you do in town or on your time off is up to you as long as you're up to your work when you return, but there will be no smoking and no drinking on this property."

Caught in the middle of washing his face, Jake could only stare up at her, water dripping from his chin and arms.

"Did you bring any whiskey with you?" Carrie asked.

"Well, yes, ma'am, but it's just a little."

"Give it to me."

"What?"

"I said give me the bottle of whiskey."

"It's over in the barn, but it's only a drop."

"You can bring it to me after breakfast, but I want your promise you won't bring any more to this station."

Jake took some time drying his face, and it was clear to Lucas he was gauging his chances of getting away and deciding they weren't very good. "Okay, but it sure takes the heart out of a man to know he can't have his drop of whiskey every now and then."

"A drop you could have and be none the worse," Katie said

sternly, once again standing at Carrie's shoulder. "It's the swallows you take to keep it company that'll get you skinned alive."

Jake looked hard at Katie. He was never very good in the morning, and it wasn't easy for him to work up an interest in a second female with that little widow woman around, but this other gal was a mite nippy, and he thought he'd better check her out before she did him some damage. He peered past Carrie and was surprised to see a young, ruddy-cheeked Irish girl, fully as large as he was, staring back at him with wrathful eyes. She looked mad enough to lay him out with a frying pan.

"Don't you be staring at me with your beady eyes, Mr. Jake Bemis," Katie said, speaking sharply and waving a threatening finger under his nose. "Get yourself cleaned up before you come into me kitchen, watch your manners and don't track mud all over me floors, and maybe we will get along okay. I already promised Mrs. Simpson I'd treat you with Christian charity, but you be giving me any cheek, and I'll lay the side of your face open. Then you'll have to catch your own dinner for I'll not fix it." Having delivered herself of that warning, Katie returned to the kitchen and started beating the flapjack batter with unwonted energy. Jake was the last to go inside.

"Wonder why she's beating her batter thataway," Jake muttered to no one in particular. "Must be something in it she means to kill?" He shuffled over to a chair and dropped in it. "All right, lassie, you can put a helping of that breakfast you're so proud of on my plate. I'll let you know if you've got any reason to be giving yourself airs."

"You keep a civil tongue in your head, or I'll be letting the air out of you," Katie said, whirling on him. "Don't you even know enough to wait for a lady to be seated first?"

"Never knowed any ladies," Jake explained, getting up while Lucas held a chair for Carrie, who was looking from Jake to Katie with gathering dismay. "From what I can gather, it's a waste of time, them being so full of themselves they can't take no notice of a poor sort like me."

"I'll have you know Mrs. Simpson is a lady."

"Sure she is, but she's different. There ain't no shilly-shallying about her. You cross her, and she'll shoot you. Simple as that."

"Is that all you respect? A gun?"

"You got to be a fool not to respect a gun," Jake said. "Or dead," he added after a moment's reflection.

"Please serve breakfast, Katie," Carrie directed, hoping to head off what promised to be an explosion. "You and Jake can compare philosophies later."

"I'd sooner milk a wild cow."

"Probably be more purpose to it," Jake muttered. "At least you'd have something when you was done jabbering," he explained after they all looked at him inquiringly.

"Meals are served the same time every day of the week regardless of the stage schedule," Carrie intervened, hoping to prevent Katie from picking up Jake's gauntlet. "Lunch at noon, and dinner at six o'clock. We don't eat with the passengers, but there's always something left if you're hungry. There's nearly always a pot of coffee on the stove, but if not, you're welcome to fix it yourself."

"And you be sure to leave me kitchen orderly," Katie warned. "There's too much to be done for me to be cleaning up behind no-account men."

What have I done? Carrie asked herself as they ate in uncomfortable silence. Who would ever have thought mild-mannered Katie would have taken such a violent dislike to Jake or that she would be so vocal about it? And poor Jake hadn't even had a chance to do anything to annoy her. True, his appearance at the table could use some improvement. He looked as though he'd never taken the bath Carrie had interrupted. He might not actually *be* dirty, but he looked disreputable enough that Carrie decided it would be good for the station if she helped Jake clean up his appearance.

"I bought some work clothes for you," Carrie informed Jake. "You can change after breakfast, and I'll wash your own clothes and put them away for you."

"You talking to me?" Jake asked, surprised. "What's wrong

with my duds?" he asked, looking at himself to see if there was something about him he hadn't noticed.

"You have the appearance of rolling in the dust with the horses, that's what," Katie announced. "You'd better have Mr. Barrow strip him to the skin, ma'am. And if I were you, I'd boil everything he brought with him. I'd take me oath he is infested with lice."

"Now don't you go getting excited about stripping me, young lassie. It won't do you no good." Katie looked as if she was about to take a knife to him; Lucas did his best to hide a grin while Carrie thought in dismay that it might have been easier to live with Baca Riggins than it was going to be to live with these two.

"To blazes with ye!" Katie stormed, her Irish brogue thickened by anger. "The female wanting to do anything to yer unnatural self except throw ye on the manure pile is no better than she ought to be," she declared, righteous wrath stoking the flush in her cheeks. "And if ye dare say another word to me, I'll make me a giblet of yer innards."

"If it's all the same to you, Mrs. Simpson, I think I'll finish my breakfast on the porch. I don't know how you keep up your appetite with that gal screeching about the place. It's just about turned me off my food." Jake shuffled toward the doorway. "Must say, though, she's got a mighty fine way with a stove." He took a bite from his plate as he backed out the door, then caught it with his foot as it swung shut to keep it from banging.

"There's them in Ireland what would shoot a man like that," Katie said. "Bless Pat, the blarney fool left his coffee." She rose and flounced through the door. "You forgot this," she said, setting his cup down with a thump.

"No, I didn't," insisted Jake. "I didn't have any more hands. I knowed you'd bring it to me. There's some females that just can't resist pointing out a man's mistakes."

"I've no doubt, but it would take a whole room full of females to catalog your shortcomings," Katie said with a snort.

"Seems like somebody put a burr under that filly's saddle," Jake said as though to himself. "I doubt if it would be worth taking out though. Too tough for any man to chew."

"Now that will be enough, both of you," Carrie declared, deciding if things didn't stop now, there would be no way the three of them could coexist. "We have to work together, and rather than picking at each other, I want you to look for ways to get along."

"I'm agreeable. I'm a peaceable man, even if I am a little ripe."

"From the smell of you, I would say rancid be the better word."

"I said that's enough," Carrie repeated, and both were quick to catch the note of steel in her voice. "Katie, you stop criticizing Jake for every breath he takes, and Jake, you stop baiting her. We've got too much work to do to waste our time like this. I'm determined to make this the best station on the whole route, and it's going to take all the energy and cooperation you have. Is that understood?" Both protagonists nodded their understanding, but Carrie had an uneasy feeling the battle had hardly begun.

Carrie and Lucas accompanied Jake back to the barn. "About all you have to do is keep the horses and harnesses in good shape and be ready with a fresh team whenever a stage comes in," Lucas said.

"The schedule is posted on the wall in the station, but I'll make a copy for you to keep out here," Carrie told him. "I also insist that the barn be kept neat, the stalls mucked out every day, and the tack room kept orderly. I want you to replace those nails with wooden pegs. They will tear up the harnesses sooner or later."

"You ain't looking to give a man any time to himself, are you?" asked Jake.

"I'm not paying you to sit back on a bale of hay or doze in the tack room. I want an inventory of our feed and hay. I need to know how much we require on a regular basis, and how much extra to lay in for the winter."

"She's worse than any man I ever knew for laying on the work," Jake complained to Lucas. "I'll be worn down before the month's out."

"No you won't," Carrie informed him. "The alcohol will be completely out of your system, your muscles will have some tone, and you won't shuffle and stumble along like a man twice your age."

"Ma'am, you're nearbout as bad as that Irish gal. Don't you like men at all?"

"That has nothing to do with it," Carrie replied, blushing lightly and being careful not to glance at Lucas. "I don't like mess and I don't like sloppy work. When I pay for a job to be done, I expect it to be done well."

"I knowed I should have left for Denver the minute you turned your back."

"I'd have gone after you."

"That's what I figured. It's the only reason I'm here."

"Now get out of those clothes, and give me any others you brought with you. If what I bought doesn't fit, you can exchange them for some that do, but I'll deduct these from your wages and you can buy any extras you need next time you're in town. I'll wash your own clothes and put them away for you." She handed Jake a wrapped bundle that contained some Levi's and several checked flannel shirts. He looked at the bundle with downcast eyes and mumbled softly under his breath, but he went off and Lucas soon returned with the clothes he had been wearing.

"What have I let you talk me into?" she asked, in not entirely feigned trepidation. "I've practically got a full-scale war on my hands."

"Don't blame me."

"Why not? You're the one who recommended Jake. In fact, you egged me on until I practically *had* to agree to hire him."

"You noticed that, huh?"

"Of course I did. I'm not blind or stupid."

"Not stupid, but I'm not sure about blind." Carrie gave him an inquiring look. "Blind not to see I'd rather be talking about you. Won't you sit with me a little while?"

"I've got an armload of clothes, a house full of work, and you want me to sit talking to you."

"Well, I'd actually rather do something else, but I figured talking was about all I was going to get in broad daylight." Carrie looked at him with pretended condemnation, then broke out in an amused chuckle.

"You're almost as bad as Jake."

"Will you sit with me?"

"No."

"Not ever?"

"Not now."

"When?"

"I don't know. When I finish my work, I guess."

"You'll be dead before you finish your work. I know women like you. They're never satisfied unless they've finished one job and have two more waiting to get started. Sit with me this afternoon."

"I can't. I've got two stages coming through."

"Then how about tonight?"

"If I have time."

"I'll have none of that. Agree right now, or I'll kidnap you and drag you off into the hills."

"You probably would," Carrie said, aware of the pleasurable feelings creating havoc inside her, "but I wouldn't like that."

"I promise you would."

"Lucas Barrow, you're the most brazen man."

"No, I'm not. I can't believe how tame I've been acting. If my uncle could see me now, he'd swear I had a wasting fever and send for the doctor. I've never taken so much time to court a female in my life."

"Is that what you're doing, courting me?"

"I'm not just aiming to pass the time of day. I've got other work needing to be done."

"Then go do it," Carrie replied smartly. "I wouldn't want to hold up your schedule."

"Hold up my schedule, hell! You've already ruined it. Will you walk with me tonight?"

"Okay, but you're going to have to behave yourself. Katie is keeping a sharp eye on us."

128

"We could go up to my cabin. She couldn't see us there."

"No we won't."

"You can't blame a man for trying."

"I can and I will."

"Shrew," he said, but it sounded like an endearment.

The battle resumed at lunch. Jake washed before he entered the station, but he was unshaven and his hair was uncombed.

"I would appreciate it if you would shave each morning," Carrie said after they sat down. "I don't care whether you do it before or after breakfast, but it will give the passengers a much better impression if everyone is neat and well groomed."

"Then you'd best do something about that mop of his hair," Katie pointed out. "It won't make much difference if you clean up only half his head and let the other half go to seed."

"It just needs to be cut."

"There's a barber in town," Jake said, hopeful of being allowed into town for at least a few hours.

"There's no need to go into town," Lucas said. "I'm sure one of these ladies can trim it for you." Jake looked as if he'd rather have surrendered his head to a bobcat, but he brightened when neither woman was quick to volunteer.

"I've no doubt I could do it," Katie finally offered. "I cut me brothers' hair often enough."

"I ain't letting no damned female loose on my head with a pair of scissors," Jake protested. "I'm liable to end up bald."

"Jake Bemis, I won't have you cussing or blaspheming in me presence," Katie warned him, a martial light in her eyes.

"Lord help us. First Mrs. Simpson takes away my whiskey and my clothes. Now you're trying to take away my words and my hair. Pretty soon there won't be nothing left of me."

"Good," Katie state uncompromisingly. "Then maybe the good Lord can start over afresh. *Somebody* sure made a mess out of you the first time."

After they finished eating, Katie directed Jake to carry a

chair out into the back yard. She draped one of the smaller tablecloths over him and prepared to begin work.

"You remember that you're cutting a man's hair, woman. I take some pride in my looks."

"I've no doubt, but the rest of us take fright," Katie retorted.

"I wonder how long before one of them murders the other?" Lucas wondered as he and Carrie lingered over their coffee.

"Oh, I don't know," Carrie said, looking suddenly as if she had thought of something that was about to make her break out with laughter. "I think Katie likes him a little."

"Likes him! Are you crazy? She hasn't stopped digging at him since he set foot in the door."

"A woman doesn't pay all that attention to a man she's not interested in. Watch what she does, and pay no attention to anything she says." Lucas looked as though he thought the idea was lunacy, but as he listened to the exchange between the two in a new light, he wasn't quite so sure. It certainly wasn't the way he would have courted a woman, or wanted one to court him, but then he wasn't a woman. Men were predictable. You could nearly always plan on them behaving according to pattern, but you never could tell what a woman was going to do, especially a woman in love.

It wasn't too long before Jake emerged from under the tablecloth with a thoroughly competent haircut and a totally difference appearance.

"He's not so bad looking now," Carrie remarked rather surprised. "And he looks at least ten years younger."

"You keep your eyes on me, Carrie Simpson," Lucas ordered, his voice not entirely free from anxiety. "I won't stand for competition from the likes of Jake Bemis."

"You've got to be in the running before you can be said to have competition," Carrie retorted.

"You just make sure I'm the only one running."

Carrie got up with a toss of her head and took their coffee cups to the sink, but she decided it was wiser not to answer him until she was more certain of her own feelings.

"That you, Jake?" Bap Turner asked when Jake brought out the team for the afternoon stage.

"Who the hell do you think it is?" demanded Jake. "I ain't got no twin brother." Suddenly apprehensive, he looked over his shoulder to see if Katie was anywhere within hearing distance then donned a satisfied smile when he saw she was nowhere around.

"You just don't look right."

"You'd look peculiar too if you had two females fussing over you all the time, trying to change everything about you until your mother couldn't recognize her own son. I damned near ruined my britches when I looked in the mirror and saw a stranger staring back at me. Felt like I was shaving somebody else's face."

"You better watch that cussing," Bap warned. "Mrs. Simpson don't like it."

"It makes that Irish gal powerful mad, too," Jake said with a wink as he jerked his head toward the station to indicate Katie. "Does my soul good every time I get out a good one." Bap grinned in sympathy.

"You just watch it. Mrs. Simpson is a nice lady, but she don't put up with any stuff from nobody."

The evening air was rapidly turning cool as Carrie and Lucas wandered out to a bench under a tree in the station yard after dinner. The dark velvet of the night sky was illuminated by thousands of glittering stars suspended by invisible threads. A brilliant full moon bathed the landscape in a silvery sheen, making everything as clear as day, but an eerie quiet and an unnatural stillness made it all seem remote and unreal. More light poured from the station windows and filtered from the barn, but the dark shadows under the tree enveloped the two in its cloak.

"I think you may be right about them," Lucas said as he settled down beside Carrie. "She can't seem to leave him alone for a minute."

"And he's sure to respond with something guaranteed to keep her at it. If Katie's not careful, she's going to find herself in love with that worthless scamp. That's not my idea of love."

"What is?"

"Do you really want to know? I don't think you'll like it."

"Yes, I want to know, and why won't I like it?"

"You'll see." Carrie settled herself on the bench and looked up at the stars. She couldn't get over how clear the sky was, and how close the stars seemed. She wondered if her dreams were as deceptive as those stars.

"I want a husband who will love me for myself — he'll have to, I won't bring him an inheritance — and who will put me before anything else in his life. I've seen how men usually treat their wives, I was treated that way without even being married, and I'd rather be single for the rest of my life. I don't want to be left home every time he goes anywhere, and I don't want to be left out of what he does. I want him to be interested in the house and the children, and I expect him to listen to my ideas on all those things women aren't supposed to know anything about."

"Where do you expect to find someone like that?" Lucas asked, unable to hide his consternation.

"I don't know, but I'm not going to get married if I don't."

"Was your husband like that?"

Not Robert again! When was she going to tell him that she'd never been married so she could drop this pretense? It had seemed harmless enough in the beginning, but now it was beginning to intrude into nearly every conversation, making her original deception, no matter how innocently entered into, seem like some kind of monstrous lie. There never seemed to be a time when something wasn't hinging on her answer, a time when it didn't seem as if she had used Robert to manipulate the conversation, or Lucas. And that made it even worse, that it would seem that she used Robert against Lucas. If he saw it that way, it would be very difficult to change his mind.

"I was only married to Robert for a few weeks," Carrie be-

132

gan, yielding to the necessity of keeping up the pretense, "but he really wasn't very different from my father and brothers. He was not a strong man, and I admit that's part of the reason I agreed to marry him" — at least that part was true — "but I could see him deciding things that affected me without even telling me about them or shunting me off to a corner with the other women while the men talked over the important things."

"I can tell you feel strongly about this."

Lucas couldn't keep the dismay out of his voice, and Carrie couldn't miss hearing it. She experienced a sinking feeling in her heart, a sense of cold traveling from her extremities in the direction of her heart, but she would not stop. No matter how great the pain or disappointment, no matter how much she wanted to hang on to her slender hopes, she was determined that she could tell no new lies. She had come to Colorado expecting to be alone. If he left, she would have no less than she had expected.

"Yes, I'm afraid I do. You see, all my life everybody just assumed that I would cook and clean and care for them without ever asking if I wanted to, if there was anything else I wanted to do with my life. I was a prisoner and I wasn't even married. That's why I agreed to marry Robert, why I insisted we leave Virginia, and why I took the job at this station after he died. I won't ever go back to being the nonspeaking, nonthinking partner ever again. I'd rather live and die an old maid than sell myself into that kind of bondage."

Carrie realized she had allowed herself to get rather excited and her voice had scaled upward during her speech. She stopped, partially ashamed of voicing her views so stridently and partially surprised by her own words. She had always known she would fight before she would allow herself to be thrust back into the role her father and brothers expected of her, but she had never fully understood what it was she wanted for herself. Well, she still didn't fully understand it, but she was a lot closer to achieving it than she'd been before.

"Is there room in that scenario for someone who falls a little short of the ideal?" Lucas asked. He wondered why his voice sounded so forlorn. He had been rather startled by Carrie's views and, yes, disapproving, but he wasn't giving up.

"I'm not sure, but I guess it would depend on how far short he fell. Most men are ready to swear on their mother's grave they love their wife and children more than life itself. My brothers are like that, but they don't mean it. Both of them courted my sisters-in-law with traditional Southern charm, giving them presents, hanging on their every word, and swearing they would give their last breath to spare them the slightest suffering. Yet the minute the honeymoon was over, they expected the house and everyone in it to revolve around them. No, I've had that, and I gave up my home so I would never have to tolerate it again." Carrie paused to allow her heart to slow down. "I guess I sound a lot like a hysterical female, but I mean every word I've said."

She wondered what it would be like not to see his silver-gray eyes following her every move, his lean body negligently lounging nearby just in case she needed him, his lips never touching hers again. Oddly enough, she felt angry rather than sad, angry that her chance to come to know this man should be snatched from her grasp after a tantalizing few days. It was so unfair of life to dangle her ideal before her eyes and then take it away. "But I've talked too much about myself," Carrie said abruptly. "What are you looking for?"

Chapter 10

Lucas hardly knew where to begin. If Carrie had had too much family, he'd had too little. Whereas her father came home every night, he and his uncle were sometimes away from home for weeks at a time. But he enjoyed the stimulation of traveling to new places and meeting new people, and he also enjoyed the challenge of the West, pitting his intelligence and instincts against those of other men and the harsh conditions of this mountainous country.

He could no more envision himself as a banker who came home regularly every evening than he could see himself as a humble clerk who kept to his books and deferred to his wife in everything. Up to this point he hadn't felt the need for family obligations, but that was changing, had probably already changed, or he and Carrie wouldn't be having this discussion. Still, a family could never replace his need to succeed, to leave something behind that he had created out of his own wit, will, and strength. And it wasn't something he was sure he could share. How could you look at some achievement and say half of it was yours? Wouldn't you always wonder which half belonged to you, the strengths or the weaknesses, or if your half would have existed at all without the help of the other half?

Actually, now that he thought about it, he realized he'd been so busy trying to become everything Uncle Max wanted him to be, he hadn't had time to think about what *he* wanted from life. He'd always assumed he was doing exactly what he wanted to do, but now he wasn't sure.

"After what you've said, I'm almost afraid to tell you what I think I want," Lucas said, turning to face Carrie. "I should have said *try* to tell you because I'm not sure what is important to me. I thought I did, but listening to you has made me realize I never had a normal family life, and I don't really know what to expect.

"You see, I can barely remember my parents. My father was gone a lot with the cattle, sometimes for months at a time. The part of Texas I come from is miserably hot in summer and miserably cold in winter, but I find myself thinking increasingly of my mother and the home she made for us. I don't suppose she was any better at it than any other woman, but I've begun to look back on it as something I wish I had had for a longer time. When my uncle took me to live with him, he took me with him everywhere he went, but we never had a home with the care and comfort you speak of, and I think it would be important to me.

"The more I think about it, the more I realize I want all the things you say you don't want. There will be times when I won't be available to my family even though they need me and I would want to be with them, but I would expect their support for me to be as strong and unwavering as my willingness to work for their future. And I do want a family, preferably a large one. I know the loneliness of being the only child in a world of adults, of having to grow up before your time. But I don't want to come home after a long absence and be confronted with all the domestic travail any more than I expect to bore my wife with the details of my workday."

It was impossible for Carrie not to feel moved by Lucas's poignant memories of his mother, it was touching and heartwarming, but she still equated a home with the bondage she had struggled so hard to escape. When he spoke of the warmth and comfort his mother provided, she thought only of the unending hours of toil; when he spoke of the

136

need to be away from his family, she saw only the fetters that would keep her tied to one place forever. She could not see that what he was talking about could be any different from her own past experience, but she sensed that it might be, and she wavered.

"You sound a lot like my brothers." But then what did she expect? Had he given her any *real* reason to think he would be different, or was she just hoping he would be? "They think the world was created for men and that women are only the most favored of its workers." She tried not to sound as disheartened as she felt.

"But that's not what I said."

"It's close enough," Carrie replied, wondering why she felt so much like crying.

"You know what neither of us has mentioned?"

"Yes, the man or woman we hope to marry. You think that will make a difference, but that's where I have the advantage over you. I've seen new marriages close up, and I know you don't cut the marriage to fit the wife, rather you cut the wife to fit the marriage, and I'm not willing to be cut up and remade, not for any man."

"I can't imagine that any man would want to remake you," Lucas said, sitting down so close to Carrie their bodies touched. "He'd be a fool to think he could improve on what's already here."

"But we're not talking about my physical makeup," Carrie replied, trying to keep her mind on their differences and to ignore the tumult caused by his nearness. She could always become excited just by the sight of his body, but she was discovering that his nearness radiated an even more disturbing electricity, and her own body was responding enthusiastically.

"I am," Lucas replied, his lips close to her ear. "I think you're perfect just as you are." He took her ear between his teeth and nibbled ever so gently, distracting her attention and paralyzing her thoughts while his treacherous arms slipped around her.

"But I'm not at all what you want," Carrie said, struggling against the delicious feeling that was making it virtually impossible for her to remember any of their conversation. "You just said so." He was doing absolutely wonderful things to her neck, and all at once she didn't care if they were terribly wrong for each other. Everything felt marvelously right and she surrendered with a pleasurable sigh. She turned toward Lucas and his lips claimed her mouth with breathless urgency. His tongue plunged into her mouth, ravenous for the sweetness only she could offer.

Carrie felt a shattering surge of response and found herself eagerly returning his embrace, her arms around his neck, her breasts pressed against his rock-ribbed chest, her tongue as voracious as his own. Their bodies writhed and tensed as the surge of heat grew intense, as their need for each other became more feverish. Lucas reached a part of Carrie she had never suspected existed, and she was so overwhelmed by the flowering of this sensation that she was hardly aware when Lucas's hand found her breast, just mindful that her body was exploding with feelings as new and exciting as they were wondrously enticing. An alarm sounded in the back of her mind when he unbuttoned her dress and slipped his hand inside, but the firming of her nipples, and the involuntary arching of her body against his hand, destroyed any thought of resistance before it was born.

While Lucas continued to scatter passionate kisses over her whole face, her neck, her eyes, while his boldly insistent hand searched for a way past the hindering clothes to the heady warmth of the ruby nipple now clearly noticeable against her gown, Carrie felt herself buoyed and enveloped by a cocoon of bone-melting, tension-dissolving yearning, an ache so strong it made her shudder with pleasure. For a moment she could almost believe nothing else mattered.

The feel of Lucas's callused hand against the soft, warm

flesh of her breast woke her to the reality of what was happening and Carrie felt her body tense. Even though Lucas's torrid kisses made her feel faint, her arms slid from around his neck and pressed against his chest. His finger found her swollen nipple and gently massaged it, threatening to wash away Carrie's meager resistance, but she summoned up all her will and pushed herself away from him.

For a moment she was silent, her ragged breath making speech impossible. She felt like a runner who had approached the edge of utter exhaustion, where reason doesn't work and the senses almost fail, but gradually the feeling of being utterly shattered left her and she looked into Lucas's passion-shrouded eyes.

"I had to stop you," she whispered. "I wouldn't be able to face you tomorrow if you disgraced me right here in the stage yard."

"I'll be gone tomorrow," he said, and tried to take her in his arms again, but Carrie pushed him away. There was no hesitation this time. A feeling of betrayal drove all desire for surrender from her mind.

"Where are you going?" She busied herself putting her dress to rights, hoping he wouldn't see the sudden desolation in her eyes. He had warned her that he would someday drift out of her life, but somehow she had never faced the reality of what it meant until now, and she was nearly immobilized by the fear she would never see him again.

"I'm going after some more horses," he explained, his voice still hoarse with longing, his hands cupping her face, his fingers tracing the gentle curve of her cheek and jaw.

"How long will you be gone?" She tried to listen for his answer, to ignore the pleading of her body to return to his arms, to the touch of the fingers that were teaching her the meaning of ecstasy, but an awful feeling of rejection, the sickening fear that he would never come back, the humiliating suspicion that she was of no more than passing interest transformed her desire into anger.

"At least four or five days. Maybe a week."

"You didn't waste any time, did you? I'm surprised you didn't leave first thing this morning." She knew her reaction was unfair and unreasonable, but she couldn't help it.

"What do you mean?"

"I'm glad to know that concern for my safety is no longer getting in the way of your work. If you'd told me it was that much of a problem, I'd have gone into Fort Malone and hired Jake the minute Baca Riggins cleared out."

"What are you talking about?" Lucas's passion was being twisted by confusion and the result was painful.

"Merely that you are leaving virtually the instant Jake arrived."

"He's been here a whole day, and I told you from the beginning that I couldn't always be here, that I had work to do."

"True, you did, and I'm excessively pleased that you now feel free to do it." Carrie got to her feet and vigorously shook out her skirts.

"I'll be back as soon as I can," Lucas promised, warmth returning to his voice. "It shouldn't take more than a few days to find some good horses."

"Please take your time," Carrie said, her voice as cold as her mortification was hot. "The company needs the very best animals you can find."

"To hell with the company's needs!" Lucas exploded, attempting unsuccessfully to take Carrie into his arms again. "I'm more concerned with me and you."

"Then it's a good thing I'm the one who works for the Overland rather than you. I hardly think they would approve of your attitude." She didn't want to say all these things, but they kept erupting from her fevered brain. He was leaving, he was rejecting her, and only anger could hold back the choking sobs that filled her chest.

"Carrie, please," Lucas virtually pleaded, "I have so much more I want to say to you."

"I'll be here when you return," she replied. "I imagine it can wait until then. Right now I'm extremely tired."

Lucas started to press his attack, but the light in the station went out and Katie came out, headed back to the cabin.

"Wait for me," Carrie called out. "I'll walk with you." She turned back to face Lucas and he thought her expression softened a little. "Good-bye," she said, and turned and left.

Lucas dropped to the bench with a muttered curse.

Carrie woke up feeling as if she were coming down with influenza. Her head throbbed, her body ached, and she felt an impulse to roll over and die. But she knew it wasn't the flu and she wasn't going to die. She hadn't been able to sleep since Lucas left. She would toss and turn in her bed all night until she felt as if she had been beaten. She would doze fitfully, sliding in and out of dreams that were worse than reality, only to wake to a feeling of utter desolation. She could come to no conclusion about Lucas except that they would never suit.

She had had no notion of how much she had come to think about him, to feel drawn to him, and need him — until he was gone. She had brashly told him everything she wanted and didn't want without ever really imagining his wishes would run contrary to hers. That had been a terrible shock — not that he would think differently, but that the first man she had ever felt really drawn to would be beyond her grasp. But that was silly. She was more than drawn to him. She had been so busy with the station, worrying about one thing or another, she hadn't paid any attention to the real state of her feelings, and now she was flabbergasted to discover she was practically in love with Lucas. The shock was almost worse than learning Robert had died.

But how could that be? He wasn't at all the kind of man she wanted. Sure he was handsome and his presence caused her nervous system threaten to block out all other sensations, but she was no mere girl to think that a charming smile and a great body was all there was to a man, or a marriage. She had seen too much of both and knew that they were only the beginning.

Yet might it not be more important than she had originally thought? She could remember other girls becoming excited by the physical presence of a man, and now that she thought about it, she remembered that they had talked about some of the very same sensations she had experienced when she was with Lucas. These were not foolish girls either but young women nearing the threshold of adult life and encountering their first adult sensations. They, too, felt excited by the mere presence of a man, felt light-headed and tingly in every part of their body.

And that kiss! One friend admitted that her first kiss had been so overwhelming she fainted. Carrie had never believed that, but Lucas's first kiss had left her feeling weak. If she had not been seated that last night, might not his tender kiss have left her unable to stand?

She enjoyed Lucas's kisses and wanted him to kiss her again. She enjoyed the feel of his hard, powerful body next to hers, the security and warmth of his embrace, the reassurance of his presence. In fact, there was very little about Lucas she didn't like. She did wish he had more faith in her ability to survive on her own, but she wondered if that didn't stem more from worry for her safety than doubt she could survive by herself. Even if it were doubt, was that so terrible? Didn't she have doubts herself? Hadn't she needed his help? Was there anything so terrible about his knowing she was ignorant of the difficulties she faced and telling her so? It had hurt her pride, it had been something she didn't want to hear, but he had stayed to help her when he could just as well have left her to the mercy of Baca Riggins. Or he could have ridden out afterward and left her on her own to discover that she knew very little about running a station and nothing at all about what it took to survive in Colorado.

Would her father and brothers have done half of what

Lucas had done for her? She doubted it. They would probably have laughed among themselves about the foolish female who thought she could succeed at a man's job. Then they would have waited for her to fail, taking pleasure in the fact they had been proved right.

Carrie had had plenty of time to remember every word Lucas had spoken that last evening. In the more objective mood that followed she began to discover that no matter how much they sounded alike at first, the things Lucas said, and most important of all, the things he *did*, were not the same things her father and brothers said and did. And this gave her hope.

If Lucas was unlike them in those ways, maybe he wouldn't be like them in the way they took their wives for granted, ignored and depended upon them at the same time, set them on a pedestal and showed it to be a hollow honor by bestowing their attention on less worthy females, or of saying one thing and doing another. Lucas did what he said, and there was no deceit in it. Maybe he would be different if she were his wife, and it was his wife she suddenly realized she wanted to be.

She had made up her mind several nights ago to turn her back on him, but the ground had fallen away from under her decision like sand before the incoming tide. He had told her he would be leaving before dawn, but he hadn't said where he was going or why, and that annoyed her so much she decided this would be a good time to put an end to her interest in him. Then she had been certain he was not the kind of man she wanted for a husband, but now she wasn't at all sure.

She did know she couldn't stop thinking about him and that she had been trying to find an excuse to change her mind about him. The fact that she had found a legitimate reason to withhold judgment was merely convenient; she would have made one up if she'd had to, and she knew it. Something in her wanted Lucas Barrow, and it wasn't about to give up so easily. She had had the courage to come all the way to Colorado to face an unknown land and an unknown future. It certainly shouldn't be a hard thing to face up to Lucas Barrow. She wasn't sure he wanted to marry her, but he did want her, and for now that was enough because she wanted him too.

"The horses are gone." Jake made the bald announcement as he came in to breakfast as though it were of no more consequence than the fact that the water trough was empty.

"What do you mean?" Carrie asked, too surprised by such a statement to take the obvious meaning.

"They're gone. The corral is empty. Some Indians got them."

"All of them?" Carrie could hardly force her mind to accept the fact that there were no horses for the next stage. If she had learned one thing so far, it was that horses were the first obligation of a state station, and Jake was telling her that she had no horses. There wouldn't be a stage through until late afternoon, but that didn't really matter. She had failed again.

"Got Lucas's mustangs too, not that they were much good." He sat down at the table, complacently expecting his breakfast.

"Aren't there *any* horses left?" Carrie asked, hoping that somehow he would tell her they were not completely stranded.

"Just the two I had in the barn. One is the gelding you use with the wagon. The other is a mare I was thinking about making into a saddle horse for you."

"Then you can go after them?"

Jake looked up from his plate, the startled look in his eyes the first sign of emotion Carrie had seen. "You mean you expect me to go chasing after those Indians by myself?"

"Why not? You're the stock tender, and protecting the

horses is part of your job. Besides, how do you know it was Indians if you didn't see them?"

"First, I know it was Indians because they was riding unshod ponies. Second, I ain't going after any Indians by myself, not even if you take that pistol of yours after me, 'cause it's for sure the Indians will do worse. And third, I wouldn't go after them alone if it wasn't Indians because we hang horse thieves out here, and whoever took them would be mighty determined to hang on to 'em."

"Then you'll be getting nothing to eat from me," Katie said, snatching up the plate she'd just set down in front of Jake. "You don't work, you don't eat."

"You expect me to get myself killed over some bunch of horses?"

" 'Twould be no great loss," Katie said, still withholding the plate.

"I could take the mare and ride into Fort Malone to borrow enough horses for a team," Jake offered hopefully. "Sam Gibbs usually keeps some extras at the livery stable. He might know where I can buy a few more."

"That won't hold us for long. I've got two stages coming through tomorrow and the teams need more than a day's rest. I'm going to need all those horses."

"The horses from town will hold us for a day or two, and I can get some men to come back with me and go after the horses."

"Will they?"

"If you pay them. It won't take many. There's always a few standing around willing to take any job for a few dollars. Now if you will tell that Irish hellcat over there to give me my breakfast, I can be on the way to Fort Malone inside thirty minutes." Katie set the plate before him with a loud thump, but her look of angry disapproval didn't change. "It's a shame I won't have time to go over to the saloon. They have the best whiskey in Colorado. And there's always a game going for a man who feels lucky, and some girl or two standing around if he doesn't." Jake

145

couldn't resist a quick glance at Katie's outraged countenance.

"You should be ashamed of yourself, talking like that in front of Mrs. Simpson," Katie said, her eyes flashing in indignation. "I don't know why she hired you, and I don't know why she keeps you. Seems to me horses don't need your help to get lost."

"Where do you think the Indians took them?" Carrie asked, oblivious of their words. "I didn't think there were any camps near here."

"There aren't. Probably a few braves ran them off for their own use. Indians are always looking for more horses."

"How long have they been gone?"

"No more than half an hour. That's what woke me up."

"You mean you saw those Indians stealing the horses and you didn't try to stop them?"

"Ma'am, you don't see Indians and you don't hear Indians unless they want you to see or hear them. They made that noise so I would see who took them horses. Besides, I couldn't follow them in my underwear, and I couldn't shoot at them because they were around the bend in the canyon by the time I got to the window."

"So they don't have much of a head start. Can you track them?"

"Sure, but those Indians are clever. They'll find some way to cover their trail."

"Then if we wait until you get back with those men, we won't be able to find them?"

"Naw. It'll just take us a few days longer."

"But I don't have a few days. You've got to go after those horses now. I'll go with you."

"I done told you, Ma'am, I don't go after Indians alone."

"I wish Lucas were here. He'd know what to do," Carrie said more to herself than Jake. "*He* wouldn't sit around while those thieves got away with my horses."

"No, ma'am, he probably wouldn't, but then Mr. Barrow is good with guns and he's good with his fists. He *likes*

146

to stick his neck out to see who'll shoot at it. I ain't good with guns or fists, and I don't like being shot at."

"Then I'll go alone," Carrie said, suddenly making up her mind. "I'll take my pistols and the mare."

"You'd better take a shotgun if you're going to go after Indians."

"Why? I'm an excellent shot with a pistol."

"I know," Jake shuddered, remembering his humiliation in the bathhouse, "but any Indian will take a chance if he's facing a pistol or a rifle. There ain't any man, Indian or White, who's going to take a chance when you're pointing a shotgun at him."

"Good. I'll take *two* shotguns, and you make sure you get back with some men as fast as you can." Carrie hurried out of the station and Jake turned back to his breakfast.

"Jake Bemis, do you mean to sit there and let Mrs. Simpson go after those Indians by herself?" Katie intoned like the voice of impending doom.

"Do you think I can do anything to stop her?"

"No . . ."

"Then I mean to let her go."

"But not alone. There's no telling what might happen. She could get killed."

"You heard me trying to tell her that, but she wouldn't listen. Some people you just can't tell what they don't want to hear."

"You be scared, Jake Bemis," Katie suddenly cried at him. "You be a pigeon-hearted coward who would rather protect his own skin than help that kind, good *lady* who gave you a job." Jake looked up, clearly surprised by the vehemence of Katie's attack.

"Now look here, you ain't got no right—"

"You be a bloody bastard," Katie shouted. "Get out of me kitchen before I kill you." Katie grabbed up a knife with a twelve-inch blade she had used to slice the bacon and whirled on Jake, the knife raised above her head. "I said *get out!*" she cried, and rushed for the stunned Jake.

Jake moved faster than he'd ever moved in his life. He was out the door and halfway to the barn before Katie reached the station steps. "That female's crazy," he muttered to himself when he reached the safety of the barn. "They're both crazy, and if I don't get out of here while I have the chance, I'll be crazy too."

In the kitchen Katie leaned against the door, the knife still held in her slack grasp, and sobs wracking her body. She was crying because she was afraid for Carrie, she was crying because she was shocked she had used such language, and she was crying because Jake Bemis was even less of a man than she had thought.

Jake hadn't been on the road to Fort Malone for more than two minutes before he started mumbling to himself. "You're well out of this mess, Jake Bemis," he said aloud. "You can be halfway to Denver before that Simpson dame ever finds those Indians. And you'd better be farther than that when Lucas finds out you let his woman go off by herself. He's going to come hunting your hide if she gets hurt, and you *know* she's going to get herself killed sure enough. She don't know any more about Indians than you know about women." He rode for a few more minutes. "If Lucas wanted his woman watched, why didn't he do it himself? He knows I can't make her do anything. I doubt he can either." He rode a little farther. "That Irish gal sure did get upset. I thought she was going to slice me up like a side of beef. I don't understand it. She's never liked me anyway." He rode a few yards more, then with an oath, he swung his horse around and headed back to the station at a gallop.

"You're a fool, Jake Bemis," he said aloud to himself. "You're going to end up with your hide full of arrows and no thanks for risking your neck. You should never have left Ohio. Nobody could prove that kid was yours."

Lucas kept his mustangs tightly bunched. He had been lucky to find a good-sized herd within two days' ride. It had proved relatively simple to turn part of the herd and head it in the direction of the station. Along the way he cut out the horses he didn't want and let them drift back to the main herd until he had ten good horses left, sturdy, hardy mustangs with plenty of Spanish blood in them who were sure-footed and long on stamina. He intended to find that herd again though. There were still a lot of good horses left in it.

As he rode, his eyes watching the horses to cut off any escape or tendency to stray, his mind was on Carrie and their last talk. He hadn't thought of much else for five days, and the closer he came to the station, the more thoughts of her filled his mind.

He couldn't accept the idea that they would never be able to work out their differences. He had had time to think of what he wanted, and he was even more certain than ever that he wanted everything Carrie said she was determined to avoid, but no matter what either of them said, he could not give up Carrie. The thought of not seeing her again, of losing her forever, was just not acceptable.

He could see her as clearly as though she were there, her perfectly shaped body, so small and dainty when compared to Katie, but her spirit bigger and more stubborn than any women he'd ever known no matter what her size; her eyes that twinkled when she was amused, but were usually hard with determination; her lips, pursed in defiance, her turned-up nose practically pointing straight into the air as she craned her neck to see him; her soft skin, pink with exertion and determination; the smell of lavender which always hung about her. It all seemed so vivid he was nearly tempted to reach out and touch her, to pull her into the crook of his arm and keep her there, safe from all harm for the rest of her life, even though she would probably continue to insist that she could take care of herself.

Just thinking about her caused desire to rise in him, but nothing like he'd ever experienced before. It was no sudden sweep of animal hunger erupting because he had the means or opportunity to appease it. It was something much more quiet, much more pervasive. At first he thought it was something he could ignore, a poor substitute for what he'd enjoyed with other women. He wondered if that was how you felt about a *lady*, the kind of woman you wanted to take for your wife. But it didn't take him long to realize he had misjudged his feelings. They didn't seem to pick him up and shake him hard, but then they never let him down either. It was as though he was in a perpetual fever. It was there over meals, during his work, in every free moment, and all through his dreams. It wasn't something that came on him hard and then left him alone until its next attack; it was a permanent state of unrest.

And it didn't take him long to realize it was growing in intensity, approaching the magnitude of the feverish attacks he had experienced before, only this time the attack was a siege, a twenty-four-hour-a-day assault on his self-control. He had thought that getting away from Carrie for a while would help, and it had. It was more difficult to be constantly in her presence and be kept at arm's length than to know she was a hundred miles away and absolutely beyond reach. Yet his longing for her did not decrease, his need for her did not wane, his determination to win her did not waver.

Carrie had never allowed him to do more than hold her in his arms, and not very often at that, but he was certain there was a vibrant, loving, passionate woman captured in her shell, a passionate woman tightly encased by a fierce determination not to become the slave of any man, a loving woman who was only looking for a person who would love her with equal singlemindedness, a vibrant woman unwilling to waste her strength on a man incapable of appreciating it. Lucas was determined to be the man who would set Carrie free from all her inhibiting fears, who would release her from the bondage of experience, who could convince her to seek the joys and pleasures of a full, loving relationship. He didn't yet know how he would do this, but every time she struggled a little harder to prove her independence, he became a little more determined to rid her of the need to struggle.

It never occurred to him, as he guided his band of wild horses back to the station, that struggle and challenge might be just as necessary for her as it was for him.

Chapter 11

The tracks made by the stolen horses were the first signs Lucas saw to indicate that something was awry. The hoofprints had been badly trampled by his own herd before he noticed them, but it was relatively easy to see that the hooves were headed in the opposite direction and that they were shod whereas his wild horses were not. Lucas tried to come up with an explanation which would account for the tracks and not involve Carrie, but he couldn't.

The second sign was impossible to ignore. His corral was empty and the bars were down. That made it easy to drive his mustangs into the corral, but he knew something was wrong and headed for the station at a gallop. He was greeted by the sight of the empty corral behind the barn and moments later by Katie running from the station, calling and waving to him as though her life depended on it. A chilling fear seized Lucas. Where was Carrie, where was Jake, and did their absence have anything to do with the missing horses?

"Indians stole the horses," Katie said, between gasping breaths as Lucas slid out of the saddle, "and Mrs. Simpson has gone after them by herself."

For an endless moment Lucas was unable to move. Visions of what the Indians might do to Carrie if they caught her, and they would catch her if she didn't recover her senses and turn around, raised the hair at the back of his neck.

"Quick, tell me what happened," he demanded, snapping out of his trance.

"They took the horses just before breakfast," Katie told. "Jake wouldn't go after them, so Mrs. Simpson went herself."

"Did she take any guns?"

"Her pistol and two shotguns."

"But she doesn't know how to use a shotgun. She told me so herself."

"I only know what she took."

"Where is Jake?"

"He went to town to borrow some horses and to hire some men to go after the horses with him."

"And he let Carrie go alone?"

"He tried to stop her, but she wouldn't listen."

"How long has she been gone?"

"Maybe a couple of hours."

"Is there another horse in the barn?"

"No. Jake took the only one." Lucas didn't wait to hear any more. He leapt into the saddle, wheeled his mount, and headed back to where he first saw the tracks. He prayed he would catch up with Carrie before she found the Indians. He wanted the privilege of wringing her neck himself.

Carrie had no trouble following the tracks of the stolen horses. She had never been trained to track anything, in fact she had never tracked anything in her life, but a child could have followed the trail of the nearly twenty horses, all except two of them equipped with iron shoes that left clear impressions on the sand, numerous scuff marks on rock, and churned-up earth at entrances to and exits from streams that were impossible to miss. No, following the horses was not the problem. The question teasing Carrie's mind was *what was she going to do when she caught up with them?*

It was all well and good to say the horses were her responsibility and she couldn't let the Indians steal them, but it was quite another to face real, live Indians who were not likely to give up their booty just because she asked them to. And suppose she did somehow manage to capture the horses. What was she going to do with them? She had never herded loose animals in her life. It had taxed all her ingenuity to figure out how to get the harnesses on the team that first day. These horses weren't in a corral; they were in the hills, free of any restraint.

Carrie kept up her pace, but she became more anxious as the minutes went by and she still hadn't found answers to her questions. Time and time again her mind said that if only Lucas were there she wouldn't have to worry. Lucas was away chasing mustangs, and she had to figure out how to recapture the horses herself.

She hadn't been on the trail very long when she heard the sound of a galloping horse behind her, and she nearly panicked. Suppose one Indian had somehow gotten behind her and they planned to pin her down by attacking from opposite sides. Frantically Carrie looked for a place to hide, and finally drove her mare off the trail into the mouth of a small canyon. It never occurred to her to cover her tracks; her only thought was to get out of the way of the oncoming horse.

She had barely slipped into her hiding place when she recognized Jake as he galloped by. Calling his name in welcome relief, Carrie drove her mare out of the canyon and gave chase. Jake had not gone far when he, too, heard the sound of a galloping horse behind him. He turned with a curse only to see Carrie racing toward him, and he slowed his horse to allow her to catch up with him.

"I was never so glad to see anyone in my life," she said, almost laughing with relief. "What made you change your mind?"

"I thought about what Lucas would do to me when he heard I let you go off on your own, and a few Indians didn't seem so bad anymore. A fella can't die more but once. I'm not sure but what I prefer an arrow through the heart to having my guts torn out right before my eyes."

"Lucas doesn't care what happens to me," she said, self-consciously blushing, wanting Jake to say more.

"You can keep telling yourself that if it's what you want to hear. Me, I ain't such a fool, and I know that Lucas is just about eat up with thinking about you."

"What makes you say that?" Carrie asked, desperate after five lonely days for any proof that Lucas still cared for her.

"You don't know much about men out here, do you?"

"They aren't different from men anywhere else."

"God almighty, and you were going after Indians by yourself! Ma'am, back East a man might make up to a girl, take her places, make all kinds of promises, and have every intention of leaving town the next day. Out here, if a man looks at a woman, he's interested; if he speaks to her, you'd better keep your hands off; if he follows her around, and ma'am, your shadow don't follow you any closer than Lucas, then she is his woman, and any man who thinks otherwise is asking to get killed."

Carrie blinked. "But suppose the woman doesn't want to be followed about?"

"I don't know about that, but I do know she's a staked claim until the first fella gives her up." Carrie wasn't at all sure she approved of that practice and was inclined to argue the point, but Jake had lost interest and turned his attention to the problem at hand.

"Wonder why these Indians don't seem to be making any attempt to hide their trail. We ought to come up to them pretty soon. How are you planning to get these horses away from them?"

"I was hoping you were going to tell me that."

"I just knew you were going to dump it back in my lap. Before I get shut of this station, I'm liable to think a shotgun wedding's a Sunday afternoon picnic."

Lucas slowed his horse to a canter. The trail was easy to follow, but his mount had already covered a lot of distance this morning, and he had no idea how much farther he would have to go today. He kept a careful watch, but he had seen nothing in the tracks to indicate that Carrie had come up to the Indians yet, but by this time he had figured out that there was a second horse with Carrie. He had no explanation for that unless the Indians had somehow surprised her and she was being forced to ride with one of them. The horse was shod, but that only meant that someone else had found her, maybe an outlaw, maybe Jason Staples. Fear for what might happen to her made him try to plan ahead, but he knew there was nothing he could do until he found them and got a look at the situation. It would depend on how many Indians there were as to whether he would attack right away or wait until dark. He didn't know of any Indian village or encampment nearby, so they would probably have to travel at least one more day before they reached their camp. They would be unlikely to do anything to her until their reached their destination. That was small consolation, but it did give him time.

He was getting close now, and he had to be exceptionally careful so they wouldn't see him before he saw them. He was Carrie's only chance, and if he got himself killed, well, he preferred not to think of the consequences. If he could somehow get Carrie's attention without alarming them, he knew she was intelligent enough to keep quiet and wait for him to make the first move. He just wondered what she would do on her own. Carrie had never been one to sit back and wait for someone else, and he couldn't imagine her doing that now. And that worried him a lot. She didn't know how much danger she could be in.

He suddenly pulled his horse to a stop and listened intently. He thought he had heard the sound of a horse whinny. His own mount's ears were pricked forward so he was certain he was coming up to someone. He kept to the side of the trail hoping the loose dirt would muffle the sound of his approach and he moved forward as quickly as he dared, his eyes sweeping the area for a sign of anything unusual and his ears keenly alert for the slightest sound.

Then he came around a curve in the trail and he saw them, two riders well down the trail, a man and a woman, the woman undoubtedly Carrie and the man most likely Jake. They were riding with no attention to their back trail, intent only upon catching up with the Indians. Lucas spurred his horse forward, not daring to call out or fire his rifle for fear the Indians would be close enough to hear. It was Jake who first heard his approach and without waiting to look around, he drove Carrie's horse off the trail into the brush.

"You can both come out," Lucas called as he pulled up his horse at the spot where they had left the trail. Relief banished his fear and he was suddenly furious. "You're not going to lose your scalps today, though I've a good notion to take your hide off myself."

"Lucas," Carrie called with happy relief and quickly left her place of hiding. Jake was not so anxious to put himself in the path of Lucas's anger, and he tarried in the shadows a little longer.

Lucas was so thankful to hear the sound of her voice he felt dizzy with relief. "Whatever possessed you to take out after Indians by yourself? Didn't they teach you anything in your schools back East? I won't put up with this kind of nonsense."

"But they took my horses," Carrie said simply.

"You could always buy or borrow some, or wait for me to round up some more mustangs."

"But I needed them for the stage this afternoon. The company wouldn't be inclined to keep me on if I let anybody who wants come in and help himself to the stock."

"The company, the company, *the company!*" Lucas repeated in a crescendo. "Can't you ever think of anything but my blasted Overland Stage Company? Indians aren't just anybody. Not even a *man* would be expected to go after them alone, even if there are only two of them." In the heat of the moment, no one noticed Lucas's slip of the tongue.

"And if a *man* can't do it, it's foolish for a woman to even think about it, is that it?" Carrie demanded, her eyes dangerously bright.

"It usually is," Lucas said, then added, "but not always." It was a small concession, but it mollified Carrie.

"How do you know there are only two Indians?"

"By the tracks. Now where is Jake? Come out of those bushes, you sniveling coward, or I'll wring your neck for you."

"You'll do nothing of the kind," Carrie fired back. "He volunteered to help me even though he told me to wait for him to hire some men from town."

"You should have listened to him."

"But they might have gotten away."

"It's better to lose your horses than your scalp. Hasn't anybody ever told you that Indians are not especially friendly?"

"I didn't expect them to be. I came armed and so did Jake."

"You may be armed with guns, but as far as knowledge of the wilderness or Indians is concerned, you're no more able to defend yourself than a baby."

Carrie wasn't feeling nearly so glad to see Lucas anymore. In fact, she was thinking what a nice hole one of those pistols could make in his hide.

"Come on, I'm taking you back to the station. Than Jake and I will go after those horses."

"Why go back? You'll lose too much time. They can't be too far ahead."

"Because I'm not tackling any bunch of Indians with a woman in my camp. I couldn't concentrate, and that's a good way to get killed."

"But I can help, and three guns are better than two."

"I can't take the chance on you being captured. Suppose the shots bring their friend. We'd be outnumbered, and you have no idea what the Indians do to women."

"He's right, Mrs. Simpson," Jake said, speaking for the first time. "It would be much better if you let us take you back."

"That's a foolish waste of time," Carrie stated indignantly, "and I won't allow it."

"I'm not one of your employees and I'm not asking," Lucas told her, anger making his eyes hard. "Now turn your horse around or I'll do it for you." Carrie suddenly spurred and whipped her horse forward, but Lucas had anticipated her move, and he reached out and grabbed the bridle of the bucking horse. Carrie was furious!

"Take your hand off that bridle, Lucas Barrow, or I'll use my crop on you."

"Not unless you want it across your backside," Lucas replied, and Carrie had no doubt from the blazing anger in his eyes that he would be as good as his word. "You may be intent upon getting yourself killed, but you're not going to do it where people can say I should have taken better care of you."

"Leave me alone. I don't want you to protect me. I'm not your responsibility."

"I know that, but out here menfolk feel obliged to take care of a woman, *all of them*. Other people, not knowing what a stubborn, hard-headed female you are, might think I neglected my obligation." Carrie reached for her shotgun in anger, but found her scabbard empty.

"I thought we'd all be a mite safer if I was to hold on to the weapons," Jake explained apologetically. "I don't mean to be disrespectful, ma'am, but you're wrong, and the sooner you let Lucas take you back to the station, the sooner we can get after those horses."

"You forgot my pistols."

"No I didn't," replied Lucas, leading her horse back toward the station. "You'd never shoot me in the back."

"Maybe not, but you'd better not turn around, or I'll shoot you between the eyes." Carrie couldn't swear to it, but she thought she saw Lucas's shoulders shake. If he was laughing at her, the black-hearted, bullying monster, she *would* shoot him in the back and be proud of it. But instead she sagged in her saddle and allowed herself to be led home. No matter how furious she was at having to go back without the horses or how much she would have liked to murder him for the high-handed way he had treated her, she was honest enough to admit she had bitten off more than she could chew. At least this once she probably was better off back at the station, but she would die before she would admit it to Lucas.

She looked at his broad, powerful back as he sat easily in the saddle, powerful legs hugging the side of his horse, the reins held loosely in equally powerful hands, and realized how relieved and happy she was to see him. It was impossible to feel threatened when he was watching over her. She tried to drive away the memory of his kisses, of how it felt to be held in his arms, but it was impossible to be this close to Lucas and ignore him. It was almost as though his body reached out to hers and found an answering response. She felt the now familiar surge of excitement, the acceleration of her heartbeat, the release of adrenaline, and she felt supercharged, as though her body were threatening to jump out of its skin.

Suddenly she didn't have any time to think of Indians or missing horses. Lucas was all that filled her mind. He had come back and had come after her. He was furious and had acted like the pigheaded male he was, but he had come after her, and she knew that whatever he was looking for in a woman, no matter how much he was sure they didn't fit, he could not give her up. And for now, that was enough.

The lines of anger were set firmly in Carrie's face. If there was one thing she meant to do before she grew much older, it was to prove to that insufferable Lucas Barrow that no matter how much she might want to have him and his big shoulders around, she'd be damned if she was going to depend on him to help her run her station. She had been almost in charity with him by the time they reached the station. He had been wise enough not to open his mouth and give her any more reason to be angry with him. Unfortunately, he could not see that what worked perfectly in one situation might not work at all in another, and he had made the serious mistake of leaving without saying anything. Well, he had said *one* thing, but it would have been better if he'd preserved his silence.

"I'll be back to get you in a few hours. You be ready."

"Get me?" Carrie echoed furiously.

"Yes. We've got a lot of talking to do."

"You set one foot on this porch and what you'll be *getting* is the business end of a shotgun," Carrie had shouted just before she slammed the door hard enough to pull one of the slats loose.

"Unless you're good at trimming wildcat claws, you'd better stay on your side of the corral tonight," Jake said, a half grin on his face as they headed back after the Indians.

"Unless you're good at dodging bullets, you'll do nothing to attract my attention. I still might skin you alive for letting Carrie go off alone."

"What was I supposed to do," Jake asked plaintively. "Tie her up?"

"If you had to."

"You know what she can do with a pistol."

"She's still just a woman."

"That *woman* is more than I can handle, and I ain't afraid to admit it. I don't mind doing what I can, but if she makes up her mind to do something, I'm getting out of her way."

"Then you'd better make damned sure nothing happens to her," Lucas replied, and spurred his mount into a gallop.

"You'd think somebody would give me credit for going with her," Jake called after Lucas. "After all, I'm not too keen on getting my hide ventilated with Indian arrows."

Lucas didn't answer him.

It was beginning to look more and more to Jake as if he had gotten himself into a situation where it was impossible for him to win. Just my luck, he thought. Fall into the best job I ever had, and it's liable to cost me my neck.

Carrie didn't know any of the things Lucas said to Jake, but it probably wouldn't have made any difference. Her anger boiled over.

"Did you tell Lucas where I had gone?" she demanded of

Katie before that sorely worried young woman could welcome her back.

"To be sure I did," Katie said, giving Carrie an impulsive hug. "How was I to know Jake had gone after you? I was worried you would get into trouble."

"Don't you ever tell that man a single thing about me ever again, or you can go look for a job somewhere else," Carrie stormed. "I will not be hounded and pandered to and made to feel like an empty-headed fool by that great hulking cowboy!" she exploded, wishing she could get her hands on him for just one minute. "Do you know what he did? He forced me to return. He didn't ask, he didn't try to convince me that I should. He just grabbed hold of my horse's bridle and forced me to come home."

Katie started to speak, then changed her mind.

"I've been surrounded by rude, selfish, egotistical, unthinking men my whole life, but never have I run into one that carries the art of presumptuousness to such Olympian heights. He wouldn't even let me stay and help, said he couldn't *concentrate* with a woman about, just like I was a head cold or something." Carrie stalked across the room and threw herself into a chair. "And that horse can keep on wearing her saddle until they get back because I'm not taking it off even if it does give her a rash.

"You just wait until he gets back. I'm going to give him his walking papers. He's not to set foot in this station, do you hear, not for coffee, not for meals, not for *anything!* If he wants to play rough, I'll show him what rough is. I'll write Duncan Bickett and get him replaced. Anybody can break mustangs. I don't have to put up with this kind of insolence from a no-good drifter."

"I don't think he is a drifter, ma'am. He doesn't act like one." Katie tactfully declined to point out that Carrie had been the first one to doubt Lucas's announced profession.

"He acts like he thinks he's God, but you see if I don't get rid of him. I didn't come two thousand miles to escape a houseful of domineering males to fall into the clutches of another one." Carrie paced the room for a while then settled

162

back down in her chair, a fierce frown on her brow. She looked up when Katie nonchalantly headed for the door. "And don't you dare unsaddle that mare. She's my horse, and I can take care of her just fine by myself." With that Carrie got up and stalked out of the station.

Katie let out a long breath very slowly. "Faith, has she ever got it bad."

Unsaddling the mare gave Carrie something to do while she cooled off, and it wasn't long before she started to worry about Lucas. For a few moments, that made her angry all over again, but it didn't last long, and soon she was imagining all the things that could go wrong. Lucas had been certain there were only two Indians, but what if more had joined them since then? What if they were ambushed? She didn't know anything about Indians.

You idiot, she said to herself. If the Indians are harmless enough for you to go after alone, surely two men can handle them. But Carrie would not be pacified by that argument. Thinking about what might happen to Lucas had the double benefit of also telling her what might have happened to her. She was honest enough to admit she had been extremely foolish to start off alone and very lucky she *hadn't* found the Indians.

But he had no right to treat her as he did, she thought, her anger flaring briefly once more. But all the fire and energy was gone out of it now and she could only think of the danger to Lucas, and Jake. What would she do if either of them were killed?

For a moment Carrie could hardly think for the wild pounding of her heart. But when her mind was able to grapple with thought, she almost wished it were paralyzed again. She was in love with Lucas, and that was a fact she didn't want to face.

Carrie's legs gave out from under her and she sat down right where she was. She ignored the inquisitive looks of the mare, the straw that was getting into her hair, or the dust that was soiling her skirt. That could all be fixed; she wasn't sure her heart ever would be.

Up to a point, Lucas was everything she wanted in a man. Just thinking about being near him caused her blood to warm. He was strong, decisive, and he had the most exciting body she had ever seen. He was handsome, he could be charming, and he was definitely exciting to be around. Just about everything a girl could hope for in a man, *up to a point*. Unfortunately, at that point he turned into just about everything she disliked and distrusted in men. He was egotistical, autocratic, overbearing, stubborn, temperamental, and probably a dozen other things she hadn't yet had time to discover. He also thought a wife should be hedged about by senseless restraints, and that was much more of a barrier than being a drifter.

She would have preferred to marry a man with a greater goal in life instead of a drifter someone who wasn't hiding out in the remote parts of Colorado from whatever it was he had done back East. But she didn't really mind that as much as she'd thought. He was good with horses, better with men, and could do practically anything that needed to be done around the station. If they could manage to get over their differences, they could run it together, but it was those differences that kept intruding on her hopeful dreams of the future until she was sure she was doomed to die an old maid.

She thought of what her family back in Virginia would say about her choice of husband and she almost broke out laughing. She realized that her sisters-in-law would probably be just as attracted to him as she was, but he did not fit into their notion of what a socially acceptable man was, and they would ultimately turn their backs on him no matter how regretfully. Her brothers would probably find him an enjoyable companion, but they would never invite him into their home. He would be kept for those mysterious activities which men indulged in on their own, far away from the watchful eyes of the females of their families and the inquisitive ones of their children. As for the older ladies in her town, those dowagers who considered themselves the arbiters of public conduct, she didn't even want to think of the mayhem his appearance would create in several socially prominent parlors. Those that didn't pass out from shock would probably take to their beds for the better part of a week.

Well, she didn't care. She would happily put up with his dust and sweat and Levi's if he would only come back safe.

Chapter 12

"When do you think they'll get back?" Carrie asked for the twentieth time that afternoon. "All they had to do was find the horses and drive them back. They'll probably even head home on their own."

"There's no way I can know for certain," Katie had returned that answer the same number of times.

"But Jake and I must have been close to the horses when Lucas found me. It shouldn't have taken them more than a few hours, yet it's been six hours since they left. And I'll have a stage in here in less than thirty minutes expecting to find a fresh team waiting for them." Several attempts to forget her worries by immersing herself in work hadn't succeeded. Neither did they fool Katie into thinking it was the horses Carrie was most worried about.

"Well, you'll not do anything about that team now, but there'll be a stage full of hungry passengers in that yard any minute now, and you can do something about that. I could use a hand with these potatoes, and the beef stew needs to be stirred every few minutes to make sure it doesn't stick."

Carrie knew that stirring the stew wouldn't keep her mind off Lucas, but she couldn't stand about doing nothing, so she picked up the big wooden spoon and began to move it slowly through the thick, aromatic mixture. She had been at odds with Lucas over one thing or another almost from the first moment she had met him, but from the moment she realized she loved him, fear banished all thought of their differences

166

and started to eat away at her optimism and assurance that she could do everything. Lucas had always seemed like an indestructible power. Whenever something went wrong, he was there to fix it; whenever there was a problem, he was there to solve it; whenever she needed him, he was there whether she wanted him or not. Without realizing it, she had come to think of him as the one unchanging constant around her, the one person who was part of every equation in her life.

Now she was forced to consider the possibility that he had been hurt or captured. The longer he was absent, the more terrible became her fears until she had to face the possibility that he was dead. Carrie would never have believed anyone's death could have affected her so. Her mother had died when she was four, but no one had died in her family since then, and she had grown up with the feeling that people who came into her life were going to be there forever. She couldn't accept the fact that Lucas might never return, that he might never come up the steps to the station to have his dinner, that he might never be around to make sure that everything went right for her. He had become a part of her thinking, a part of her life, and she didn't know how to go on without him.

"The stage is coming. I just heard the driver's yell," Katie announced, bringing Carrie out of her thoughts. "We'd best get the food on the table. 'Tis late, and they'll be near-about starved."

The two women worked quickly to set out the food before the passengers could burst through the station door. Carrie had been in charge of the station for just a week, but already the reputation of her food was beginning to spread up and down the line.

"I've got to speak to the driver before he starts to unhitch the horses," Carrie said to Katie. "Do you think you can handle everything for a few minutes?"

"Sure. If not, they can always get up and serve their own plates."

The driver was Jerry Blake, the only one of the regulars who had not accepted Carrie yet, and he had already started

167

to unhitch the team. He would have to be the one driving today, she thought irritably. He was the one least likely to understand any shortcoming on her part. She wouldn't put it past him to report her to Duncan Bickett.

"Don't unhitch that team," Carrie called. "Indians stole our horses this morning, and we haven't gotten them back yet. You're going to have to use the same team over the next stage." Blake stood up from where he had been undoing buckles.

"They're pretty worn out. Don't know as they'll make it to the next station."

"They will if you take it slowly." Blake looked as though he was about to disagree. "You have no choice unless you want to stay here until Lucas and Jake return," Carrie told him.

"Should have gone to Fort Malone. Bound to be some extra horses around somewhere."

"Actually, that was my original plan. Jake headed to town, and I went after the horses."

"Would have thought it would have been the other way around."

"I suppose you would, but then you're a man." Blake stared at her, unsure of how to take that. "Nevertheless, Mr. Barrow caught up with us, and he and Jake went after the horses."

"Still should have gone into town."

"Possibly, but it's too late for that now. You'll just have to make do. I'll give the team some oats. That may help some. Now you might as well come inside and eat your dinner. Take your time. You're already behind schedule, but having to use a team for two stages ought to be enough of an excuse to keep you out of trouble." Jerry Blake looked at her sharply, a little threateningly Carrie thought, but he refastened the buckles he had already loosened. Then with a last questioning look he turned his unhurried steps toward the station.

Carrie moved off to the barn to find and fill the feed bags for the team. She was glad to be away from the hearty cheerfulness of the passengers—they were always so pleased to be let off the stage for a short while—and she was glad to be by herself. She had always found that when she had a problem or was upset for any reason, she preferred to be completely alone. The presence of others only seemed to perpetuate her state of mind, especially if the people around her were in a good mood and required her to pretend to be in one too.

She moved about the barn, getting out the nose bags, hanging them up, and filling them with oats, but everything reminded her of Lucas. He had slept in the barn and he had worked with the horses; her association of him with this place was so strong she felt certain he would walk through one of the doors any minute.

She went outside to give the horses their oats, but every minute he was gone, she became more and more certain that something had happened, that she would never see him again. She thought of all the things she hadn't said to him, the times she hadn't thanked him, or hadn't done so properly; the times she had been irritated or angry or ungrateful when she was really so thankful he had offered to help; of her new feelings for him which she might never get a chance to express; the chance to see if their love could triumph over the obstacles that stood between them. There was so much she hadn't said or done because she was so busy with the station, trying to prove that she could succeed on her own, refusing to accept or acknowledge his help and her need of his help because it would take away from her own success.

Yet what was her success when measured against the loss of someone so important to her? She knew she could handle the station better than most men, so was it necessary that she prove it? Well yes, it was, but was it more important than Lucas? No, but Carrie realized that if she had been forced to choose between one or the other, she would have a difficult time deciding which to give up. She didn't know what Lucas would ultimately mean to her life, but even if she were to marry him, she realized that proving her independence was critically important to her. It wasn't this particular job—it could have been anything from running a saloon to a general store—it was just that this was the only chance she would be given to stand on her own two feet and it was vital that she succeed. She realized finally that if she was going to even consider the compromise that being Lucas's wife promised to require of her, then she was going to have to know she would live without the help of a man before she could give up her freedom.

Admittedly it was all in her mind, but her whole perception of life was in her mind, so telling herself it was *all in her mind* was just an attempt to circumvent the difficulty. The more she realized the importance of Lucas to her life, the more she realized the necessity of proving to herself that she could do without him. She wondered if he would understand that. Probably not. She wondered if she would ever get a chance to try and explain it to him.

She sat down in the chair under the tree, *his* chair, the spot where she had first seen him, and she thought of him just sitting there, a lump of vital energy just waiting for a chance to explode. And Lucas was like that, always there, always ready, always waiting for the opportunity to do something for her. She brushed a tear away. She couldn't start crying now. She wasn't a crier. She hadn't cried since her mother died, and besides that, the passengers were beginning to come out of the station and there would be no end to the questions and sidelong glances thrown her way if they saw tears. As far as she could gather, women were supposed to be just as hard and tough as men, and if they ever did cry, which of course they probably wouldn't admit, they would only do it in private or in the company of another female. So Carrie rose to her feet, put on her brightest smile, and went to meet the passengers.

"You set the finest table on the whole Overland line, ma'am," one of the passengers said, a plump middle-aged banker type. "But you'd better keep an eye on that Irish gal, or some hungry rancher is going to steal her away from you."

"Thank you, sir, but I prepare half the food, so I guess I could prepare the rest if I had to."

"Well now, you might be in some danger yourself. I hear tell it gets mighty lonely being a widow."

"Maybe you have also heard that widows are mighty hard to please." The man laughed heartily.

"Maybe, but it would be near-about impossible to find a man who wouldn't be pleased with you."

"Thank you, sir, but if you don't get on the stage, you're going to be late getting home, and I doubt that would please your wife."

"None at all," he agreed, and took his place on the stage. Jerry Blake sauntered out last of all, picking his teeth and in no hurry to get started. Carrie removed the nose bags and then waited for him to climb up on the box.

"There's two stages coming through tomorrow," he said insolently. "You're going to have to find horses from somewhere."

"I'm aware of the schedule and the number of horses required, Mr. Blake. I assure you there will be horses for every stage that comes through here tomorrow."

"I doubt you'll find changes for two teams in town. There ain't many extra horses about just now."

"I'll manage." Carrie had tried, but she just couldn't like Jerry Blake. The fact that he didn't every try to like her didn't help.

But just then everyone's attention was drawn to the sound of horses' hooves, lots of them, and Carrie turned around to see a herd of horses approaching at a fast trot. Lucas was back! They had found the horses and he was back!

Without a second's hesitation she was racing toward the corral, the tears she had resolutely held back under the tree flowing freely now. She hadn't realized just how tense she was, how intently she had been listening for just this sound, and now the relief was awful and wonderful at the same time. The corral poles were just as the Indians had left them, and oblivious to the dust and the danger of being struck by a shod hoof, Carrie hurried up to help point the herd toward the opening to the corral. But no matter how much she tried to keep busy to distract herself, her eyes searched for Lucas, and her heart beat faster when she saw him bringing up the rear, herding the last reluctant horse into the corral. Her heart swelled with pride. This was her man, she thought, a man who went after Indians as though it were no more than an ordinary task, a man who considered protecting her to be an accepted part of his daily life, of seeing that all that was important to her ran as she wanted it to run, a man who only lost his temper in her interest. How could she ever have doubted what he meant to her? How could she have allowed anything such as different ideas about marriage to lead her to think she could live without him? This was *her* man, and she fervently hoped she was his woman.

"Jake, you go help Jerry unhitch the team while Lucas and I harness a fresh one." Carrie settled down to work, hoping to give herself time to recover. She hurried to the barn, caught up as many harnesses as she could carry, and went back to where Lucas was already cutting out the team. The horses were still worked up and she had to hold the first two so he could throw the harnesses over their backs, but they quickly settled down as he started fastening all the hooks and buckles, and Carrie went back for the rest of the harnesses.

"What have you been crying about?" Lucas asked as he suddenly looked up over the back of the horse he was working on.

"I haven't been crying," Carrie insisted. "It's just all this dust has made my eyes water."

"You'd better splash some water on your face before you go back, or people are going to start asking questions." Carrie didn't dare meet his eyes. She didn't know whether he believed her, she didn't even want to know, she only wanted to hide her tears. She didn't know why she should be so ashamed to admit she cried with happiness and relief, she supposed it was because she had no idea what had been going on in her heart and head since that talk on the porch, but she knew she wasn't ready to face the people on the stage or their questions. She bathed her eyes in the cool water from the trough, dried her face quickly, and was ready to face Jake when he led the old team to the barn.

"Blake's anxious to be off. Says you're going to cause him to be late and get him in trouble."

"He has all the excuse he needs, and he knows it," Carrie said.

"Looks like one to cause trouble if you ask me."

"But not one to know how to handle it," Lucas said, coming up with the fresh team.

"The sooner we get this team hitched up and the stage on its way, the sooner we can see about getting you some dinner," Carrie said. "I've had enough of Jerry Blake for one day already."

"I could do with some food," Jake said. "I ain't had anything since breakfast."

"And I haven't eaten at all today," Lucas said. "I broke camp early, thinking how much better the food at the station would taste than anything I could rustle up."

"And instead of a hot meal, you were met by another crisis you had to solve," Carrie finished for him. "Just consider yourself close to sainthood and you won't feel so hard used." Lucas smiled in spite of himself.

"I'd think myself hard used if I was forced to become a saint," he said with an easy chuckle. "I've got several things in mind for my future that I'm not sure are allowed to saints, and I don't plan to give them up."

"You don't have to worry," Carrie replied, happy to be indulging in the old give-and-take with Lucas. "Sainthood is about the least likely handicap you'll be asked to shoulder in this life. Now finish up here and wash up before Katie decides the kitchen is closed for the night."

A few minutes later Jerry pulled away, only a few minutes behind schedule. "Now there's one widow who looks like she's found exactly what it takes to please her," observed the banker as the stage rolled on to the road and out of sight of the station.

"Tell us about the capture," Katie asked after the two men had satisfied the worst of their hunger. She had been virtually dancing with excitement ever since they got back. "Was it hard to take them away from the Indians? Did you have to kill anybody?"

"We want to know every detail," Carrie added. "We've been counting the minutes all day, and you can't begin to know all the things that have occurred to our imaginations."

173

Lucas looked at Jake, who looked at Lucas and suddenly Lucas started to laugh.

"What's so funny?" demanded Carrie. "You have no idea how awful it is to wait, not knowing when you are going to come back, or if you'd be back at all. After what you told us about the Indians, I imagined you killed, wounded, all sorts of terrible things."

"I almost hate to tell you, but there were only two Indians, and they were both boys."

"Boys?"

"About fifteen or sixteen."

"They're braves nevertheless," Jake said, not intending to make light of any Indian. "A rifle doesn't take into account the age of the man firing it."

"They were just trying to prove themselves," Lucas said. "They probably heard that Baca Riggins was gone and didn't know you had a stockman."

"In other words," Carrie observed, "they thought it would be no problem to run off the stock with a woman trying to run the place."

"I didn't say that," Lucas replied quickly. "Boys no older than those two have stolen stock from grown men all over the West. Anyway, it wasn't much of a problem to find them. It just wasn't easy to get the horses back without hurting anybody."

"That's what took us so long. Lucas didn't seem to care that they nearly killed him while he was trying to spare them the discomfort of a bullet hole."

"If you had been able to shoot a little better, you could have kept the second one tied down longer, and I wouldn't have had to fight them both at the same time."

"And you never saw a neater job of it," Jake said admiringly.

"Nonsense. It's no feat to defeat two boys."

"Don't listen to him. If he'd been any less clever on his feet, I'd be bringing you back his carcass instead of the horses."

"You got anything for desert?" Lucas asked. "I feel hungry enough for two people." Katie produced what was left of a peach cobbler and Lucas directed his attention to his food. Carrie busied herself with refilling all the coffee cups and putting on a new pot.

"I'm going to need some extra horses," Carrie said. "I don't want to be this shorthanded again."

"I got a good bunch up at my place," Lucas said. "Why don't you come up after dinner and look them over?"

Carrie was so flustered she put the coffee beans in the pot without grinding them, and had to take them out again. She was not prepared for Lucas to invite her to his cabin, and certainly not in front of Katie and Jake.

"It'll be dark before long, and I've got to help Katie with the dishes." She didn't know whether she wanted to go or not.

"You go on," Katie said. "I can finish up by myself."

"I won't let you," Carrie said firmly. "Besides, I have a few chores I need to attend to right away."

"Well, I'll be there if you change your mind. The horses aren't going anywhere either." Lucas rose to his feet. "Mighty good, as always."

"That'll be a quarter." All three people stared at Carrie as if she'd said something blasphemous.

"You talking to me?" Lucas asked.

"You can't mean to be charging Mr. Barrow for his meals?" Katie demanded.

"Yes, I do. I didn't charge him before because he was doing the stock tender's work and it didn't seem fair, but now I have to. You're not an employee of the Overland Stage Company or a passenger on one of its stages, so I'm required to charge you for the food you eat. I probably shouldn't be feeding you at all, but after all you've done for the station, I don't think I could refuse you."

"If I was you, I wouldn't pay a cent," Jake advised Lucas indignantly. "Nobody was ever charged for eating here when Baca Riggins was running the place, and I don't remember there was ever any fuss made about it."

"I don't like to have to do it, but I would be dishonest to my employer if I didn't."

"What about my bringing back the horses?"

"I plan to write the company and tell them of your services in their behalf and request that they pay you for these services, but in the meantime I'm going to have to ask you to pay for your meals." Everyone looked at Carrie, but it was the expression on Lucas's face that concerned her the most. She couldn't say just what she saw there—respect, dismay, doubt, wonder—they were all too confusing and too elusive. She did know that she had succeeded in upsetting him and not at a very good time.

"I'm sure the Overland will be overjoyed to know they have an incorruptible servant jealously watching over their purse."

"Please, Lucas, don't make it any harder. Wouldn't you expect me to charge for extra meals if it was your company?" For a moment there was a startled look on Lucas's face before he broke into a rich laugh.

"Yes, I would. I've a mind to write the company myself and tell them what a pearl they have in you."

"Please don't, but I'd appreciate a good word to Duncan Bickett if you get the chance. I expect Jerry Blake hasn't exactly been singing my praises."

"I don't think Duncan pays much attention to the likes of Jerry Blake," Jake said scornfully. "He's much more likely to listen to the passengers when they tell him how good your food is and how promptly everything is done."

"Well, if you're going to spend the rest of the evening passing around compliments, I'm going to clear on out," Lucas said bruskly. "The offer's still open if you want to see the horses."

"I don't think I'll be finished in time," Carrie said, but she seemed less definite about it this time.

Carrie knew she was procrastinating. She could think up as many little jobs as she wanted, she could give herself as many reasons as she could think of as to why she should go back to her cabin and go to bed early, but she knew that no matter what she said to herself, she was going to Lucas's cabin. She also knew it had nothing to do with the selection of horses. She had to talk to him, to tell him of her feelings and to tell him that she had never been married. She didn't know how he was going to react to that, she had a feeling he had already endured about all the deceits and surprises he could take from her, but she had to tell him. If they were ever going to have a chance to become more than friends, she had to be completely honest with him.

She knew she had to go, but she was afraid, nevertheless. Going up to the cabin meant risking a kind of physical closeness she had never experienced, and she wasn't sure she was ready for that.

She admitted to herself, with a pleasurable shudder, that she didn't really know what it meant to be physically joined with a man, but from everything she had been told, it couldn't be too earth-shaking. The married women she knew all spoke of the physical act, when they spoke of it at all, with a kind of forced tolerance, implying that only lewd or loose women could actually enjoy such a coupling. They were willing to endure it for the sake of children, or to satisfy the bestial appetites of their husbands, but they professed to feel great relief when participation was no longer required of them.

Carrie didn't know any lewd or loose women, but she had often wished she could talk with one for about an hour. However, the opportunity had not presented itself so far. Her friends had all professed to believe the same thing as their mothers, but Carrie had often noted that her younger sister-in-law would grow excited and start to giggle whenever her brother said he wanted to go to bed a little early. It was no secret why he wanted to go to bed, and Lucinda didn't try to pretend she wasn't anxious to go with him.

In addition to this, there was the considerable evidence of a long history of many a husband's involvement with women other than their wives. It seemed unlikely that so many men, and women for that matter, would brave the most terrible stigmas organized society could devise if there weren't something very necessary, indeed very wonderful, to be enjoyed. Carrie couldn't help remembering the response Lucas's kisses had aroused in her body. And when he touched her breast! She couldn't find words to describe how she felt, but it was a wonderful feeling and she longed to experience it again. Maybe that was how Lucinda felt. Carrie wished now she had thought to talk with her sister-in-law about her relationship with Sam instead of merely considering her an additional burden in a household left for her to manage.

Personally, Carrie thought it probably was the union of minds, the sharing of day-to-day life, and the rearing of children that bound two people together rather than their physical attraction; men did seem to devote most of this kind of attention to women who were not their wives, but she decided it was probably best to keep an open mind on the subject. Lucas had already upset several of her most firmly held canons. There was no telling how many more he would topple.

Chapter 13

It was impossible to miss the path to Lucas's cabin. Funny she'd never been this way before, Carrie thought as she made her way up the slight incline and around the shoulder of a hill toward the cabin. Perhaps it was because Lucas was always down at the station. And it's not like this place is a part of him, she told herself. It's just an old cabin the company provides for the wrangler, just like the cabin they provide for you.

She came into the clearing and found herself next to the corral. The mustangs had gathered near the side of the corral near the path and they scattered at her approach, their nickers sounding softly in the evening air. Knowing all the while that she was merely putting off the moment when she had to face Lucas, Carrie turned her footsteps aside to the corral. She had come to discuss horses and it made sense for her to look over the livestock before she started to discuss them. It was also perfectly understandable that she could concentrate on what she was doing better if she was alone. It was always more difficult to think when someone was talking to you.

Lucas was right, she realized, when he said he had gotten a fine group of horses. Even a quick appraisal told her there were several horses in the corral as good or better than any she had seen in the station corral so far. She had a particular liking for a sorrel mare that seemed less afraid of her than the others. She didn't have a saddle horse of her own and maybe that little mare would be just the horse for her.

"Any particular horse you like?" The sound of Lucas's voice made her jump, and she turned as he came toward her, feeling just as guilty about coming as she felt about not having had the courage to go straight up to his cabin.

"I was looking at that sorrel mare. It hadn't occurred to me until Jake mentioned it this morning, but I don't have a saddle horse." Lucas's glance slid away from Carrie and found the mare which had left the group of horses and come halfway across the corral toward them. He leaned on the fence next to her, his foot resting on the bottom pole. Immediately Carrie felt the temperature of the night change and she found the shawl she had thrown over her shoulders to be too warm.

"She acts like she's been around people before," Lucas observed. "Maybe she's even had a saddle on her back."

"Does that mean she belongs to someone else?"

"Not unless she's wearing a brand, and I don't see one. Would you like me to break her for you?"

"Could you? What I mean is, does the company own the horses yet? Are you obliged to give them all to the company or do you sell them one by one?"

"You mean since you're charging me for food, you expect me to charge you for this horse?"

"Of course. I wouldn't expect the company to provide a horse for my private use."

"I don't know what the company policy is on horses for personal use, though I imagine any use you made of it would have to do with company business, but these are my horses, and I'll make you a present of the mare."

"Oh no, I insist that you allow me to pay for her."

"And if I refuse?"

"But why should you?" Carrie demanded, both curious and a little irritated at his stance. "These horses represent your livelihood, the way you make a living."

"I just realized that I've never given you a present, and this will make up for that oversight."

"But why should you give me a present?" Carrie asked. She

felt a tightness in her chest, a constriction around her heart. Why did being around him always make her so nervous? It was impossible to consider being constantly near a man who caused such chaos in her mind and body. And no man would want to spend the rest of his life with a woman who acted like a perfect idiot every time he stepped into the room.

"Because I want to give it to you." Lucas reached out and brushed her cheek with his fingers. "There's something about you that makes me want to shower you with gifts." Carrie felt even more miserable. She felt like three separate conversations were trying to take place simultaneously, the one about the mare, the fact that she had discovered that she was in love with him, and her confession that she had never been married at all. In the end she was unable to get anything out and Lucas had to break the silence.

"Come on up to the cabin. I have a pot of coffee on." He reached out and took her hand, and it was all Carrie could do to keep from jumping. It was just like the bite of static electricity except that its energy was not dissipated and her whole body felt charged with sparks arcing across the lines of her nervous system.

"Those horses will make a nice addition to our teams. How long does it take you to break them?"

Lucas had to give a tug to her hand before her feet began to move. "It depends, but I ought to have the first of them ready inside of a couple of weeks. It's teaching them to respond to the reins and run in harness that's the hard part."

The hard part is walking hand in hand with you and pretending I'm not about to stand on my head from the upheaval inside my brain, Carrie thought. She hesitated involuntarily as they reached the cabin door.

"It's not much of a cabin, even for a man," Lucas said, "but it's free." The cabin was made up of two plain rooms, one behind the other. The front room took up most of the space and was the living, cooking, and eating area. A large fireplace took up one end with a mantel free of objects and a bear's head mounted above it. A large sofa was placed before the fireplace. At the other end of the room, a small cooking stove with a flue going straight up to the roof provided the heat. There was no table and no chair other than the sofa. The spaces between the logs had been filled in with mud, and the whole whitewashed with lime, but dust and soot had turned the walls gray. An oil lantern suspended from the ceiling in the middle of the room provided the only light other than that coming in the two small windows.

"This place could use a good cleaning," Carrie said, self-consciously seating herself on the sofa. That wasn't what she wanted to say, but she wasn't sure what she *did* want to say. Nevertheless, she had to say something, and that was certainly safe enough.

"You're welcome to have a go at it anytime you like. I don't pay good wages, but I might be talked into providing coffee and a little something extra." Lucas set two cups of steaming coffee on an upended log in front of the sofa and sat down next to Carrie. "Don't you want to know what the something extra might be?"

"I haven't decided if I'm going to clean up the place. I suppose it does belong to the company though no one said anything—"

"Can't you forget the company for one evening? Would it be completely out of the range of possibility that you would clean it up because it belonged to me?"

Carrie didn't know where that statement was meant to lead—there were so many possibilities—but she was too nervous to make a rational choice among them. Lucas was resting his arm on the back of the sofa, and his fingers were touching her shoulder, moving back and forth ever so lightly, and it was driving her crazy.

"I suppose I could," she managed to say, "but that would just reinforce your male idea that God created woman merely to cook and clean for man."

"Did it ever occur to you that the roles men and women have assumed were dictated by impersonal considerations like size, strength, and childbearing and nurturing?"

"Of course it did. I'm not a fool. And if we were still living in a primitive society, I would expect to fall into the traditional pattern."

Lucas leaned over and took a sip of his coffee, but he didn't move his hand and his fingers were now at the nape of her neck.

"Tell me something about your husband," he said unexpectedly. "Why did you marry him?"

Now, Carrie said to herself, tell him *now*, but instead she said, "I married Robert primarily to get away from my family. I know that sounds awful and I suppose it was, but I was desperate to escape the prison they were building for me and Robert was the only chance I saw."

"Surely a young woman as pretty as you would have offers of marriage."

"You have no idea what a toll the Civil War took on Virginia's men. Many were killed, others disappeared, still others just never returned. There weren't many men in our town, but the only ones to come back were my brothers, Robert, and two who already had sweethearts. Our whole county was devastated so there was no incentive for people to move in.

"But that wasn't the only reason. I knew Robert would never force me to become anything I didn't want to become or do anything I didn't want to do. When I talked him into finding a job away from Smithfield, I knew I was stronger than he was." Carrie didn't like the look in Lucas's eyes; it made her feel defensive. "There's nothing wrong with that. Many women are stronger than their husbands, and they have very happy marriages."

"Did it work out the way you had hoped?"

Tell him, you fool, tell him now, or get up and walk out of this cabin and never come back. Carrie tried to say the words, but they wouldn't come out. She didn't know what she was afraid she might lose, but she knew she would lose more if she didn't tell him the truth right now.

"I never married him."

"What?" Lucas exclaimed, sitting forward and looking at her very intently. His fingers were still.

"I never had the chance. I told you he died in St. Louis of a

183

fever. That was true, but he died before I got there. I have never been married."

"Then what is your name?" Lucas demanded. "Your *real* name."

"It's Terwillinger. Carolina Marsena Terwillinger." There was a moment of stunned silence. "Now you can see why I prefer Carrie Simpson."

"But to tell everyone you were married."

"I knew there'd be no problem in my coming to the station if they thought my husband was taking it over. Duncan Bickett would never have allowed me to stay here a single night if he had known I was an unmarried woman of twenty-two. I knew I would soon have to tell everyone I was a widow, but a widow has much more freedom and standing in a community than a single woman. I also knew I had to be a great success if they were to let me stay, and I was determined to give myself every chance." The fingers on the nape of her neck were moving again.

"Have you told anyone else you were never married?"

"No."

"Not even Katie?"

"I've told no one."

"Then why did you tell me?" Carrie hardly knew what to say and those fingers on her neck and shoulder weren't helping.

"I had to. I didn't feel I could just go on pretending forever." Lucas cocked his head to one side, a definite I-don't-believe-a-word-you're-saying look on his face.

"I knew I wasn't being honest with you, and it was important that I was."

"Why?" God, he was relentless.

"I don't like lying to people, even for a good reason."

"Then why haven't you told Katie and Jake?"

"I don't intend to," she confessed. "I'm depending on you to let me go on with the pretense. Even if I'd been here for years and was accepted by everybody, I'd still prefer to be thought a widow. It makes everything so much easier."

"Okay, I understand that well enough, but why did you

184

elect to tell me and not the others?"

"I don't know."

"Yes you do, and I intend to find out why. I promise I won't ever lie to you, but you've got to promise you won't ever lie or pretend a lie to me again."

"Why?" she asked, thankful she could get in a question before he drove her to the wall in his inexorable search for the true nature of her feelings.

"Because what I feel for you allows no room for anything except the truth. It's too important to me and too precious to both of us to risk losing it because of a lie."

"What are you talking about?"

"You want me to go first?"

Carrie was thankful for Lucas's understanding, but when one hand slipped down over her shoulder, drawing her against his powerful chest, and the other hand found and captured her fingers, she wasn't sure that she hadn't surrendered more than enough ground to give support to any notions of ownership he might have.

"I can remember just as clearly as if it were happening right now the very minute you stepped off the stage. You didn't know I existed and your only thoughts were for Baca Riggins and the station, but it was as if a trumpet call announced your arrival, as though God said, *Here she is, Lucas. If you don't do something about it, you have no one to blame but yourself.* I just sat under that tree, too confused to know what was really happening to me and having no idea how to draw myself to your attention. I know you weren't pleased to meet a man like Baca Riggins, but I was glad because I knew it would give me a chance to do something for you that would force you to pay attention to me."

"Did you anticipate I was going to be so difficult?" asked Carrie. "I can't imagine that females are in the habit of giving you the cold shoulder."

Lucas chuckled. "No, but from the first I suspected you were different. Once you drew down on Baca Riggins, I knew it."

"Are you trying to tell me you fell for me after no more

than a glance?" Carrie felt mighty comfortable. She hoped his explanation wasn't going to be too short.

"No. I didn't fall completely until the next day when I sat up in the loft and watched you figure out how to get a harness on that team."

"So that's where you were," Carrie said, leaning slightly forward. "I always wondered." Lucas gently pulled her back against him.

"I knew then that you were clever and resourceful as well as strong and determined. It's not often you find all those characteristics in one person."

"You make me sound like a list of qualifications."

"Everyone is a collection of character traits that appeals to others. There's nothing wrong with saying I like a girl with strength of purpose as opposed to one who agrees with every foolish thing I say."

"Maybe men think like that, but a girl likes to feel like she's wanted for herself, no matter what her list of desirable traits might be, and not because she's a collection of characteristics which make her a good choice."

"You're not going to be reasonable about this are you?"

"Not if by reasonable you mean to list off the things you like about me. Suppose some of those things change? They do you know. Are you going to want to pitch me out the door?"

"I didn't know we were talking about doors to homes and long-term arrangements."

"You know what I mean," Carrie said.

"Yes, and no. I never made a list of the things I like about you. I never got a chance. By the time I knew what was happening, it was too late."

"Me, too," Carrie admitted, now anxious to tell him some of the things which had been filling her heart to overflowing. "I knew I liked you, I mean who can help liking a man who's got shoulders and a backside like you." Lucas's brows drew together and Carrie giggled. "I couldn't help that. Men talk about women like they can be dismantled into their component parts without knowing that women do the same thing. I

186

could tell you a few other things I like about you."

"Somehow I think I'd rather you didn't." Lucas looked decidedly uncomfortable, and Carrie suspected she was the first *nice* girl he had ever known who had had the courage to mention the attractiveness of his body. Somehow it made her feel a little less at a disadvantage, more of an equal in this very new game she was playing.

"I liked you from the first, even after you told me you thought I ought to go back and wait for my husband."

"Only part of that was concern for your welfare," Lucas said. "I knew I was becoming, had *already* become, dangerously attracted to you, and I couldn't possibly consider compromising a married woman."

"You would have sent me back to Robert without ever saying anything?" Lucas nodded. "Nothing at all?"

"If I had ever once told you what I felt for you, I would never have been able to make myself stay from you."

"What did you feel?"

"I didn't know at first. It was something I had never felt before, maybe because I was too busy or maybe because I never met anyone who could pierce the armor I built around myself. Anyway, the more I saw you, the more I was drawn to you. Not just physically. I was familiar enough with *that* feeling to recognize it, but I wanted to be with you all the time, hold you in my arms, protect you, all things I'd never wanted to do for any woman before."

"Never?"

"Never. And I wanted to do this so much I could hardly sleep." Lucas leaned forward and kissed Carrie gently.

"Is that why you stole that kiss?"

"I kissed you hoping it would make you stay away from me, but it was a mistake. After that *I* couldn't stay away from *you.*"

"I liked it too," Carrie confessed. "The only man I'd ever kissed was Robert, but I felt like it was a duty, not something I especially wanted to do again. But I remembered your kiss. At first I was angry, but soon I wanted you to kiss me again." Lucas obliged.

"Does that mean you've learned to like me a little?"

"Do you think I'd be sitting here like this if I didn't?" Carrie asked, indignantly trying to sit up but Lucas wouldn't let her. "You got to be an obsession. It grew worse after you told me everything I hated about being a woman was what you wanted in a wife. I suddenly understood it meant I would have to give you up. That was when I realized I would dislike that very much."

"How much?" Lucas asked before he kissed her quite passionately.

"Very much." Lucas kissed her again, quite ruthlessly this time. "I couldn't possibly give you up," Carrie murmured, half out of her mind with happiness. "Couldn't possibly give you up at all."

"Is that why you told me you were never married?"

"Yes. Somehow I thought it was important for you to know that no one had ever touched me in the way you have. I thought I liked Robert well enough to marry him and perhaps I did, but it was nothing like this. I was quite unhappy when they told me he had died, but I didn't feel like a part of me had died with him."

"And that's how you feel about me?"

"How many hints do I have to give you before you guess that I'm in love with you? Don't you Western men leave a girl any self-respect at all? I hope you realize you've reduced me to the level of a strumpet. Back home no girl who hadn't been on her last prayers for years would dare admit she loved a man before he confessed he loved her. Even then half of the women would rather die an old maid before they'd do anything like that."

"You must waste a lot of time back East."

"No, because our men aren't so slow," chuckled Carrie, but her chuckle was abruptly cut off by Lucas's passionate embrace. He may have been slow to start, but there was nothing backward about him now. He had leaned her back in the sofa until she was virtually lying down, penned to the sofa by his taut, heated body. He was kissing her mouth, eyes, and ears, but Carrie had never been so conscious of a man's body, never so aware of the answering response from her own. Robert had never had that effect on her.

"Do you realize I'd spent the whole evening plotting how to get you up here?" Lucas asked as he gazed lovingly into her eyes.

"All you had to do was ask."

"Do you mean you would have come, just like that?"

"I'm sure no self-respecting girl would make such an admission, but yes, I probably would," Carrie admitted. "If you hadn't come down to the station every day I would have come before now."

"Which just goes to show how much I know about tactics, and women," Lucas said before he applied himself to Carrie's lips once more. This time his tongue snaked out, invading her mouth and inviting her tongue to invade his. Carrie felt the welling need inside her become more insistent as his voracious tongue searched out every part of her mouth, tasting its sweetness, sharing its warmth. She was becoming increasingly aware of his chest pressing against her sensitive breasts, the length of him pressed against her body, the heat of him scalding her flesh.

Lucas's hand slid from behind her shoulder and under her chin. Tenderly he caressed her neck then slid his hand down to her shoulder. Carrie felt herself going limp and sinking farther into the cushions, but when Lucas's hand slipped down inside the bodice of her dress, she heard herself gasp for breath and felt her whole body tense. His fingers were rough and cool, her skin tender and overheated, but within seconds she was so overwhelmed by a new flood of sensations she forgot the differences in heat and texture. Lucas's dexterous fingers had quickly unbuttoned the front of her dress and chemise to uncover her breasts. His powerful hands cupped her breasts and she felt them begin to stiffen with desire. When his fingers found and lightly massaged her taut nipples she thought she would moan; when his lips found her rosy peak and covered it with moist warmth, she did. Lucas moaned in response, and before Carrie could get her breath, he had swept her up in his arms and was heading for the small room at the back of the cabin.

It was hard to see his face clearly in the shadowy light of the room, but it was impossible to miss his presence. Carrie lay there almost paralyzed as Lucas undid the remaining buttons on her dress, too stunned to move, too overwhelmed with an unsuspected driving need to be able to think. All she knew was that at least there were no more barriers between Lucas and herself, and it was the most wonderful feeling in the world.

"My God, you're beautiful," Lucas rasped as he removed her chemise. "Even more beautiful than I thought."

"You don't mind that I'm so tiny?"

"You're perfect." Lucas let his fingers wander over her breasts, circling the rigid tips and making ever widening circles as they descended to the warm, creamy flesh of her body. Down her side, over her belly, and along her thigh his fingers traveled, leaving blazing trails of singing sensations which slowly engulfed Carrie's mind until she was barely conscious of anything but the aching desire building within her.

"Now you."

Lucas's startled, inquiring gaze met her warm, beckoning look. "I want to feel you next to me," she said. "I want to feel the warmth of your body, your rough strength." Lucas didn't make her wait.

"I've dreamed of this moment," he whispered as he lowered himself on the bed next to her. "It's kept me awake nights wondering how you would look, how you would feel in my arms."

"Are you disappointed?"

"No. Are you?"

"I knew I wouldn't be," she answered, snuggling close to him. "I knew that the first time I saw you."

Lucas kissed her, roughly and hungrily, crushing her tender breasts against his chest. She put her arms around him, feeling the strength and power of his muscles, the breadth of his shoulders, the overwhelming sense of his presence. Then Lucas's hands began to caress her body, traveling over every inch of her soft skin, searching out every point of sensitivity, fondling and teasing until she arched against him, nearly crazy with need.

Lucas's hands drifted lower until they stroked the softness of her inner thighs. Instinctively Carrie relaxed and opened to him. She could not contain a tiny gasp as Lucas's fingers invaded her inner self, but the sense of shock was almost immediately obliterated by a rush of desire, a sudden and powerful need to draw him to her, to press his flesh against her flesh until they were one.

"It may hurt a little at first," Lucas whispered as Carrie felt something hard and hot nudge against her. Spirals of aching need shot all through her body like fireworks in the night sky. When he stopped moving, she felt an insistent need to pull him deeper until she had engulfed him, but he remained where he was, teasing, tantalizing, toying with her until she thought she would go crazy.

"Please," she moaned.

"It's going to hurt," he said, but Carrie didn't care anymore. She pressed against him and still he did not enter her; she pressed harder and still he withdrew. Frantic with desire, she flung herself at him just as he plunged toward her. There was a momentary flash of sharp pain and then a burst of pleasure so brilliant and pervasive that it wiped out all memory of discomfort.

Now Lucas entered her fully and Carrie drew him into her, needing him as much as he needed her, wanting to consume him, demanding that he touch something at the very core of her being. Carrie could hear his breath coming quickly and in short, rough gasps and the sound created an equally insistent urgency in her. She had never felt more wondrously alive in her life.

Wave after wave of pulsating desire swept over her, picking her up, flinging her upon the shore and then washing her back out to sea to be borne ashore once again on a still higher crest. Carrie wondered how long she could stand it, certain she would be destroyed by the fury of the sensations exploding all through her. Suddenly she was aware of a difference in Lucas. His breath was ragged and his movement no longer smooth and controlled. Gradually his body became stiff, his movements uneven until, with a roar of release, he drove deep into her, scalding her with his heat. Carrie felt her body respond with equal tension and they clung to each other, their bodies racked by spasms of exquisite pleasure, their minds filled with nothing but each other.

Then with a sigh that came from the very depths of their beings, they fell apart, exhausted and temporarily emptied by their passion.

Chapter 14

A sixth sense warned Lucas of danger and he woke with a start. Without a moment's hesitation he drew on his pants and reached for his rifle.

"Where are you going?" Carrie asked drowsily, the mists of sleep still clogging her brain.

"There's somebody outside," he whispered. "Stay here while I have a look." Carrie sat up, clutching the bedclothes to her bosom. Was it Baca Riggins? Had he come back as he'd said?

Lucas tiptoed to the front window and looked out, being careful not to offer himself as a possible target. He saw nothing at first. The yard was empty and he heard no sound of anyone moving around the cabin. Then one of the horses whinnied and he looked toward the corral. The mustangs were moving about restlessly, but it was several moments more before Lucas saw the young Indian creeping along the edge of the corral toward the gate; he was going to open it and stampede the horses.

"It's those fool Indian boys," he called to Carrie in a loud whisper. "They're after the horses again, and they may have brought their friends along this time."

"What are you going to do?"

"Stop them, of course."

"But they're boys. You can't kill them."

"I won't hurt them if I can help it, but if I let them take our horses, nothing will be safe. I've got to stop them." As he slipped noiselessly out the cabin door, Carrie jumped out of bed and began to dress. She had no intention of lying quietly in bed while Lucas battled Indians, boys or not.

But before Lucas had gone more than fifteen steps, the morning stillness was rent by an Indian war cry, and the boy stood up from his crouching position and reached for the corral gate. Taking quick aim, Lucas squeezed off a shot, and the corral post beneath the Indian's outstretched hand dissolved into a shower of splinters that pierced his skin like a barrage of sharp needles. The boy let out a startled yell and leaped for the cover of a nearby tree. But the gate was unlatched, and a second Indian boy inside the corral began herding the horses toward the gate. Lucas put two shots into the ground in front of the herd; the shower of dust and stones caused the lead horse to rear and those behind him to run up on one another's heels. Catching sight of Lucas where he knelt in the open, the Indian boy drew a bow, but before he was able to loose the arrow, a bullet from Lucas's rifle shattered the bow in his hands.

With two Indians down and busily occupied pulling the painful slivers of wood from their flesh, Lucas darted for the open gate. If the horses got out, they wouldn't stop until they were back in their familiar grazing ground, and that was a hard three-day-ride away. He reached the gate and was in the act of sliding the bar back into place when a whisper of clothes against leaves came to his ears; he whirled just in time to see a third Indian attacking with tomahawk raised. There was no time to take aim or dodge the blow; Lucas threw himself to the ground, hoping to confuse the boy long enough for him to get in a position to defend himself. The crack of a pistol sounded at that moment, and the tomahawk disintegrated in the stunned Indian's hand. Lucas whipped his eyes toward the cabin in time to see Carrie, wearing nothing but one of his shirts, turn her pistol around toward the Indian in the corral and take the feather out of his bonnet with another shot.

Their surprise attack having failed and their weapons and themselves in total disarray, the three boys scrambled to

194

their horses and galloped off.

But before Lucas could congratulate himself on having broken the attack without a serious injury to anyone, he heard a shout from the corral behind the barn and the sound of thundering hooves told him the stage teams were being driven off at a gallop. "There's more of them down at the barn," he yelled to Carrie and disappeared down the path at a dead run. Only the sheer fear of being caught in such a state of provocative undress kept her from chasing after him. Instead, she ran to her cabin to put on her *own* clothes and prepare to help Lucas.

The Indian boys had meant to coordinate their attacks on the separate corrals, but Lucas's unexpected shots had caught the two boys behind the barn still in the midst of their soundless approach. At the sound of shots, they had darted forward, one opening the gate and the other yelling and screaming to stampede the horses. They were through the gate and heading for the road before Jake could roll out of his bed and reach for his shotgun. The boys were too far away for the scattered shot to cause them any serious injury, but before the boom of the big sixteen-gauge gun had ceased to echo through the hills, several pellets were painfully buried in their skin and they had caught a glimpse of Lucas vaulting down the path. Unwilling to face lethally accurate gunfire from two sides, the Indians abandoned the horses, headed for their mounts, and took out for the hills at a dead run. The bullets Lucas sent whistling around their heads encouraged them to drive their ponies to even greater speed.

"Them the same boys we took those horses from a few days ago?" Jake asked as Lucas reached the barn, still panting from the sprint down the mountain from the cabin.

"Looks like it, only they brought a few of their friends along with them this time."

"Did you hit anybody?"

"No. I just gave two of them a handful of splinters."

"I didn't really hurt anybody either."

"Did they turn out all the horses?"

"I still got the mare in the barn, but it don't make no difference. Those horses won't run far from their feed. I expect they'll be back before the stage pulls in."

As it turned out, they were back even sooner. When Lucas and Jake rounded the corner of the barn, their surprised gaze fell on Katie driving two of the horses back toward the corral.

"Seems to me like you can't keep up with your horses even when you've got a barn and a corral to do the work for you," Katie said disgustedly, herding the horses past a suddenly lackadaisical Jake and into the corral. " 'Tis a mystery to me why Mrs. Simpson keeps you about the place."

"Probably because she likes to see a pleasant smile and hear a kindly word once in a while," Jake responded, choosing this particular moment to scratch vigorously at a part of his body normally considered unsuitable to receive attention in public.

"A hyena can smile," Katie shot back, "but that doesn't make it any less a carrion beast nor any easier on the eye."

"Are you saying I'm hard to look at?" Jake demanded, acting as though there was nothing unusual about his wearing long underwear in the barnyard.

"I'm saying you're not fit to be consorting with decent folks," Katie responded sharply, "you with your dirt and your shoddy ways."

"Supposing I was to take a bath in that there horse trough?"

"I've no doubt you'd get wet through and smell worse than a hound dog," Katie stated with a toss of her head and turned toward the station.

"Damned sharp-tongued female," Jake said loud enough for Katie to hear him. "I bet she wouldn't need no knife to take the hide off a rabbit." Katie continued on her way without any sign that she had heard him.

"You're wasting your time with her," Lucas said, a trace of a smile on his lips. "I don't think she likes you at all."

"I ain't wanting no part of that uppity female neither," Jake said, then grinned happily. "I just like to get a rise out of her now and again."

"Watch it. You get too much of a rise, and you're liable to find yourself squaring off before a preacher."

"The female ain't been born who can get me inside a church," Jake swore. "My pa weren't never married, and I ain't going to be either. First thing you know women start trying to change you. They pick at a man until his life ain't worth a bent horseshoe. They want you to go to church, stop cussing and drinking and gambling, come home of evenings, and spend some time looking after the children. That ain't no life fit for a man. Why, I'd rather be shot and tortured by one of them Indians. It hurts like hell for a while, but it don't last forever."

Whatever else of his philosophy on women and marriage Jake may have been willing to share with Lucas had to be saved for later. A stranger was coming up the road from Fort Malone driving the remaining horses before him. He was a nice-looking young man, and one neither of them had ever seen before. He rode his horse easily, as though he was used to being in the saddle, but he was dressed like a man who was accustomed to living and working in town, his only concession to riding being a pair of expensive boots, most of which were hidden under his pant legs.

"These horses yours?" he said, addressing both men as he rode up. "I found them down the road a piece and figured they must have gotten loose from here."

"Just some Indian boys playing a prank on us," Jake said nonchalantly. "I would have had to go after them myself, so I'm much obliged to you for saving me the trouble."

The young man said no more while Jake put the horses in the corral, but once the gate was closed, he turned to Lucas. "Brian Kelly is my name. I'm fairly new to this part of the country."

Lucas gave him a long, slow look before his gaze shifted to the horses in the corral. "Lucas Barrow," he said at last, "and that's Jake Bemis."

"You work around here?"

"Yeah," Lucas replied without amplifying his answer.

"I'm looking for Katie O'Malley," Brian said after a pause. "I was supposed to meet her here about a week ago, but I got held up. I'm engaged to marry her." Jake's head came up with a snap, but Lucas continued to look at Brian out of the corner of his eyes. "Is she still here?" Brian asked.

"Yeah."

"Do you know where I can find her?"

"Up at the station I expect."

Brian paused. "What does she look like?"

"Step inside and you can answer that question for yourself," Lucas replied. Brian stood there a minute more, undecided, then with a nod of his head headed off toward the station.

"So Katie's man did show up," Jake said.

"Yeah. Fancy that."

"I don't," Jake said, hostility rampant in his voice. "I don't trust nobody dressed up as slick as a wet otter."

"I guess it doesn't matter what you fancy as long as Katie's happy."

"Who was that?" Carrie asked, coming up from the direction of her cabin. She had just had time to change her clothes and tidy herself up. She was careful to avoid looking at Lucas just yet. She knew it wouldn't be long before everyone knew she'd spent the night with him, but she wasn't ready for that quite yet.

"Katie's young man," Lucas informed her. "It seems he was held up."

"Oh damn!" That exclamation brought startled looks from both men. "I can't help it," Carrie said, not in the least apologetic. "I'm as concerned for Katie's happiness as either of you, but I don't want to lose her. What am I going to do for a cook?"

"I think the question is what is Katie going to do?"

"Well, I can't stand here all morning waiting to find out. I'm going up to the station, and I want both of you to come along with me. It won't look so much like prying if we all come in naturally like it was time for breakfast. And don't you laugh at me, Lucas Barrow. I know I shouldn't, but I can't help it."

But nothing had been decided when they entered the station. Nervous and ill at ease, Katie was going about her preparations for breakfast, her eyes held firmly on her work. Brian had taken a seat at the long table as though prepared to wait until Katie lost her shyness, but Carrie knew instinctively that it was not timidity that was causing Katie to hesitate.

"Good morning, Mr. Kelly. I'm Carrie Simpson, the station manager." Brian stared at Carrie in open surprise and admiration. It was clear he had not expected to find a woman running the station, but it was even more obvious he hadn't expected to find someone like Carrie at Green Run Gap.

"How do you do. Glad to make your acquaintance." Brian's gaze wandered over Carrie's petite, shapely body in a manner that made Lucas's whole body stiffen, but Carrie was more displeased that he would continue to lounge in his chair. Even in Colorado, it was the custom for a gentleman to stand when he was introduced to a lady.

"I was just explaining to Katie why I was late."

"Why *were* you late?" Carrie asked, deciding that if he had no delicacy of manner, then she need have none either. "Leaving a young lady alone and unprovided for can have serious consequences in this country."

"I marked the wrong week on my calendar," Brian said with a ready smile. "I threw the letter away and didn't even think about it until I was setting out today and remembered that the date was supposed to be the seventeenth and not the twenty-fourth."

"I've been telling him why I can't leave right now," Katie announced as she served the plates with unusually hurried and awkward movements. "At least not until you can find someone to help with the cooking." There was something in Katie's voice that made Carrie look at her more intently, but Katie kept her eyes on her work.

"Are you sure?" Carrie asked. "It shouldn't take more than a few days to find somebody."

"You know you can't do all this work by yourself," Katie repeated, her head still bowed. "You tried before, and you nearly wore yourself out. He's waited a whole week extra. It won't hurt him to wait one more."

"It's okay, Mrs. Simpson," Brian assured Carrie, his eyes still glued to her body. I'm going to be away a lot for the next couple of weeks. I will come back when I return to Fort Malone."

"Then you must stay and have breakfast with us before you go. That's the least I can do for you for bringing the horses back."

"You needn't thank me for that. They were all over the road. I was going to have to do something about them before I could get by."

Breakfast was an uncomfortable meal. Katie didn't raise her eyes from her plate, Lucas spoke only when spoken to and then in monosyllables, and Jake seemed to have something in his craw. It was left to Carrie to carry on the conversation with Brian. He seemed an amiable young man, certainly a nice-looking one, and Carrie became more convinced as the meal progressed that Katie should marry him. There couldn't be many young men like him in the West.

"I've been with the Overland Stage Company a little more than three years," Brian was saying in a voice almost entirely free of the Irish brogue that so strongly colored Katie's speech, "but one day I hope to buy myself a ranch, maybe in Arizona."

"A thing like that takes a heap of money," Jake observed.

"That's why I don't have one yet," Brian admitted with becoming modesty. "But I'm expecting to come into some money soon, enough for a ranch I hope."

"You mean you're coming into an inheritance?"

"Yes." The pause before he answered was so slight Carrie wondered if maybe she had imagined it.

"If you change your mind about staying here, you can send a message into Fort Malone," Brian said to Katie as he rose to his feet at the end of the meal. "I'll be around for a few days yet."

"I'll start looking for someone to replace her immediately," Carrie assured him when it was obvious Katie wasn't going to answer him. "I wouldn't want her obligations here to stand in the way of her future happiness."

But after the men had gone, Katie didn't seem too eager to discuss her engagement to Mr. Brian Kelly.

"He's a handsome young man," Carrie said, trying to get around Katie's unaccustomed reserve. "And he looks like a nice, steady type. It's not often a girl finds a husband who has a dependable job and plans for something even better." At last Katie looked up, and Carrie was surprised by the hunted look in her eyes. "What's wrong?" Carrie asked, immediately troubled.

"I don't know," Katie admitted uncertainly. "I don't understand it. I was sure I wanted to marry Brian—I haven't been thinking about much else for months now—and I never had any wrong feelings about it. But I no more set eyes on him than I felt all funny, like something wasn't right."

"But what could be wrong?"

"That's just it. I don't know. I know it sounds like I'm daft, but I can't help it. I can't go marrying any man I don't feel right about."

"Are you trying to tell me you don't love him?"

"I never looked to be in love, at least not like you and Mr. Barrow," Katie said, shocking Carrie right down to her toenails. "All I wanted was a steady man who would provide for me and the children. All I asked was that he be no drunkard."

"But you don't know anything about Mr. Kelly's habits. What makes you think he's a drunkard?"

"It's not that. There's something else that don't be right."

"But how can you say that when you've just met him? I thought he looked like an exemplary young man, just about the nicest-looking I've seen out here, and I think you ought to drop that pan right where you stand and run after him as fast as you can. He can't have gotten far. If I were to ask Lucas to go after him . . ."

"Would you take him in place of Mr. Barrow?"

"I don't know what you mean," Carrie protested, badly shaken. "I don't know that Mr. Barrow is in love with me. He certainly hasn't asked me to marry him."

"He's in love with you, and you with him for all you haven't gotten around to talking about marrying, but that's not what I mean either," Katie said, a plea for understanding sounding in her voice. "Brian has the appearance of being everything you say, but he hadn't been in the room more than a minute when I realized he couldn't hold a candle to Mr. Barrow. And he never will," she declared passionately. "But even worse, I found I trusted Jake more than I could trust him. *Jake!*" she reiterated as though she were talking about some reptilian creature. "I pray every day you'll send that man back to where you found him. He's filthy, slovenly, and has the soul of a drunkard for all he's been sober since he started working for you, and I wouldn't marry him if the Virgin Mary herself was to get down on her knees and ask me. If I can trust *him* before Brian, then something's terribly wrong, and I'm not budging from here until I know what it is."

"If you want to know what I think, and I don't suppose you do or you would have asked, I think seeing Brian has given you cold feet and you're just looking for an excuse to put the wedding off until you've had a little time to think things over. That's fine with me. Take all the time you want, but don't wait too long. And if you decide you *do* want to marry him, you can leave at any time. With Jake and Lucas to help me, you know I can handle things for a little while. Now I'll finish up here. You go on back to the cabin and see if you can sort things out in your mind." Katie tried to protest, but Carrie would hear none of it and she soon went off, her brow furrowed with uneasiness.

Carrie quickly finished the cleaning up, wondering all the while what could have caused Katie to take such a fright at Brian Kelly. He wasn't her kind of man, but that didn't change the fact that he was extremely presentable. To have been engaged to someone like him before she ever left Ireland, Katie was a very lucky young woman. Much more so than she had been with Robert.

Thinking of Robert started a comparison with Lucas in Carrie's mind, but it only took a few seconds for her to realize they had so little in common it was impossible to compare them. You can't compare horses and potatoes anymore than you can compare Irish whiskey and Brussels lace. Not that Robert or Lucas was anything like Brussels lace, she thought to herself with an inner smile. She visualized Lucas in his tight jeans and flannel shirt, dusty and sweaty from working with the horses. There wasn't a thing about him that was soft or malleable, but she couldn't get him out of her mind and that in itself was ironic. Here she was, stranded in the middle of Colorado because she was running away from hard, selfish men. And after having chosen a manageable man for her husband for the very reason that he was manageable, what did she do but fall in love with the first absolutely inflexible man she met?

Carrie smiled to herself. There had been nothing granite or immovable about Lucas last night. She could still feel his strong, sinewy limbs, smell the clean smell of plain soap on his skin. He most often faced the world with a closed expression that gave the impression of a tough, relentless man, yet when he looked at her his eyes seemed to come alive, to deepen and glow with warmth. His firm mouth would curve into a half smile which made him appear to be smiling at himself as much as her. He was a man who wouldn't give much away, but he was also a man who didn't let anything get away, not if he wanted it. And Carrie fervently hoped he wanted her.

She looked around the room to satisfy herself that everything was clean and ready for their preparations for the next meal before she stepped out on the porch. The sun shone brightly on the wooded hills and towering mountains, but the morning air was still cool. A refreshing breeze brushed Carrie's cheek as she leaned against the porch post, her cheek against the age-stained wood, her mind far from the vista spread before her.

Everything was so different here, so unlike what she was used to in Virginia, she wondered if she would manage to make the adjustment. Life asked so much more of a woman here, not just the work she was willing to do but the responsibility she was willing to accept. Back home there was always someone close by to help—family, in-laws, neighbors, somebody who had known you since birth and who would take an interest in you even after you had died. There was no such network of interwoven dependency out here. She could disappear tomorrow and only a few people would ever know she had existed; even fewer would mourn her passing. She wondered how many men had died alone, killed by disease, Indians, animals, other men, their death unattended and unmourned? Was she willing to take on that burden? Was she willing to bring a family into a world where the struggle for survival began the moment they entered the world and ceased only after they had left it?

But wasn't that the way it was in Virginia too? True, there were no mountain lions and Indians hiding in the woods, but a terrible war among supposedly civilized men had caused more suffering than Indians and animals ever could. Was she any worse off out here? It seemed that the only difference between living in Colorado and Virginia was in the things you had to struggle against. And the struggle went on in both places—nothing was going to be given to her—and she could be made just as miserable by a struggle in her mind as she could by a struggle to find enough food and shelter to survive.

No, she was glad she had come to Colorado. It demanded a lot that would never have been asked of her if she had remained in Virginia, but in exchange she had the freedom to decide what she wanted to be, the freedom to try to achieve something new without having to endure the censure of a rigidly structured society. Colorado and much of the rest of the West was filled with people just like her, people who couldn't fit into the interwoven, interdependent social structure of the East, people who demanded more room and fewer restrictions.

She was under no illusions about Lucas. He seemed made for the life he led—in fact, he seemed to thrive on it—and he would want someone with his same goals and lust for life. He would need someone with his same strengths, his same ability to carve a path for himself where none existed and be able to go forward despite any opposition. Could she do that? Was she that strong? She would never know until she tried, but did she have the right to burden him with a wife who had not been tested by the kind of ordeals he considered an everyday matter?

Carrie's train of thought was suddenly broken by the sound of someone moving about in the station. Irritated by the unwelcome interruption, she set about trying to reconstruct her chain of reasoning, and it was several moments before her mind registered the fact that the noise couldn't be Katie getting ready to prepare lunch. Neither would it be Lucas or Jake because they never came in by the back door or passed her without saying a word. All of a sudden her whole mind was focused on the sounds and she immediately knew something was wrong. The person in the kitchen was no one she knew and had no business being there. Had Baca Riggins come back? It seemed she was going to be plagued by that man for the rest of her natural life. All her weapons were inside and she wasn't about to step into the station unarmed; instead she peeped in at the window.

She couldn't see much of the room through the small space between the curtains, but she could see a shoulder and occasionally a bit of back, enough to know it was no grown man who was raiding her kitchen. With swift decision she lifted the latch as quietly as possible and stepped inside.

Carrie was stunned to see a young boy, she guessed his age to be no more than ten or eleven, with his head and hands almost lost in the pot containing the remainder of last night's stewed venison. His clothes were old, dirty, and almost falling to bits. He was barefooted, so thin she was certain he hadn't eaten a full meal in months, and looked as though he'd been living wild for quite a long time. Immediately her heart went out to him.

"Would you like me to heat up that stew for you?" The boy's head came up like a deer when it smells a cougar, his eyes wide and staring, a look of caution combined with one of desperation in their brown depths. He froze, unwilling to leave the food but unsure of how far he could trust this strange woman.

"If you'll wait a few minutes, I can have a whole meal ready," Carrie said, being careful to move slowly toward the cupboard where she kept the leftovers so as not to frighten the boy. "Meantime you can wash up. There's a bucket of water along with some soap and a towel just outside the door." The boy continued to stare, but his body seemed to relax ever so slightly. "Go on," Carrie encouraged. "It will take a few minutes to get things ready, and I can't have you at my table until you wash your face and hands." The boy remained still for a few minutes more, but Carrie gently removed the pot of stew from his hands and began to take bowls and pots from the cupboard and set them on the stove. While she set the table and poured a large glass of milk, the heat from the stove released the fragrant smell of warm food, and the boy's stomach began to churn.

"You'd better hurry," Carrie said, "or the food will get cold before you're washed up." He still looked undecided, but the delicious aromas of the food Carrie was ladling into the plate decided him. He disappeared through the door only to reappear in what seemed like mere seconds, dripping wet but considerably cleaner.

"That's much better," Carrie said, setting a slice of pie next to his plate. "Now sit down." The boy sat down, but he didn't eat. He looked up, apparently waiting to be allowed to start.

"You don't have to wait for me. I've already had my breakfast," Carrie said. The boy hesitated only a second more before he began to eat twice as fast as Carrie thought it was possible for a human to eat, but she didn't stop him. She sat down and waited for him to finish.

"Would you like anything else?" Carrie asked when he at

206

last looked up from his plate. "There's plenty more." The boy shook his head. "Okay, then suppose you tell me something about yourself. My name is Mrs. Simpson. I run this station. Do you live nearby?" The boy didn't answer. "What's your name?" Still he didn't answer. "Okay, you don't have to talk, but will you nod your head if I ask a question?" The boy hesitated, then nodded.

"Good. Now let's see. You're not going to tell me your name? No, I didn't think so. Can you write?" The boy shook his head. "Do you have any family? Mother? Father?" The boy shook his head. "Where do you live? Is there anybody to take care of you?" Again he shook his head. "Have you been staying by yourself?" He nodded. "Well, we can't have that," Carrie said, making up her mind. "Would you like to stay here with me? I will give you all the food you can eat, and all you have to do is a little work around the station to help me and Katie. She's the lady who cooks the food you just ate." The hesitated before he nodded once again.

"Good. Now we have to do something about your clothes. You can't go around looking like that. Do you have any more clothes?" He nodded. "Can you get them?" He nodded again. "Fine. You go right now to wherever you've been staying and bring me everything you own, especially your clothes. And hurry back. I'm going to need help carrying water for the wash pot. Now one last thing. I've got to have something to call you. I can't just say *boy* every time I want you, so I'm going to call you Found. I know it's not a particularly good name, but it'll have to do for now. Now you be off, but hurry back. You don't want to be late for lunch. And Found," Carrie said as the boy started toward the door, "I'm glad you're going to stay with us." The boy blinked at Carrie then disappeared through the door.

Chapter 15

"I didn't know what else to do except tell him he could stay with us," Carrie said, explaining Found's presence to Katie. "I just couldn't let the poor child go on living by himself."

"And what makes you think he's been living in those hills without a family?" demanded Katie, pausing in stirring the pot of beef soup. "I've no doubt he's some shiftless vagrant's lad they be sending to nose out what he can, most likely to see if we're worth robbing."

"He's nothing of the sort," Carrie said, affronted that Katie thought she could be taken in so easily. "You wait until he gets back. You'll understand as soon as you see him."

"If we do see him, in daylight that is," Katie added. But Katie didn't have to wait long. She had barely begun to set out the plates for lunch when the boy soundlessly reappeared in the doorway, his arms loaded with his worldly possessions.

"You got back just in time," Carrie said, giving him a smiling welcome. "Put those things in one of the rooms in the back. We can decide what to do with them after we eat. Now wash up. The men will be coming in from the barn any minute now, and they'll want to eat as soon as they get here."

"Faith! He be nothing but a filthy orphan lad," Katie exclaimed. "I'm warning you, Mrs. Simpson. You send him off first thing or he'll be after robbing you blind."

"Now Katie . . ."

"Don't you *Now Katie* me," Katie said, her complexion pink with exasperation. "I don't know what it used to be like where you grew up, but there was dozens of orphans where I come from and a more shiftless, light-fingered bunch you'd be hard-pressed to find. And don't give me any story about how all he be missing is love and he'll straighten right up once he's clean and has a soft bed to sleep in. Once a sneak and a thief, always a sneak and a thief, that's what I say. You just wait and see if I'm not telling the truth."

"For goodness' sakes, he's only a child. And his clothes are almost falling off him. The poor thing is hardly more than skin and bones."

"Begging your pardon, ma'am, but I can see that without you telling me. I can also tell a shifty eye when I see one. I be warning you, Mrs. Simpson, you keep that boy and you won't be able to feel easy in your bed." Found had reentered the room in time to hear Katie's last words. "And don't you be giving me any of your innocent and pitiful looks, for all your name is Found. I'd be more satisfied if it was Lost. And I'd be better suited still if that's what you *were*."

"You should be ashamed of yourself, Katie O'Malley," Carrie said, sparks of anger glittering in her eyes as she guided Found to his place at the table. "He's never going to be lost again if I have anything to say about it."

"And what's Mr. Barrow going to say?" Katie asked, a challenge in her eyes. "*That's* what I be wanting to know."

"I don't see that he'll be called upon to say anything at all," Carrie responded, just as stiffly, "but I know he will feel exactly as I do."

"That's to be seen," Katie said, and turned back to her food.

"It most certainly is," Carrie replied, but she wished she felt as sure as she sounded.

"What's *he* doing here?" Jake demanded the minute he set eyes on Found.

"He no more than showed his face at the doorstep, than Mrs. Simpson ups and takes him in," Katie said. "And nothing I can say will change her mind."

"You know who he is?" Carrie asked.

"Yeah. He's a squatter's kid. Name's Willis McCoy. His folks live in one of the canyons somewhere back in the hills. I've seen them in town a couple of times." Carrie looked at Found again. He didn't look like a child who had been cared for, even by very negligent parents.

"How long ago was that?"

"Last fall sometime. Must have been about six months ago."

"Are you Willis McCoy?" Carrie asked Found, but he merely hung his head. "Did something happen to your parents? Are they sick?" Found raised his head and the empty, lost look in his eyes told Carrie they were more than sick. "They're dead, aren't they?" she asked, her voice soft and full of sympathy. Found dropped his head again. "What happened to them? Can't you tell me?"

"He could talk if he chose to," Katie said, some of her earlier antipathy dissolved by the moving plight of the boy.

"Let me have a go at him," Jake said, making a threatening move toward Found. "I bet I can loosen his tongue."

"You lay one finger on this child, Jake Bemis, and I'll horsewhip you with one of your own harnesses," Carrie said with such fierce anger Jake stopped in his tracks and stared at her in surprise. "He will talk when and if he wants to, but until then you're both to treat him with kindness. And don't you dare threaten or frighten him, or you'll have me to deal with, and I don't frighten very easily."

"I didn't know anybody thought you did, but why do you feel the need to announce it so fiercely? Are you expecting trouble?" It was Lucas, and he was smiling endearingly at Carrie. Her anger melted and color rushed to her face, but she refused to let her disconcerting reaction to him shake her determination to ensure Found's well-being.

"I was just making it clear to Katie and Jake that they're to be gentle with this child. They don't seem to think he can be trusted."

Lucas walked over to Found and lifted his face by putting his hand under his chin. "I don't know why not. He looks like a right good specimen of the human race to me. Might even be handsome if he was cleaned up and properly clothed."

"He most certainly will be, and don't you call him a specimen again. His name is Willis McCoy." Found shook his head vigorously.

"It's not your name?" Carrie asked. "I guess Jake meant that was your father's." Found shook his head again. "Then what is your name?" He was still.

"I think he's trying to tell you he doesn't like his name," Lucas said. "Is that it?" Found nodded.

"What do you want us to call you?" Found looked up at Carrie, his big brown eyes open and trusting. "I was only calling you Found until you could tell me your real name." Found nodded his head vigorously. "You want to be called Found?" she asked, surprise in her voice. Found nodded again.

"Faith, that's peculiar," Katie commented. "I wonder why?"

"You never know with a squatter's kid," Jake said. "They're a shiftless bunch set on stealing anything that's not tied down."

"You should be ashamed of yourself, Jake Bemis, lumping everybody into one category just like nice people can't be poor."

"He can't help it, Mrs. Simpson. Scamps and rascals is all he knows anything about," Katie said scathingly. "He's after judging others by what he knows himself."

"I'm not surprised you were run out of Ireland," Jake said, sitting down at the table so he could see Katie out of the corner of his eye and pulling one of the full plates toward him. "With a tongue like yours, you could stir up a full-scale rebellion all by yourself." Lucas caught Carrie's eye over Found's head and winked. She smiled and blushed in return.

"I took out of Ireland because it was full of drunkards and shiftless no-accounts," Katie replied promptly, "too many of them blessed with a handsome smile and a tongue ready to wrap itself around any handy lie. If I'd known I was going to meet the same kind of varmint in Colorado, I'd have taken meself off somewhere else."

"If travel is what you've set your heart on," Jake said, filling his mouth with as much food as he could fit inside at one time, "then you go settle your tongue on Fort Malone. I'll wager a month's pay that inside a week they'll be taking up a collection to send you anywhere you want to go."

"You two can abuse each other some other time," Carrie admonished, trying to suppress a smile. "Right now I'm more interested in deciding what to do with Found."

"I don't want to do nothing with him," Jake insisted. "I ain't got time to teach him how to live indoors like a human, not with me worrying every minute that he might be stealing the bits out of the horses' mouths."

"I'll take him," Lucas offered. "He looks like a handy boy to have around." He glanced over at Jake. "Besides, there's nothing over at my place to steal. You like horses?" he asked Found, and the boy nodded shyly. "Good. I've got a dozen to break to harness, and I could use some help."

"I'm glad that's settled," Carrie said, hard-pressed to keep from gazing in a decidedly love-sick manner at Lucas, "but he's going to have to sleep in the barn with Jake. There's no room at your cabin or ours. And I don't want him sleeping at the station by himself, not at first anyway."

"Where am I going to put him?" Jake asked plaintively. "There ain't but one bed in the tack room."

"Let him sleep in the loft if you like, but I don't want him sleeping by himself until he gets used to being here."

"I don't know why. If his parents are dead, instead of gone off and left him, which wouldn't surprise me at all, squatters being the sorry lot they are, he's plenty used to being by himself."

"I'll have no more argument," Carrie stated firmly. "He stays with you."

After that, the conversation turned to other topics even though Jake continued to mumble periodically under his breath, but when the meal was ended, he stood up and spoke roughly to Found. "Get your things and come on with me if you're coming. I ain't got time to waste waiting on no orphan boy."

"I'd like to know just what it is you're in such a hurry to do, you being so important and all?" Katie asked scornfully.

Jake turned to Katie and deliberately started to scratch the small of his back while he glared at her with an assumed posture of male arrogance. "It'd be a waste of my time to try and explain it to you. God didn't make women with an understanding of a man's business, with the exception of Mrs. Simpson here," he added hurriedly. "Now you gather up your belongings, young Found, and let's be about our business so others can do the same," he finished up with a meaningful glance at Katie.

"I think you ought to consider new sleeping quarters for Jake," Lucas intervened hurriedly before Katie could respond to Jake's barb. "With this many people working here, it might be a good idea for someone to sleep at the station. It'd be best for security."

"Don't you be looking at me," Jake said. "I prefer horses to people."

"Seems a little unfair to the horses," Katie observed without pausing in her clearing of the table.

"We'll work that out later," Carrie said, encouraging Jake and Found to leave before Katie could think of anything else to say. Lucas got up to follow them, but when Katie turned her back, he winked at Carrie and nodded his head in the direction of the door, indicating he wanted to see her outside. Carrie flushed in spite of herself, but a minute after he left, she excused herself and hurried outside. He was waiting for her on the porch.

"I never got a chance to talk to you this morning."

"I know, but there didn't really seem to be anything to say."

Lucas looked at her questioningly.

"I thought I made it very plain how I felt about you," she said, swallowing with difficulty. "I don't know much about how men think of their relations with women, and from what I have seen, I don't think I want to know any more, but when a woman gives herself to a man, she's given all there is."

"That's what I wanted to talk with you about."

"You don't have to say anything you don't want to. I'm not going to start acting possessive . . ."

"Now look here," Lucas said sharply, taking Carrie by the shoulders and spinning her around to face him, "I will not be lumped with any other man you've known. I neither know nor care what they would do, or what you think of men in general. I act for myself and don't need to follow anybody's lead."

"If all this is leading up to an offer to make an honest woman of me, you can save your breadth," Carrie said, almost choking on her words. "I didn't ask anything from you last night, and I don't intend to start today."

"Yes, you did ask something of me. You asked for the most valuable and important thing a man can give to a woman."

"I wanted it, but I didn't ask for it," Carrie whispered, not daring to look up. She was so acutely aware of Lucas standing next to her, her arms still held in his powerful

214

grip, his powerful body forming a shield between her and the rest of the world, that she had trouble keeping her mind on her thoughts.

"I want to give you what you never asked for," Lucas said, emotion making his voice tense. "I want to learn to give you as much as you have given me. I'm not very good at it, I've never tried before, but I want to learn. Will you help me?"

"Are you sure you want me to?"

"Of course. Why would you doubt it?" Carrie found herself staring at the buttons on his shirt.

"I can love you and you can love me just as we are now, and things may stay the same. But if you start trying to love me and I keep on loving you more each day, then after a while you may find things aren't what you want them to be. You say you're a drifter. I don't think you are. You're something else, but that doesn't really matter. What matters is that you've never been tied down and you don't want to be tied to me. I could stand it if you decided to leave now. It would hurt, but I could stand it. If you stay around studying how to love me more, I think your leaving would drive me crazy." Lucas started to speak, but she put her fingers to his lips. "I haven't asked anything of you and I don't mean to now, but I'm not made of stone. We're too different. We've already been over that. Let's just take what we have while we can."

"Do you really want that?"

"Why not?" Carrie asked, not daring to raise her eyes.

"Look at me," Lucas demanded. Carrie's eyes remained glued to his vest and he had to force her head up. "Do you think I just want to make love to you until these horses are broken and then disappear?"

"I don't know what you want from me. You never told me."

"Yes I did."

"No you didn't," Carrie replied with spirit. "You painted some preposterous picture of connubial bliss which seemed to have you married to a mindless slave, possibly one of those Eastern harem girls who are used to the slave-and-master routine, who would wait patiently at home while you gallivanted about the world, who would take care of your children and see that everything ran perfectly in your absence, and who would be perfectly happy on your return to act like she had no brain at all and couldn't do a thing without you. Somehow I can't see myself fitting into that picture."

"I don't see myself in it either. Even though you make that compliant harem girl sound mighty attractive, I've already set my heart on a pint-sized redhead with blue eyes and a nagging temper who promises to make me miserable for the rest of my life."

"I'm not promising you anything for the rest of my life."

"But you said you loved me . . ."

"I do, and I expect I always will, but I'm still not ready to make a life-long commitment to you."

"I don't understand," Lucas said. "If you love me and I love you . . ."

"Then we're two people in love. That's all it means."

"But didn't you expect to marry the man you fell in love with?"

"I did until I was prepared to marry Robert without it," Carried admitted candidly. "Now I'm not sure, not that you've asked me or that I expect you to, but one doesn't have to follow the other."

"I thought they did in every woman's mind."

"Now who's lumping everyone into the same boat. I haven't gotten used to loving you and I haven't given up on being married, but after our talk the other night, I realize it will take a great deal more than love for us to make a successful marriage."

"Such as?"

"First there has to be total honesty between us. Second, there must be a commonality of goals, and third, there has to be agreement on how to reach those goals. As far as the first is concerned, I've finally been honest with you, but you still haven't told me anything about yourself." Lucas had the grace to look uncomfortable. "And we haven't even discussed the others."

"Must we complete each step before we go on to the others?" Lucas felt it wasn't yet time to tell her the whole truth.

"I don't know. I'm not sure anymore."

"Does that mean you won't come up to the cabin again?"

"No, but it does mean you can't ask any more of me than you're ready to give of yourself."

Their attention had been so tightly focused on each other that they hadn't heard Jake approaching until he was practically at the porch. He was dragging Found by the ear with one hand and holding a small leather bag with the other.

"I told you he was a no-good thief. Look what I found wrapped in one of his shirts." Found made a grab for the leather bag, but Jake held it up out of his reach. "It's a leather pouch of some kind with the initials J.B. on it and it's full of money. *Gold* money, I'll have you know. Now where would a kid like him be getting gold, let alone it's not his leather pouch."

"Give it to me," Carrie said, stretching out her hand, "and let go of his ear. It must be uncomfortable."

"But he'll get away."

"I doubt he'll leave without his money," Carrie said. But when she had opened the pouch, she was less sure of herself. The name "Jonathan Blake" was scratched into the underside of the flap and the pouch was nearly full of gold coins. "Do you know how much is in here?"

"No. I started to count it, but the brat was grabbing at it so I couldn't keep the figures in my head."

"Here, let me," Lucas said. Carrie handed him the pouch and he counted the money swiftly. "There's about two thousand dollars here. A dangerous amount of money

217

for a boy to be carrying around."

"Is this your money?" Carrie asked. Found had not taken his eyes off the pouch since he had been dragged up to the porch, and now he looked directly into Carrie's eyes and nodded his head ever so slightly. "Could you tell me where you got it?" He didn't move by so much as a hair's breadth. "Found, I don't think you stole this money, but it's most unusual for a child to have such a large sum in his possession. I would like to know where you got it, and I need to know who this Jonathan Blake is. Is this his purse? If so, what is your money doing in his pouch?" Still Found didn't move.

"You're wasting your time asking him questions," Jake said. "It's plain as a pikestaff he stole it. No kid has that kind of money, especially not a squatter's kid. I know for a fact his folks could hardly find the money to pay their bill at the store."

"That's not the issue here, Jake. All I want is for Found to tell me how he came to possess such a large sum of money."

"I told you you're wasting your time. He stole it sure as—"

"Be quiet, Jake," Carrie said, speaking more sharply than anyone had ever heard her speak before. "Please, Found, can you tell me where you got this money?"

"We're not going to hurt you, son," Lucas added, trying to see if he could reach the silent youngster. "If it's your money, no one is going to take it from you."

"Of all the crazy things—" Jake began, but a cold glance from Lucas cut him short.

"Please, Found, tell us where you got the money." But the child would not answer Carrie. He just stood there, staring at her out of those big brown eyes like a St. Bernard puppy. "I think I'd better keep it for the time being," Carrie finally said. "You might lose it, or someone might take it from you. I'll put it in the cupboard at the station until I get a chance to take it back to the cabin."

Carrie would have sworn not a muscle moved in the boy's whole body, but somehow he looked deflated, defeated, and her heart went out to him. The accusing look in those big eyes made her feel like a traitor, and she had to battle a momentary impulse to give him back his money and forget the whole incident, but she knew she couldn't. If it was his money, it should be kept someplace safe for him. If it wasn't, well, she'd deal with that when she had to.

"You go on back to the barn with Jake, and we'll talk about this later." Jake turned away, his quick, awkward stride indicating his disgust with the way Carrie had handled the whole situation. Found stood looking at Carrie a moment longer, and then he followed after Jake, his slow dragging footsteps telling an entirely different tale.

"Looks like you got more than you bargained for this time," Lucas said, his tone thoughtful as his eyes followed the boy. "What are you going to do? Do you think he stole the money?"

"No I don't."

"I don't either, but where could he have come by such a sum? That's the savings of a lifetime."

"I don't know. If he would just talk. Why won't he say anything?"

"Fear, and a distrust of other human beings, I suppose. I think that boy had been very badly treated by someone. And I'll lay you a bet it was someone he thought was going to take care of him."

"The money's gone," Carrie almost shouted, forgetting she was alone. She had put the money in one of the cupboards while she went about her work and had gone to get it to take back to the cabin with her. But it was no longer there. Found must have taken it, but how could anyone enter the station, take the money, and leave without her or Katie seeing them? Sure, they hadn't been in the dining room all the time, but they had never been far away for very long. Quickly she made her way to the barn.

"Jake, do you know where Found is?" she asked. Jake was seated outside under a tree, repairing one of the harnesses.

"Lucas was going to take one of the horses he's breaking for a ride, and he told me to send Found up to watch the cabin. I ain't seen him since."

"Where did you put his clothes?"

"In the tack room. I ain't had time to do anything more. I figured he could sleep in the loft if he had a mind to." Carrie turned her steps in the direction of the tack room, but she knew before she got there that Found's clothes would be gone.

"Well I'll be damned," Jake said in amazement. "He's run off already. It's a good thing we took that money from him. I told you he was a thief."

"He's not a thief. He told me that money was his, and my taking it away is the very reason he left. I had no good reason not to believe him, and I ought to have let him keep it."

"Do you mean he stole that money again?"

"He *never* stole it," Carrie insisted. "We were the ones who had no right to it, and I'm going to tell him so the minute I find him. You said his folks lived in one of the canyons in the hills behind the station. Tell me how to find it."

"You can't go traipsing off after that brat alone," exclaimed Jake. "Lucas will have my head if I let you go alone."

"I have no choice. Lucas isn't here, and Found will never come to me if I take you along. I'm sure he thinks you're the cause of all his troubles."

"Now see here, just because I thought he had no business with so much money . . ."

"I should have tried to believe him and offered to keep

220

it for him, but I should never have taken it from him. If I knew anything, it was that he has been badly treated by someone, and now I'm afraid that in his eyes we've done the same thing. I've got to find him."

"Then take Katie with you."

"I can't. There's a stage due in less than an hour. Just tell me how to find the place, and tell Lucas to come after me as soon as he comes in."

"He's going to kill me," Jake said, sorrowfully anticipating his demise. "He's going to cut my guts out and roast them over a fire with me watching."

"Stop trying to make me feel sorry for you, and tell me how to get to that cabin."

But an hour later Carrie was wishing she had waited for Lucas. It had sounded so easy to find the canyon when Jake had described it to her, but she soon found that to someone used to paved roads and street signs, all canyons looked alike; it was impossible to tell the gray ones from the red ones or the narrow openings from the wide. She was able to tell a sandy floor from one strewn with rocks, but except for the willow and pine trees, she could hardly tell what kind of plants she was looking at. In one swift and awful lesson, she had more than amply proved Lucas's contention that she was totally unprepared to travel unaccompanied in the wilderness.

Carrie's mare had not been happy with the saddle from the moment it was place on her back, and she became more difficult to handle the farther from the barn they went. Carrie had been able to follow Found's tracks at first, but they had long since disappeared and the mare seemed to resent her habit of retracing her steps to see if she had overlooked something. Then a covey of quail erupted from a low bush practically under her feet, and the mare reared, unseating Carrie just as she was in the process of leaning down to get a better view of a suspicious-looking footprint in the sand. Carrie managed to hold on the pommel and keep one foot in the stirrup, but she could not regain her seat, and the mare was galloping down the trail. She tried to pull up the runaway horse with only one hand on the reins, but the mare knew she was in control and made a spirited attempt to rip the reins out of Carrie's grasp. Realizing she couldn't hold on long with only one foot in a stirrup and her body leaning off to one side, Carrie turned her attention to getting her leg back over the saddle.

She had a firm grasp on the pommel, and she was able to gradually ease her weight over the center of the mare's back. Given a little more time and the requirement that the mare continue to run a straight course, she would have been able to get her leg over the saddle and probably her foot back into the stirrup. However, the mare made an abrupt turn, and Carrie lost her grip and tumbled to the ground, where she lay still.

Chapter 16

Carrie didn't know how long she lay on the ground. She wasn't conscious of the passing of time, but her body felt hot from the sun and she knew she must have lain there for some time. She was suddenly aware of something soft touching her forehead. For a split second she was petrified that it might be some wild animal, but almost immediately she knew it was a hand. A small hand. She tried to open her eyes, but they wouldn't move. She tried to move her body, but it seemed to be part of the ground and she nothing more than a spirit caught in its stony crust. She heard a sniff, then what sounded like a soft sob. She tried to move her lips, but nothing came out. Oh why couldn't she do anything? Had she broken her neck? Was this what it was like to be dead? She felt as if she were trapped inside a lifeless shell, unable to communicate with anyone outside of herself.

A drop of water landed on her cheek to be quickly followed by others, and her eyes flew open of their own accord. It was Found. He was leaning over her, gently touching her face with the tips of his fingers; it was his tears that had wet her cheek. Suddenly she felt as though her spirit moved back into her body and she was herself again. She smiled.

"It's all right, Found. I just fell off my horse." The boy drew back in frozen surprise. Carrie was shocked to see fear erase his grief as though it had never been there.

"It's not your fault I fell, and I'm not mad at you," she told him, sensing at once that he thought she was going to hold him responsible for her accident. "I was worried about you when I found the money was gone. I knew you had run away because I thought you had stolen it, but I don't think you're a thief, Found. I never did, and it was wrong of me to take your money. I was just worried about your having the responsibility of such a large sum, but I'll never take it from you again. And I won't let anybody else take it either." Carrie tried to sit up, but her head ached and the landscape swam before her eyes. She was tempted to lie back and not move until the agonizing pain had gone away, but it would be dark in another hour, and they had to find some place to spend the night.

"I'm afraid I'm lost, Found. Do you know where we are?"

The boy had gradually relaxed during Carrie's speech, and he nodded.

"Good. Is your cabin close enough for us to reach it before dark?" Again the boy nodded. "Then we'd better get started as soon as I can get my feet under me. I don't want to spend the night out in the open. I have no idea what kinds of wild beasts wander over these hills at night, but I don't think I want to find out." Carrie managed to get to her feet with Found's help. She felt a little unsteady, but she could stand. "Okay, I'm ready, but remember I'm used to living in a house in a town. I'm going to have to depend on you to take care of me until we get back to the station."

Found took her hand and started to walk slowly down the trail, but they hadn't gone very far when he turned off into a canyon that promised to be bigger than any Carrie had passed yet.

"Is your house up here somewhere?" Found nodded. "Did you stay here after your parents died?" Again Found nodded. "You poor boy. That must have been awful, having to live all by yourself in the house where your parents died. Well, you won't have to do *that* again. I'm going to fix up one of the bedrooms in the back of the station for you. You're too big to need Jake to stay with you, and I need someone to stay in the station to scare away robbers." She looked at the wild, forbidding loneliness of the landscape and she shivered inwardly. "Anybody who could stay out here by themselves can't be afraid of anything as harmless as a thief. And just as soon as I get a chance, I'm going to take you to Fort Malone and get you some new clothes. I think you ought to have a horse, too. How would you like that mare I was riding, the one Jake keeps in the barn?" Found's eyes widened in disbelief, but there was the beginning of a smile on his face. "Well, you can have her. I don't like her, and to tell the truth, I don't think she likes me very much either. I'm sure a clever boy like you would have no trouble handling her. Lucas, Mr. Barrow that is, is going to give me one of his mustangs so you don't have to worry about me not having a horse. Then as soon as you're a little bigger, I can send you into Fort Malone to pick up the supplies. It'll be a big help to me not to have to make that trip."

Carrie continued to talk to Found about anything that came into her head. It was exactly like thinking out loud, and it made the trip to his cabin seem easier and shorter. Besides, she couldn't stand to walk through the falling twilight in complete silence. It was beautiful country, or at least it would have been if she had been astride a horse, it had been daylight, and Lucas had been at her side, but she didn't feel too much like taking in scenic wonders right now.

She was beginning to feel very tired when, without explanation, Found led her off the path and into the tall brush that nearly choked the canyon. He was gone before she could open her mouth to protest, but it was only a moment before he returned and beckoned her to follow him once again. In a matter of minutes they rounded some stones that had fallen from the canyon wall eons ago,

225

and Carrie found herself staring at what was probably the poorest cabin she had ever seen. She stopped where she stood and took stock of the situation. The cabin would probably give them a roof over their heads, but she was certain it leaked and doubted the doors could be secured. The small yard was littered with the debris which inevitably collects where humans live. There was no shed or coop to be seen. Carrie decided that if Found's parents had ever kept chickens, pigs, cows, or horses, they had been forced to fend for themselves. Not that the cabin looked as if it would offer much protection to its human occupants either.

She started forward toward the cabin, but stopped. Out of the corner of her eye she noticed a grave marker. When she turned she saw there were two of them. She looked toward Found. "Are those your parents?" He nodded, but the soft, open friendliness was gone from his glance. There was an odd mixture there which Carrie couldn't quite interpret. It looked like a cross between anger and fear, but it was such an unexpected mixture Carrie thought the failing light must have misled her. The markers were starkly simple, two crossed sticks with nothing more than the initial and the last name. In a few years there wouldn't be anything to show these people had ever lived. Privately she thought that was quite sad, but then she remembered that they would live on in Found, and she felt less melancholy.

"I'm just about to die of thirst," she said to Found. "Is your well still good?" Found lowered the battered metal bucket into the well and came up with it half full of water, but Carrie didn't like what she saw. The water was dark and brackish. "I can't drink that," she said, drawing back. "It might give me cholera or something." Without a word, Found disappeared and reappeared a moment later with a small bucket of cool clear water. "Where did you get that?" she asked. "I didn't see any stream." Found pointed to a part of the canyon wall that looked exactly like every other part of the wall. Carrie could see nothing until she followed him to where water seeped out of the rocks and collected in a series of small rock basins. "I would never have thought to look for something like this. I could have died of thirst with plenty of water here all the time," she said, thinking out loud again.

They returned to the cabin and were about to enter the front door when they heard the sound of more than one horse coming up the canyon. Before she could think, Found was pulling her hard by the hand, virtually dragging her into the surrounding brush. Carrie thought it was probably a good idea to know who was coming before she revealed her presence, but her reluctance to meet strangers didn't account for the look of terror in Found's eyes. Clearly someone had been in the habit of coming to this cabin who frightened him badly. But they had hardly settled into a hiding place among the scrub pines when Carrie caught sight of Lucas's head above the low-growing vegetation. Her first impulse was to rush toward him in relief, but some second thought kept her in her hiding place.

He came up the trail looking as if the only thing in the world he wanted was to make sure she was safe. His eyes were glued to the ground and lifted only occasionally to make a sweep of the surrounding canyon walls. His haggard expression testified to the worry that had been his constant companion since he reached the station to find her gone, and the slump of his body in the saddle betokened the dread with which he followed her trail. Suddenly her conscience gave her a sharp prod, and Carrie knew she couldn't prolong his misery a minute more. She stood up and walked into the cabin yard to await him.

Yet no sooner did Lucas set eyes on her than his expression turned to black thunder, and she could have sworn lightning would flash from his eyes any minute. It was really quite touching, and if it hadn't been so serious she would have laughed out loud. She would have to try hard to remember how he looked before he saw her, because it was obvious she was in for a rough time.

ing. Under the circumstances, one of them saying things they didn't mean was going to be quite enough.

When he came closer, she saw he looked more relieved than angry and he was leading her mare, and she was so relieved to know she wasn't going to have to walk back to the station she didn't much care what he said to her.

"I was hoping you would have returned to the station earlier," Carrie said calmly, trying to act as though nothing out of the ordinary had occurred. "Then you might have caught up with me before that treacherous animal ran away."

As soon as Lucas reached Carrie, he was off his horse and sweeping her up into a powerful embrace. "Are you all right? When I found your mare coming back down the trail, I was worried you might be lying somewhere with a broken neck." Carrie hadn't expected this reaction, and it was some time before she could catch her breath and answer him.

"I didn't fall," she said, trying to reassure him. "I sort of tumbled off." Lucas didn't understand. "I was about to dismount when she was startled by some quail. I would have gotten back into the saddle, but she made a sharp turn and I tumbled off."

"Were you hurt?"

"No. Anyway, Found came along right after that, and he's taken very good care of me." The glance Lucas threw the boy was anything but grateful.

"If I had one grain of sense, I'd leave you this horse, turn around, and never come near that station again," Lucas said as he released Carrie from his embrace. "You are the stubborn, hardheaded woman I've ever met, and I have to be crazy to even think about marry-

you be talking about?" Carrie said, trying face. "Found ran away because we took his money when we had no to come after him."

"You didn't have to come by yourself."

"You weren't around, and Katie had to stay to meet the stage. I figured he wouldn't come out of hiding if he saw Jake."

"I know all about your brilliant reasoning. I had it out of Bemis before I broke his stupid neck. I still can't believe that I was the one who recommended that prize fool to you."

"As I remember, you gave him a glowing recommendation."

"You're not going to get me off the subject on this one, my girl. You blatantly ignored what I said after you went chasing those Indians. You started out in country you'd never seen, you went off alone when you knew nothing about finding your way around a wilderness, and you did it on a horse not accustomed to a saddle. And what for? To chase after some boy who can take good care of himself without any help from us."

"That's not the point," Carrie replied, refusing to be put in the wrong. "I adopted him without even asking him if he wanted to be adopted, and then we practically accused him of being a thief. I couldn't let him run off thinking we weren't his friends. A child his age needs someone to take care of him, even if he can get along by himself."

"I quite agree, but you took a damned awful risk running off in strange country. You could have gotten lost or hurt yourself. Who knows what could have happened."

"Well, fortunately nothing did, so you can stop worrying about it."

"So you're going to go on thinking you were right along?"

"I won't have to think for myself at all. You'll be o[nly] happy to tell me what to think." Carrie was findin[g in]creasingly difficult to remember that Lucas had b[een wor]ried about her. "Should we go back, or do you[think we] ought to spend the night here?"

"Why ask my opinion? You're the woodlan[d]

can dash about without regard for consequences that plague normal folk. I'm sure you can do anything you wish."

"Well, I can't give you the spanking you deserve," Carrie said angrily, "though the mere thought of it gives me considerable pleasure."

"If there's any spanking to be done, my dear Carolina Marsena Terwilliger, *I'm* the one who's going to do it."

"You'll do nothing of the sort, so stop acting like a self-appointed dictator, and let's start back. I don't want Found to be out too late."

"You don't want Found to be . . ." Lucas was unable to finish the sentence, and his unsuccessful attempts to get another off the ground restored Carrie's good humor.

"I'm sorry I upset you, Lucas, I really am, but I couldn't wait. And I truly thought I could catch up with Found and be back within an hour. It was so easy to follow the Indians I'm afraid I assumed it would be equally easy to follow Found. I never stopped to realize he probably knew as much about living out here as the wild animals."

The sincerity of Carrie's apology prevented Lucas from taking his frustrations out on her, and that made him furious. He had come back to find Carrie gone on a wild-goose chase and Jake calmly working on his harnesses. It was a good thing Katie had come out to the barn when she did, or he might really have broken Jake's neck. And it would have served him right too, the half-baked idiot. He had virtually tricked Carrie into hiring a man he thought would look after her when he wasn't around only to dis— the fool was letting her wander over half of Colorado making only the feeblest attempts to stop

a pleasurable hour rehearsing all the say to her and what he would like ght up with her only to have it all e found her mare running loose. ed by the most awful images of

Carrie lying at the bottom of a ravine or canyon with her neck broken, or of her lying on the trail at the mercy of any man or animal that came along. It had been the worst thirty minutes of his life.

And now she had apologized very nicely, just like the Southern lady she pretended to be when it suited her purpose, and made it impossible for him to tell her that she had much more in common with a mountain wildcat than a lady. Of course, he probably preferred the wildcat, but that wasn't the point. If this girl wasn't broken to bridle, she was going to drive him to do something drastic, and so far he was making no progress at all. Now she was sitting on that no-account mare and smiling as if she was actually proud of herself for getting in the saddle unassisted.

"Climb up behind me, Found," Carrie said. "You can't walk all the way back."

"He can ride with me," Lucas said, doing his best to hold his temper in check. "You'll have enough to do to stay on that horse."

"How ungallant, and after I explained how it happened. It's partly your fault anyway."

"My fault!" Lucas's voice practically rose to a squeak.

"You had no business going off all afternoon without telling me. I couldn't very well wait for you when I didn't know when you would return, or even *if* you would return."

"You *knew* I was coming back," Lucas said, turning abruptly to face her while he helped Found climb up behind him. "You did know that, didn't you?" Carrie's gaze dropped before his flashing eyes.

"Yes, I knew, but I truly couldn't wait. I'm sorry." Lucas ground his teeth. His anger wasn't appeased and Carrie didn't seem the least bit sorry for what she had done. It was possible she was sorry to have gotten him so upset—although he wasn't even sure of that—but he had no doubt that should a similar occasion occur tomorrow, she would do the very same thing, even in worse circumstances.

Maybe he'd been wrong about her being half Southern lady. Maybe she was two completely different people. When she needed help, or wanted any kind of assistance, she could become the most charming, the most beguiling mite of a woman he had ever known. But if she wanted something, she didn't hesitate to step out of the *lady* role and pick up any other characteristics she might find useful. If there was ever a female who had earned her red hair, it was Carrie Simpson. Yet corner her, and you'd find yourself facing not a Colorado wildcat you could tackle with a clean conscience, but the Southern lady again, inviolate and absolutely out of reach behind her prim smile and starched petticoats.

And it didn't matter in the least that Lucas knew what she was like out of those petticoats. Without having to think about it, Lucas knew that what she had given him was like an honor bestowed on him, a kind of sacred trust that he couldn't violate no matter what she did. It was the most priceless thing a woman can give a man, and he was bound to protect her with his very life; and he knew he would do just that. Damn! He hadn't even asked her to marry him, and he was already bound hand and foot. Never again would he underestimate a pint-sized female from Smithfield, Virginia. If he had any sense at all, he'd get on the nearest horse and head back to Texas. All they had there were Mexican bandits, hard-bitten gunslingers, a few million wild longhorns, and three kinds of poisonous snakes.

"You know you may not be able to keep him," Lucas said after they'd traveled a few minutes in silence. "He should be the responsibility of the court, and they will insist that a search be made for any relatives."

"Naturally," Carrie said, turning in the saddle to face him. "But I don't think we should do that until Found gets over the distress of being abandoned. It's quite possible we can do permanent damage if we upset him again too soon." Lucas could think of few people less likely to be upset by change than a boy who'd survived several months in the wilds by himself. He was much more likely to become unhinged from the trauma of going to school or having to wear shoes and a clean shirt.

"How long do you think you should wait?" It was a dangerous question, probably stupid as well, but somebody had to ask it, and he was the only candidate.

"Oh, I don't know," Carrie replied innocently. "I think Found ought to tell us that."

"And how are you going to tell since he refuses to talk? And I'm sure he is equally unable to write!"

"How clever of you to put your finger on the crux of the matter so quickly." This was the first time Carrie had ever given Lucas credit for having the answer to anything, and he knew he was in trouble. "We'll know he's ready when he starts to speak."

"But that could be months," Lucas protested.

"Yes," Carrie said sadly. "I'm told that these things can affect a child very deeply."

"Carrie Simpson, you know very well you're just manipulating the situation, and doing a damned good job of it, I might add. You have no intention of turning this boy over to the court anytime soon, if ever, and you're not the least bit sorry about the trouble, or worry, you've caused me."

"You were worried about me, Lucas? I thought it was Carolina Marsena Terwillinger you were concerned for. That was the name you mentioned, wasn't it?"

"Careful, girl. I've never wrung a woman's neck, but you're just about to give me ample reason to overcome my scruples."

"I do hope you mean to tell me whose neck you're wringing before I've drawn my last breath, Carrie's or Carolina's."

"Both!" Lucas nearly shouted, the words exploding from his lips. "For it's both of them you use, first one and then the other, to plague a man and keep him off balance."

"I promise not to do it again."

233

"You can't help it. It's in your blood."

"And you can't help charging around acting like Sir Galahad, certain I can't do anything for myself and will come to grief if I'm out of your sight for as much as an hour."

"Just look at what you've gotten yourself into since you've been here. I never knew a woman with such a talent for stirring up things."

"And just look at what I've done without your help."

"You've had Katie and me here the whole time and then Jake. Now you'll have Found too."

"Lucas Barrow, no wonder you're unwed. If you don't change your condescending attitude, you're going to stay a bachelor unless you can talk some poor ignorant soul into marrying you before she has any idea what a hide-bound woman hater you are. Can't you give me credit for anything?"

"I don't hate women. I thought I'd given you proof of that."

"I'm not talking about physical interest," Carrie said scornfully. "I was talking about your absolute certainty that a woman can't do anything herself."

"I never said that."

"You may not have stated it in so many words, but your every action screams it."

"I was under the impression that women liked to be pampered and cared for."

"Pampered and cared for, yes, but not suffocated. It's a wonderful feeling when a man treats you like something precious. It makes you feel like the most important person on the face of the earth."

"Then why—"

"But no woman wants to feel a man is taking care of her because she's incapable of taking care of herself. You'd be treating her exactly like you would a baby, spending lots of time making sure she's comfortable and happy, but looking elsewhere when you wanted companionship. I don't want to be your equal in strength, I know I can't be, and I don't want to be able to do everything you can do—there are plenty of things I can do that you can't—but I don't want to be despised because of my weaknesses or shortcomings any more than you do."

"I never said I was per—"

"And you have both, even if you are a member of the mighty male sex."

"If you'd ever let me finish a sentence, you might not be under so many misapprehensions. Of course I realize that might force you to give up all your prejudicial thinking, but then you just might have a chance to learn what *I* think, rather than what you *think* I'm thinking."

"I don't think we should talk anymore until we reach the station," Carrie said, urging her mare to pull ahead. "It's getting us nowhere, and it'll probably upset Found."

"Of course it doesn't matter to you that *I* might be upset or that *I* might want to keep on talking?"

"As a matter of fact it does, but not very much at the moment."

Lucas was so angry at this point he didn't trust himself to speak. Once he had cooled down, he didn't know what to say, so he accepted Carrie's ending of the discussion and followed her back, all the while making plans for her total and utter capitulation.

"The saints be praised," Katie exclaimed as she came running down the steps to greet them when they rode into the station yard. She had been standing on the porch under the light of two blazing lanterns, and the relief in her face was easy to see.

"You might praise me just a little bit for finding her," Lucas remarked sulkily. "I'm certainly not going to get any thanks from Sacajawea over there."

"I've been worn down with worry over you," Katie rushed on, too taken up with her own agitation to have time to care that Lucas's eyes flashed with anger. "You should have been back hours ago."

"It was a long way," Carrie said, "and I didn't see any

point in pushing the horses, not with Lucas to protect us." A choking noise made Katie turn and Carrie struggled to cover a smile, but there was no sign of amusement on Lucas's face when he finally got off his horse and moved within the ring of light.

"I hope you've saved me something to eat," he growled as he climbed the steps, leaving Carrie to dismount by herself. "And I trust you don't mean to charge me this time," he said, swinging swiftly back toward Carrie. "Chasing after you across half of Colorado should have earned me at least one meal."

"Make sure Mr. Barrow has all he can eat," Carrie said to Katie. "I wouldn't want to think I didn't have a proper appreciation for myself." Carrie winked at Katie, who turned away quickly to hide a grin. "You come too, Found," Carrie said. "You deserve the best seat in the house for finding me."

Lucas didn't say anything, but Carrie could tell he was hurt, and it wasn't just male vanity this time. He was really hurt, and she quickly moved to correct her mistake.

"That wasn't a fair thing to say. You both found me, and I'm equally grateful to both of you." But it didn't work. Lucas had had time to get over his initial fear that something had happened to Carrie and then his reaction of unreasoning anger at her attempt to find Found by herself. He had moved on to thinking about tonight as it affected his dreams of their future, and Carrie could tell that what he was thinking was not making him happy. She suddenly wondered if she had gone too far. Proving to a man that you could take care of yourself was a far cry from convincing him you could do without him altogether. It would be disastrous if he should get the idea she *wanted* to do without him. She wasn't sure just yet what she did want, but she knew she didn't want to lose him. Still, from the gathered brows and the fact that he hadn't said a word during the meal, she concluded that this was not the time to try to retake the ground she had lost. It would be much better to allow him a good night's sleep and hope he would have calmed down by tomorrow.

"Come on, Found," Lucas said when he had finished his coffee and gotten to his feet. "It's about time we cleared out and let the ladies clean up. Besides, I want to see if Jake's still alive."

" 'Tis no thanks to you if he is," Katie said, surprising Carrie by the sharpness of her tone. "I wouldn't be surprised if he has the marks of your fingers on his neck for several days to come."

"He should be glad he's still alive and able to have bruises. I don't know how a great fool like him escaped being murdered anytime these last twenty years." Katie didn't answer Lucas, but the clatter of the plates as she stacked them made certain Lucas knew she wasn't in agreement with him.

"Did he really assault Jake?" Carrie asked when Lucas and Found had gone.

"It's not for me to say what happened before I got there," Katie said, dropping the plates into the hot soapy water so carelessly Carrie was surprised some of them didn't break, "but if I hadn't arrived when I did, Mr. Barrow would be standing his trial for murder. Jake's face was as black as night, and I would have taken me oath he was already dead. I won't be telling you that Jake isn't a great trial, but the poor man couldn't do no more than make hoarse, rasping sounds for close to an hour afterward. A man like Mr. Lucas doesn't know his own strength, especially when he gets angry, and he shouldn't be going about taking things out on people who are nowhere near up to his weight."

"He was quite angry then?" Carrie inquired, unable to deny a twinge of pleasure.

"I can't remember that I've ever seen anybody that mad, not even me pa when he was drunk, and he used to be ready to take on the whole village when he'd had enough whiskey. You'd better be glad you weren't here, because if you were, you'd still be wearing the marks of the spanking he would have given you."

"He was *that* mad?" Carried asked, feeing guilty for taking pleasure from Lucas's misery but enjoying it nevertheless.

"I should say he was. Unless you want him to haul you into town and marry you for spite, you'd better make sure not to set him off again. The poor man was in such a taking, I don't think he could stand another thing without his mind becoming unhinged."

A muffled giggle escaped Carrie. Katie looked up from her dishwater, prepared to be filled with righteous indignation, but the unholy gleam of amusement in Carrie's eyes overset her gravity, and both women fell into a prolonged fit of helpless laughter.

Chapter 17

The next day Found was at the mustangs' corral before Lucas stepped out of his cabin. Lucas had endured a wretched night, and seeing the instigator of the latest round of his troubles only served to renew his feeling of injustice over the manner in which Carrie had treated him. This was one pair of ears that needed pinning back, and he intended to see it was done right away. His ambling walk changed to a purposeful stride which had become an angry stalk by the time he reached the corral. He reached down, picked the boy up, and set him on the fence rail.

"I've got something to say to you, Found, and I want you to listen closely because I don't intend to say it again." The boy stared back at him out of guileless eyes, but Lucas didn't let that stop him. "You had no way of knowing what was going to happen when you ran away yesterday, you probably still don't understand what a can of worms you opened, so I'm going to try to explain very simply the way things are around here. Nobody asked you to come up to this station and get yourself caught stealing food, but if there is one thing that gets to a woman faster than a bolt of lightning, it's a hungry kid who's fresh out of family. The only way you could have done the job quicker would have been to wrap yourself up in a blanket and leave yourself on the doorstep.

"Anyhow, once you got yourself caught, Mrs. Simpson still gave you a chance to leave. She asked you if you wanted to stay. Now I have nothing against you staying here, in fact, I sort of like you, but we're not talking about me. We're talking about Mrs. Simpson. Once you told her you wanted to stay, the damage was done and the gate slammed shut behind you. There was no backing out and no changing your mind. You *had* to stay here. If you hadn't wanted to, you should have thought about it before you nodded your head. You do want to stay here, don't you?" Found was still for a moment, then he nodded his head.

"Then you stay, do you hear me? I won't have any more of this running off or running away, whichever it was. I guess you were upset about us taking your money, but we didn't mean any harm, really we didn't. I don't hold it against you for taking your money back, I probably would have done the same thing, but don't you ever run away again because when you do, you endanger Mrs. Simpson as well. You didn't think she was just going to let you leave and forget about it, did you? If you did, then you don't know Mrs. Simpson. That woman would have followed you all the way across this country if need be. It wouldn't have mattered to her that half the country is still covered by Indians who will scalp her as soon as look at her, or worthless white folks who would probably do even worse. She'd have kept going until she found you. Now I know it's not a very smart thing to do and no sensible man would set out to go somewhere by himself when he didn't know a thing about the country or living off the land, but womenfolk don't think like men, more's the pity. You can't ever predict what they're going to do, but you can be sure it will cause some poor man a heap of trouble.

"But that's beside the point," Lucas said, realizing he was getting sidetracked by his own sense of ill-usage. "What I mean to say is if you don't stay here and make sure you're where she can keep her eye on you every minute, I'm going to tan your backside so bad you won't be able to go anywhere for quite some time. You can kill yourself if you like, you can even go back and live in that tumbled-down cabin if that's what you want, but Mrs. Simpson will break her neck trying to help you, and I won't have you helping her to do it. Now you make up your mind right now. Either you're going to stay as long as she wants you to, or you're going to leave *today*."

Lucas turned away from the boy. He felt a little ashamed that he'd put the issue to him so roughly, but he had to make him understand what he was doing to Carrie. He simply couldn't allow anything to happen that would cause her to run off again. Twice she had escaped any serious consequences, but it was pressing her luck to think she would be able to do it a third time. Lucas wouldn't let himself think about the things that could happen. He had been mad enough last night to think it would serve her right if she received a good scare from some Indians or one of the gangs that kept hideouts in the remote canyons all through the state, but today the thought of such an eventuality served only to fill him with a cold fear. It was obvious he was not going to be able to make Carrie understand the danger of such little jaunts, so he was going to have to see to it she didn't have any reason to light out without him to look after her.

He picked up the rope he had brought with him, uncoiled it, and began to recoil it again more to his satisfaction. "After all I've said, do you still want to stay with Mrs. Simpson?" he asked Found, and the boy nodded without hesitation. "Good. I hoped you would, but now you're going to have to help me take care of Mrs. Simpson."

"Katie too," said Jake, who had come up to join them in time to hear Lucas's last remarks.

"Women don't see things like a man," Lucas continued, "and sometimes you have to think for them."

"But you can't let them know what you're doing, or they'll take the hide off you quicker than boiling water." Lucas could see that Jake's wandering off into personal revelation was confusing the boy. Of course, Carrie's way of thinking had confused him too, but he wasn't discussing that now.

"Look, Found," he said, starting over, "Mrs. Simpson comes from a different part of the country where nothing is

241

like it is out here, and she doesn't understand the way some people act. She doesn't believe they will do anything bad to her, but we know different." Found nodded his head in agreement and Lucas felt encouraged. It was the first time anybody had gotten an unsolicited response from the boy. "She thinks everybody is good, and even though I've told her they aren't, she won't believe me. So we're going to have to see that nothing happens to her. And the most important thing is to make sure she's never left at the station by herself. There's no way of knowing when someone will come riding up the road, or who it will be. Do you understand? Will you help me?" Found nodded eagerly.

"There's more. I'm not sure you're going to like it, but if you mean to stay here, you might as well know," Jake added, determined Lucas shouldn't overlook any of the hardships of living under a woman's dominion. "Women put a lot of importance on things that a man wouldn't give much thought to if he was left to himself. And it doesn't do any good to try to reason with them. They're not going to change. Some of the things they can get upset about real quick are being dirty, bad table manners, cussing, drinking, smoking, and tracking manure into the kitchen. Katie will near-about kill you if you don't scrape your boots real good. And all the while they expect you to work like a pack horse and turn over your pay to them. Makes you wonder why any man would ever let himself get talked into marrying. Sounds like that kind of life just wouldn't be worth living, but of course you won't have to worry none about cussing unless you make up your mind to start talking."

"It's not as bad as Jake makes it sound," Lucas said, unable to repress a grin at the crusty bachelor's chafing over the constraints imposed by female companionship, "but he's right about having to learn to live differently. I know it'll be strange for you at first and it won't be easy to learn how to do things all over again, but you'll have to if you want to make Mrs. Simpson happy."

"Katie too," added Jake. "That female can be downright tyrannical when she has a mind to."

"There's still one more thing. Can you read or write?" Found hung his head. "I didn't think so, but I expect Mrs. Simpson will want to teach you. Are you willing to try to learn?" Found raised his head, and it was clear from the eager light in his eyes that he would swallow all of the indignities previously named if he could just learn to read and write.

"Okay, we've given you a lot to remember, but I want you to think it over. You've got to make up your mind to learn to live like Mrs. Simpson wants you, or you have to leave right now. It can't be any other way. Now let's see if you know anything about horses. Can you catch that sorrel mare over there and bring her to me." Found took the coiled rope Lucas held out to him and jumped down into the corral.

"Do you think he'll stay?" Jake asked, his eyes on the boy as he worked his way through the milling horses toward the mare.

"Yes, I do, and I think he'll do everything he can to do exactly what Carrie wants of him."

"Poor little blighter," commiserated Jake. "Makes you think living in that cabin might not be so bad after all."

"I didn't want to scare him off, but I can't take a chance on his doing something to cause Carrie to run off by herself again. And if *you* ever let her out of your sight . . ."

"I'll make sure I'm halfway to Arizona before you get back," Jake said emphatically. "I like Mrs. Simpson. She's got a lot of guts for a female, but I'm not about to get my neck wrung because of the fool things she does." Lucas directed a threatening glare at Jake, but the shorter man didn't back down. "You know damned well she's the most unpredictable woman, and she won't do what you tell her no matter how many reasons you give her."

Lucas didn't like to agree with Jake, but he had come to grief too may times when trying to change Carrie's mind to refuse to admit the truth. The woman was enough to make a grown man groan with desire, but she would also make him howl with fury.

"Would you look at that," Jake said, interrupting Lucas's train of thought. "Slipped the noose over that mare's head just as neat as you please. That kid's pa may have been a sodbuster, but he knows something about horses."

For some reason Jake's words struck Lucas all wrong, and it took him a minute before he could figure out why. He hadn't seen any signs of ground being plowed at Found's cabin except for a vegetable garden near the house. Whatever Found's father was doing, it wasn't farming. He watched Found leading the mare over to them, and an idea came to his mind.

"I'm glad to see you know something about horses. You can help me break this bunch, but we're going to let Jake here take this one. I've got some questions I want to ask you." Found looked puzzled and a little disappointed he wasn't going to be able to work with the mare, but he calmly listened while Lucas explained to Jake what he wanted done. Lucas watched Jake work with the mare for a few minutes, and once he was satisfied he was doing exactly what he wanted, he turned back to the boy.

"Maybe you can help me with something, Found, something that would help Mrs. Simpson too." The boy stared at Lucas impassively. "Do you remember when I said you had to help me protect the women?" Found nodded. "Well, protecting them is more than just doing what they want you to do. There are some people around here who want to stop one of Mrs. Simpson's stages and take something that doesn't belong to them. They're already robbed one stage, and I'm sure they're still around somewhere planning to do it again." Lucas had decided to tell Found about the robbery on a hunch, but the boy's reaction told him his hunch had paid off. Found's expression changed from one of bland inquiry to nervous, self-conscious fidgeting. Clearly he knew something.

"I'm going to let you in on a secret," Lucas said, squatting down so he could be on the boy's eye level. "I haven't told anyone else, not even Jake or Mrs. Simpson, so you've got to promise you'll keep it a secret. Is it a deal?" Found had stopped fidgeting for a moment. At last he reluctantly nodded his head. "Okay, I'm not really a wrangler. The reason I'm here is to catch those thieves before they can steal any more gold. And I need your help. They may intend to come here to the station, and if they do, they mean to hurt Mrs. Simpson and Katie. Now, I don't want that to happen, but I haven't been able to find any trace of them. Do you know of any strange men moving among those hills behind your father's cabin? The man I'm looking for is just about as tall as I am, weighs about forty pounds more, has a rough beard and uncut blond hair, and wears two black-handled guns tied down with the handles forward. He usually goes by the name of Jason Staples." Found's complexion lost its color, and the boy looked petrified.

"I don't want to scare you, son, but it's important to catch this man, not only for Mrs. Simpson's sake and the gold, but for everyone else. He's a dangerous man, so if you know something, I want you to tell me. Anything will help, even if it's not much."

Found looked too scared to move. "Maybe it would be for your protection too," Lucas added. "Why are you so afraid of him?" Found didn't speak. Instead he turned away and Lucas thought he was going to leave, but it turned out he was looking for a stick. When he found one that suited him, he returned to where Lucas was still squatting. He started to draw something in the bare earth beside the corral. For the best part of a minute Lucas couldn't figure out what it might be, since Found wasn't a particularly good artist, but after a while he recognized the series of canyons that reached into the mountains from behind the station.

"I know those canyons," Lucas told him. "What are you trying to tell me?" Found continued to draw, adding more canyons and valleys and passes to the ones he had already drawn until he reached a part of the surrounding area Lucas had not yet explored. In the middle of a series of twisting, almost blind canyons, Found began to scratch out rough pictures of riders on horseback until he had eight of them.

"Are you telling me that is where Jason Staples is hiding?" Found shook his head. "But he did camp there at one time?" Found nodded. "Do you know of any other places he stayed? Please, Found, it is important that you tell me everything you can." Lucas was certain the boy knew something else, but he didn't know if he would tell him what it was. "You do want me to find him so he can't hurt Katie and Mrs. Simpson, don't you?" Found nodded and started to draw again. It was a picture of a cabin in the canyon where Lucas had found them the night before.

"Do you mean he used your cabin? Did your father know what he was doing? Did he help him?" Found stared at Lucas with such a vacant expression that Lucas decided not to press him for more information. Something had happened that had scared Found very badly, but he had found out far more than he had expected. It just might turn out to be his first solid piece of evidence that the Staples gang was in the area.

"Jake," Lucas called, going over to where the stocky man was still working with the mare Lucas meant to give Carrie. "I've got to be gone most of the day. Take Found back up to the barn with you when you finish with the sorrel. You can teach him to muck out stalls or repair harnesses. Maybe he can help you with the teams. I'll tell Carrie what I mean to do, but I'm depending on you to make sure she doesn't follow me. You too, Found. If I come back to find she's stepped one foot off the place for as much as five seconds, you've both drawn your last breath."

"But what am I going to do if she won't listen?" asked Jake, already certain his end was near.

"Tie her up if you have to, but make sure she doesn't leave this place."

"You can't tie up a woman! It's not proper."

"Is it more proper to be dead?"

"I guess it wouldn't hurt her too much," Jake decided, reversing his opinion with alacrity, "but if she takes her gun after me, my death will be on your conscience."

"It'll be there either way, won't it?" said Lucas as he

246

moved toward the house.

"I don't think he's got a conscience," Jake complained to Found. "He don't really care what happens to the rest of us as long as that woman of his is all right. Come on, let's go back up to the barn. It won't do us any good to try and watch her from here."

Lucas found Carrie still in her cabin, and as he expected, she was not happy with the news that he would be away most of the day.

"But you were gone half of yesterday. Can't you break the horses in the corral?"

"This has nothing to do with breaking horses. You told me some time ago you didn't know what I was, but you were sure I was something other than a wrangler. Well, you were right. I'm breaking horses for the company as a cover, but I've been sent here to find the gang which robbed one of our stages of a gold shipment four weeks ago. The company is certain they mean to try it again, and it's my job to stop them."

For reasons Carrie didn't have the time or inclination to explore, all of Lucas's talk about outlaws and danger hadn't seemed very meaningful before, but now that he was actually going *in search* of gold thieves, it seemed very significant indeed. She had expected all along that he would ultimately tell her what his real purpose was at the station, but she'd never imagined it would be anything dangerous, and she was almost too shocked to think. All she could think of now was that if anything happened to him, he would never know all the things she hadn't told him. Now she regretted the time she spent teasing him when she could have spent it telling him how much she loved him, time she could have spent listening to *him* say how much he loved *her*. And there were all those unresolved differences standing between them, differences she suddenly realized were not terribly important after all.

"Why would they stay around here if they already have the gold?" Maybe he wouldn't have to go. Maybe they had already left Colorado.

"There's an even bigger shipment coming through, and the company is certain they're waiting around for it. At least we expect they'll come back to try for it."

"But why? They already have one shipment."

"No amount of gold is ever enough for these people. They would rob a stage every week if they had the opportunity and then turn around and waste the money. They don't think of stealing enough to buy a farm or a business, or even to have enough to live on the rest of their lives. To them it's a way of making a living, very much like the way you look at your job here at the station. When they've spent what they have, they expect to get more the same way."

"But they can get killed."

"Most of them do, sooner or later, but there's nothing you can do to make most of them take up a decent job. It's not merely the only way they know to get money. They actually despise people who work for a living."

"But you can't go after them by yourself. There's bound to be several of them." She had to think of something to stop him. If outlaws could get killed, Lucas could too.

"Eight to be exact, and I do have to go by myself. I'm not trying to catch them, just find out where they are."

"You're just trying to make me feel better." Lucas took her in his arms.

"No, I'm not. It wouldn't do me any good to catch them now. There's no way I can prove they stole the gold unless I find them with it, and they're bound to have hidden it somewhere long ago. I want to find their hideout, try to figure out what they intend to do, and then catch them when they try to rob the stage."

"You promise that's all you'll do? You will be careful, won't you?"

"You sound like you're actually worried about what might happen to me."

"Of course I am, you idiot," Carrie said. Lucas had never thought he would like hearing himself called an idiot, but when Carrie said it that way, it sounded like a caress.

"I couldn't have told it from the way you acted yesterday."

"You know exactly what I was doing and why," Carrie said, too desperate and upset to pretend she didn't know what he was talking about. "You were trying to coddle me and I wasn't going to have any of it, but this isn't the same thing. Wouldn't those men shoot you if they thought you were going to spoil their plans?" Lucas nodded his head. "That makes it altogether different. I don't want you to go. I'm sorry if the company is losing its gold, but they can always find some more. Where are they going to find another one of you if those villains decide to shoot you full of holes?"

Lucas held her tightly and kissed her hard on the mouth. "I'll take very good care of myself. I have a debt to collect."

"What are you talking about?"

"You owe me for treating me so abominably yesterday after I went to the trouble of looking for you. I mean to collect this very evening."

"And just what might you mean to collect?"

"We can decide that later."

"Don't start making too many plans. After all, I have to be consulted in this, you know."

"I know, and I plan to consult you quite thoroughly."

Carrie felt a shiver of desire race through her, and she clung a little tighter. "Do you really have to go?"

"Yes, and you are not to follow me under any circumstances."

"Lucas Barrow, I thought we had already decided—"

"This has nothing to do with me trying to coddle you. I don't know what I'll be walking into. I may not find anybody, or I may find the whole gang, but I'll need by whole concentration on what I'm doing. If you were somewhere about, I wouldn't be able to think for worrying about you. The most dangerous thing you could do would be to follow me. One of us would be bound to be seen, and they would be sure of getting both of us if they had one."

"This really is that dangerous then?" she asked, realizing fully for the first time what he might be facing.

"Deadly dangerous, but that's all the more reason you

should stay close to the station. If they did find me, they wouldn't have any reason to suspect me. I'm just a wrangler looking for a way to earn some extra money, but you work for the company, and they would know you wouldn't have any reason to be that far from the station unless you were looking for them." Carrie felt a cold chill. She had been told about the dangers of the frontier many times before, but they had never seemed very real to her until now.

"I promise I will wait here, but you've got to promise me you won't do any more than try to find where they are hiding. I don't want you attempting to capture them or sneaking into their camp and pretending you want to become one of them so you can learn their plans." Lucas grinned sheepishly. "I know, that's just the kind of thing you think would be very clever, but if you find them, I want you to come right back here. I'll write the company and tell them to send somebody else to go after these men."

"You really don't want me to get hurt, do you?"

"Sometimes men can be remarkably thickheaded," Carrie said, worry making the tone of her voice sharper than she meant.

"Men are no different from women," Lucas assured her. "I want to hear you say you love me just as much as you want me to say it to you."

"Then say it, you blockhead, and maybe I will."

"I love you, Carrie, alias Carolina Marsena Terwillinger, alias Mrs. Robert Simpson. I love everything about you from the tip of your rioting copper curls to the bottom of your tiny feet, and I intend to go on loving you for a long time yet. You're such a thin-skinned, sharp-tongue virago I haven't had much chance to either tell you or show you that I love you, but I plan to start doing so the minute I get back."

"And I love you too, you narrow-minded, egotistical medieval overlord, and I just might pull in my horns long enough to let you show me. When I first saw you, I thought you were different, but you're just like every other man I've ever known. Still I love you anyway. I guess I'm going to have to figure out some way to put up with you because I'm finding it harder and harder to think about giving you up."

"You mean you'll—"

"I'm not making any promises about anything past tonight. Every time you start ordering me around, I remember that you're exactly the kind of man I swore I'd never have anything to do with, but every time I see you, I forget all about my vows. I'm much more weak minded than I ever thought, but I'm not so stupid as to ignore the fact that the things we want are exactly opposite of each other."

"I don't think we're all that far apart, not really. I'm sure you'll find I'm not so terrible."

"I never thought you were terrible," said Carrie, remembering the wonderful feeling of being in his arms. "You're just impossible. Please, Lucas, don't push me toward anything. I love you as I never thought I could love anyone, but I've endured life with my father and brothers and I know that love isn't always enough. It's easy to fall in love—I did it without even knowing it was happening—but there are so many things that go into making a loving relationship into a successful marriage it scares me. I don't want to end up being constantly angry with you or at cross-purposes. That would kill everything we have to share before it has a chance to grow into something wonderfully warm and permanent. I want to *know* I will want to live with you as much thirty years from now as I do today."

"You don't have to worry about thirty years from now," Lucas said, impatient at her reluctance to listen to his persuasion. "After living with you for thirty years, how could I help but love you even more than I do now?"

"It won't be as easy to love me after the children have grown up and you realize you have to look at the same old wrinkled face across the breakfast table for the rest of your life."

"I'll love them because they're your wrinkles."

"That's an absurdly foolish thing for a grown man to say."

"Is it any more absurd to say that I love your red hair and crazy temper because they're yours? Or that I don't like

251

your taste in shoes, but that I don't care because I love the rest of you too much for it to matter?"

"That's not the same thing."

"Yes it is, or it's close enough that it doesn't matter. Why are you always discounting the power of love? Don't you believe it can overcome our differences?"

"I guess it can if it's strong enough."

"Are you saying my love for you isn't strong?"

"Of course not," Carrie snapped, feeling cornered, "but marriage is forever. I would rather live out my days alone rather than have to face you across the table each day and see your eyes grow cold when they rest on me, your body draw back when I pass, have you stay away from home rather than spend time with me."

"But you know I would never do that."

"Lucas my love, you may not intend to do any of those things, but if I can't bring to the marriage what you want and need, then you will ultimately be unable to help yourself. You will fall out of love just as inevitably as you fell in love, and it will happen whether you want it to or not."

"You've got to be the most unromantic woman in the world," Lucas said, trying to banish some of the seriousness of her mood. "Here I am, a fairly good example of the American male, doing his best to sweep you off your feet, swear eternal fidelity, swear to worship you forever, and all you can do is tell me love is a partnership and you're going to have wrinkles. Don't you think there's more to you than skin, hair, and eyes?"

"I know there is, but I'm scared."

"You spent too much time watching your brothers."

"I had little else to do all those years while I cooked and cleaned. But we've got to stop talking about this now. I don't want you to be worrying about it while you're out in those hills. Keep your mind on business and get back here with a whole skin."

"That's not much of an invitation to return."

"It's all you're going to get." Suddenly Carrie smiled. "If I make it too interesting, you might get distracted and end up with a bullet in your head. I don't think I would like that."

"There's no room for anything else in my head or my heart. You've filled them both."

"Get out of here. If you start thinking as silly as you're talking, you'll never make it back with a whole hide." Lucas managed to get his arms around Carrie and extract several more substantial kisses from her far from unwilling lips. In fact, he was so bemused and contented, he rode away whistling, and Carrie hoped the effect would wear off before he found any outlaws.

Chapter 18

Lucas turned into the yard of Found's cabin. It was on his way, and he decided it might be a good idea to have a look about before he went any farther. If the outlaws, or any one of the outlaws, had been using this place recently, they would have left some signs of their presence, and right now Lucas needed to know when they had been in the vicinity almost as much as where they had been.

The cabin looked deserted and forlorn in the morning sun. Lucas rode in slowly, not expecting to find anyone there but ready in case he did. He dismounted, and tying his horse to a tree, he approached the house carefully, his hand never far from his gun. A quick look about convinced him no one had used the cabin recently, and neither the back room, which had obviously been used as a bedroom, nor the loft, which was probably where Found had slept, had been used in quite some time if the abandoned field mouse nests were any indication. There was no food in the cabin either, but it was impossible to tell if the odds and ends he saw lying about belonged to Found's father or to some man who had been here since. He made a careful inspection of the ground nearest the cabin, but any tracks that might have been left had been obliterated by wind and rain.

He unexpectedly found a shed behind a large rock outcropping; he was even more surprised to find signs that it had been occupied recently, within the last week if he could judge by the droppings. The graves in the front yard were much older than that. Someone had been here, and it wasn't Found. A brief inspection of the surrounding canyon walls turned up a small cave which had clearly been occupied off and on over a long period of time. From the old clothes and other discarded items, Lucas gathered the occupant had been Found but that this was no casual playground. It had been used recently, at the same time the horse had been stabled in the shed, Lucas guessed. Whoever he was, Found felt he had reason to stay out of sight. Lucas decided to go over the cabin again, but he found nothing to shed new light on the situation. Clearly, the cabin had not been used as a hideout for the whole gang. No more than one or two men had stayed there, and then only briefly, probably even less than a day.

Lucas got back in the saddle and headed back up the canyon at a trot. He had spent much more time at the cabin than he had intended, and he would have to hurry if he was to reach the canyon Found had indicated and return that night.

The hidden canyon was not many miles from the station, but the terrain was extremely difficult and Lucas found he was unable to travel quickly. There were times when he had to retrace his steps, a promising trail leading to a boxed canyon or a trail only a deer could negotiate. The hills were heavily wooded with spruce and aspen, and at times it was difficult to get through or see where he was going. Lucas was unfamiliar with the area, and he lost valuable time picking his way between the ridges and through canyons that stood in his path. Soon it was well into the afternoon, and he realized he might have to spend the night in the hills. It would be dangerous to retrace his route in the dark, but maybe he could find an easier way in, the one the outlaws took *into* their hideout.

Lucas would never have been able to identify the canyon when he came to it without Found's map. The ground was very rocky and the few hoofprints the outlaws had left behind had almost been eradicated. Lucas unholstered his gun and walked his horse forward very slowly, keeping his eyes and ears open to the slightest sound or movement. But if the footprints were to be believed, no one had been here for a couple of weeks, maybe even longer. The canyon curled in on itself like a giant snail's shell, and Lucas could soon see why it was such an excellent hideout. Every step he took seemed to bring him to the end of a boxed canyon, but as he approached what looked like a flat wall, it would curve around to the left. It was unlikely that anyone who didn't know the canyon would even bother to go to the end.

After winding around for nearly a hundred yards, Lucas came to a large opening in the rock formation that contained the canyon. It formed a tiny valley with enough grass and water to keep a few horses fed for several days. Unless it could be approached from the top of the mesa, this was a perfect hideout, completely hidden and impossible to attack. It was an ideal spot for the outlaws to wait until the stage came through and again after the holdup until the hunt had been called off. Lucas wouldn't know until he checked it out, but he guessed that one of the trails leaving the canyon would take him close to the route the stage would take after it left Green Run Pass.

Lucas inspected the canyon closely, but the campfires and the droppings of the horses confirmed his suspicion that no one had been here for several weeks. There was no reason to stay and he headed his horse out of the canyon, but he couldn't help looking up at the canyon walls. They rose almost vertically for a hundred feet or more to the floor of the mesa above. If it was possible to reach the top, he could observe the outlaws with almost no risk of being seen himself. With a little luck, he might even be able to overhear some of their plans.

He reached the canyon entrance and continued on to the north beyond the canyon. He inspected each rock face and canyon he passed, but none offered a way to the top. He reviewed the route he had traveled to reach the canyon, and he was certain none of them offered a route to the top either. He continued north for another hour, checking on each likely spot until he came upon some deer tracks leading to what appeared to be another unscalable canyon wall. But this canyon, too, made an unsuspected turn to the right, and Lucas found himself in a part of the canyon where the walls must have been made of softer rock. The rim was much decayed, and he was able to make out the faint footprints leading between the boulders going upward. Lucas followed this for a short while until the trail narrowed and there was barely room for Lucas himself to continue. He left his horse on a wide ledge, and in a few minutes he found himself standing on the grass-covered top of a mesa deeply scarred by the many canyons that had been carved from it. Even on foot, it was a rather short trip to a spot where he could overlook the hideout. He would be able to come here every few days or so to see if the outlaws had returned. He intended to set a trap for them.

Carrie eyed the neatly dressed man with dislike. She didn't like having a stranger from the company office in Denver descend upon her station without warning, but she resented even more deeply the fact that he was obviously not prepared to trust her with the reason for his visit. To top it all off, he had refused to tell her why it was necessary for him to wait on the station porch until Lucas returned. From the way he was acting, you'd think Lucas was his boss instead of the other way around.

Lucas was the other and more serious cause of her irritability. She had expected him back before supper, but it had gotten dark half an hour ago, and he still hadn't returned. Carrie had worked hard all day to keep her mind off what Lucas was doing and what could be happening to him, and then this man arrived, determined not to leave until he had seen Lucas. With his presence as a constant reminder, Carrie was painfully aware of Lucas's absence and the slow passing of the hours.

"Didn't you tell me you expected Mr. Barrow to return before six o'clock?" the man who had identified himself only as Mr. Anderson asked. He had refused to wait inside the station, and had to leave his self-appointed position on the porch to come inside where Carrie and Katie were finishing up the last of the dishes.

"I said I *thought* he would be back by then," Carrie responded shortly, "but I didn't promise anything. Mr. Barrow is not an employee of this station, and I'm not responsible for his whereabouts or the schedule he keeps."

"But I've got to talk to him as soon as possible," the man insisted. Just as though his insisting would make Lucas appear, thought Carrie to herself.

"Then set yourself back down on that porch," Katie said, not mincing words. "You won't be missing him when he comes for his supper, and you won't be putting yourself in the way of our work getting done either."

"I would like some coffee, if you don't mind."

"There be the pot," Katie said, indicating the large blue porcelain coffee pot on the stove. "I expect your ma taught you how to pour."

"You were a little hard on him, weren't you?" Carrie commented after Mr. Anderson had filled his cup and gone back outside.

"I don't like clerks who act uppity, and that man's a clerk if ever I saw one. He just thinks because we be ladies he can act self-important, but he's hooked the wrong bull this time."

Carrie smiled absently at Katie's response, but her mind was consumed with worry over Lucas. She had made him promise not to tackle the outlaws by himself, but he was no more likely to abide by his promises than she was, she admitted ruefully. If he thought he had the least chance of ending this now, she knew he wouldn't hesitate. She doubted that the fact there were eight of them and only one of him would change his mind. That man was as stubborn as he was irresistible.

She tried not to picture him too vividly in her mind—it clouded her judgment, and she desperately needed to keep her head about her. She knew she was growing more deeply in love with Lucas every day, but she wasn't one step closer to agreeing to marry him. And she knew that no matter how much discomfort that caused her now, it was nothing to the agony it could cause her in the future. She had been a fool to allow herself to fall in love with a man she wasn't sure she could marry, but it was too late to tell herself that now.

She also tried not to remember his invitation for that evening, an invitation her body was all too ready to accept. Even now she could feel his hands on her body, feel the warmth of his skin against her breasts, feel the heat of him inside her. It made her almost too weak to stand. She could see his marvelously sculpted torso, the deeply tanned skin smooth and taut over firm flesh, his wonderfully defined muscles moving effortlessly, and she was filled with a longing to be back in his arms. The vivid memory of his hungry kisses was interrupted by the sound of an arrival outside, and Carrie heard Lucas's deep, rumbling voice as he addressed the man who was waiting for him.

"What are you doing here, Harry? I didn't think Uncle Max could get along without you," Carrie heard Lucas call out in happy greeting. She had to remind herself of the pot she still held in her hand, as well as that disagreeable stranger, to keep from rushing outside to meet him.

"It's your uncle I've come to see you about."

"Well, come on inside. You can have another cup of coffee while I eat my dinner." Carrie forced herself to move toward Lucas and greet him as she would any other working acquaintance, but Lucas had other ideas. He strode into the kitchen and swept her up in a hot and eager embrace. The fact that both Kate and Harry stared at them with open mouths didn't seem to bother him in the least. After a split second's consideration, Carrie decided it didn't bother her either.

259

"I want you to meet Carrie Simpson," Lucas said when he returned Carrie, breathless and blushing, to her own feet. "I've been trying to talk her into becoming my wife, but she's still holding out."

"Faith and begor!" exclaimed Katie, who threw the dish in her hands up in the air without the slightest regard for where it would come down or the dangerous fragments to which it was speedily reduced. "You never said a word to me, and all the while I be watching for just such a sign."

"I haven't had time to think it over," Carrie muttered, her mind scrambling wildly for some plausible excuse. "He just asked me."

"You don't waste time thinking when a presentable man asks you to become his bride. You take him up afore he has the chance to change his mind."

"Maybe you should talk to her, Katie," Lucas said, teasing Carrie. "She won't listen to me."

"I won't listen to either of you until your supper is on the table and Mr. Anderson has a chance to tell you what he's been waiting half the day to say," Carrie said, briskly moving to lay the table while Katie started filling a plate from the pots that were being kept warm on the stove. Mr. Anderson had not eaten earlier—he had insisted on waiting until Lucas returned—so Katie filled a second plate for him.

"Katie and I will leave you to your dinner," Carrie said when both of them had been served. "The coffee is on the stove. Just put the dishes in the sink and make sure the fire's out. Good night, Mr. Anderson. You can have your choice of the rooms at the back of the station." Lucas glanced up, his mouth full and his eyes questioning. "I'll be at the cabin if you need anything," Carrie added, unable to leave the question in his eyes unanswered.

The two men ate in silence. Only when they had each finished two slices of apple pie did they attempt to share their news with each other.

"I've located the Staples gang's hideout," Lucas said.

"They haven't been there for some time, but I expect they'll return about the time the shipment's due. I just wish I knew how they find out when the gold is scheduled to go out."

"Your uncle is certain someone inside the company is selling information, but that's not why I'm here. You have to come back to Denver with me."

"I can't go until after the shipment, in two weeks."

"He won't be alive if you wait that long." Lucas paused in the act of taking a sip from his coffee, his eyes locked with Harry's.

"He's dying then?" he asked simply.

"Yes, and he knows it. You're all he has, and even though I know he would never tell you this, he would rather lose that gold shipment than die without seeing you again. I know he's been hard on you, but he loves you."

"Hell, he's been hard on everybody his whole life," Lucas said, trying to control the emotion that threatened to choke the words in his throat. "If he hadn't been tough on me too, I'd have thought he didn't like me." They sat in silence for several moments, Lucas remembering the man whose larger-than-life personality had shaped the years of his youth and early maturity.

"How much longer does he have?"

"We ought to leave with the first stage in the morning."

"I'll leave at daylight on horseback. I have an extra mount if you want to come with me."

The older man smiled. "There's nothing about me that lends itself to being astride a horse."

"There are times when I wonder how you ever managed to survive out here, or why you even tried."

"Your uncle is the only one who could have gotten me out here or pulled me through. Now if you have no objection, I'm going to make use of that bed Mrs. Simpson offered me." He paused and studied Lucas with added concentration. "Did you mean what you said earlier, about asking her to be your wife?"

"Yes, but she hasn't agreed yet."

261

"A widow, mmmh. Does she know who you are?"

"She's not a widow, and she doesn't know who I am." Anderson's eyebrows rose in question, and Lucas chuckled. "Her fiancé died before they could be married. She knew the company wouldn't allow her to take over the station in her own name, so she came out here, told everyone she was married, and that her husband would follow in a few days."

"Rather enterprising young woman. Quite nice-looking too. I think your uncle would approve." Lucas gave a shout of laughter.

"They'd fight like dogs for the first five years and end up being crazy about each other." He suddenly sobered. "At least they would if they could have had the chance." He stood up abruptly and emptied his coffee cup in the sink. "I'll see you in the morning. I've got things to do before I go to bed."

But Lucas paused on the porch steps. He had known his uncle was dying, but now he realized he had never faced the reality of his death. Somehow he had always assumed it would be sometime, but never now. He supposed it was because Max Barrow was the only relative he had left in the world. Oh, he supposed there were some kinfolk left in Texas — his mother had brothers and sisters after all — but he didn't know them and they might as well not exist for all he felt a part of them. Carrie was the only family he had left now.

He started toward the cabin. It was odd that even though she had not yet agreed to marry him, he already thought of her as part of his family. And he was right about Uncle Max. He would not approve of Carrie and her newfangled ideas about female independence. He was a firm believer in the superiority of men, and just as firm a believer that a woman's one and only place was in the home. Maybe it was because he'd been familiar with so many whores and saloon floozies, but Uncle Max would not compromise on what he saw as the rightful sphere for a proper lady.

When Harry told him his uncle was dying, Lucas

thought briefly of taking Carrie to Denver with him, but he had just as quickly cast it aside. Neither of them was likely to sit quietly and keep his opinion to himself, especially his uncle. And once Uncle Max had had his say, Carrie was bound to let him know that *she* thought, and then the fat would be in the fire. It would end with Lucas having to take sides, and that was something he could not do. As sad as it was, the two most important people in his life could never meet.

His step quickened when he saw Carrie waiting for him on the porch.

"Bad news?" she asked apprehensively. She had known from the beginning it would be.

"My uncle is dying. I have to leave for Denver first thing in the morning."

"When will you be back?" What she wanted to ask was *would* he be back.

"I don't know. Harry says Uncle Max can't last more than two weeks."

"Two weeks!" Carrie hadn't meant to sound so upset; it just popped out of her mouth.

"I don't know, but I will have to stay until . . ." Lucas left the sentence unfinished.

"I understand," Carrie said, forcing a smile on her face in an attempt to banish the feeling of dismay. "It's just that I didn't expect it. You never told me anything about your uncle."

"I didn't realize his illness was so serious until Harry told me."

"Who is Harry anyway?" Carrie asked, remembering her irritation of the day. "The way he acted, you'd think he was the personal assistant to the owner of some big company."

"That's just his way," Lucas said evasively. "No one could ever figure out why he left St. Louis."

"Someone else escaping his murky past?" Lucas laughed so loud Carrie had to hush him. "Be quiet, or you'll wake Katie."

"Then let's move away from the door," Lucas said, ushering Carrie down the steps and toward his cabin.

"If you're leaving at dawn, you ought to get to bed," Carrie said, making a halfhearted attempt to stop at the bottom of the steps. Her whole being was tense and overwrought because of Lucas's presence and his going away. She didn't know how long it might be before she saw him again, and her body stiffened in protest.

"Not before I get an answer from you, young woman," Lucas said, making sure that Carrie kept moving toward his cabin.

"You haven't asked me properly," Carrie retorted, and stopped again in the middle of the path. "How dare you ask me to marry you by telling your Mr. Anderson that you had *already* asked me to marry you?"

"What was I supposed to do, tell him to go outside and wait?" Lucas said, starting Carrie moving again. Just the feel of her in the circle of his arm was enraging his senses, making them wildly impatient to have all of her to himself.

"You didn't have to tell him anything," Carrie said, aware that Lucas was irresistibly maneuvering her toward his cabin, and knowing too that she wasn't offering much resistance. "Besides, I told you I hadn't made up my mind."

"But that was yesterday."

"Do you think I am some sort of weather vane that I can change my mind so quickly?" Lucas tightened his circle of his arms and Carrie almost lost the thread of their conversation.

"I don't want you to change, just make up your mind," Lucas said, drawing her body against his so that they touched from shoulder to hip to thigh as they continued along the path under the brilliant moonlight.

"I don't think we should do anything until you come back from Denver," Carrie said, aware that she was at last squarely facing the expectation that she would spend her future with Lucas, aware that with him so close it seemed impossible to do anything else. "Your uncle's death may

264

change everything."

"Nothing will change my love for you," Lucas said, and Carrie felt her heart swell with happiness. "When Harry told me Uncle Max was dying, the first thing I thought about was taking you to Denver to meet him."

"I don't think that's a good idea," Carrie began, suddenly terribly nervous.

"Neither do I. He wouldn't understand you. Hell, I don't understand you half the time, even after you explain what you mean, and I love you."

"I told you before, loving me is not enough."

"Maybe not, but the more I love you, the more I *want* to understand. I want you to be my wife, and I don't want to spend the rest of my life with someone I don't understand."

Carrie leaned against Lucas as they walked, aware of the feel of his thigh against hers, of his hand curving just under her bosom. The nearness of his body excited her, and she was startled to find the thought that he would always be near equally thrilling. Rather in awe of what was happening to her, she wondered if Lucas could have such a profound effect on her already, what might happen in the long years ahead?

The prospect made her shiver with anticipation, a feeling that Lucas took to be anticipation of a different nature. The long days he had spent away from her had whetted and teased his appetite for her company, but the feel of her body in his arms had roused his physical desire to a warlike pitch, and he felt as though he would explode if he had to restrain himself much longer.

Carrie had never seen such a brilliant night. The sky seemed to be filled with stars which shone uncommonly bright in the clear, thin air of the Rocky Mountains. The moonlight bathed the hills in a shimmering pale glow and turned everything into a glittering, almost magical fairyland that transported Carrie from the world of ordinary mortals into a realm occupied by Lucas and herself alone, a realm completely removed from the mundane considerations that made ordinary living so difficult, a realm where two people could think of nothing but what they meant to each other.

Suddenly Carrie felt almost overwhelmed by her love for this man who walked at her side, this man who struggled against a lifetime of experiences to understand her, this man whose love and devotion had not wavered no matter how much she struggled against him. And she knew without asking that no matter what she did, he would always be there, waiting for her to stop fighting her past, longing to hold her in his arms, wanting her by his side forever. Why had she ever doubted that he embodied everything she longed for? Why was she perversely running away from the very thing she most wanted to run toward? Was her relentless struggle to achieve her independence going to condemn her to a lonely and solitary future?

"Hold me, Lucas," she pleaded, suddenly turning to him and putting both her arms around him. "Hold me tight."

"What's wrong?" Lucas asked, more than willing to enfold her in his arms but unable to understand the hard edge of alarm in her voice.

"I'm afraid."

"What of?"

"Myself."

"That doesn't make any sense."

"I'm afraid of what I might do that I can't help, that I'll do something I don't want to do. My daddy used to say I was my own worst enemy, and I never understood what he meant until now."

"Listen to me," Lucas said, pausing on the path only a few yards from his cabin, gripping her shoulders, and turning her to face him. "All you need is time to sort things out in your mind, and you'll have plenty of it while I'm in Denver. In the meantime, I want you to concentrate on me. Don't think about the future and don't think about the past. Just think about how much I love you and how much I'm going to miss you while I'm away. I never knew it could be so hard to leave you, but if my uncle weren't dying right now, there's nothing this side of heaven that would get me to go to Denver."

Carrie slipped out of his grasp and into his embrace. "I don't want you to leave either. It seems you just got back from going after those mustangs, and I never thought I could miss anybody so much in my life. It's going to be worse this time."

"It's going to be better," Lucas said, guiding her up the steps and into the cabin as he talked. "You're going to marry me as soon as it can be arranged, so you can pass the time planning your wedding, deciding what kind of dress you want, and designing a house big enough for at least six children. Do you realize I haven't lived in a real house since I was six?" Lucas said, ignoring Carrie's strangled protest at the mention of six children.

"*You* can spend your time thinking about houses and children," Carrie said as Lucas pulled her back when she would have lighted the single lantern suspended from the center of the ceiling. "I'm going to spend my time thinking about one stubborn, ruthless, rather wonderful wrangler. I want to know if I will be just as contented to stand in his arms in the dark as I am now."

"Ask yourself whether you'll be just as anxious to wake up with his face on the pillow next to yours. Because that's just about all I can think of now. Having you in my arms, your body against mine, is driving me crazy."

"Is there an antidote?" Carrie asked, her voice sinking into a whisper.

"Only one," Lucas replied, and his lips sank to hers in a hot, hungry kiss. "But I've got to see you," he said, pulling her into the bedroom and taking down the small lantern that hung from the ceiling. "I will always want to see you when I make love to you." The lamp was quickly lighted. "Do you know what your hair looks like in the light?"

"No," Carrie whispered, her lips nuzzling his neck, her whole body pressed tightly against his.

"I saw a forest fire at night once, the flames leaping brilliantly against the black of night, their light creating an aura around them. That's what your hair reminds me of, tongues of dancing flame."

"What about the rest of me?" Carrie said, urging him to continue. "I'm more than a head of hair, you know."

"Oh, I know," Lucas answered, and his body moved against hers meaningfully. "I could spend hours describing you. I have spent hours thinking about you every day."

"I can think of better ways to spend the time," Carrie said, and standing on her tiptoes, pulled his head down until his lips touched hers in a tender kiss which increased in intensity as it lasted longer and longer. Lucas's hands moved over her back, down her sides, and then upward to cover her breasts. Carrie's whole body shivered in anticipation and she pressed herself ever more firmly against the hardness of him.

Carrie pulled away enough so she could unbutton Lucas's shirt and run her hands through the slight covering of soft hair on his chest. Then she pulled his shirt out of his pants and slid her hands across the bare skin of his back. Lucas's hands slipped from her breasts to her buttocks and pressed her hard against him, driving a moan from deep in his throat.

"I want you," he muttered finally. "By God, I want you so much it hurts." With swift, numble fingers, he undid the buttons and the back of her dress and dropped that garment to the floor. While Carrie struggled to rid him of his shirt, he unlaced her petticoat and she was left standing in her shift. That was soon gotten rid of. "You're beautiful, you know," Lucas said, gazing at her in wonder. "You're the most beautiful sight in the whole world." The buckle of his belt dug deep into her soft flesh as he pressed her against him once more, covering her face, neck, and shoulders with an avalanche of torrid kisses. Then sweeping her up in his arms, he gently lowered her to the bed.

"If you're thinking of joining me," Carrie said, provocatively making room for him, "you're going to have to do something about that belt. It nearly disemboweled me."

"Gladly," Lucas returned with a grin that had too much hunger, too much need in it, to have any room left for humor. He stifled a sigh of relief as he undressed and lowered his body on to the bed next to her.

"I thought of this moment at least once every minute for the last week," Lucas said as he buried his face in her bosom. "It drove me so crazy I almost came back without the mustangs."

"Don't talk anymore," Carrie whispered, desire making her voice husky. "Just make love to me. Make me believe you will love me forever as much as you love me tonight."

Lucas did not need a second invitation. He cupped Carrie's firm breasts with his hands and then tortured their ruby nipples, first with his fingertips and then with his hot, moist tongue. When her body began to writhe under his touch, his right hand relinquished its hold on Carrie's left breast to his fevered lips and snaked down her side, over the mound between her legs, and into her silken heat. Carrie's body arched convulsively at the invasion, then responded to his expert stroking by growing ever more impatient to gain relief from the gnawing need that was building within her.

"Please," she murmured as her own burgeoning desire began to block out her consciousness of everything else. When Lucas ignored her pleas, she roughly drew his body down to press against her sensitive breasts, and throwing her limbs around him, she attempted to draw him within her body. Almost at once, she felt Lucas's manhood thrust between her legs and she opened her body to receive him, shuddering with relief and heightened tension as he sank deep within her.

Immediately Lucas moved into a smooth, even rhythm and in minutes Carrie's whole body was screaming for release. Higher and higher, faster and faster Lucas drove her until she thought she would cry out.

Then Lucas seemed to stiffen and his movements became less smooth and controlled. Carrie could hear his breath begin to rasp in his throat, could sense the tensing of his body as he was held ever more firmly in the jaws of his own raging desire. Responding to his body, Carrie, too, tensed, awaiting the explosion that would bring with it fulfillment.

No longer attempting to control the pace of their lovemaking, Lucas drove deep into Carrie's body, barely conscious of anything beyond his own blissful torment. His muscles gathered and bunched, and with one final powerful thrust, he flung himself at Carrie and the built-up tension burst all about them, causing their bodies to lock together until their limbs were as tightly entwined as their souls.

Chapter 19

It had been the longest week of Carrie's life. His horse saddled and ready to go, Lucas had awakened her just before he left. "I didn't dare wake you earlier," he had admitted as he took her into his arms, "or I might not have been able to tear myself away." He had kissed her swiftly while she was still asleep and was gone before she was awake.

The last seven days had taught her what loneliness was. Stages had come and gone, meals had been prepared and dishes washed, and decisions had been made and orders given, but she moved through her daily routine hardly aware of what she did. Jake and Katie made sure that one of them was with her most of the time. Even Found came by to check on her. Several times each day she would look up from what she was doing to find his big brown eyes staring at her, wide with curiosity. His was an open gaze, but somehow those soft, innocent eyes made her feel that Found understood and sympathized with her loneliness. She guessed Katie and Jake understood too. All of them were alone. The only family they had was each other, and Lucas's absence seemed to pull them closer together.

In the middle of the afternoon of the eighth day, the front door of the station burst open and Katie's terrified shriek brought Carrie out of her mental paralysis.

Jake, his hands clutching a bloody wound in his side, was roughly shoved into the room by a man Carrie had never seen. Jake sank into the nearest chair as the man staggered over to the table, leaned on it for support, and pointed a rifle at them. His leg appeared to be badly wounded, but the light of desperation in his eyes warned Carrie that it was going to make him more dangerous rather than less.

"Don't anybody do anything foolish, or I'll finish killing this here fool," the man threatened, his teeth showing surprisingly strong and white. "They can't hang me no higher for two murders than they can for one."

Murder! This man was a killer, Carrie realized in stunned disbelief, and he would probably kill her or Katie just as soon as he would Jake. He was not an unattractive man, but he was unshaven, unkempt, and looked as if he might be flushed with fever.

"What do you want?" Carrie asked, struggling to keep her voice steady and not show the terror that filled her mind.

"Food, and something to bind up this leg. I also want a horse. Mine is finished." Katie had been standing immobile since they entered, but now she suddenly came to life and ran to where Jake sat slumped in the chair.

"Get away from him, or I'll put a bullet between his eyes. Then you won't have no cause to worry over him." Katie stopped in midstride, unable to move backward or forward, her eyes still on the blood dripping from Jake's side.

"Can't you see he's bleeding?" Carrie demanded, unable to believe what was happening. "His wound must be cleansed and bandaged before he loses any more blood."

"I ought to know how much he's bleeding. It was my knife that was nearly stuck in his heart."

"You did this!" Carrie exclaimed, though she didn't know why she hadn't known it immediately. "Why?"

"He had some foolish notion about warning you I was about."

"Well of course he would," replied Carrie, recovering sufficiently from her shock to move to the drawer where they kept the clean towels. "He works for me. It's his job to warn me of intruders."

"Get away from that drawer, lady, or I'll shoot you!" the

intruder warned, and fired a shot into the wood floor at Carrie's feet.

Carrie had been badly frightened when the man burst into the station and she saw what he had done to Jake and realized what he might do to all of them, but when he shot into the floor, *her* floor, anger washed over her like rushing floodwater. She whipped around to face the killer, her fearless gaze challenging his, her body held proudly erect. "You would shoot a woman in the back?" Scorn sounded loud in her voice. "I was led to believe that Western men respected women, that at the very least they were honorable, not cowards and bullies." Right away Carrie knew she had said the right thing. The man was angry and in considerable pain, but he had pride and Carrie could see it stiffen his trembling body.

"I'd kill any man who said half of what you said to me, lady, but I've never harmed a woman in my life."

"Considering the direction in which your rifle is pointed, you can't expect me to believe that." She had to think, to outmaneuver him. Jake was wounded and Katie was petrified by fear. It was up to her to get them out of this situation.

"I didn't want you to get no clever notions about doing something fancy."

"What kind of fools do you normally point your rifle at? I wouldn't attempt to reach for a gun when you were already pointing one at me."

"You were reaching into that drawer . . ."

"I have towels in here which I need to clean Jake's wound, and I intend to get them. You can watch me closely if you like, and you have my permission to shoot me if I attempt to pull out a gun."

"Don't touch that drawer," the stranger threatened.

"If you're going to shoot me anyway, I might as well die trying to be useful." Carrie didn't know what drove her to defy this man. He was clearly desperate and he was also in great pain. There was no way of knowing what he would

273

do. She turned her back on him and carefully opened the drawer, but she moved so the killer could get a good view of its contents. "You can see it's only towels." Carrie removed several and handed them to the still immobile Katie. Katie looked from Carrie to the killer, unable to make her limbs move, certain he would kill her if she moved a single step without his permission.

"Go on and clean him up," the man growled. "Just make sure you don't do nothing stupid." Katie rushed to Jake's side and pulled away his hands. It was difficult to tell how badly he was cut because of the blood and the torn shirt.

"Strip him to the waist," Carrie ordered, "while I get some water." For the next several minutes both ladies were busy until the wound had been cleaned well enough for Carrie to see it wasn't serious.

"It's just a cut across his ribs," Katie said at last. "It's not a bad thing at all."

"If he hadn't been so quick on his feet, it'd be serious enough," the man said. "I mean for people to do what I say."

"And what is it you want us to do?" demanded Carrie.

"Give me some food and a horse."

"You're welcome to any food we have. I won't see any man go hungry, even a murderer."

"I'm not a murderer," the man stated with sudden vehemence.

"But you said—"

"I said they couldn't hang me no higher for two murders than for one. I didn't say I'd done the one."

Carrie paused, her curiosity and sympathy engaged. If this man wasn't a killer, then why was he threatening them? "Why don't you have a seat at the table, Mr.—"

"The name's Butler, Sam Butler. I suppose you've heard of me."

"No, I can't say I have," Carrie told him as she moved to take food out of the pantry and lay the table.

"You be careful with those pots and pans, ma'am. You suddenly show up with a gun in your hands and your friends are going to die first."

Carrie turned to face him. She was completely calm now. "It's clear *you* haven't heard of *me*. If I pick up a gun, *you* will be the one to die."

"She can do it too," Jake said, grimacing with pain as Katie began to bind the open wound. "She can shoot the ash off a cigar and never touch the fire." Sam eyed Carrie in disbelief. Her back was turned to him as she worked at the stove, but she showed no evidence of the fear his presence usually evoked in people. He didn't believe she could shoot the way Jake said, but this woman was different somehow. He had better keep an eye on her.

"I have plenty of food I can serve you here, but I don't have much you can take with you," Carrie said to Sam as she placed a plate in front of him. "Suppose I tell you what I have, and you tell me what you can use."

"Suppose you just sit down over there," said Sam, wondering why this woman wasn't afraid of him. He had looked over the whole station before he jumped Jake, and there was no one about, but she acted as though half the United States Army would be at her door in two minutes. "You just sit real still while I eat. I get jumpy when I'm eating."

"You probably have extremely poor digestion from eating badly prepared food in too great a hurry," Carrie suggested. "You should take more time over your meals."

Sam looked as if he trusted Carrie less and less every minute, but she poured out two cups of coffee, checked to see if Katie needed any help, then calmly sat down at the table across from him.

Sam ate slowly at first, keeping his eye firmly fixed on Carrie, but the excellent food began to work on him, and before long his attention was evenly divided between Carrie and his plate.

"Now suppose you tell me what this is all about," Carrie said as she handed him a piece of pie and refilled his coffee cup. "Surely you don't make a practice of holding people hostage and stealing food they would have been happy to give you quite freely."

"I don't make a practice of holding nobody hostage, and I don't steal nothing neither," Sam said angrily. "I don't say I ain't come mighty close to the edge from time to time, but I ain't killed nobody who wasn't trying to kill me first, and I ain't taken nothing from nobody I wasn't paid to take."

"I don't find that kind of slipshod morality the least bit admirable," Carrie told him frankly, "but that doesn't explain what you're doing here now and why you attacked one of my employees."

"Because of this hole in my leg," Sam said, pointing to the leg which he had stretched out awkwardly in front of him. "I didn't shoot myself."

"Who did, and why?"

"The damned sheriff from Tyler's Mountain and that posse of his. He's got it into his head that just because a man was shot dead in the street and I was in town at the time, I must have been the one to shoot him."

"There's either more to it than that, or you're lying to me," Carrie said bluntly, her gaze unwavering. Sam blinked in surprise, looked like he didn't quite know how to proceed next, and then decided to trust Carrie with the truth.

"We'd had an argument earlier, that fella and me, in the saloon, and I told him I'd kill him if he ever crossed me again. But I went to get something to eat after that, and I never even thought of him again until they burst into Carla's room thinking they'd find me with my pants off and be able to take me easy."

"You were in . . ." Carrie couldn't put it into words.

"Yes, ma'am, I was, but I was just visiting. Carla's a friend from back home in Indiana. And it's a damned good thing she is, or I'd never have gotten out that window, clothes or no clothes. As it was, they got me in the leg."

"And you've ridden all this distance without taking care of that wound? It might become infected."

"Lady, there's a posse on my heels, and they mean to

hang me when they find me. This leg being infected won't make no difference if I'm dead."

"But if you didn't kill that man, there can't be any witnesses. And without witnesses, there's no case against you."

"That sheriff's been wanting my hide for a long time. This is his best chance to get it, and he knows it."

"You ought to let me look at that leg. I've got some medicine over here . . ."

Carrie got up from the chair as she spoke and turned toward where Katie had laid out all their medicines as she took care of Jake. Just as she glanced up, she saw the door to the back of the station open ever so slightly and the barrel of a rifle slide silently through.

"No, Found!" she shouted. Lulled by a stomach full of good food and the fearlessness of this unusual woman, Sam had laid his rifle down while he ate his pie. It was that, along with Carrie's sudden shout, that kept anyone from being killed.

Just as Sam dived out of the chair and rolled away from the table, Found's rifle shot splintered the back of the chair where Sam had been sitting. In the seconds it took Sam to throw his body away from the chair, draw his gun, and aim toward the doorway, Carrie sped across the room, and threw herself in the line of his fire.

"Stop!" she shouted as she pulled Found from behind the door, took the rifle from his hands, and hid him behind her own body. "For God's sake, can't you see he's just a child!" Sam had already shot, but his aim was spoiled as he rolled and the bullet embedded itself in the door frame mere inches from Carrie's head.

For several seconds everyone was too numb from shock and fear to move.

"Put that rifle on the table, and I just may let the lot of you live to see tomorrow," Sam said when he stopped breathing too rapidly. "I didn't know there was anybody else here. Where the hell did you come from, kid?"

Found didn't reply, and Sam impatiently waved his gun at

Found. "I said where'd you come from?"

"He can't talk, at least he never has," Carrie explained, holding the boy even tighter and still shielding him with her body. He was probably up at Lucas's cabin checking on the horses. It's part of his job."

"Is there somebody else here I missed?" Sam demanded, wondering if he had stumbled into some kind of mirage.

"Lucas is the wrangler," Carrie told him, "but he's gone to Denver. I don't know when he'll be back. Now sit back down and finish your coffee. There's no need for you to be lying on the floor."

"Not until that rifle is on the table. I ain't taking no chance on that kid plugging me in the back."

If Carrie had believed Sam was a killer, she would have risked a shot. As it was, she laid the rifle on the table, being careful to keep Found behind her. "Found only tried to shoot you because he thought you were threatening me. I don't see how you can blame him for trying to do what you said you would do to us."

"Lady, that kid don't have a posse out after him."

"If you didn't shoot that man, you don't have to be afraid of the sheriff or his posse. You can wait here until they come, and then tell them what you've just told me."

"Can't you understand what I'm trying to tell you, lady? They don't *want* to find I'm innocent. That sheriff is the kind that likes to throw his weight around, and I'm the kind that just naturally objects to that sort of thing. Anyhow, the long and the short of it is, I embarrassed him in front of his own town a few years back, and he's been after me ever since. I ain't no outlaw, but I ain't no sissy either, and there just don't seem to be a lot of people ready to stand up for me."

"Why not?"

"Look, lady, I have a short temper, a pair of handy fists, a fast draw, and a reputation for being a tough man to tangle with. I been trying to outrun that reputation for five years now, but there's a lot of people back there who think they

278

have something against me."

"It seems to me, Mr. Butler, that it's about time you reformed your way of life. Someday one of these people is going to shoot you first. Surely you can't expect to continue tempting Fate."

"Lady, *you're* tempting Fate."

"I'm just trying to point out the absurdity of threatening four people who've never done you any harm, not to mention the cut you gave Jake."

"Let's mention it," Jake said, speaking for the first time. "It hurts bad enough."

"I've got to get out of here," Sam said, getting up from the table. But his leg collapsed under him and he stumbled to the floor. Carrie started toward him, but Sam whipped over and brought up his gun.

"No, you don't. I'm not done up yet."

"Maybe not, but you will be if you don't let me look at that leg. You know you can't ride."

"Yes I can. Just give me a few minutes."

"In the meantime, let me look at that leg."

"Lady, don't you come close to me."

"Look, if you're afraid we'll do something to you, let Katie tend to your wound and you can keep your gun on me." He looked at her as if she were crazy. "You will lose that leg if it's not attended to. How are you going to outrun that sheriff then?"

"Okay, but the first person that moves won't get six inches. And you be careful with that knife," he growled at Katie. "Make sure you cut the pants, not me."

Carrie pulled Found over to a seat next to her and sat down right in front of Sam. "Okay, Katie, we're all seated."

Katie cut away the material with painstaking care, revealing the swollen and discolored flesh. "The bullet's still inside," Katie said. "If it doesn't come out, he's liable to get blood poisoning or gangrene. Either way he'll be dead as a hare inside a week."

"It'll last until I can get out of here."

Carrie knew the only way she was going to get him to let them tend his wound was to attack his pride, and she didn't hesitate. "Don't you think Katie is capable of removing the bullet, or can't you stand the pain?" she asked, her skeptical gaze an open challenge.

"I don't have time."

"How much of a lead do you think you have on that posse?"

"Probably three or four hours."

"That's more than enough time. Jake, give me your pocketknife. I'll sterilize it while you get the whiskey. Found, you get me that lamp out of the back room. Katie's going to need more light." Sam tried to keep everyone in his sight, but it was impossible. As long as that crazy redhead was running things, there was no way he could control the situation. Well, she could get the bullet out of his leg. He'd be damned glad of it, as a matter of fact, but as soon as it was bandaged up again, he was getting on a horse and getting out of there. He'd rather face a posse than this woman.

"Give me a swig of that whiskey," he said when Jake returned with the bottle. Jake looked questioningly at Carrie, but it was Katie who answered.

"I guess it's okay for him to have some, but don't you get your hopes up. There's no bullet in you."

Carrie folded a towel and gave it to Sam to bite on, but it was no use. As soon as Katie cut into the wound, he fainted.

"He's been out for nearly an hour," Katie said, coming into the dining room from the back bedroom. "What are we going to do with him if that posse arrives?"

"You wouldn't be asking that question if it had been you he tried to cut up," Jake said irritably.

"That was a mistake, but if he's being accused of a murder he didn't commit, we've got to help him." Jake was about to mention that he failed to appreciate the distinction

280

between crimes, but he lost Carrie's attention when Found came silently into the station. "Did you hide his saddle and gear?" The boy nodded. "Do you think anybody could recognize his horse among the mustangs?" He shook his head. "Good. He ought to be safe at your parents's cabin until his leg is well. Do you think you can get him there?" Found nodded. "Okay. Now you go sit with him for a while and give Katie a rest."

"Do you think you ought to be doing this, Mrs. Simpson?" Jake asked as Found obediently headed toward the back room. "If the law is after him, they won't take kindly to your interfering."

"I don't mean for them to know that I interfered. Besides, it serves them right for trying to hang an innocent man."

"But you don't know he's innocent."

"He says he is, and I believe him."

"I do too," added Katie.

"I'm inclined to take his side, I must admit," Jake said reluctantly. "He just doesn't seem like the murdering type to me, but you can't ever tell."

"If the sheriff has proof, I suppose we can't hide him."

Found came rushing from the back room, gesturing frantically behind him. Carrie looked up in time to see Sam emerge from the doorway, walking with great difficulty, but walking nevertheless.

"Where are my guns?" he demanded, clearly uneasy without his weapons.

"They're right here," Carrie said, indicating the guns and other property spread out on the table. "Everything is here."

"You have no right to take a man's guns," Sam said. "It makes him feel naked."

"I had no intention of keeping them, but if you had been *naked* more often, maybe you wouldn't be in so much trouble."

"Ma'am, there's probably a good bit of truth in what you say, but it ain't going to help me now. I appreciate what you done for me and the way you've treated me so kindly, but

I'd better be going. I've lost too much time now. I'll just gather up my things and fetch my horse . . ."

"Let Found do that for you. We hid him for you."

"Lady, I don't understand you. Don't nobody stick his neck out for a stranger. It don't get you nothing."

"But I'm not trying to *get* anything. You were in difficulty, and I helped you. Now wait here until Found returns with your horse. He's an orphan, but his family had a cabin back in the woods . . ."

The back door burst open and Found tumbled into the room, wide-eyed and gasping for breath. He took Carrie's arm and pulled her toward the window and pointed. Carrie felt cold fear grip her heart when she saw about a dozen men riding into the station yard. It was the posse after Sam, and there was no way for him to escape.

Chapter 20

In a flash Carrie realized the posse intended to capture Sam and that he would resist arrest. There would probably be shooting, and someone might get killed. By deciding to help him, she had placed Katie, Jake, and Found in the middle of a dangerous situation, and if anything happened to one of them, it would be her fault.

"Into the cupboard," Carrie ordered, pointing to a small closet used to store her cooking staples and separated from the room by a curtain.

"He can't hide there," Jake exclaimed. "He'll be practically under their noses."

"They're going to want to search the place," Carrie said, "and I don't see why I shouldn't let them. About the only place they won't look is this room. Come on, Sam. We're almost out of time."

Sam looked at Carrie, and for a brief moment she could tell he was weighing his chance of making a run for it. Abruptly he ducked into the closet and allowed her to stack the sacks of flour and bags of sugar to cover his feet and legs. She wondered whether he had done it because he trusted her or because he had no other choice.

When the sheriff reached the station door a few moments later, Carrie and Katie were busy preparing dinner.

Jake was seated at the table drinking coffee, his shirt buttoned over the bandages, and Found was busy filling the wood box. The bloody clothes had been thrown into the wash pot out back, and Sam's rifle lay hidden on top of a cabinet. Carrie stepped out on the porch to meet the sheriff as he rode up.

"Howdy, ma'am," he said, pulling his horse to a stop without dismounting. "I'm Sheriff Tate from over Tyler's Mountain."

"What can I do for you, Sheriff?"

"I'd like to speak to the manager of this station."

"I'm Mrs. Simpson, Sheriff, and I manage the station."

"But you're a woman."

"I'm glad you noticed."

"Where is your husband?"

"Dead."

"You mean you run this place all by yourself?"

"I didn't say that. I have a stockman, a girl to help me with the cooking, and a boy for chores. We also have a wrangler who helps out when we need him."

"Lady, you shouldn't be here without a man. There's no telling what can happen to a woman alone."

"But I've just explained that I'm not alone. Now did you have some reason for being here, or did you think it your civic duty to warn me that a woman can't survive without a man to hold her hand?"

Sheriff Tate was inclined to pursue the argument, but he had a feeling he was not going to get around this woman, and he didn't want to be embarrassed in front of his men. Besides, this lady was young and stunningly good-looking. The men in his posse wouldn't take it kindly if he gave her a bad time. The way some of the boys were staring at her right now, they'd be more likely to clean out her barn, fetch water, and chop enough wood to supply the kitchen stove for a week.

"We're on the trail of a dangerous criminal, ma'am."

"What did he do?"

"Murdered a man, shot him in the back when it was dark and he was too drunk to defend himself."

"But why are you here?"

"We trailed him here. To your barn, as a matter of fact."

"You trailed him here?" Carrie asked, stunned. "How?" She hadn't planned on this. If they knew Sam was here, what could she do?

"We got an Indian tracker, ma'am. He can follow a hawk over rock."

"Well, he's not here," Carrie said. "At least if he is, we haven't seen him."

"Mind if my boys look around?"

"Not at all. Why don't you come inside and have a cup of coffee while you wait?"

"Don't mind if I do," the sheriff said, climbing down from the saddle as the posse broke up to begin their search. "I've been in the saddle since dawn."

"You hungry?" Carrie asked, moving through the door to allow the sheriff to enter. "We could fix your men something to eat if you're willing to pay for it. We just started dinner."

"That would be mighty nice. We brought our own food, but we're not very good at turning it into something tasty."

"Help yourself to the coffee. It's strong and there's plenty of it." One of the posse came hurrying in.

"Sheriff, we found signs of blood in the barn."

"You'll find more in the bedroom and on the rags in the wash pot," Carrie said. "I wouldn't be surprised if you found a good bit on the ground between here and the barn. This is Jake Bemis, my stock man," She said, pointing to Jake. "He had an accident this morning. It took us a while to patch him up." Jake pulled open his shirt enough for the sheriff to see the bandages, just as two more men entered the station, one of them obviously the Indian tracker.

"We found his horse in a corral up the canyon."

"Any sign of Butler?"

"No, but there's a set of tracks leading out of that corral

that can't be more than an hour old."

"How can you tell that?" asked Carrie. Her eyes cut to where Found stood behind Jake's shoulder, but his face was expressionless. She didn't know what had happened; she had to play for time.

"I don't understand it myself, ma'am, but this here Indian can read a trail just like he was seeing it made. What do you figure happened, Mort?"

"Must have come in here and taken one of their horses in place of his. I don't see any other signs of him."

"And none of you people saw or heard anything?" the sheriff asked, a little suspiciously, Carrie thought.

"We haven't been out of the station since Jake came up here bleeding all over the place. It took both of us to fix him up and the boy here to bring in clean water. We haven't had a stage since early this morning, and I guess we just haven't been paying much attention." Carrie could see from the disgusted look on the sheriff's face he thought that was just like a woman, but she didn't care what he thought as long as he believed Sam Butler was a long way from the Green Run Pass.

"Well, I suppose he's a long way down the trail by now. If you'd dish up that food, ma'am, we'll eat and be on our way." Katie served the plates and Carrie handed them around as the men took their place at the table.

"Here's some supplies in exchange," said one of the men as he set down a small bag of coffee, some flour, and a side of bacon.

"You needn't have done that, but I appreciate it." Carrie picked up the coffee, went over to the storage closet, and pulled the curtain partway open. She placed the coffee on the shelf, and was in the process of putting the flour away when Sam sneezed. Carried jumped six inches, and grabbed for the flour to keep from dropping it. Collecting her wits as quickly as possible, she brought the back of her hand up to her nose, as if she were trying to stifle a second sneeze, and turned around to find herself practically nose

286

to nose with the sheriff.

"Allergies," she muttered, blocking his view into the closet and not moving an inch from where she stood. "I should never have tried to put up the flour myself, but Jake can't do it, not with his side cut open, and I didn't think to ask one of your men."

"You allergic to a lot of things, ma'am?" The sheriff asked, his suspicions not entirely allayed.

"Not too many, but sometimes it seems like it," Carrie said. She decided against faking a second sneeze. The sheriff was watching her too closely. "That's the reason the doctors advised me to come west."

"Let me put up the bacon away for you," one of the men offered.

"Put it on the cutting block next to the stove. I think we'll fry a little of it for our own supper," Carrie said. She could not allow anyone in that closet.

The sheriff resumed his seat at the table. "You sure do have a mighty powerful sneeze for a little woman. I would have sworn it was a man that sneezed."

"Are you saying you think I'm hiding this criminal you're chasing, this killer, in my food closet?"

"Now ma'am, I never said . . ."

"Search the closet," Carrie said, flinging the curtain back but being careful to open it only partway. "You can also search the rooms in the back and the wash shed. You'll find blood in both places."

"We don't need to search the station, ma'am, and we know there's nobody hiding in your closet." Carrie let the curtain drop back into place, hoping there was no look of relief in her eyes to betray her to the sheriff.

"I want you to be sure in your own mind he isn't here."

"Lady, I don't expect two women and a boy, not to mention a lamed stock man, to be messing around with anyone like Sam Butler. He shoots people for fun. Why, he'd just as soon kill you as look at you."

"How do you know that?"

"What do you mean?" asked the sheriff, startled that his word should be doubted, especially by a woman.

"Just what I said. Have you seen him shoot people rather than have to look at them or just for the fun of it?"

"Well no, but he's—"

"Then how can you say he would shoot a person just as soon as he would look at them?"

"Ma'am, this Sam has a mighty powerful reputation."

"Has anyone else ever seen him shoot people for the fun of it?"

"Lady, Sam Butler has killed people before, several times."

"Were any of those killings just for fun, or were they in self-defense?"

"They was all in self-defense," one of the men spoke up.

"Did anyone see Mr. Butler shoot this man in the back? You said it was dark."

"Lady, there are about twenty men ready to swear they heard Sam and Newley arguing in the saloon about three hours earlier."

"Three hours! You're not going to tell me that this Mr. Butler person was still mad after three hours, or that he hid in some alley and waited three hours on the chance Newley would come by. From what you've said, he's too hot-tempered to wait, and much too bold to hide."

"Well, I don't know that he actually did hide."

"Sheriff, if I were Mr. Butler, we were in Virginia, and you accused me of murder without having the least bit of evidence except that I had had an argument with someone, I would take you into court and sue you for slander and defamation of character. The very least that could happen would be that you would lose your job. From what Mr. Barrow has been telling me about the way things are done in Colorado, the injured man would be within his rights in taking a gun to *you.*"

"Now see here . . ." The sheriff was not used to having his reasons subjected to careful scrutiny or to dealing with a woman who handled words better than most men handled a gun.

"I don't know whether this Butler person shot this Newley person or not," Carrie went on, "but it looks like you don't either. Did you organize this posse to take him back to stand his trial?"

"We was actually planning to save the judge the trouble . . ."

"I wouldn't think that trying to establish the innocence or guilt of a person should be considered too much trouble for a judge. If so, then maybe your judge should look for another job. After all, that's what both of you are paid to do, isn't it?"

"No, it ain't," the sheriff said, glad to finally have an answer she didn't expect. "I'm paid to put a stop to the killing and shooting and to put anybody in jail who tries to do otherwise."

"But you don't have any evidence Mr. Butler did any shooting, so how can you put him in jail?"

"Look, lady, why are you so all-fired interested in Butler's future?"

Carrie decided to ignore that and just push on. "Did this Mr. Butler shoot any of those people he killed in the back?"

"No, he didn't, Mrs. Simpson," one of the men spoke up, the one who'd spoken before, "and I been trying to tell these hotheaded fools for the last three and a half days that they was making a big mistake. Sam don't take nothing off nobody, but he don't shoot people in the back either. He's too fast."

"But you said they was having a go at it with their fists, and that Newley swore he would get even with Sam," the sheriff sputtered.

"Sure he did, but Newley was drunk. Everybody knows Newley is always saying something foolish when he's drunk, but he's not crazy enough to go after Sam Butler when he's sober. Sam didn't say nothing. He knowed Newley was all hot air."

It was obvious to Carrie the sheriff didn't know what to do next. She could also see he was furious at having the steam taken out of his posse.

"I suggest you wait until you have more evidence the next time you start to arrest someone," Carrie said. "Colorado might not be a state yet, but I can't see the territorial governor liking people being hanged without evidence. If you were to hang someone in Virginia just because you overheard him having an argument, it would be called a lynching." That was an ugly word, and it had a powerful effect on the members of the posse.

"We may not be a state, like your precious Virginia, but we have laws against lynching out here too," the sheriff said indignantly.

"I'm glad to hear that. Now if you've all finished your dinner, I suggest you find a place to camp until you make up your mind what to do." Over the noise of the self-conscious shuffling of feet came the sound of a horse approaching the station at a gallop. The rider rode up to the station, bounded up the steps, and burst through the door. The man was a stranger to Carrie, but he obviously knew the sheriff for he went straight up to him.

"It was Crosby who shot Newley," he announced, obviously relieved to have finally delivered his message. "His landlady found Newley's ring, wallet, and his gun in Crosby's room when she went to straighten up. You wouldn't think even Crosby could be such a fool as to leave that stuff lying about for anyone to find."

"Why did he do it?" demanded the sheriff, uncomfortably aware that Carrie's point had just been proven. "He didn't even know Newley. He had just got into town."

"Knew him back in some town in Missouri. Seems Crosby got himself into some trouble and skipped out, question of some money stolen from a bank and two guards killed. He figured Newley would turn him in for the reward, so he shot him before he could talk."

There was a good deal of milling about, the men muttering among themselves, but within a short time they had all murmured their thanks for the food, mounted up, and ridden out. Carrie sank into her chair with a weary plop. The adrenaline which had supported her through the last few hours was gone, and she felt as weak as a kitten.

"I never saw anyone pull a posse's teeth like you done, ma'am," Sam said as he emerged from the closet. "You gave them such a licking they wouldn't take me back if half a dozen swore they saw me shoot Newley."

"I'm just glad I was able to prevent an injustice," Carrie said, wondering why she didn't faint. "I really don't believe they were going to hang you without any evidence." She suddenly wished Lucas were here. She hadn't had time to think about him while she was facing the sheriff and his posse, but right now it would feel awfully good to be able to collapse into his arms.

"Believe it," Sam said emphatically. "The sheriff was right when he said things are different out here. You can't wait to try everybody that kills someone else."

"I didn't say anything about a proven murderer," Carrie said, "but saying that things are different is just a flimsy excuse. I won't listen to any accusation without some solid evidence."

"I'm sure glad you feel that way, ma'am. I don't think I will go back to Tyler's Mountain anytime soon, but it's nice to know I won't have a posse on my backtrail."

"Good. Then you'll be able to rest up a few days until you feel well enough to travel."

"Thanks, ma'am, but—"

"I won't have any buts," Carrie said firmly. "I'm the one who got you out of this mess, so now you owe me a favor, and I'm calling it in. I want you back in bed, and I don't want you on that leg until I say you can get up."

"Is she always like this?" Sam asked Jake.

"Always," Jake answered promptly. "And you don't know the half of it. You wait until she starts putting you to work."

"He ought to have to do your work," Katie suggested.

"Thanks just the same, but I'd rather not," Jake said, not liking the idea of having anyone like Sam Butler working with him, especially if they both had to sleep in the barn.

"Then he ought to be leaving just as soon as he's able," Katie said, looking at Sam with dislike. "Just because he didn't kill that Newley doesn't mean he didn't cut Jake with a knife. Who's to say when he'll get upset over something else and do it again?" Jake was obviously surprised by Katie's defense of him.

"You don't have to worry about that. I'm leaving," said Sam.

"Not tonight," Carrie said, and there was no give in her tone of voice. "Maybe you shouldn't stay, but I won't have you trying to ride a horse for miles with that leg, and I won't have you doing it tonight either. You sleep here tonight, and tomorrow you can let Found take you to his cabin. And I mean for you to stay. I intend to go out and check on you."

"She will too," Jake told him. "She don't trust anybody when she can't see them."

"You also owe me one top-quality mustang." Everyone looked at her as if she had suddenly started talking gibberish. "Unless I'm mistaken, those hoofprints the tracker saw were left by one of Lucas's mustangs Found turned loose when he put your horse in the paddock. Isn't that right?" The boy nodded. "That was a smart thing to do, and I'm proud of you. I always knew you were a clever boy." Found tried not to show his pleasure at Carrie's compliments, but he turned pink with embarrassment and pleasure.

"Now I think it's time we all went to bed. I'm exhausted. I don't know when I've felt this tired. And the stage comes early in the morning. Found, I want you to stay here with Sam in case he needs anything during the night. You're to come get me if it's anything serious. Are you going to be okay in the barn by yourself, Jake?"

292

"Sure. I don't feel too good right now, but I'll hold together a bit longer."

"You make sure you don't do anything to pull that cut open again," scolded Katie, "and you take it easy around those horses tomorrow. You can get Found or one of the drivers to help you."

"I ain't such a weakling I need help with horses just because of this little scratch," Jake protested, but he looked at Katie a little differently, and for the first time he didn't say anything to annoy her.

"There's a roast beef dinner waiting for you downstairs," Amelia Crabapple said to Lucas when she came into his uncle's room at dusk. "And there's pie and plenty of coffee."

"I don't want anything now. Maybe I'll have some coffee later."

"Mr. Barrow, you can't stay in this room forever, never moving and not eating. It's not right. You've not set foot out of here for three days. You know your uncle won't be coming out of that coma, or whatever it is that's got hold of him now."

"He might."

"No matter. He wouldn't know if you took a few minutes to get a bite to eat and tidy yourself up a bit." He was such a handsome young man, and Amelia hated to see him look so downcast and shabby.

"I'll have plenty of time after Uncle Max is gone. I don't have much longer while he's here."

"But he doesn't know what's going on around him. He won't know."

"I will," Lucas responded simply.

"I knew you'd come," Max Barrow said as his eyelids fluttered open, his normally thunderous voice reduced to a

293

hoarse whisper. "Did you find those gold thieves?" He obviously didn't remember that Lucas had reached Denver a week ago and had seldom left his side since.

"Not yet," Lucas replied, "but I will."

"Don't waste your time on them. Go find yourself a wife. You're the last Barrow left."

"I did find the woman I want to be my wife, but so far she won't agree to marry me."

"What do you mean the gal doesn't want to marry you? Is she crazy or something?" Even as weak as he was, the question contained some of the fire and energy Lucas had always associated with his uncle.

"No. As a matter of fact, she's the smartest woman I ever saw."

"She can't be, not if she's refusing to marry a man as good-looking and rich as you." Max tried to raise himself up on his pillow, but he barely had the strength to lift his head.

"Look, boy, when a man reaches the end of his life he doesn't want to leave nothing behind except buildings or companies. He wants to see children, something permanent he's created. It took me sixty years to learn that, so don't you forget it. You marry that little girl of yours and put down some roots."

Uncle Max didn't remember the hours they had spent talking quietly either, hours spent saying things they had always been too busy to say before.

"You shouldn't talk so much, Uncle Max," Lucas said. "You look tired."

"What you mean is I look like hell." He chuckled softly. "Wouldn't old Frank Adams give every nickel he ever stole from me to be here now. Well, you just hold on, Frank. It won't be long before I'm wherever you are, and I sure as hell am not going to start agreeing with you just because I'm dead." He paused a minute until his breathing became easier. "Dying on your back in some hotel is hell, boy, a damned sad end to a good life. Don't ever let it happen to you. Get yourself run over by a train or shot by some fancy whore. At least old Frank went with his pants on."

Lucas reached out for the frail, veined hand and his uncle's fingers tightened in his grasp.

"There's not many things I regret, but I'm sure sorry your daddy didn't live to see how you turned out. He'd be mighty proud of you."

"I had a good teacher."

"Yeah, they threw away the mold when they made old Max. If they'd made one or two more of me, we'd've torn this country apart." Max's eyelids closed and his soft, shallow breathing was the only sign of life in his tired body.

"No, they don't make them like you anymore, Uncle Max," Lucas whispered as he brushed a tear from his eye. "I'm going to miss you."

Max's breath was labored and his last words had been a whisper, but after a minute Lucas could tell he was trying to say something more. When he finally spoke, Lucas had to lean his ear close to his lips.

"Don't bury me in Texas. I want to be buried where I'll have you and your children to keep me company someday. Don't leave me with strangers, do you hear."

"I hear you, Uncle Max," Lucas answered, having great difficulty talking himself. "I'll buy a family plot. Is that what you want?"

The old man was too weak to answer, but he mouthed the word "yes."

For a long time afterward Lucas talked to him, telling about the family he hoped to have, about Carrie and how she was just as stubborn as he was. Occasionally he would feel the fingers move within his grasp or the grip tighten almost imperceptibly and he knew his uncle could still hear him.

"I guess we'll have to name the first boy after you. It won't seem right not to have a Max Barrow around." Lucas paused, longer than he had before, and when he spoke again, his words came out slowly and with great effort.

"I'm going to miss you, Uncle Max. I love you."

Lucas thought he felt a tremor just before his uncle's fingers fell away and his hand lay limp in Lucas's grasp.

His Uncle Max was dead.

Chapter 21

"I'm sure all the boys are sorry for what they said after you first came here," Bap was telling Carrie as he bolted down his breakfast. "Even Jerry Blake finds a good word for you now and then, and I thought hell would freeze before he said anything nice about a female excepting that Quaker woman that raised him."

"It's not important now," Carrie said, refilling his coffee cup. "That's all over with."

"But it *is* important," Bap said, taking a swallow of the hot coffee and burning his tongue. "Duncan Bickett is coming to inspect this station, and from what I hear he's planning to take it away from you."

Carrie nearly dropped the coffee pot. "How do you know? Are you sure?"

"Of course I'm sure. Do you think I'd go about spreading gossip?" Bap asked, his masculine pride injured.

"No . . ."

"Haven't I just been telling you how some of the men were bad-mouthing you. Well, it seems that someone finally got around to telling Duncan your husband was dead and no man was coming out to help you, and that decided him to come right away. He has some man from Denver that's interested."

"But he can't just give the station to someone else without even giving me a chance. I mean, it's not fair for him to come here with the *intention* of giving it to someone else."

"That's why the boys are feeling so bad. We everyone of us tried to tell him he'd be making a mistake, even Jerry, but you know Duncan. Once he's made up his mind, he don't change it very often. There's also been some talk about making this an overnight station."

"That would mean another building for the guests and extra help to take care of the rooms."

"Yeah, and Duncan thinks you need a man for that."

"I've never met Duncan Bickett so I don't know anything about him, but if he thinks he's going to come in here and run me out before he even bothers to see what I've done, he's got a big surprise in store for him."

"What you going to do?"

"When is he planning to get here?"

"Tomorrow on the noon stage."

"Then he'll have to eat lunch before he begins to look around," Carrie said to herself, having already forgotten Bap. "Katie," she called, turning with sudden resolve. "I want the entire kitchen and dining room scrubbed from top to bottom. I'll help you as soon as I get Jake and Found started, but this entire place has to look like it's brand new by noon tomorrow. I'm glad Sam's finished whitewashing the station. We'd never have had time to get that done before tomorrow."

"I still can't believe you got Sam Butler to whitewash anything," Bap said, amazement and awe showing in his regard for Carrie. "That man's been known to knock people down for just talking to him disrespectful."

"Sam's a fine man when he's treated fairly," Carrie said absentmindedly. "Jake and Found will have to clean every piece of harness. I just hope Found has finished replacing the wooden pegs."

"I'm glad he started staying at that cabin," Katie said,

298

still thinking about Sam. "Every time I sat his food down in front of him, I would start thinking of what he did to Jake, and it would make me so mad I wanted to take me knife to him."

"I wish Lucas were here," Carrie said without even hearing Katie. "He would know what to do."

"Ain't nothing going to impress Duncan more than seeing this station operate like it does every day," Bap volunteered. "You don't have to do nothing special."

"You do when you're a woman," Carrie responded bitterly. "A man could get away with just giving moderate service—Baca Riggins got away with even less than that—but I have to make sure I don't overlook even the smallest detail. I'm going to have to leave Katie to take care of you while I go find Jake and Found. I hope they have time to sweep out the barn," Carrie said as she was going out the door. "And then there's my cabin. Oh lord, I wish I had known just one day earlier. There's so much to be done."

"From the stew she's in, you'd think she had nowhere to go if she left here," Bap commented.

"Nowhere she wants to go," answered Katie.

"With her looks, all she has to do is go to Denver, and she'll have men asking to marry her before the sun goes down."

"She's had offers of marriage aplenty, but that's not what she wants." Bap's eyes widened in question. "Mr. Barrow has been after her for days now," Katie informed him in a conspiratorial whisper, "but she can't make up her mind whether she wants him more than she wants this station."

"Lucas asked her to marry him?" Bap said, nearly shouting the words.

"You don't have to act so amazed. Mrs. Simpson is a beautiful woman, and a real lady. She's good enough for a whole lot more than Mr. Barrow will ever be. I know she hasn't been a widow long, but she was hardly married, so it seems to be no point in wearing weeds for a man who was never your husband."

"So Lucas wants to marry Mrs. Simpson," Bap said to himself, unaware of Katie's reply. "Well, I'll be stripped naked and washed with lye soap."

"The way you're carrying on, you'd think Mr. Lucas was an earl or something. What's so special about him?" Bap opened his mouth to speak but closed it tight instead. Katie looked at him with suddenly narrowed eyes. "You've been with this stage a long time, haven't you?" Bap nodded absently, his eyes still not focusing on Katie. "So there might be a lot of things you've had time to find out that the rest of us don't know?"

"I know a whole hell of a lot you don't," Bap said, getting up and heading toward the door, "and it's going to blow the roof right off this place when it gets out." He marched out, leaving Katie to stare after him, wondering whether he really did know something or if he was just an old man who was trying to make himself feel important.

Lucas had to look a second time when he rode into the stage yard. The station had been transformed since he left, and it hardly looked like the same place.

The yard in front of the station had been swept clear of debris, and everything made neat and tidy, but the most striking change was the station house itself. It shone white and clean from a fresh coat of whitewash, glaring brilliantly in a landscape of green, brown, and gray. Carrie had even dug up some flowering plants from the garden and surrounding woods and planted them in tubs to give it a touch of color. He wouldn't have believed it if he hadn't seen it himself.

Lucas had hardly swung out of the saddle when he heard his name uttered as a near shriek and he turned in time to see Carrie come catapulting through the station door. He guessed he would live the rest of his life and never experience a moment of greater satisfaction than seeing her race headlong toward him with a look of ecstatic delight on her face. It sent a jolt of adrenaline through his body that banished the fatigue of eight hours in the saddle. Throwing his leg over, he leaped out of the saddle and swept her off her feet when she threw herself into his arms.

Carrie clung to Lucas, her arms encircling his neck, her lips pressed hungrily against his in a kiss that blotted out everything around her. She had known she missed him and that things were never quite as wonderful as when he was around, but only now did she realize she also felt incomplete without him. It was as though only part of her had been able to function in his absence. But Carrie knew this instinctively, and no such thing as logical thinking reared its ugly head to ruin the joy of their reunion.

"By God, I missed you," Lucas murmured when he could catch his breath.

"Me too," insisted Carrie, holding doggedly to her grip on his neck, her feet dangling several inches above the ground. "I didn't know how utterly miserable the absence of one wrangler could make me. My sisters-in-law would say I've got a bad case."

"I hope you've got a near mortal one. I want you to feel so awful you'll never want me to leave again."

"You dreadful man," Carrie laughed, tightening her hold around his neck. "The first time I admit to a weakness, and you immediately take advantage of it."

"If I only could," Lucas replied, and tightened his hold on her, reluctantly fighting down the excitement that was coursing through his veins before he embarrassed himself in front of the several pairs of eyes he was sure were watching. "I've bloodied my head butting it against your stubborn resistance," he said, kissing her again. "By now I'm too desperate to act like a gentleman. I'm determined to get you any way I can."

"Well, put me down," Carrie commanded without loosening her hold on his neck. "I think we've made enough of a spectacle of ourselves." Lucas lowered her to her feet slowly, his lips sinking to meet hers in one more kiss. "I thought you would never come back," Carrie murmured when she emerged from his embrace. "Don't you ever leave me that long again." Then she remembered his uncle and sobered. "Your uncle?"

"He died two days ago. We talked a lot about you, but I'll tell you about that later when I can get you to myself. Tell me, what is going on around here? I almost thought I was in the wrong place."

"Oh, I almost forgot, and here you are mussing me up in the middle of the station yard. Thank goodness he didn't come while you were kissing me."

"Don't you mean while *you* were kissing *me?* And who is this *he* you're talking about?"

Carrie blushed furiously in spite of herself. "Duncan Bickett, and if he had seen us just now, he would never believe I wasn't brought up to kiss men in public, especially since I'm neither married nor engaged to you."

"We're going to fix that. That's another one of the things I want to talk to you about."

"We can do that later," Carrie said, a telltale blush touching her cheeks. Lucas did not fail to notice that for once she didn't say she hadn't made up her mind; neither was she so undecided or standoffish now. If she was willing to kiss him in public, and she had kissed him just as thoroughly as he had kissed her, then maybe she was ready to agree to marry him. His loins tightened at the thought of having her to himself twenty-four hours a day, and he had to turn his attention back to her improvements to cool his senses.

"Duncan Bickett is coming to inspect the station, and Bap says he means to take it away from me," Carrie said by way of explaining who she was expecting and why.

"And all this is supposed to convince him to change his mind. You're dressed up like you're going to the Christmas cotillion. And I had hoped it was for me."

"How could it be when I didn't know when you were getting back?"

"Don't you think you're a little overdressed?" It was a statement, and Carrie could see Lucas wasn't going to understand.

"Of course, but I'm trying to make the strongest impression I can."

Lucas looked at the rioting copper curls, the turned-up nose and pursed mouth that he had dreamed of for days, skin that courtesans would envy, and a figure that no dress could hide, and he decided that Duncan would have to be three parts dead for Carrie *not* to make a powerful impression on him no matter what dress she wore.

"You still don't want me to have the station, do you?"

Lucas knew Carrie wouldn't understand his answer without a long explanation—she probably wouldn't understand it under any circumstance right now—and he decided to skirt the issue. "What I think doesn't matter right now, but if you mean do I want to help you convince Bickett he's wrong, the answer is yes."

Carrie looked as if she didn't care for that answer in the least, but before she could ask Lucas what he meant by it, she heard the call of the stage driver and then the sound of the stage itself.

"I've got to be up at the station when the stage pulls in the yard," Carrie said, her preoccupation with the inspection and her desire to welcome Lucas battling for her attention. Business won. "You go take care of your horse or whatever you do when you come back from a trip. I'll come up to your cabin after Duncan leaves."

"Don't you want me to stay here with you?"

"No. Don't misunderstand," Carrie added quickly, "but I don't want Duncan to think I depended on anyone but myself."

"It's really important to do this by yourself, isn't it?" Lucas asked, and Carrie was not so absorbed with her own affairs that she didn't notice the plunge in his spirits. It was almost as if he had hoped she would have changed her mind while he was gone. But she hadn't, and she wasn't

303

going to.

"You know it is, and you also know why. This is the first chance I've had to do something on my own, and I can't fail."

Lucas almost started to tell her what she was doing to him, that he had spent the last seven days and nights thinking about her, planning their future together, dreaming of holding her in his arms again, but he didn't. She was filled with impatience to be off, and he wasn't sure she could stand still long enough to listen to him.

"You won't fail. There isn't a station on the whole line that can compare to the way this place looks now, and there's none that has the food either. Since Jake is one of the best stock men, all Duncan can do is decide that you're the best station manager in all of Colorado and give you a new contract. The company would be foolish to do otherwise. They've already been hearing about you in Denver."

"Really? You're not just saying that to make me feel good?"

"Yes, really, but I'll tell you about that later too. The stage will turn the corner any minute." He kissed Carrie quickly, and picked up his horse's reins. "I'll be back shortly to hear the verdict."

Carrie watched Lucas as he turned away from her and led his horse off toward the cabin, and the sight of his long, powerful limbs and his tightly encased rear end caused a knot of desire in her stomach. In spite of the chill in the breeze coming down from the mountains, she felt herself flush with the heat of desire, with the warmth of a remembered embrace, and her whole body felt charged with the excitement of his presence. She found herself thinking of the coming night in his cabin, and suddenly it was very difficult to remember Duncan Bickett and the inspection.

Carrie felt a wild impulse to forget the station and Duncan Bickett and run after Lucas, to tell him that nothing mattered in the world but the two of them. His long ab-

304

sence and his unexpected return had cleared away any remaining doubts as to whether she loved him and wanted to marry him, but she could feel the station almost within her grasp, and she couldn't let it go. Everything she had dreamed about since the day she decided to leave Virginia, everything she had worked for since she came to Colorado, all of it could be hers within a matter of minutes. How could she turn her back on it just now?

The sound of the wheels of the stage as they crunched the small stones in the road captured her attention. For a second she stood poised between Lucas and the station, unable to make up her mind as the two battled for her heart.

"You better hurry if you don't want Mr. Bickett to find you standing in the yard," Katie called from the porch. "You can't surprise him that way." For one second longer Carrie remained undecided, then she dashed inside the station. By the time Duncan Bickett stepped down from the stage, she and Katie were discreetly watching through the curtains inside the dining room.

"His eyes are as big as saucers," Katie said with a delighted giggle. "I fancy he's never seen a station like this." The look of stunned surprise on Duncan's face was plain enough for all to see. Even though he was the first out of the stage, all the other passengers had alighted and filed past him before he could stop staring at everything around him.

"Well, it's time," Carrie said as she prepared to step out on the porch to welcome her guests. "Wish me luck."

"You don't need it, ma'am. Everything here is perfect. And I'll take me oath he's never set eyes on a woman as pretty as you. He won't be able to think except to do what you tell him."

"I'll settle for his being very impressed," Carrie said as she stepped outside to greet the passengers. She was beginning to know some of the regulars by name. She asked one man about his wife and another about his business, then she turned to wait for Bickett with poised calm. She was determined she would not go to him or give him the satisfaction of knowing how anxious she was.

"Looks like you slumguzzled him before he even got his feet on the ground good," Harry said with a wink at Carrie as he followed the others inside.

"You'd better hurry up if you expect to get anything to eat," Carrie called to Duncan after a minute had passed. "They don't usually leave much." Recalled to his senses and remembering the purpose of his visit, Duncan came hurrying toward the porch only to slow down once again when he got a good look at Carrie.

"Bap didn't exaggerate," he said, almost to himself. "You certainly are beautiful."

"Why, thank you, Mr. Bickett, but as much as I appreciate the compliment, it's not going to save you any lunch."

"You know who I am?"

"Bap told me you were coming."

"I'm here to make a thorough inspection of this station and evaluate the job you've been doing," he said, mounting the steps to join her.

"Don't you mean rather that you are here because of the men's complaints that a woman is running this station, not that the station is being badly run?"

"Well, yes, I guess I am, though all complaints have to be considered no matter what they are."

"I agree with you, but we can talk about it after you've eaten."

Lunch was a silent meal—everyone took eating seriously, and there was no conversation wanted or accepted until the coffee and pie had been passed around.

"Hadn't you better see about the horses?" Duncan said to Harry when he asked for his second cup of coffee. "You've got to be off soon."

"That's already taken care of," Carrie said, not pausing in pouring coffee for all the passengers. "Jake changes the horses while the driver eats. It saves time and gives Harry and the other drivers more time to relax."

"I heard Bemis was your stockman," Duncan said. "Sounds unlikely from what I hear about him."

"Jake does work for me," Carrie replied, and was pleased to see Duncan's eyebrow rise in surprise. "I also have a boy who helps him. I have meant to have a new team ready, but Lucas had to go to his Uncle Max's funeral, and he hasn't gotten around to breaking the last of the horses."

"Lucas Barrow?" Duncan asked, showing a surprising amount of interest.

"Yes. He just got back from Denver before the stage pulled in. I expect he'll be over to get something to eat before long."

"Lucas eats here?"

"Yes, but he pays for his meals," Carrie was quick to add. "I wouldn't think of letting him eat at the company's expense."

"You make him pay?" Duncan looked as if he had swallowed something down the wrong way.

"Of course. I don't expect the company to feed everyone who happens to be at the station." The passengers began to drift out, and Harry got up to leave.

"I guess it's time I was going, Mrs. Simpson. The food was good as usual."

"I would say it was excellent," Duncan said. "Is it always like this?"

"Every time you come through, day or night," one of the passengers said. "I've never seen anything like it, not even in Denver. And the place looks brand new. You can't know how different it is from when Baca Riggins was here."

"Yes, I can," insisted Duncan, turning back to Carrie. "That's the only reason I didn't come out the minute I heard you had arrived. I figured anybody who could get rid of Baca deserved a chance. But at that time I thought you had a husband on the way."

"That's why I let you go on expecting him. Would you have let me stay if I hadn't?"

"No, ma'am, I'd have been out here the next day. I'd have run the place myself if I had to."

"That's what I figured. Now let's go look at the rest of the station. You didn't come here to talk about my family history."

"No, but your being a woman is going to make me have to do it sooner or later. Is that girl the one who does the cooking?" he asked, gesturing toward Katie.

"I share the cooking with Katie. I hired her to help me get started, and she decided to stay."

They moved outside and Duncan was struck again by the neatness of the grounds and how good the station looked with the new paint and the tubs of flowers placed all around.

"You can always tell a woman's touch," he remarked. "There's not another manager on the whole line who thought to get his station painted recently, and none has ever set out flowers."

"Surely they have wives."

"Not like you, Mrs. Simpson. You're beautiful, you're dressed like something straight out of San Francisco, and you're obviously a lady. There's nobody else like you in Colorado, except maybe in Denver." Frank admiration was in his gaze and Carrie hardly knew whether to be pleased or scold him for staring so rudely. Lucas did it for her.

"You can put your eyes back in your head, Duncan," Lucas said, coming up behind them before Carrie could see him. "I've already got my eye on this girl, and if you try to steal her away from me, I'll shoot you dead right here."

"You knew she was here by herself?" Duncan asked Lucas, surprising Carrie because it was obvious Duncan felt Lucas's answer was important. "And you approved of it?"

"It's not my place to approve or disapprove," Lucas said, giving Duncan a meaningful glare. "I have nothing to do with running the stations or choosing the managers."

"I know that," Duncan said, recovering quickly. "I just

308

didn't realize you were helping out here."

"I'm not," Lucas said. "I'm breaking horses."

"Mr. Barrow has been a great help to me, especially in the beginning, but the station operates without his assistance now. In fact," Carrie said, eyeing Lucas sternly, "I'm still waiting for that new team he promised."

"You'd better go check out the barn, make your decision, and get out of here before she puts you to work," Lucas said, looking at Carrie with embarrassing warmth. "The woman is a demon for work, and she thinks everybody else likes it as much as she does."

If it was possible, Duncan was even more impressed with the barn than the station. The dust had been whisked from the windows and rafters, the stall leavings neatly composted out back, and the floor swept clean. Jake and Found had worked on the tack room until it was spotless. Everything in the room was neat and orderly, and every harness, newly cleaned and glowing in rich blacks and browns, hung on its own wooden peg.

"You couldn't have done all this in the last day?"

"Mrs. Simpson doesn't like for anybody to have time on their hands," Jake told him. "If she comes out here and I'm not busy, she finds something for me to do. I generally prefer to find my own work."

"Well," Duncan said, coming out of the barn and looking around once more, "I must say I've never seen anything like it. I only have one question. How would you handle an outlaw?"

"Have you ever seen this lady shoot?" Lucas asked. "She can take the fire off the end of your cigar."

Jake could see Duncan didn't believe him. "That's how she got me to work here."

"I heard about that, but I didn't know whether to believe it or not."

"Would you believe she got me to whitewash the station for her?" Sam Butler unexpectedly came around the corner of the barn.

"Now that I *won't* believe," Duncan said, staring at the notorious gunman.

"I came in here several days ago, wounded and with a hungry posse on my heels," Sam said, more to Lucas than to Duncan. "She fixed up my leg, sent the posse back to Tyler's Mountain with its tail between its legs, and made me rest up until my leg was fit to ride. A little whitewashing seemed small payment for all that."

"That ain't all she done," swore Jake, "but you wouldn't believe it if I told you. Hell, I saw it myself, and I still don't believe it."

Lucas stared at Carrie in stunned surprise, shock at the risk she had taken battling with pride that she could stand up to an outlaw, as well as a bloodthirsty posse it seemed. He *had* to marry her and take her off to Denver. Either she was going to get herself killed, or she was going to turn the whole territory on its ear.

"It really wasn't as dangerous as it sounds," Carrie said, silently pleading with Lucas to believe her. "I'll tell you about it later."

"I certainly hope so," Lucas said before he turned back to Duncan. "What do you think?"

"What do *you* think?" Duncan asked, turning the question back on Lucas.

"If you want my opinion about her work," Lucas said after a moment's hesitation, "I think there isn't a better manager on the line."

"There certainly isn't one with a place that looks like this. The passengers have been after me to make this the overnight stop. With your cooking being what it is, I'd be hard-pressed to find a reason to put it anywhere else."

"Does that mean I still have the job?" Carrie asked, unable to wait any longer. This was what she'd been working toward from the first day she arrived. She had even shunted Lucas and her love for him aside in her efforts to make sure that nothing would go wrong today. Now success was within her grasp, and she couldn't wait another second to know if she had succeeded.

"For as long as you want it and can keep things going like they are," Duncan said. "I'd be a fool to give it to anyone else."

It took all of Carrie's self-control not to give a shout of triumph. "Are you going to make it an overnight station?"

"I can't answer that yet. That's a decision for the company office, but I'm going to recommend it."

It would have been easy for a less perceptive man than Lucas to see that Carrie hardly knew how to contain her happiness. It also wouldn't have taken one with much insight to see that he didn't share it. Certainly he was proud of her achievement and he was glad she had proved her ability to the extent that she had won a renewal of the contract, but the station had always stood between them, a bar to her becoming his wife, and he didn't see that her resounding success was going to make things any easier or increase the chances of a decision in his favor.

So far he had been unable to make Carrie see that she was using the station as an excuse—maybe he had only just seen it himself—and that she didn't need it anymore. She was still fighting doggedly against the possibility of being treated the way her family had treated her. He wasn't sure she could see that she could give up the station, marry him and move to Denver, and still maintain her independence. To be perfectly honest, he didn't know how he was going to explain it to her, but he couldn't imagine anyone imposing on Carrie ever again.

And if Jake was to be believed, she could handle outlaws and posses as well. Lucas tried to remain optimistic, but he had a dark presentiment that things were not going very well for him just now. He could also see that this was not the moment to press his case. Carrie was too excited over her victory to be able to pay attention to anything else right now. She was positively dancing in place, just waiting for Duncan to leave so she could share her victory with Katie and Jake.

He felt left out, and he resented it. Recognition of her success required that it be achieved independently of him — it followed that her success should be celebrated just as independently — and it angered him that he was not a part of her achievement. He felt almost like the enemy, and it was a feeling he disliked.

She would have to choose between him and this station sooner or later, and he decided it might as well be now.

Chapter 22

Half an hour later Duncan had mounted the horse he had brought tied to the back of the stagecoach and ridden back to Fort Malone. Lucas walked up behind Carrie and put his arms around her. She turned into his embrace with a happy smile. "Do you think you could give me a few minutes now?" he asked. "I'm feeling terribly jealous."

"I'm sorry," Carrie said, immediately remembering that Lucas had lost his uncle and that she had not taken the time either to sympathize with him or to share in his feeling of loss. "It's just that I've worked so hard for this and now that I've finally got the contract, I can hardly believe it. It's like losing your sense of direction all of a sudden and having nothing to struggle against."

"Listen to me for a few minutes and see if I can't give you something to think about."

Carrie tried to clear her mind of her own concerns. She wanted to listen to Lucas, she really cared about his loss, but it was hard to keep her feelings of happiness from bubbling over. She had proved she could run the station, and Duncan had acknowledged it with the most concrete admission possible, an extended contract.

"Uncle Max only lived a few days after I reached Denver, but we talked more in that time than we ever had in our

313

lives. I told him about you, told him I had asked you to marry me but that you couldn't make up your mind to give up your freedom yet. He said he wished I had brought you to see him."

"I would have liked that," Carrie said. "It would have been nice to meet at least one member of your family."

"I suppose I have some relatives back in Texas, but Uncle Max was the only one that counted. I told him quite a bit about you. He said you must be crazy not to jump on me like a hen on a June bug. I told him you weren't at all partial to June bugs, but he seemed to think you might learn if you tried."

"Lucas, what kind of nonsense did you tell that poor man?" Carrie demanded, her attention finally caught. "You had no right to worry him with the things we say to each other."

"He wasn't worried. He just wanted to tell me he made a big mistake one time, and he didn't want me to make the same one."

Carrie could tell from the look in Lucas's eye that what he was going to say was very important to him, that it would be very important to both of them, and suddenly she was nervous.

"He asked me to do just two things for him, and both of them surprised me. There is a woman back in Nebraska he almost married, and I guess he wished many times afterward that he had. Anyway, she's not doing too well now, and he wants me to look after her."

"What will you do?"

"I'll have to go see her."

"That's a long way," Carrie said, thinking that it would mean he would be gone almost as long as when his uncle died. She had missed him terribly. She didn't want him to be away from her that long again. "What was the other thing your uncle did that surprised you?"

"He told me to get married, have a family, and put down roots." Lucas felt Carrie stiffen in his arms, but he didn't stop. "He told me that nothing else a man did in his life

314

mattered a whole hell of a lot, nothing else lasted unless it was in the minds and hearts of a man's own flesh and blood, his sons and daughters. It was just the opposite of what he had done with his own life, and he didn't want me to make the same mistake."

Carrie hardly knew what to think. She was standing in the ring of Lucas's arms, vibrantly aware of his body, of the delicious excitement of merely being near him, but she had just won the right to operate what could become the most important stage station in Colorado, and she couldn't bring herself to give it up. It wasn't that she didn't want to get married—she did and Lucas's holding her in his arms made it hard for her to think of anything else—but she felt her contract could be the beginning of a new and exciting kind of life, and she was being asked to give it up without having had a chance to experience its benefits.

"You know what I asked you to think about while I was gone?"

"What?" Carrie said, trying to get her thoughts back on their conversation. "I can't remember. So much has happened."

"You know you remember," Lucas said, making her look him straight in the eye. "I asked you to marry me, and you were heartless enough to say you had to think about it." He had decided he wasn't going to let her off anymore. She had to give him an answer now.

"Well, I did have to think about it. It wasn't a decision to be made lightly. There are so many things that we don't agree on."

"I know. You keep saying that, but you still haven't answered my question. Will you marry me?" He knew she loved him, she had admitted it. If he could just get her to agree to marry him, they would be able to work everything else out.

"I *want* to marry you, but I'm not sure I should."

"What the hell does that mean?" Lucas demanded.

"I love you," Carrie said, wondering how to explain her indecision, "much more than I ever thought possible. I've

315

been terribly busy since you left and I've had lots of things to worry me, but never for one minute did I forget you, how wonderful it felt to be in your arms, or how much I wanted to be there again. There were some nights I ached for you so I couldn't sleep, and I would get up and pace the room. I even came over to the station one night and scrubbed the stove again just to have something to do. It nearly drove me crazy."

"Then why are you still unsure?"

"You know there are still so many things we can't agree on."

"We can work them out."

"I don't know. You've been different since you got back from Denver. I could tell it almost the minute you got off your horse. I think your uncle's words had a much greater effect on you than you know."

"But I told you weeks ago that I wanted a family and a home."

"You had some doubt in your mind then, I don't know how much, but there was still a question, some room to negotiate. I don't think you have any uncertainty now, and I don't think there's any room for compromise. I think you know in your own mind you will never be happy without the kind of home you had when you were a boy."

"Carrie, there are bound to be many things we don't see eye to eye on. We don't have to work them all out right now." He could feel her slipping away, and he didn't know what to do to bring her back. She was hiding behind walls of her own making, and he had to find some way to convince her to tear them down.

"Where are we going to live?"

"In Denver."

"But I've just been given a new contract to run this station. I can't leave."

"You can give it to someone else."

"But I've worked hard for this contract. I don't want to give it to anyone else. Why can't we live here?"

"Because the company office is in Denver, and I can't do

316

my job from here." This wasn't the way Lucas wanted to tell her about his job.

Carrie stared at him in stunned surprise. "Do you mean to tell me that you're more than just an investigator sent out here to spy on some outlaws?"

"You might say I was second in command to my uncle," Lucas said, realizing he had made a mistake in keeping this information from Carrie for so long. "In fact, you might even say that he owned the company."

Carrie went rigid in his arms. He tried to tighten his hold on her, but she impatiently pushed his arms away.

"You *own* the Overland Stage Company? You don't merely work for it or have some stock in it?"

"I own it, all of it. Uncle Max founded the company, and I'm his only heir."

"Does Duncan Bickett know who you are?"

"Yes." Lucas could see what was coming next and he didn't like it, but there was nothing he could do about it. She was going to be mad as hell, and he didn't blame her. He should have told her before he left, but it was too late to know that now.

"So when he was asking you what you thought about this station, he was really asking you whether he should give me the station or not?"

"No, he was not," Lucas said as emphatically as he could. "Duncan might want my opinion because I was around here more than he was and knew more about how well you operated the station, but hiring the managers is his job and he knows I don't interfere. Neither did my uncle."

"But he would be reluctant to go against your wishes if he knew what they were." There was no way out of this one, and Lucas knew it.

"Look, Carrie, I know what you're thinking and you're wrong. Duncan doesn't have to try to make me happy. He knows he's too valuable to the company for me to ignore him, and he knows we think too much of his opinion to go against it without some damned good reason."

"But he still wouldn't want to disagree with you unless he

317

had to?"

"No, he wouldn't," Lucas admitted, unable to get out of it any longer, "but if you think he gave you the contract because of me, you're mistaken. You can go into Fort Malone right now and ask him."

"With you riding along with me, standing at my side while I asked him?" Carrie said, her feelings of betrayal making her furious. "I wouldn't waste my time on such a fool's errand."

"Naturally I would stay here."

"It wouldn't make any difference. He would know why I was asking." She was so thoroughly furious and hurt and bitter and confused she could hardly speak. Everything she had worked for, all the things she had tried to do to improve the station and make the customers happy, everything was meaningless next to Lucas's yea or nay. She hadn't proved anything at all. She was right back where she was in Virginia, dependent on the approval of some man.

"Why didn't you tell me you owned the company from the first?"

"Why didn't you tell me you had never been married?"

"I've already answered that."

"Well, now I'll answer you. No one was supposed to know who I was or why I was here. I came to look around, and I couldn't do that if everyone knew who I was. They would have been watching my every move."

"Why didn't you tell me?"

"There was no reason to tell you at first, and then there never seemed to be a good time. Why didn't you tell me you had never been married until just before we made love?"

Carrie had no answer for that.

"My being president probably wouldn't have made any difference if I hadn't happened to be here when Duncan arrived. And I didn't tell him I'd asked you to marry me. I just told him to keep his hands off."

"You might as well. It was the same thing."

"Look, Carrie, I know how important it was for you to win this contract, but I promise you Duncan didn't give it to you because of me. Look at this place. Do you see anything that reminds you of the dump you found when you stepped off that stage? And there's no question that the food and the service are better. You did that and you know it. I had nothing to do with it. In fact, if you had listened to me, you'd be in Denver right now as my wife. You don't owe any of this to me."

"But I'm a woman."

"Yes, and I think Duncan has seen that it can be an asset to the company. As long as he feels you can run the station and protect it, everything you do of a feminine nature is a plus. It will be even more so if this becomes an overnight station." He almost said when. That would have told her that it was *his* decision, and he would never have gotten her to believe him after that. "Also, if this becomes an overnight station, there will be more people here on a full-time basis and your ability to run the station will be more important than your ability to protect it." Lucas could see that Carrie was wavering, but she wasn't convinced.

"But you're still asking me to give up this station and go to Denver with you?"

"Yes. I can't run the company from here even if I wanted to, and since I intend to move into railroads, I have to be where the railroads are."

"So I'll become just a housewife, just like any other woman."

"Look, I'm not going to beat around the bush. I want you to be my wife and the mother of my children. I want you to be my companion, my friend, my comfort, and my solace. I don't want you to become my vice president, and I don't want you starting another company on your own. I know you need to feel you can do something without depending on a man, but I thought you had proved that to yourself."

"I don't know that I have, and I don't know that I want to give up what I've got just yet."

"One of us will have to give up our job for the other. Logic and economics say it should be you."

"Why?"

"Don't ask stupid questions just because you don't like the answer you're going to get," Lucas said, his temper getting worse. "You'll never earn much of a living managing this station, and it certainly wouldn't be enough to raise a family. And my being your wrangler won't make much difference either."

"But as the wife of the company president, I could have a big house, servants, and the best of everything for my children."

"Yes, you could. You would also have a lot more freedom to do what you want as an individual. If you stay here, you'll be tied to these buildings, this very spot, because you will have to be at the beck and call of the passengers every time they come through. This station will have to be the most important thing in the world to you, no matter what else is happening in your life, no matter how much you want or need to be somewhere else. That wouldn't be true if you married me."

"But I would be dependent on you."

"Carrie, don't you understand that marriage is a partnership, that I can't do it alone, even if I am the one to go out and earn the money?"

"I know, but why do I have to give up my position?" Carrie knew she was being irrational, but she couldn't help it. It seemed that circumstances were hemming her in again just as tightly as they had in Virginia.

"Why is a job automatically so important, so valuable because a man is doing it? Don't you think it takes ability and dedication to be a good wife and mother?"

"You have the gall to ask me that?" Carrie snapped, all the remembered wrongs and slights springing to her mind. "I who worked day after long day for my brother and never got a word of appreciation? Don't you know that *any female* can be a mother."

"No they can't, any more than anybody can be a good station manager or a good cook or a good wrangler, any more than any man can be a good father. It takes talent and practice. It also takes dedication to see that job through to the end. You can have children because you're a female, but you will be a good mother because you'll work at it."

"I know all that," Carrie said impatiently, still feeling that circumstances were against her, "even if I'm not acting like it. I also know that you want a home and that you want me in that home all the time. I know you want children and that you want me to raise those children for you while you go out and earn millions so we can be rich."

"Is there anything wrong with that?"

"What if I don't want to be rich? What if I don't mind staying here for the rest of my life and being at the beck and call of every out-of-patience passenger that comes through here?"

"I want more for you than that."

"But suppose *I* don't? Have you ever considered that?"

"No. I never thought anyone would dislike being rich."

"I don't dislike having money, but I would dislike having a husband who was always away trying to make more money. I would rather have him at home, as would his children. Do you remember telling me how much you liked your home when you were a little boy?"

Lucas nodded.

"Well, you were remembering what it was like to be at home *with* your mother and father. The house you were in, the clothes you wore, and the food you ate weren't important. What really mattered was who was in that house with you. I don't want to take away your company and I would never want to deny you your right to build it into anything you wanted, but I can't live as the second, or third most important thing in your life. I don't necessarily want to work with you, but I don't want to be left out of what you are doing and thinking. I don't want to be a wife who sees that the children are fed, who keeps your bed warm and satisfies your needs, but who is shunted aside when it comes to the important things. Are you willing to give up your company and take a job that will demand less of your time?"

"I don't know," Lucas said, suddenly feeling like a balloon someone had punctured. "But that's not what I'm asking you to do."

"Yes, it is. Yours may be the more important job and it may make us richer, but it's just the same. If I can be a mother without running this station, maybe you can be a father without being a company president."

Lucas realized that they were at an impasse. He had never thought of giving up his company, it had been a part of him ever since he could remember, and he doubted if he could turn his back on it, even for Carrie. But the thought of losing her frightened him to death.

"I do love you, Lucas, more than I've ever loved anyone in my life, but I've got to be at peace with myself as well," Carrie said finally. "I can't marry you if it means I'll be wanting something else all my life and wondering if I would have been happier if I'd done things differently. That would make us both miserable. And you need time to decide whether the home and family you want are going to fit into the same life with your company."

"How long do you need? The gold will be going through in a few days, and I have to go to Denver after that." It sounded as if he was pushing her, not thinking her time wasn't important.

"And if I haven't decided by then?" It sounded like a challenge.

"I'll come back, and I'll keep coming back until you agree to marry me. I know we have a lot of things to work out, but we will work them out because we love each other and we each want the other to be happy. As long as you love me, it will be all right."

"I love you with all my heart," Carrie said.

Carrie couldn't remember when she had spent a more miserable afternoon and evening. The news of Duncan's inspection must have traveled through the air. Two stages had come through, and everyone knew she had won a renewal and that they were considering making her station an overnight stop. It seemed as if everyone who had ever ridden the stage was anxious to offer their best wishes and predict that she would soon be running the most famous stage station in Colorado.

Much to Carrie's bewilderment, the repeated congratulations and predictions of success served to irritate her rather than boost her spirits. After seeing the last passengers off, she threatened to lock herself in her cabin before the next stage pulled in, but no one seemed to be interested in her disordered spirits.

She hadn't seen Lucas all afternoon, and whenever she spoke to Katie, she got the feeling her thoughts were elsewhere. She did notice that Katie found more than one occasion to go to the barn, and even though Jake had enough work to keep him busy all afternoon, Carrie saw him in the station yard twice.

Found should have been the least affected by the contract, but he seemed to be the most affected by Carrie's ill temper. He was constantly underfoot, repeatedly wanting to know if there was anything he could do to help, until Carrie lost her temper. "If you would just talk, I could understand what you are trying to say," she said, speaking quite sharply. "Surely you must trust us by now."

"The poor laddie has not gotten over what happened to him before he came here," Katie said, taking Found in her arms and giving him a protective hug. "Jake says he still has nightmares about some men and what they did to his family."

"I didn't mean to be so abrupt," Carrie said, feeling quite angry with herself for not being able to control her feelings. "It's just that I'm rather upset right now I think I could use some time alone."

But Carrie found that fifteen minutes of her own company was too much, and it was a relief to head back to the kitchen and help Katie with dinner. Lucas came up to eat with them, but he didn't ask her about her decision and he didn't say anything about her coming to his cabin later. He acted as if they were old friends and nothing out of the ordinary was happening. When he walked out the door with a cheerful good night, Carrie felt desolated. It was almost as though he didn't care about her answer. She told herself he did care, that he was just giving her time without putting any pressure on her, but the nagging fear that she might have finally put him off one time too many wouldn't go away.

"I've decided not to marry me Brian," Katie announced quite suddenly after Jake and Found had returned to the barn. They were putting things away for the night and getting ready for the next morning. "I'd like to stay here if it's all the same to you."

"You know I'd be delighted to have you. In fact, I've been wondering how to talk you into working here after you got married, but are you quite sure you don't want to marry Brian?"

"Yes, ma'am, I am. I never thought much about the man I was to marry before I came here and watched you having such a hard time figuring out what to do about Mr. Barrow."

"What do you mean?" Carrie asked, suddenly defensive.

"You know what I mean," Katie said. "Everybody on this place knows he wants to marry you, that he has been wanting to for some weeks, and that you be trying to make up your mind what to do. Well, you see, I never thought I would have such a choice, that I would be allowed to make up me own mind about me husband, so I just accepted the first man that asked for me. But I been listening to you talk, and now I know I don't have to do that if I don't want to."

"What did I say?" Carrie felt rather guilty that it had been her words that had convinced Katie to refuse Brian. It was bad enough she was making her own self miserable. She had no right to ruin Katie's life as well.

"It wasn't always things I overheard you saying to Mr. Barrow. It was things you did too. Seeing you run this station and all the time standing up to these men, I realized that I could decide what I wanted to do, that I didn't have to marry Brian. Well, I have decided, and I don't want to marry him. I mean to tell him as soon as he comes back."

"But what are you going to do?"

"I've a fancy to go on working here for a while yet. Could be someone will turn up that appeals to me. Maybe I've got me eye on somebody already." Katie blushed quite vividly and abandoned all attempts to be mysterious in a rush to confide in Carrie. "He's nothing like what I ever thought to marry, ma'am, and I don't know but what I'm crazy to think on it. I doubt we'll agree on two things in our whole lives, but I've been happier since I've met him than I ever was before. And besides, he needs me."

"It's Jake, isn't it?"

"It would have to be now, wouldn't it? The only other man I see every day is Mr. Barrow, and you'd claw me eyes out if I was to so much as *think* about him." Now it was Carrie's turn to blush vividly.

"It could have been one of the drivers," Carrie offered, trying to recover her composure. "I'm not personally fond of Jerry, but Harry and Bap are very nice. Of course it could have been one of the regulars on the stage."

"I'd rather have that Sam Butler of yours than Jerry Blake. Bap is old enough to be me father, and Harry is making up to a girl in Fort Malone."

"Oh," Carrie replied, nonplussed. She didn't know how Katie knew so much more about the men's lives than she did.

"No, it's Jake, and though I know we'll probably never settle on anything without a having a set-to beforehand, I can't think of anybody else I want to marry more."

"But doesn't it bother you knowing that you disagree on much?"

"Sure it does, just like it bothers you about Mr. Barrow, but a man and wife are bound to have disagreements. Working them out is just a natural part of being married. Besides, it can be a lot of fun if you go about it right."

"But you don't mind becoming the wife of a confirmed woman hater?"

"Jake's no woman hater, but I don't mind cooking and doing for me man. I guess I'm kinda looking forward to it. After taking care of me father and brothers for so long, I had come to believe I hated it, but I know now that isn't so. You see, I never wanted to prove I could do anything a man could, and I never wanted to be independent. I guess I'm really not very much like you after all. I just want a husband and a home and family, and I want it with the man who will make me happy."

"I'm sure you'll be very happy," Carrie said, mumbling a formula in an attempt to disguise her own feelings of jealousy. It staggered her that she could feel so strongly envious of the very thing she thought she scorned when she left Virginia. What had happened to her in the weeks since she had come out here? Had she changed her mind? Didn't she still have the same goals? She had told Lucas she did, but was she sure?

"Can you finish up without me?" Carrie asked Katie.

"Sure. There's almost nothing left to do."

Carrie wandered outside on the porch, sat down in one of the rocking chairs, then almost immediately got up and walked out into the yard. Without knowing why, she found herself under Lucas's tree in his chair. If it helped him to think, it might help her also.

Carrie had talked with Katie often enough to know that they had suffered almost identically at the hands of their families, and that both of them had left home rather than continue to endure such treatment. But if this was so, how could Katie want to marry Jake? He firmly believed that women were inferior to men, and there was hardly anything he and Katie could discuss without having recourse to some very harsh language.

Because she loves him and doesn't want to live without him, something shouted in Carrie's brain. That's all that matters and she knows it. But it's *not* all that matters, Carrie argued back. A husband and wife have to think the same way, want the same things. You and Robert felt alike and wanted the same things, the voice replied. Would you rather be married to him than Lucas? The answer came back a thundering negative.

But she would have to give up the station and everything she had worked so hard to achieve.

What will you have in ten years if you keep this station? the voice asked. What will you have in those same years if you marry Lucas? Is the station worth what you will have to give up? Carrie realized there was no comparison; there was not even the shadow of a doubt in her mind.

She visualized herself sitting under this same tree, ten or twenty years from now, still single and still manager of this station, and watching Lucas get off the stage followed by his wife and children. Even though it was only her imagination, Carrie felt a stab of jealousy that was so sharp and deep it really hurt. No, it was closer to hatred than jealousy, and it had nothing to do with the clothes the woman wore or the fabulous jewels at the throat. She hated the woman because Lucas went home to her, because he held her in his arms at night, because he confided his hopes, dreams, and fears to her. But she also envied the woman her family, the bright hopeful pledges of Lucas's affection, her own gift to the future.

In that moment she realized that the stage station was meaningless in itself. Its only importance rested in what it represented, and if that was true, she didn't need the station at all. She would never need it again.

She had already proved she was capable of accomplishing something by herself, and she didn't want to spend the rest of her life proving it over and over again. There was so much more to life, and she realized that everything she wanted to do somehow included Lucas. True, she'd been angry at him when she'd learned he owned the company and she'd thought she had gotten the contract because of him, but she realized now that wasn't true. Now she had no more need of the station, or anything else outside Lucas's arms.

Carrie looked off in the direction of his cabin and wondered what he was thinking. He hadn't pressed her at dinner, he probably didn't expect her to make up her mind for several days to come, but she had made her decision and she wanted to tell him now. Properly speaking, she should wait for him to come to her, but if she was going to spend her time doing things differently, then she might as well start acting differently right now. She had sent him away, after all, so maybe it was appropriate that she go to him.

Chapter 23

Lucas's thoughts were less comforting. Carrie had never made a secret of her determination to prove herself capable of being independent of a man, but her courage and determination were part of what had made him fall in love with her. He expected they would argue over something for the rest of their lives, but he had been certain their love would help them solve any problems that came between them. It had *never* occurred to him that she might ask him to give up his company. That struck at the very foundation of his life, posing fundamental questions about what he wanted for Carrie, himself, and his future family, and it had caught him unprepared. But of one thing he was absolutely certain. He could not live without Carrie.

It was impossible to say how she had become so important to him in such a short time. Maybe she always had been. He didn't know if he believed in predestination, but the moment she stepped off that stage into the Colorado sunshine he felt as if she had stepped into the center of his life, and he would have killed Baca Riggins if he had hurt her. It was all too easy to remember her loveliness, the perfection of her body, or the way she made love—in fact, it was impossible to forget any of these things—but his love had sprung to life before they made love and could never have grown to such magnitude because of her physical beauty alone. They were knitted together just as inextricably as though he were one half and she the other half of a single body, he the right arm and she the left. He could never feel complete again without her.

His life had been a shambles since she had entered it, soaring to the heights of happiness because of her love only to plunge into depths of despair by her refusal to marry him and then be flung into the whirlpool of fear by the hare-brained things she did without a thought for her safety. There was something irresistible about her, a spirit and energy that made her exciting to be around, and Lucas wondered if trying to protect her from the dangers she so blatantly ignored wouldn't make him old before his time.

Yet here he stood, trying to take his need of Carrie, his need of his job, and his need for a family, and meld them into a single channel of life, but one broad enough for both him and Carrie to swing abreast. When seen from a distance, it hadn't looked very difficult. Faced with the difficult choices of the present, it looked impossible.

Lucas's thoughts were interrupted by a timid knock, and then the door opened and Carrie stood in the threshold of his cabin.

Lucas was certain that he had memorized every feature of her face, every curve of her body, every nuance of expression that came into her eyes, but though she looked more beautiful than ever tonight, there was something slightly different about her. But at that moment their differences didn't matter; Lucas held out his arms and Carrie walked eagerly into his embrace.

It was impossible to find words to describe how good it felt to hold her in his arms. Out in the station yard he had felt the eyes of others on them, the tension of the inspection, the presence of the station itself all coming between them, muting their welcome, restraining their reunion. The tension still intruded, but for the moment they felt as one, and he was content to feel her close to him, to feel the warmth of her body, the excitement of her nearness.

"I missed you terribly," he said, and kissed her hungrily. The smell of lavender was a familiar memory that welcomed him into its embrace. No matter what happened, no matter

330

what it cost him, he could not lose her. Not ever.

"I missed you too," Carrie said, snuggling against his chest. "I was never so miserable in my life. I don't ever want you to leave me again."

Lucas felt his hopes soar, felt expectant energy rush through his body. "Does that mean you'll marry me?"

"That's what I came to tell you," she said, pushing him away so she could look up at him with her tantalizing smile. "Yes, I will marry you."

Lucas felt something inside him explode like a rocket, but he pulled hard against the rush of exhilaration. "What are your conditions?"

"I have none." Lucas couldn't believe his ears. Again he had to restrain himself from whooping for joy. Maybe she didn't think of restrictions the same way he did. "But what about your independence, the station?"

"What about it?" she asked, looking up at him with a provocative, hooded look he knew was calculated to drive him out of his mind with desire.

"Woman, you've driven me crazy ever since I set eyes on you. You knew I loved you, that I wanted to marry you, that I could hardly think straight when you were in my arms, but you always had your heart set on something else and couldn't make up your mind to marry me. Now, just hours after you repeated nearly every reason you had for refusing to marry me, you waltz in here and tell me you want to get married and that you have no conditions."

"That's what I said."

"What did I miss? Where's the catch?" He didn't mean it like that, but he just knew there was something wrong.

"Lucas!" Carrie exclaimed, sincerely shocked and hurt. "Why do you think I want to trick you?"

"I don't," he replied, still unable to believe she really meant it, "but you held me off so persistently, and I can't see what's happened to make you change your mind."

"I love you."

"You loved me this afternoon, but it wasn't enough then." He was beginning to believe it now. He was trying hard to restrain himself, but he could feel it coming.

"Maybe it's your good looks and money."

"I don't know anyone who's less affected by my good looks and money," Lucas replied, impatiently waiting a real, convincing reason.

"Your money, yes. Your body, well, that's something else again." She pulled his face down to hers and kissed him with all the hungry passion he could want.

"Watch it," he said, taking a deep breath. "You do that again, and we won't get around to finishing this conversation until tomorrow."

"Is that such a bad idea?"

"No," Lucas replied, struggling manfully to hold his rampaging desire under control, "but I don't think I can stand to get my hopes built up only to have them dashed down again. And I can't go on making love to you if you're not going to marry me."

"But I've already told you I want to marry you."

"I know, but what caused you to change your mind? I haven't even said I'd give up anything." He had a presentiment of disaster.

"I don't want you to give up anything for me."

"I know what this is," Lucas said, holding his head like he had a splitting headache. "You've got a twin sister, and you've sent her in your place to make sure I'm battered into submission before you give me your terms."

"Lucas Barrow, I have a good mind not to marry you after all."

"See, I knew it was coming."

"Now you just listen to me, you bull-headed man. I had lots of reservations this afternoon, but I asked myself one very important question, and I got a surprising answer that turned all my other questions and answers out into the dust."

"What was that?" Lucas hardly dared to breathe.

"I asked myself what I would have if I didn't marry you, and I saw myself sitting here still worrying about horses, food, maybe outlaws and Indians, and working at the same thing year after year. Then before I could realize what a dismal picture that was, I pictured you getting off the stage with your wife and family. Lucas, I *hated* that woman. I didn't even know her, but I would have killed to take her place. I realized I wanted to be your wife, and the station and independence and everything else didn't mean anything when compared to that. And the children, oh Lucas, if you're going to be rich, can we have lots of them? I didn't realize how much I wanted to have your children."

Lucas gave a whoop that nearly scared Carrie out of five years of her life, picked her up like she was a ball, and swung her around until she was too dizzy to stand up. He felt as if he were living in a dream. After being afraid for so long that Carrie would refuse him in the end, it was hard to believe that everything he had ever wanted was being handed to him without any strings or reservations. Carrie held on to him, trying to get the whirling room to stand still, while he danced a jig that would have done justice to a drunken Irishman.

"You are willing to give up everything for me?" he asked in disbelief when he could finally stand still.

Carrie laughed. "To be perfectly honest, and I don't know that I should have been, I don't know if I could have given it up, but I found I didn't want it anymore. Maybe I never did. Maybe I just thought I did because I was so unhappy. When I saw how the other women were content to act like China dolls, I wanted to scream and rebel. I could never live like that again, but I know you won't ask me to. You want to protect me too much and I expect there'll be times when I want to do something you'll disapprove of, but Lucas, I'd rather fight with you over anything, no matter how trivial, than live without you and have all the independence in the world."

Lucas's heart was so full he couldn't speak. That Carrie should be willing to give up everything she had worked for because of him filled him with wonder and amazement. What could he offer her in return for her sacrifice?

"It seems odd that you should have asked yourself almost

the exact same question I asked myself," Lucas said.

Carrie looked up into his eyes, and the look of utter happiness and contentment told him he didn't have to do anything, that she would accept him just as he was now, but he couldn't do that. She deserved more.

"I asked myself what would I have in twenty years if I devoted all my time to the company, and it didn't take me long to realize that I would be missing what I told you I wanted, what *you told me* I wanted from a home, the people who were there. I thought of my sons as little boys, doing all the things I was unable to do and my missing that part of their lives because I was at a board meeting or on a trip. I thought of my daughters becoming young women and finding young men they wanted to marry, but most of all, I thought of you and all the moments when the magic that is you makes something so very special out of something so ordinary. I love to look at you because you are beautiful, I want to make love to you because it's wonderful beyond anything I ever imagined, but I would lose so much more if I couldn't share all those ordinary hours in your life. I made up my mind I wouldn't miss them."

"But you can't give up your company. I don't want you to do that for me."

"I don't mean to give it up," Lucas said, "but I won't let it become the only thing in my life as Uncle Max did. There are plenty of men who can run a company just as well as I can. And I can't think of a better use of money than to have the time to be able to spend with you."

"You really mean it? You're not saying pretty things like my brothers did to their wives, and then they ended up going back to things just as they always were?"

"I really mean it. I'm sure there'll be plenty of times when you don't think I'm living up to my bargain. You tell me, and I promise something will change."

"But that's your life's work."

"Yes, but it's not my life. I want you to solemnly promise to warn me if I ever start to forget that. I don't want to die like Uncle Max, regretting people I never got to know, regretting a life I never had time to live."

There was no rush to their lovemaking that evening, no hurry, no sense of urgency, only a gradual realization that they could look forward to sharing the pleasure of their bodies with each other for the rest of their lives. They undressed each other in silence in the soft light of the lantern. Carrie finally gathered the courage to gaze openly at Lucas's body, to take in the beauty of his carefully sculpted legs and thighs, the tightly muscled derriere that had long excited her senses, the powerful chest and shoulders that gave her such an electrifying sense of strength and security.

But it was his handsome face, above all, that gave her the satisfaction and the sense of being wonderfully blessed, for in his face resided the person she had fallen in love with. The silver-gray eyes that could snap closed like a shutter to his mind or caress her like liquid moonlight; the soft, dark brown hair perpetually in boyish disarray that made her long to take him in her arms and brush it back from his brow; his soft, gentle lips that smiled when he was happy and roused her body to such wanton desire; his firm jaw, lean cheeks, long straight nose, and thick brows that imparted an immediate awareness that he was a man of immovable principle and unwavering support—it was this face that laughed, scolded, invited, cajoled, that had become the focus of her life, and she could not gaze upon it enough.

But the fire Lucas had painstakingly lighted in her body and was just as carefully building into a conflagration soon claimed her attention, and his beloved features became a mirror of the passion that swept through her, turning her into a pool of distilled desire. Lucas carefully and methodically stoked the fires in her body until she was aware of nothing but her own pleading need and the hot, rigid, masculine body which was its only answer.

Their joining was slowly achieved, but the electricity that arced through her body, making every inch of her sensitive to the touch of Lucas's fingers, lips, and tongue, was augmented rather than diminished by this deliberate assault on her senses. Carrie felt herself losing touch with reality, floating off on wave after wave of thundering desire until she was immersed in a sea of sweet ecstasy and then washed up on the shore of utter fulfillment.

Even before Carrie opened her eyes, even before her mind had come to grips with consciousness, she felt wrapped in a cocoon of happiness. There was warmth, comfort, and a feeling of contentment. She opened her eyes and they fell on Lucas. He lay sleeping next to her, his sheet thrown off to reveal the upper part of his muscled body, his hair mussed by their passionate lovemaking. She smiled and started to ease herself gently out of the bed. She didn't want to wake him. He was sleeping heavily, still tired from his nights of sitting with his uncle and his long ride back. His hand reached out and pulled her down next to him.

"I thought you were asleep," she said as her fingertips brushed the lashes of his still closed eyes.

"A man who sleeps too soundly can't tell when danger approaches."

"Well, you're not sleeping outside in some canyon, and I'm not a wild beast."

"You seemed pretty wild to me last night," he mumbled, enjoying the warmth of her body. "Growl for me again."

"Stop it," Carrie said, giggling guiltily. "I don't growl, and I didn't last night either."

"Must have been me I heard." Lucas growled in her ear. "Does that sound familiar?"

"Yes," she said, unable to keep from laughing. "I heard it so often I thought I was in the middle of a dogfight."

"Dogfight!" Lucas exclaimed, erupting from the bed like Neptune from the sea. "Is that how you value my caresses, woman?"

"Come here, and I'll show you how I value your caresses." The invitation was unmistakable. Lucas lowered his head and Carrie encircled his neck with her arms. She pulled him down until their breath mingled in the sliver of space between them.

"Careful. You never can tell what will happen if I get too much appreciation."

"Do you dare me to find out?" Carrie challenged, a twinkle in her eye.

"Yes," Lucas said, nibbling at her lip. "I dare you to kiss me as you did last night. I dare you to touch me as you did, and I dare you to respond as you did."

Their lips met in a kiss that turned hot and then fiercely passionate. Carrie felt her body suddenly become flushed with excitement, her limbs rigid with expectation. Lucas had rolled over on his back and pulled her down to him, crushing her breasts against his chest. Suddenly she felt no inhibitions at all, just a terribly fierce longing to lose herself in Lucas. She pressed against him, as though willing her body to become part of his, her lips as hungry as his, her body crying out its need just as loudly.

Abruptly Lucas rolled over and laid her down and his body pinned hers against the mattress. Their arms wrapped around each other, their limbs entwined, their mouths sought to draw the very essence from each other.

Suddenly Carrie could stand it no more, and she opened her legs to Lucas, inviting him to join with her, to plunge into her very depths and quench the fire that flamed there. Carrie had no time to wonder how after last night there could be an unsatisfied nerve in her entire body; she only had time to realize that all of her was crying out with a deep, unquenched need, and it was a need that only Lucas could satisfy.

Carrie's body shuddered with spasms of aching pleasure when she felt Lucas enter her, slowly, deliberately sinking deep into her heated welcome. She arched toward him, drawing him further inward, urging him to reach down and down until he reached the craving that was turning her body into a crazed thing. Suddenly he began to withdraw, and she frantically wrapped her limbs around him, trying to force him to plunge deeper, but he continued to withdraw until she nearly screamed in frustration. Then without warning, he drove deep inside, forcing a moan of pure ecstasy from between her lips. Then he withdrew again, maddeningly slowly, only to plunge deep within her once more. Lucas repeated this until Carrie thought she could bear it no longer.

Then Lucas shifted the rhythm, driving deeply within her in rapid, powerful strokes. Within seconds Carrie was near the edge, ready to swoon with pleasure, then Lucas changed again, slowing down just enough to prolong the pleasure agonizing moments longer. Carrie was sure she could not stand it and fought against him, but he would not be hurried and she could only cling to him, trying desperately to hold on to her sanity as she was driven closer and closer to the edge of an abyss when her body would explode with delight.

Then just as she sensed that Lucas, too, was about to lose control, a flood of sensations swept over Carrie, and she felt the most indescribable ecstasy explode throughout her body. Swept by a wave of pleasure, she felt Lucas explode within her and felt him cling to her. For a few moments, they clung to each other, their bodies as hard and unbending as stone, then they collapsed in sheer exhaustion.

"Is it always like this?" Carrie asked after several minutes.

"It is with you."

"How can we endure it?"

"I don't know. I wonder if I can again, but then I gather you into my arms and I know I can't live without it."

"That's how I feel too," Carrie said, a lazy smile spreading across her face. "I guess we'll have to have separate beds."

"I'll sleep in yours."

"In separate rooms."

"I'd sneak in after everyone had gone to bed."

"On separate floors."

"I'd climb down the drainpipe."

"In separate houses."

"I'd follow you through the streets."

"Then I guess there's nothing for it but to share your bed. Denver society would never recover from the sight of you chasing me through the streets in your wherewithal."

"You don't mind moving to Denver?"

"Not as long as you're there. I never have lived in a big town."

"It's not much of a town yet, but it's growing fast, and it's going to become the center of the railroad industry."

"When do you have to go back?"

"Not until the gold shipment goes through. I either have to find those thieves before then, or make sure they don't take it off the stage this time."

Carrie sat up in the bed, alarm setting her features into an appearance of bravery she did not feel. "I don't want you to go after those men. It's not safe. They might try to kill you."

"They most certainly will try to kill me if they think I might keep them from getting the gold," Lucas replied with what Carrie thought was a callous indifference to her fears for his safety. "Jason is not going to give up just because we want him to. Also, I don't think he has spent the gold from the first shipment. I think it's hidden somewhere near here, and he doesn't mean to divide it up until he's robbed his last stage."

"I still don't want you to go after him," Carrie said, fear unexpectedly freezing the warmth out of the morning. "I don't care if he takes all the gold in Colorado as long as you're safe."

"I'm glad you think I'm so wonderful, but you're the only one who thinks I'm worth my weight in gold. The rest of Colorado is more likely to look for someone else to transport their gold if I don't get out there and stop Jason Staples. I've got to try to find him before the shipment goes out."

"Can't you send someone else?" Carrie pleaded. "I know there are men you can hire to do things like this."

"There isn't time," Lucas explained. "The stage comes through tomorrow. There wouldn't be time to send for anyone from Denver, and certainly not to bring in the kind of professional gunmen you're talking about."

"Are you going to put me through this kind of agony for

the rest of my life? Do you really expect me to sit home waiting to hear some common criminal has shot you and left your body for the wild beasts to tear apart?" Lucas had never seen Carrie so distraught, and he tried to allay her fears.

"I promise I will always hire professionals to investigate the robberies after this. I volunteered this time because I'm certain there's someone inside the company selling information. There is no other way Jason Staples could be privy to our shipping dates. It's almost more important that I catch the informant than the thief."

"Then offer a reward."

"I can't offer a reward bigger than the gold shipment, or bigger than all the future shipments Staples may hope to steal. No, I have to see if I can get close enough to their camp to overhear them. Maybe they will mention the man's name. If not, I'll just have to hope I can force one of the gang to divulge it after I capture them."

"You can't capture a whole gang by yourself. That's incredible."

"I'm not going to try. I expect them to attack the stage somewhere between here and the next station, and I've brought some men from Denver whom I will position along the road. As the stage passes, they have instructions to follow behind, close enough to be able to help, but far enough back not to be seen."

"Then you're not going to be out there alone?"

"Where I'll be depends on what I learn tonight."

"Tonight!" Carrie exclaimed. "Why can't you sell the stage company? You could become a rancher, a mine owner, anything."

"It wouldn't matter. It's the same all over the West, no matter what you do. This is a new country, and there are men out here like myself who want to build something out of this land. There are also men who are determined to take anything they can."

"Then we can move back East," Carrie said. "I will not endure a life where you and my children will be hemmed about by thieves and killers."

"Your children will be safe. It's just your husband who will have to contend with thieves and killers."

"That's all the more reason to move back East, at least until all this wildness is over and the men are all in jail."

"By then the opportunity will have passed."

"I told you I didn't have to be rich."

"I know, but this isn't about riches, and you know it. It's about making something, about building part of this wonderful land of ours, and you know I can't go back."

"Why not? It's stupid to throw yourself in the way of bullets for an ideal."

"Isn't that what Robert and your brothers did?"

"And look what it got them. So many fine men killed and everything ruined."

"They died for the wrong ideal, but everyone respects them for having the courage to stand up and fight for what they believed. What we have here is good and right, and I can no more turn my back and run and still be respected than you can turn around and go back to Virginia. I may be killed, but even the outlaw who shoots me will respect me. If I turn and run, even the lowest scum will think himself worth more than I am, and the honest citizens won't care who shoots me. I can't go."

"Yes you can," Carrie pleaded. "I don't care what anybody else thinks. I'd rather have you alive than some dead hero."

"I don't care what anybody else thinks either, but I care what I think, and I care even more what you would think."

"Me!" she almost squeaked. "I want you to go back East."

"Do you really? Do you think a woman who came out here alone, not knowing what she would face, but willing to face Baca Riggins even after she had seen him, do you think this same woman would respect and love a man who would run away when some thief tried to take what was his?"

"I wouldn't care as long as you were safe."

"Do you think she could love a man who wouldn't protect his property? How could she know he would protect her,

her children, and their right to a full and happy life? I don't think she could. She might try if she loved the man a great deal, but deep inside there would be disappointment and scorn. And the man would know it."

Lucas was right, and Carrie knew it. He didn't have to do the job himself. He could have hired someone to do it, but having taken it on, he could not now refuse to follow it through to the end. It's what she would have done herself, and she knew it was what Lucas would do, what he *had* to do.

She suddenly held him tight. "I'm afraid," she said. "It's one thing to face men of honor, but it's not the same with thieves."

"It's easier. Men of honor are willing to die for what they believe. Thieves only want what they can take without danger to themselves."

"You promise to be careful? I don't think I could live without you."

"I promise to be very careful. I'm rather fond of you myself. It wouldn't take much persuading to keep me lying here forever." He ran a hand down Carrie's side and she felt her whole body shiver involuntarily.

"If I thought it would keep you here, I would wrap myself around you and never let go."

"You could try it and see," Lucas prompted.

"You'll not get me with that trick," Carrie said, preparing to get out of bed. "I know you're going after those men no matter what I say, so you'd only be trying to take advantage of me again. I've got a stage coming in soon, and I can't leave all the cooking to Katie."

"You can't leave just yet. We never decided when we were going to get married."

"You never asked me."

"Well, when do you want to get married?"

"This very second, but I will settle for the day after tomorrow. Then this dreadful business of the gold thieves will be over, and I can marry you with a mind free of worry."

"I'll have the stage driver send the preacher from Fort

Malone. Or do you want to go into town to be married? You could always wait until we reached Denver."

"No, I want to arrive in Denver as your wife. I imagine there'll be some mighty disappointed women there, and it might save everyone a lot of trouble if it's all said and done when we arrive."

"You afraid I'll back out?"

"Never of that," Carrie said, bending over the bed to give him a gentle kiss. "I just want to get about the business of being your wife, and it'll be a lot less trouble this way."

"Forever the busy little bee," Lucas groaned. "I wonder if Denver has any idea of the terrible force I'm about to turn loose on them."

"You stop making fun of me, Lucas Barrow, or I'll turn my attention to your stage company, and I promise it won't be the same when I get through."

"You can have Denver. You can have all of Colorado," Lucas said in mock terror. "Just leave my poor company alone."

Carrie abandoned her dressing to teach Lucas a lesson, and she found him a more than willing student.

Chapter 24

Carrie's back was to the door when Jake hurried in with none of his usual nonchalance. "That man you were supposed to marry is coming up the road," he said to Katie. "I saw him from the hayloft."

Carrie looked up and was surprised to see Jake breathing heavily. He had obviously come up from the barn at a run. Behind his customary vacuous expression, Carrie could see an element of anxiety she had not seen in him before. Jake was obviously uneasy about something.

"Do you want us to stay, or do you want to see him by yourself?" Carrie asked, turning to Katie. She seemed to have lost a little color, but otherwise she was her usual calm self.

"Let him say his piece, and then we'll decide," she said. "For all we know, he may be coming to tell me he doesn't want to marry me."

"I don't know why he should do that, staying away as long as he has," Jake said. He was not looking at Katie, but Carrie was sure his words were meant for her.

"It would only be fair if he wanted to break it off for I'll not have him as me husband, and I mean to tell him so right off."

An uncomfortable silence followed. Katie was composing her thoughts, Carrie was wondering what Katie meant to do after she refused Brian, and no one knew what Jake was thinking. The women continued about their tasks and Jake poured himself a cup of coffee and sat down at the table. It was clear he wasn't going to move until required to do so. Carrie wondered why he had rushed to tell Katie that Brian was coming. He still loudly professed to dislike women, though he was careful not to do it in Carrie's presence, and Katie was still loud in her disapproval of just about everything Jake did. She had hoped Jake would moderate his stand on women, but lately she had begun to fear that Katie's hopes were doomed to disappointment.

Carrie moved to the window and then out on the porch when she saw Brian ride into the yard. She was struck again by how young and handsome he looked—he looked hardly old enough to be out of his teens—and she wondered if Katie was doing the right thing. He wasn't as tall as Lucas nor did his face have the same force of character, but then Katie was a much more mild-mannered individual than Carrie. She probably wouldn't want the kind of cantankerous man Carrie found exciting.

"Morning, Mrs. Simpson," Brian said as he dismounted. "I hear they're going to turn this into an overnight stop. I also heard the contract is yours for as long as you want it."

"That's Mr. Bickett's proposal," Carrie said. "It'll probably take a while before we learn what the company has decided to do."

"If Duncan Bickett recommends it, they'll do it. They think a lot of him in Denver."

Carrie didn't know what was the matter with her. She had never met a more polite, well-behaved man, but she found herself feeling like Katie. There was no reason for it, but she just didn't trust him. "I imagine you came to see Katie," she said, preceding him through the door. "She's inside." She didn't know if Brian had hoped to see Katie alone, but he displayed no signs of distress when neither she nor Jake showed any signs of leaving.

"I've come for your decision, Katie O'Malley," he said without preamble. "I'll be getting my money soon, and I want to start looking for a place."

Katie looked a little white about the mouth and her hands twisted nervously under her apron, but she didn't hesitate or stumble over her speech. "I'll be mighty remorseful if you have been putting off looking for your place because of me decision, Brian, but I find I cannot marry you. I'm sorry for it because you are a well-set-up young man, but me mind is made up and there be no changing it."

Brian looked rather taken aback, but there was little he could say, if indeed he had wanted to say anything, with Carrie and Jake both in the room. "Are you certain?" he asked after a pause. "I can give you more time if you want to get to know me better."

"She'd have to see you once in a while to do that, now wouldn't she?" Jake said, and the antagonism in his voice surprised Carrie.

"I know I haven't been as attentive as I should, but as I told you, I've been traveling for the company, and I haven't had any time to come out here."

"It wouldn't make any difference if you was to come to see me every day," Katie said, still showing few signs of the perturbation Carrie knew raged inside her. "We won't suit, and I won't marry you. Let's have an end to it."

"I'll say no more," Brian agreed, and Carrie was convinced he was genuinely disappointed over Katie's rejection.

"You can't turn right around and go back to Fort Malone now," Carrie said, "not after that long ride. Sit down and have some coffee. We still have some pie if you would like a slice."

"Thank you, Mrs. Simpson, that would be most welcome, that is, if Katie doesn't mind."

"Not a bit of it," Katie assured him. "You stay as long as you like. It won't bother me."

Katie served the pie and coffee, and Brian sat down at the table with Jake, who showed every indication of outstaying the young Irishman. Conversation languished, and after trying unsuccessfully for several minutes to fill the gap, Carrie gave up and let the silence reign undisturbed.

"You look like you're holding a wake," Lucas whispered into Carrie's ear when he entered the station a short time later. "I never saw such a solemn bunch."

"Katie has just turned down Mr. Kelly's offer," Carrie explained. "Naturally things are a little strained just now."

"Then maybe you can come outside with me. I've got a few things to talk over with you before I leave." A look of dread flitted across Carrie's face, but the others in the room were too occupied with their own thoughts to notice it.

"Who was that?" Brian asked idly when the door had closed behind Lucas and Carrie. "Somehow he doesn't strike me as the cowboy type."

"He's not," Katie said uncommunicatively.

"That's Lucas. He's the wrangler," Jake told him. "He just come from Denver because his Uncle Max died there sometime last week." Brian's gaze suddenly zeroed in on Jake.

"His last name wouldn't be Barrow, would it?"

"Yeah. Max Barrow. They just buried him a few days back."

"Are you sure of that?" Brian asked. His face seemed to retain its outward calm, but Katie was certain she read surprise and fear in his eyes.

"Sure we're sure," Jake said cantankerously. "You don't think a body would be confused about something as simple as that, do you?"

"No, I guess not," Brian agreed. He seemed to think no more of it, but Katie noticed he ate no more of his pie and took only one swallow of coffee before excusing himself.

"It's a long ride back to Fort Malone, and I think I should get started," he said. Neither Katie nor Jake disagreed with him.

* * *

"You're not leaving already, are you?" Carrie asked as soon as the door closed behind her.

"The shipment is going through tomorrow, and I'm going to meet my men first then scout around a bit," Lucas explained, leading her over to the shade of his tree. "I'm going to try to come up on them after dark. They'll be gathered around the fire then, and sound carries better at night."

"Please be careful," Carrie begged.

"That's part of the reason for going in at night. It gives me better cover."

"What will they do if they catch you?" Carrie asked, knowing all the while that she didn't want to hear the answer.

"I'm not certain, but I won't like it whatever it is, so I'm going to make sure I don't get caught. Now I want you to go about your business like nothing has happened. If anybody should ask about me, you tell them I've gone after more mustangs."

"You know I can't act like nothing has happened. And if anybody were stupid enough to believe you were going after more mustangs when the corral is full of unbroken horses this very minute, then they wouldn't have brains enough to know what to do with you if they caught you."

"That's what I like about you," Lucas said, amusement dancing in his eyes. "You're always so loving and supportive, and you've got unlimited confidence in me."

Carrie hit him in the shoulder with the butt of her palm. "I do love you, you stubborn mule, but I'd rather be supporting you in a lawful endeavour. I also have complete confidence those thieves will kill you if they get the chance. You just make sure you don't give them that chance, because if you do, well, I don't know what I will do, but I'll think of something."

"Probably clean out the whole bunch with your little pistols," Lucas said, gathering her into his embrace with a

348

fond smile.

"And don't you think you can sweet-talk me into agreeing with you by grinning at me like that. You know I can't think straight when you do."

"Yes, I do," Lucas said, still grinning as he kissed her.

"I'll recover my senses as soon as you let me go."

"Probably," Lucas said, and kissed her again.

"You can't hold me here forever." Carrie sounded as if she hoped he would prove her wrong.

"I've been thinking about it." Carrie subsided into his embrace, content to remain there even if every minute she was in his arms hadn't meant one less minute he would be exposed to danger. It seemed incredible to her that after such a long search for the one man she could love, everything should be risked for a few gold thieves. Her mother's family had already been called upon to make too many sacrifices. Bitter and disillusioned by the Civil War, her Uncle Wesley Cameron had left Virginia to lose himself in the wilds of Wyoming, and Aunt Cornelia had died of a broken heart, leaving Carrie's Uncle Stuart Cameron to raise his young daughter, Sibyl, alone. Surely no more could be expected of one family.

"When will you be back?" she asked, disengaging his arms reluctantly.

"I hope to come back sometime tonight, but it may not be until after the stage goes through tomorrow."

"Will you take Found with you? You can send him back with a message telling me what you're going to do."

"No. I don't want to have to worry about anybody else. I'll be safe enough. Now you go about your work and try not to worry."

Try not to worry, Carrie thought bitterly as Lucas rode off toward the canyons a little while later. He might as well have asked her not to breathe. She had known him for barely a month, but in the nights they had spent together, she felt as though she had become merged with him, almost as much physically as spiritually. It was no effort to feel his arms around her, to remember the feel of his strong limbs beneath her fingers, or experience the heat of his longing for her. It *was* a near impossibility to remember what it was like before she knew him. It seemed that her life had only really begun the day she stepped off that stage in front of this dilapidated station, and she was determined it was not going to end now.

She headed toward the barn, walking so swiftly and with such purpose that the swish of her skirts caught Found's attention before she called his name.

"I want you to follow Mr. Barrow," she told him. "You can take any horse you want, but I don't want you to let him out of your sight for one minute. You've lived in these hills and you know them better than he does, so you shouldn't have any trouble making sure he doesn't see you. He'll be furious if he ever finds out I sent you after him. If anything happens, you're to come tell me right away. You're not to wait a minute, do you understand, but come tell me at once."

Found nodded his understanding, and Carrie felt a little better. She might not be able to protect Lucas from the danger that threatened him, but she wouldn't be ignorant of what was happening and unable to help him either. She might be from an old Virginia family, but some of the pioneer spirit was still alive in her veins. Together, she and Lucas would carve a place out of this wilderness for themselves, and if he wouldn't protect himself while he did it, then she would do it for him.

Lucas moved through the birch grove with the stealth of an Indian. He had been unable to hear anything from the canyon rim and was coming up to the gang through the trees that lined the sides of the canyon. He had to be careful not to make any noise that would attract their attention. Jason Staples probably wouldn't kill an unknown wrangler, but Lucas didn't want to stake his life on it. The cover was sparse and grew even more scant as he neared the end of the canyon; he would never have tried this approach except during the dark of night.

There had been no difficulty in finding signs of their presence. The gang had evidently thought itself safe in the canyon and made no attempt to hide the evidence of their activity. And Lucas knew that if he hadn't already known of the hidden canyon, he would have lost their trail on the rocky ledges and sandy patches of ground that led to the mouth of the canyon.

He had already met with his men, and by now they should all be settled into their positions for the next day. He figured Staples would try to stop the stage on a steep incline about seven miles from the station. The stage would have to slow down and there was plenty of cover close up to the road which would make an ambush easy. There was also plenty of cover for Lucas's men, and by being in position before the outlaws arrived, their presence would not be detected.

Lucas reached the edge of the thicket and paused, looking around for some cover he could use to get closer. He could see the fire and the men gathered around it, but he still could not make out what they were saying. He remained perfectly still and stared into the darkness around him. He had had an uneasy feeling from the minute he had come into this canyon that eyes were following his every move, but he had paused to listen every few yards and he had failed to detect a sound. Even a bat makes some sound as it flies through the air, and these men were not bats. In fact, the men around the fire were making an unusual amount of noise. Lucas wasn't concerned with what they might be arguing over, only with getting closer, and after making sure there was nothing in the darkness around him, he sprinted on silent feet for the cover of a large bolder about thirty yards closer to the camp.

He paused a moment to catch his breath and look for his next cover. He could catch some snatches of their conversation, but he had to get even closer if he was going to be able to understand everything they said. He also had to be extremely careful. It was not a dark night and the light from the fire was illuminating some of the shadowy corners of the canyon. He sighted another boulder and was almost in the act of dashing for it when the sound of a familiar voice at the campfire caused him to freeze in his tracks, unfortunately setting his foot squarely on a twig that broke with a loud crack. Brian Kelly was standing at the fire with his back to Lucas. He had to be the one who was leaking the information.

"Mighty thoughtful of you to step on that twig," a voice spoke out of the darkness, a voice that belonged to Jason Staples himself. "Me and the boys have been watching you ever since you got here, but it was right convenient to have your location pinpointed so exactly. Now you rise up and come out from behind that rock. And if you're thinking about going for your gun, you just look around." Lucas did, and he could see at least two other men not counting the men at the fire who had stopped talking and were now looking in his direction. Lucas didn't have any choice. This was no time to attempt to escape.

"You don't seem to have left me any choice, Staples," Lucas said as he stepped from behind the rock.

"Naw. I don't like people having choices," Jason said, coming closer to Lucas. "It tends to make things a mite too complicated." He motioned Lucas toward the fire with his gun, and they moved as a group toward the light.

"Good evening, Brian," Lucas said when he approached the young man, who was obviously horrified to come face to face with the owner of the company he had just betrayed. "I see they've captured you too."

Jason shouted with laughter. "You might say gold fever captured him."

"Apparently it captured you as well," Lucas said to Jason.

"I've got it terrible bad," Staples said with a bark of a

352

laugh. "So bad I'm going to take that gold off your stage tomorrow."

Lucas was thinking rapidly. Brian had obviously told Staples about Lucas's presence, had probably even trailed him out to the canyon, and that meant he knew about the men stationed along the road. Now they were useless to Lucas and to the stage. "And I suppose you invited me here because, knowing where the gold is, I can get it more easily for you."

Jason laughed again. "I like a man with a sense of humor, especially a man who's about to die."

"I doubt that," Lucas said, gambling for time. "You may get several thousand dollars from that gold shipment, but you can get a whole lot more for me."

"What do you mean, several thousands," Jason demanded suspiciously. "There's over a hundred thousand on that stage."

"We divided it up," Lucas said. "We didn't dare risk the loss of a whole shipment again. I don't precisely know what part of it is on this stage, but it's not more than fifteen or twenty thousand. You can get much more by holding me for ransom."

"You lied to me," Jason bellowed, grabbing Brian by the throat before he hit him. "You said they'd be over a hundred thousand in that shipment."

"He had no way of knowing my uncle changed his plans," Lucas said, not wanting Jason to beat Brian too badly. Right now Brian looked like his only chance for escape, and he didn't want to lose it. "It was done at the last minute."

"Where's the rest of it?"

"I don't even know myself, but I think most of it has gone through already."

Jason was furious, dangerously so. He hammered Brian again, sending him to the ground unconscious, then kicked him viciously in the side. From the sickening crack of impact, Lucas guessed he broke several ribs.

"I ought to kill you right now," Staples roared at Lucas, pointing the gun right at his forehead.

"It won't make you one penny richer," Lucas said, knowing that remaining calm and outthinking Staples was his only chance. "I might be worth a great deal to you alive, but I'm worthless dead."

"Tie him up," Jason shouted to one of his men. "Watch that sneaking liar while I'm gone and don't let him leave," he said, pointing at Brian. "I've got plans for him when we get back."

"You're leaving?" Lucas asked. The stage didn't come through until tomorrow. Why would he be leaving now?

"Of course I'm leaving," Jason growled, and backhanded Lucas across the face. "Kelly here told me who you were, and he told me it's you who's been running the company for some time now—"

"He's wrong there."

"—so I figure you've got something planned besides those men you've got sitting out in the bushes. While I'd like to stay and beat it out of you, I can't wait that long. Get mounted up," he shouted to his men. "We're riding out in fifteen minutes. And take your bedrolls. We're not coming back." His men grumbled, but minutes later they had mounted up and ridden out, leaving a very unpleasant-looking man to guard Lucas.

"I'm pulling my bed in the shadows so I can get some shuteye," the man said sullenly. "I don't want no talking, and if you leave the fire, you get lead in you," he said to Brian, but Lucas figured Brian was still unconscious.

The hours passed slowly and Lucas had plenty of time to think of Carrie and his promise that nothing would happen to him. But how was he to have guessed Brian Kelly was the informant, or that Brian would come to the station at the very time he was setting out to spy on Staples in the hidden canyon? And there *was* over one hundred thousand dollars in gold on that stage. His uncle had talked about dividing it up into several shipments, but they had decided it would expose too many passengers to danger. Instead they had hired extra guards, and Lucas had volunteered to find Staples and set a trap for him. Now thanks to Brian somehow learning his identity, it had all come undone.

Try as he might, Lucas could not keep his thoughts from straying to Carrie. He never doubted that he would find some way out of this tangle, but neither could he entirely banish the fear that he would never see Carrie again, and all night long he was tortured by memories of the kind of love he had just begun to experience and might never enjoy again. It was pure agony, and he forced himself to rework his plans for escape again and again. But he could not keep his fears buried in his subconscious, and they emerged like dark phantoms to rob him of any measure of peace.

He was tantalized by the taste of her mouth, the feel of her lips, the texture of her skin against his cheek. He could see her copper curls, rioting against the pillow and glowing in the lantern light like a living thing, the almost black brows which could rise so imperiously in question or gather ever so slightly to underscore the provocative invitation of her dark blue eyes. He could see just as plainly as if she were at his side, the delicate upturned nose or the pucker of her full lips, her lower lip pushed forward in thought or in a pout, could remember the smell of lavender, a scent he had come to associate with her alone. And her body! Oh God, how the thought of her warm body in his arms tormented him. More than once during the night his limbs grew tense with desire and his groin swelled from an unrelieved craving to sink deep into her warm, inviting flesh. He could feel her skin against his, could almost reach out and touch her breasts, kiss their throbbing peaks, nestle his face against the column of her neck. Stifling a curse, Lucas struggled with the ropes that bound him until they cut into his flesh, and one kind of pain gave him relief from the other.

* * *

"Don't answer me, just listen," Lucas whispered to Brian when he was sure he was awake. "You've got to help me get out of here."

"You're crazy," Brian muttered through his bloody, bruised lips. "They'll kill me."

"They'll kill you anyway. You're not one of them, you never will be, and you've given them bad information. There's less than fifteen thousand dollars on that stage. The rest is already safely in Denver."

"But how? Why?" Lucas could tell that Brian was scared. If he could make him a little more scared, maybe he would help him.

"We knew someone in the organization was leaking information, so my uncle made the changes without telling anybody. Not even the drivers knew until the gold was loaded. So instead of more than fifteen thousand each, they're going to get less than three thousand. You can guess how Staples is going to like that. And we know where the first gold shipment is hidden," Lucas said, suddenly realizing where Found had gotten the gold they had discovered in his pouch. "It'll be gone before Staples goes back for it."

"You can't know that," Brian stammered, aghast that their plans could be falling apart so completely.

"It's in the cave behind the cabin," Lucas said, and could tell from the terrified look in Brian's eyes that he had hit the bull's eye.

"Quiet down there," the guard shouted from the shadows. "Any more whispering, and I'll start putting bullet holes in your feet."

"Help me get away, and I'll see that you're protected," Lucas hissed as quietly as he could. "Stay here, and Jason will surely kill you." He didn't dare try the guard's patience any further, but he saw that he had said enough to make Brian think for the first time that his life was truly in jeopardy. And as the minutes passed, Lucas could see from the

356

look in his face he was becoming more convinced. Now all he had to do was think up a plan before morning and make sure Brian was able to carry out his part.

Chapter 25

It was still dark outside the station, but Katie had the fires going and the delicious aromas of coffee and frying bacon filled the station. With an audible sigh of relief, Carrie took her first sip of coffee. She had been unable to sleep at all, and her head throbbed painfully. All night long she had been plagued by visions of Lucas captured and tortured, Lucas shot full of holes, Lucas bleeding and left to die, Lucas's body left undiscovered in some remote canyon to be desecrated by buzzards and wild animals. She couldn't stand it, and she meant to tell Lucas if he ever wanted to marry her, he was going to have to swear not to go after a gang of murdering thieves by himself. And all these men stationed along the road weren't going to be able to do him a bit of good when they weren't close enough to know he was in trouble.

"You're looking right poorly this morning, ma'am," Katie said as she observed Carrie from her position at the stove.

"I don't think I'm cut out to be a frontier woman," Carrie admitted. "It's just as well Lucas is taking me to live in Denver. I couldn't stand his going off like this. I guess it was something like this for Mama when Daddy and the boys left for the War, but you didn't know what they were facing each day, and they were gone so long with no word that it was almost like nothing was really happening. But I know exactly what Lucas is up against, and I'm petrified."

"Mr. Barrow will be all right," Katie tried to assure her. "I never knew any man better able to take care of himself."

"But there are eight men in that gang," Carrie told her. "And he didn't have to go by himself. He has lots of men out there who could have helped him, but he insisted upon going to that camp alone."

"Then I'm sure he had a good reason for it," Katie said, so serenely confident in Lucas's ability to do anything he wanted that she irritated Carrie.

"Well, he didn't have things entirely his own way," Carrie said, piqued. "I had Found follow him."

"You sent that child into those hills by himself?"

"That *child* lived in those hills by himself for months. He knows them better than Lucas ever will. Besides, no one would think anything if they saw him. Lucas would attract attention immediately."

"I guess you're right, but Mr. Barrow is going to be right angry when he finds out what you've done."

"As long as he gets back safely, he can be as angry as he wants," Carrie said. "And if he ever thinks about going after crooks by himself again, I'll dope his coffee and tie him up."

"You'll do what every woman has done who was old enough to have a husband or a son facing danger. You'll sit at home and wring your hands. Then when he gets back, you'll assure him that you expected his safe return all along. Women have been doing it for their menfolk for ages, and nothing's going to change that now."

Carrie heaved herself out of her chair—she had to help Katie with the cooking—depressingly aware that every word Katie had said was true. She swore silently. It wasn't fair for love to cause such agonies. It was supposed to be the most wonderful thing that could happen to a woman, yet from the moment she fell in love, she had oscillated with dizzying speed between the peaks of delirium and the depths of despair.

But the stage was due in at ten o'clock, and before long Carrie's thoughts were absorbed in her work; thus she was caught unprepared thirty minutes later when Found came stumbling through the door, his face immediately telling her that something was very wrong with Lucas.

He began gesturing with his hands, shaping words with his mouth, but his actions were so frenzied that Carrie was unable to understand anything of what he was trying to tell her.

"Has something happened to Lucas?" she demanded, grabbing him by the shoulders and forcing him to remain still while she spoke to him. Found nodded and Carrie's heart sank. "Is he hurt?" Found shook his head and Carrie started to breath again. "But he is in trouble and needs help, doesn't he?" Again Found nodded. "Where is he? Can you take me to him?" Found shook his head. "Why can't you?" Found began making gestures and mouthing words again. "I can't understand you," Carrie cried frantically. Found tried to draw pictures in the air and trace them on the table, but Carrie's terrified mind could understand nothing and she grew more frantic by the minute. "You've got to take me to him." Again Found shook his head. "Why can't you?" Carrie demanded, her voice rising hysterically. "Speak to me. *Tell* me why I can't go to him." She shook the child so violently that Katie had started to his rescue when he uttered his first broken sentence.

"S-Staples men . . . t-too many . . . Mr. Barrow is t-tied up." Found stumbled over his first words, as though they were having difficulty opening a passageway that had long been blocked, and then they poured out of him like a long-damned-up stream. "Miss Katie's man is one of them," Found said, throwing Katie an accusing glare. "He told Staples who Mr. Barrow was, and they were waiting for him."

"I knew Brian was up to no good," declared Katie. "I knew it the minute I set eyes on him."

"But he's not hurt?"

"No. He told them he was worth more for ransom than dead, but he also told them the gold was mostly already sent on other stages, and that made Jason awfully mad. And Mrs. Simpson, Jason is terrible when he gets mad. I know because he killed my stepfather."

"So that's why you lived wild."

"I was afraid he would kill me too. I knew too much. I know where he hid the gold."

"Can you lead us back to that canyon?" Carrie asked, totally uninterested in the whereabouts of the gold.

"There are too many of them. And Jason will kill anybody who gets in his way."

"We won't be going alone. Mr. Barrow has some men stationed along the road between here and Tyler's Mountain. I'm going to send Jake after them. Katie, you go back to the cabin and gather any weapons and ammunition you can find. Found, you tell Jake to saddle a horse as quickly as he can. And bring all his rifles back here. We're going to need all the weapons we can find."

Everyone scattered to their assigned tasks, and Carrie turned to emptying out the gun racks and laying out the weapons in preparation for cleaning and loading. The ammunition was stored under the beds in the back rooms, but she wouldn't need to get that out until later. She figured she had an hour before Jake could return with the men.

She tried to concentrate on what she was doing to drive all thought of what might be happening to Lucas from her thoughts. All night long she had imagined what might happen to him, but she had been able to tell herself she was imagining things, that Lucas said he would be safe and she had to have faith in him. Now she *knew* he was in danger, and only by concentrating fiercely on taking the guns apart and cleaning each part carefully was she able to keep the images out of her mind. Because her concentration was so intense, she was nearly frightened out of her mind when a strange voice suddenly spoke her name.

"Are you Mrs. Simpson?" the voice asked.

Carrie looked up into the coldest pair of blue eyes she had ever seen. The man was dressed respectably enough, but she knew he had not come on the stage and she had heard no horse.

"Who are you?" she asked, rising to her feet and instinctively stepping behind her chair. "I didn't hear anyone ride up," she said, trying to cover her confusion, trying to buy time to think.

"I walked," the man said, but Carrie involuntarily glanced down at his high-heeled boots and knew he hadn't walked very far.

"My horse picked up a rock in his shoe," he explained, not missing her swift glance. "I got it out, but I was hoping I might rest here a spell."

"You're welcome to sit for a while," Carrie said, knowing that no matter how much she wanted to, she couldn't turn him away, "but you can't stay here. We don't have overnight accommodations."

"I meant just long enough to have a cup of coffee and maybe a piece of pie. You expecting trouble?" he asked, noticing all the broken-down pieces of rifles.

"I wouldn't have taken them apart if I were, would I?" Carrie responded, trying to be just as cool as this stranger. She had a terrible suspicion she knew who he was, but she wouldn't even allow herself to admit that the possibility existed.

"Most likely not. You don't strike me as a slow-witted female. Must be a sluggish morning. Doesn't seem to be anybody around."

"They're around, but not here. The stage isn't due for several hours yet." That was true, and never had she wished more strongly to see Bap, Harry, or even Jerry getting down from the driver's seat. This man made her nervous, and she had decided she didn't like him. She cut the pie and set it down in front of him, but he didn't sit down. He just stood there, waiting.

"I'll get your coffee. You can sit down unless your saddle has given you a dislike of chairs."

"It's not that, ma'am," the stranger said, and a brief smile crossed his face. He's not bad-looking when he smiles, Carrie thought, but I still don't like him. I wish Jake would

362

hurry up and get here. She had just picked up a cup and the coffee pot when the sound of running feet attracted her attention, and a moment later the station door burst open.

Found flew into the room followed a few seconds later by Baca Riggins. "That's Jason Staples," Found shouted between gasping breaths. "They've got Katie and Jake tied up in the barn." Staples had turned at the sound of running feet, but before he could move out of the way, Found plowed straight into him, using his head to butt Jason hard enough to send him to the floor.

"Quick, out the back," Carrie said. She picked up a rifle stock and struck Baca a powerful blow across the back when he tried to follow Found. "You've got to find help," she hissed, ignoring Baca's slumping body and Jason's shouted curses. Jason recovered quickly enough to get between Found and the door, but the boy dashed into the back of the station and Carrie knew he would be out one of the windows and into the woods before either Jason or Baca could reach him. A couple of shots fired behind the station frightened her, but she could tell from the curses that followed they had missed and that Found was safely into the brush. Once there, no one could find him unless he wanted to be found. Now it was a question of whether he could find help and bring it in time. Carrie wondered if it would do any good. They were all helpless.

Carrie snatched up the piece of pie and flung it at Jason. "That's for your horse with the bruised foot," she said furiously.

"You knew who I was?" Jason asked, as he started to walk slowly in her direction.

"If I hadn't, I would have known from the company you keep that you were a liar and a thief."

Jason's jaw tightened angrily, but all he said was, "We've come for the gold."

"I don't have any gold, and I don't know anything about it," Carrie said, backing up and keeping the table or a chair between herself and Staples.

"I didn't expect you would. No man would entrust such important information to a woman."

Carrie vowed she would repay him for that comment before this day was done, but first she had to figure out how to get away from him. "Why are you here?"

"I told you. For the gold."

"But—"

"You thought I would try to stop the stage somewhere on the trail?" Carrie nodded automatically. "So, I hope, did Lucas Barrow. But whatever he had planned for us, we'll be long gone before that kid can find help for you or for Lucas."

"Where is Lucas?" Carrie asked, trying to show as little interest as possible.

"He's safe enough. I'll sell him to his own company if I can. Otherwise . . ." He left the sentence unfinished, but Carrie didn't need words to know what he meant. They continued to circle the table.

"Why don't you sit down?" Carrie said. "Your coffee's growing cold."

"I might, if you'll sit down with me."

"I'd rather not."

"You can't get away. My men are everywhere."

"I'd still rather not." He made a grab for her, but Carrie easily skipped out of his reach. Carrie wondered how long they would remain circling when Baca Riggins began to stir. It was only a matter of moments before Baca collected his wits enough to see what was happening, and he moved to cut off Carrie's retreat. In desperation, Carrie snatched up the coffee pot and threw its still steaming contents at him. Some of the coffee hit him full in the face while the rest soaked through his clothes to his skin. Ignoring Baca's screams of agony, Jason leapt for Carrie, but she escaped around the side of the table and was able to snatch up one of the knives they used for cutting bacon.

"Ma'am, I don't generally hold with hurting females, but I can tell you I won't take kindly to being cut with no knife."

364

"And I can tell *you* I don't take kindly to having my station invaded, my employees bound up, and my own self threatened." Jason ran after Carrie, not stopping when she managed to stay out of his reach, but Carrie's eyes were on Jason and she failed to see that Baca, staggering around as he tried to wipe the coffee from his face and pull off his shirt at the same time, had backed into her path, and they collided. She lost her balance, and in that moment Jason was on her in a flash, pinning her hand to the table and easily removing the knife from her grasp.

"I'll feel safer with it over there," he said as he tossed it into the sink they used to wash dishes.

"What are you going to do with me and the others?"

"You ought to let me have her," Baca raged, the pain from the burns inflaming his mind. "I'd teach the bitch a lesson."

"I admire her spunk," Jason said. "She's certainly worth a dozen of you."

"I don't take talk like that from any man," Baca roared.

"You'll take it from me," Jason said as he twisted Carrie's arms behind her back and stilled her vain struggles to escape. "I only let you come along because I thought your hatred might be useful. Be careful I don't change my mind. Now why don't you go see if they've found that boy. I don't think he'll have time to bring help before the stage gets here, but it's always wise to be sure."

"I'm not done with you," Baca growled at Carrie as he turned to leave. "I've got two scores to settle with you now."

"You come back in here, and you'll have three," Carrie shot back, and Baca left the station with the sound of Jason's laughter ringing in his ears.

"As much as I enjoy your company, I'm going to have to find someplace to store you while I wait," Jason said to Carrie as he looked around the room for a likely place. "Something tells me the rooms at the back of the station would not be a good choice." His eye caught the pantry door, and he dragged Carrie across the room, pulled open the door, and looked in. The pantry was a small room with no windows and walls covered with shelves lined with food. There was no escape except through the one door. "This will have to do," Jason said, and roughly pushed Carrie into the closet and closed the door. It was dark inside and she had no weapons; Carrie knew she was locked in until someone decided to let her out.

Dawn was breaking and Lucas knew if he was going to get Brian to help him, it had to be before the outlaw woke up. He had watched the young man carefully for the last hour and he was sure Brian recognized the danger of his position, but he wasn't sure how willing he was to go against a man like Jason Staples.

Brian looked up at the sky and realized that morning was only a short time away; that seemed to help him make up his mind to do something. He rose slowly from where he had lain all night, his body still stiff from Jason's kick and his handsome face covered with ugly bruises. Moving carefully to avoid making any noise, he knelt behind Lucas.

"I've been trying to figure what Jason would do," he said as he struggled with the knots, "and I think you'd better get to the station. I think it's just his style to hold one of those women. I also think he'll kill you, whether the company pays a ransom or not."

"What the hell!" exclaimed the outlaw, brought out of a light sleep by Brian's whispers. "Get away from there."

"Don't!" Lucas shouted as Brian went for a gun inside his coat. The words had hardly left his mouth before flame blossomed from the outlaw's gun and Brian staggered and fell. Almost immediately two more shots rent the air and the outlaw twisted sickeningly in the air and sank back to his bedroll. He didn't move again. Stunned, Lucas looked up to see Found come running from the cover of the same boulder he had used the previous night. He was followed by Sam Butler.

"Where did you spring from?" Lucas asked as Found finished untying his hands.

"This one will live," Sam said, looking up from a brief examination of Brian's wound. "The other one won't, but we ain't got time to jaw. The boy tells me Staple's gang has taken over the station. And if I know anything of Staples, he means to hold those women hostage. That Mrs. Simpson is a mighty fine woman, and I don't aim to see her mishandled by the likes of Jason Staples."

"Neither do I, but he's got six men with him and we're only two. Look, I've got ten men stationed along the trail to Tyler's Mountain. The first one is at the crossroads after you go down Black Mountain. We have a signal set up to draw them all back to the station in case something goes wrong. We have another for danger. The man at the crossroads is named Bill Cody. I want you to go find him and tell him to start the signal relay. Then you two hightail it for the station. Each man down the line will know to give the signal before he leaves his position." Lucas took a pencil and a piece of paper out of his pocket and scribbled a short note. "Here. This will convince Bill you're working with me. What's your interest in this?" Lucas asked as he stamped his feet hard to get the circulation going again.

"Mrs. Simpson befriended me. I was just about to get my neck stretched for something I didn't do. She actually got the posse off my tail and made me stay put until my leg healed up. You can ask the boy for the details on the way back."

"He doesn't talk," Lucas said, buckling on his guns. Found was bringing up the horses.

"He does now. Fair talked my ear off coming out here," Sam said. A groan drew Lucas's attention to Brian, and he knelt down beside him.

"Sam says you'll be okay. I'll send someone to take care of you as soon as I can."

"Just leave me my horse. I'll make it on my own." He paused a moment, then looked Lucas full in the face. "I know I made a mistake," he said, struggling to sit up on his elbow. "I wanted money for my own ranch, and I knew I'd never get it working as a clerk. Katie was right not to marry me. She knew I hadn't changed."

"You can enjoy feeling sorry for yourself some other time, young fella," Sam Butler said unsympathetically. "We've got some women to rescue, and your Katie is one of them."

"Be careful. Jason will kill anybody, even a woman."

Locked in the pantry and cut off from all knowledge of what was happening around her, Carrie felt time pass with agonizing slowness, but she knew she hadn't been there long when she heard someone enter the station. The footsteps went to several parts of the room as though someone were checking all the windows, then after a slight hesitation they came toward the closet. Carrie's body stiffened in anticipation, fearful of what was about to happen. She heard the latch lift, and then the door was carefully opened. Baca Riggins's ugly face stared at Carrie through the opening.

"What are you doing here?" Carrie demanded, determined not to show her fear.

"I've got a score to settle with you, lady, and I got a dandy idea of how to do it." He reached in to grab Carrie and pull her out, but she drew back, and reaching up to one of the shelves behind her head, she heaved a can of peaches at him. Baca ducked and the can sailed across the room, but Carrie threw a second before he could duck again and had the satisfaction of seeing a bright red mark appear across his face where the can had grazed his forehead.

"I'll kill you," Baca roared, and dived into the closet after Carrie. He grabbed one arm, but she brought another can of peaches crashing down on his skull with her free hand. When he grabbed both hands, she kicked him in the shins as hard as she could. Baca howled in agony and threw Carrie halfway across the room. He was on her before she could regain her feet.

"I swore I'd get even with you and Lucas," he said, dragging her toward the doorway that led to the back of the inn. "And when I get my fill of you, I'm going to beat your face to a pulp. Won't Lucas nor anybody ever want to make up to you again."

"You're nothing but a sneak and a coward," Carrie shot back, digging her heels in as he dragged her toward the back rooms. "You ran from Lucas and you ran from Staples, then you come sneaking behind their back to revenge yourself on a mere woman." Scorn dripped from her words and burned deep into Baca's pride.

"Shut up before I beat you right now," he raged.

"It's a poor man who runs from words," Carrie said, and suddenly spat into his face. Baca struck at her, but Carrie dodged his blow and bit hard into the fingers that held her prisoner. Involuntary reaction made Baca release his hold, and seeing the flour she had measured out earlier for the biscuits, Carrie threw it full in his face. Baca's eyes and mouth were filled with the choking flour dust and Carrie used the brief respite to get the long table between them.

"You damned hellion," Baca roared, and drew his gun just as Staples threw open the door. In a lightning draw Carrie would not have believed if she hadn't seen it, Staples drew and fired before Baca could squeeze the trigger. Baca's gun flew across the room and he grabbed at his arm. Carrie could see the blood welling up from a deep crease in his forearm.

"You're lucky I didn't kill you," said Staples, "but the stage is coming, and I need every gun I can muster."

Carrie had almost forgotten about the stage. Bap would be driving today, and he was driving into an ambush he didn't expect. He wouldn't have heard the muffled gunshot inside the station and would probably be killed if Carrie didn't do something to warn him. Making a desperate lunge, Carrie grabbed the rifle Baca had laid down on the table, and running to the window, fired two rapid shots through the panes. They were immediately answered by

369

several shots from the men Jason had hidden around the station. Carrie's body sagged with relief; the stage was warned it was headed for trouble.

"Only a stupid fool like you would leave a rifle lying around where she could get at it," Jason swore at Baca as he snatched the rifle from Carrie and threw her into the closet once more. "Get to the window. They know we're here now. There's going to be hell to pay before we get that gold."

Chapter 26

Sam pulled up at the crossroads. The trail was empty and there was no sign of Lucas's men. "My name's Sam Butler," he shouted into the surrounding hills, "and I've got a message for Bill Cody from Lucas Barrow." When nothing but silence greeted his call, he tried again. "Staples has changed his plans, and every man on the trail is needed at the Green Run station."

"How do I know you're not one of Staples's men?" a voice called, surprisingly close to Sam.

"If you know me, you know I have no truck with killers. Besides, I've got a note here in Lucas's hand." Still only silence. "I can't wait long. There's women at that station. If you're not coming now, we'll do it without you, and you can just head on back to Denver."

A tall blond man emerged from the brush at the roadside, his rifle aimed at Sam's heart. "Drop that note and ride off a piece with your back to me." Sam complied, and the man picked up the note without taking his eyes off Sam. "Turn around," he said a moment later. "What's the message?"

"Staples is waiting for the gold at the station. We're pretty sure he's holding everybody there hostage, and that includes two women. You're to give the signal that will bring the rest of your boys to the station pronto. You and me are to go on ahead. The shooting will warn them to keep their heads down."

371

"Why isn't Lucas here?" asked Bill as a sharp whistle brought his horse loping out of the brush.

"He went ahead to see about liberating the little lady who runs the place. He just asked her to marry him."

Bill gave a long, low whistle as he climbed into the saddle. "I wouldn't be in Staples's shoes right now for all the gold in Colorado." He fired three evenly spaced shots from his rifle, and then followed it with two very quick shots. "That'll bring the rest of them," he said, putting his spurs into his horse's side. "Let's go."

Sam was already three jumps ahead of him.

"There's no use for you looking to me to save you," Jake said irritably to Katie. "I'll be hard-pressed to figure a way to keep from having my own hide hung up on the barn door."

"Why should I be looking to the likes of you for help?" Katie inquired, her eyes flashing derisively. "To be sure it would take a man like Mr. Barrow to handle those ruffians. You do be a dreadful poor example of the breed when set next to him."

"You don't look so wonderful yourself compared to Mrs. Simpson," Jake shot back. "That woman would have us out of here in a jiffy."

"*That woman* wouldn't need to. Mr. Barrow would do it for her."

"You two shut up your arguing. You been at it tooth and toenail most of the night, and I'm sick of it."

"Why should I be caring what the likes of you be sick of," Katie asked him impudently. "Any one of me five brothers could whip you whilst they be drunk." The man glowered at Katie then turned back to watch the yard. "I could whip you meself if you weren't such a coward as to come at me from behind and then truss me up like a Christmas goose. 'Tis a poor example of menfolks you be."

"I said shut up before I make you," the man yelled, losing his temper at Katie's baiting.

"Ye might as well go casting at the moon as to try to shut me up," Katie said, her glance clearly challenging him. " 'Tis a task you're not man enough to handle."

"We'll just see about that," the man said, rising from his crouched position and heading back to where Katie and Jake were trussed up across from each other in one of the horse stalls.

"It won't hurt nothing to let them talk, Sully," his companion advised without taking his eyes from the road down which the stage would come. "A sharp tongue never cut no ropes."

"That Irish setting hen is getting on my nerves. My bandanna in her mouth ought to quieten things a bit."

Katie struggled to get out of reach and then to dodge Sully when he leaned around her to put the bandanna in her mouth. While his back was turned, Jake shook off the ropes Katie had worked loose during the night and threw himself at Sully. The sounds of a tussle drew the attention of the man at the window, and he turned around to see Jake and Sully rolling over in the hay, Jake's hands on Sully's throat. He hurried across the stable to help his companion, unaware that Katie had scrambled into the adjacent stall and stood waiting for him, a large shovel poised over her head. When he drew his gun and aimed, waiting for Jake's back to be to him, Katie brought the shovel down on his head with such force it left an impression in the metal. The man slumped to the floor and Katie scooped up his rifle and took his guns. Just about then Jake rolled over and banged Sully's head into the six-by-six post at the end of the stall divider and he, too, subsided into oblivion.

The sound of shots from outside drew their attention. "Let's get them tied up," Jake said as he began dragging Sully over to one of the twelve-inch support beams in order to tie his feet and legs around it. "It sounds like the stage is coming in. I didn't do too bad," he said after the men were safely secured to the poles.

"I suspect you might turn out to be rather respectable as long as you had a good woman to keep your nose to it," Katie said as she picked up a rifle and hurried to one of the windows.

"A man never has to wonder why you left Ireland," Jake fumed. "They chased you out."

"I came here to get away from drunkards and braggarts," Katie said. "From what I've seen, I was better off where I was."

"It's for damned sure *we* were," Jake snapped. He picked up a rifle and prepared to take out his frustration on the outlaws.

The repeated shots from inside the station told Carrie that the stage had reached the yard. She rattled the door as hard as she could, but the latch was caught. If she could just figure some way to open the door. Baca and Staples would be too busy shooting to pay any attention to her, and she might be able to get away. But she could think of nothing she could wedge between the door and the frame that was strong enough to lift the latch on the other side.

Suddenly she remembered a set of knives she had bought and stored in the pantry, but her hopes fell just as quickly. The knives couldn't turn the right angle either. If there were just some way to remove the door jamb. The knives! Maybe she could pry the door jamb loose with the knives. Carrie felt around in the dark until she found the box. She opened it and carefully felt for one of the knives. The blades were thin and not very strong and she didn't know if they would work. She inserted one knife between the door jamb and the frame and pulled. Nothing happened, so she pulled harder. The knife blade snapped. The sound was lost in the noise of the rifle shots, and Carrie shoved the second knife into the slot, but it, too, broke when she applied pressure.

Carrie tried not to lose her head. She had only one more knife, and she had to make this one work. The first two knives had made a thin slot in the door jamb, and she pushed the knife in all the way up to the hilt. She was sure the blade must be showing outside the door and hoped neither Baca or Staples would turn around. Gradually she applied pressure, keeping the pressure on the thick part of the knife and the knife handle. Carrie felt a sudden snap and thought the last knife had broken, but she was relieved to discover that the wood had parted from the frame and she would work her knife up under the latch.

In seconds she had the door open, but what should she do next? The knife was still in her hands, but she didn't think she could use it. Just the thought of driving it into living flesh made her queasy. She felt about in the closet and her hands closed around one of the Smithfield hams she had brought with her. It was hard as a rock. If she could just sneak up behind Staples, she might be able to hit him hard enough to knock him out. She didn't know what she would do about Baca Riggins, but she would think about that when she had to.

Carrie eased open the door, and the first thing that came into her line of vision was one of the windows at the back of the station; what she saw at that window literally took her breath away. Lucas had raised the window and was climbing into the room. And he had a gun pointed at the backs of the two men at the front windows.

For a moment Carrie was too weak with relief to move. Lucas was safe! Lucas was here! He had come after her. Then she realized he was trying to capture two men separated by about twelve feet, each of them armed and each of them willing to shoot to kill. She must take out one of the men, and Jason was the one nearest her.

Praying the hinges would not squeak, Carrie threw open the pantry door to attract Lucas's attention. It worked, and for a split second Carrie thought Lucas was going to shoot *her,* but he recognized her in time to release the pressure on the trigger. Pausing only a second to recover her wits and her strength — seeing the gun swing in her direction had left her as weak as water — she motioned toward Jason and raised the ham over her head to indicate what she meant to do. Lucas understood at once, and together they each approached their victim, each of them painfully aware that if either of the outlaws turned around too soon, someone was likely to die.

Oddly enough, it was Baca who sensed that something was wrong and turned to see the pantry door ajar and Carrie approaching Jason with the raised ham. He swung his rifle around and opened his mouth to call to Jason at the same time, but a blast from the barrel of Lucas's gun sent a bullet deep into his shoulder. Baca's rifle fell from his grasp, but even as he screamed with pain, he reached for it again.

Jason Staples whirled at the sound of Baca's scream. Unfortunately for him, the direction of his turn brought him directly into the path of Carrie's Smithfield ham, and she sent him sprawling. Carrie saw Jason reach for the gun in his holster even as he fell, and then she saw Lucas dive on top of the outlaw leader. Fearful for Lucas's safety, she picked up Jason's dropped rifle, aimed a shot at Baca's rifle, which sent it spinning out of reach, and then turned her weapon on Baca himself.

"I'm a little upset right now. I don't know much about a rifle and my nerves aren't too steady, so if you don't want a bullet in your heart, you won't move an inch."

Carrie couldn't keep her eyes off the two men rolling on the floor, especially since she saw that Jason had somehow gotten a knife in his hands. Lucas didn't weigh as much as the outlaw and Jason was using his weight to his advantage, but Lucas was stronger and more agile, and after a terrific struggle, he was able to knock the knife from Jason's hand. It slid in Baca's direction, and he was unwise enough to reach for it. A blast from Carrie's rifle put a bullet into the floor next to the knife and raised a shower of splinters that embedded themselves into the soft flesh of Baca's palm. His hand looked like the back of a porcupine.

"I've about lost patience with your stupidity," Carrie said to Baca, who stared at her in stunned surprise. "Next time I'll shoot you instead of the floor." Baca had had sufficient proof of Carrie's marksmanship and nerve, and he sank back against the wall.

Meanwhile, Lucas had succeeded in getting atop Jason

and he was able to rap his head sharply against the floor. Lucas drove his fist into the jaw of the momentarily dazed outlaw, and before Jason could recover himself, Carrie placed the barrel end of her rifle against his forehead.

"Don't move," Carrie said, anger flooding over her now that Lucas was no longer in danger. "After what you've done to my station and my people, I just might kill you."

"I wouldn't think of it," Jason said, accepting his defeat with amazing calmness. "I always thought you were more of a man than Baca."

"Listen!" Lucas said, and Carrie realized that it was quiet outside. "The fighting's stopped." The door burst open, and Sam Butler and Bill Cody rushed in, guns drawn ready to fire.

"I should have known it," Sam said when he saw Jason Staples lying at Carrie's feet. "If she could beat a whole posse to flinders, I don't know why I thought she would have any trouble with one no-account outlaw."

"You two all right?" Bill asked Lucas. "This place looks a wreck." Carrie hadn't had time to notice, but the cans of fruit, the spilled coffee, flour, and Baca's blood along with fallen chairs and shattered windowpanes and tattered curtains had turned the model dining room into a total disaster.

"We're okay," Carrie assured him with a smile. "This place will fix up a lot easier than either of us would."

"Get to your feet, both of you," Lucas ordered. "You've got a long ride ahead."

"Baca, you should have taken your beating and run," Sam Butler said to the sullen ex-station manager. "When you joined up with Jason Staples, you bought into his troubles. But then you always were a stupid man."

Jason and Baca were herded out into the station yard, and Carrie saw men converging on the station from several points around the property, several of them with captured outlaws walking before them. She heaved a great sigh of relief when she saw Katie and Jake emerge from the barn, but her relief was short-lived. Jake was wounded and leaning on

Katie and Found for support.

Most surprising of all, the stage was still moving. The reins had been tied so that the horses had to always turn to the right, and it had been going in a huge circle about the yard all during the fight.

"That was a right neat trick," Sam said, noticing the direction of her glance. "As long as the stage kept moving, none of the outlaws had a chance to jump aboard, and your men yonder had themselves a shot at every outlaw each time that stage went around. You got yourself some crew here."

"It's Lucas's crew. I can't take any credit for anyone but Katie and Jake."

"And yourself," Lucas said, unable to conceal his pride. "You're not a bad player to have on one's side."

"I can tell you she's a damned fierce customer as an enemy," Sam observed. "I heard you was fixing to marry her."

"You heard correctly," Lucas said, putting his arm around Carrie and pulling her to him. "Just as soon as we can get these men into town. I'm told there's a preacher in Fort Malone with lots of time on his hands, and I intend to claim a few minutes of it."

"You'd better not get itchy feet. That's the wrong woman to step out on."

"I know gold when I see it," Lucas said, "and I can assure you this is the real thing."

Carrie turned her head away, embarrassed by the compliments in front of so many people and saw Bap's head slowly come into view at one of the stage windows.

"Is anybody going to stop those fool horses, or do I have to risk my neck climbing up to the box?"

"You just hold on," Jake said, suddenly acting a lot less decrepit. "You might fall off, and I wouldn't want the stage to run over you." When Bap's features took on an air of self-importance, he added, "One of the horses might break a leg, and it would be a shame to lose a good animal."

* * *

An hour later, the stage had been sent on its way to Denver. Brian had staggered in with the body of the dead outlaw, and Lucas's men had taken him and the whole Staples gang and headed toward Fort Malone. Everyone else was seated around the table in the station. Jake's wound had proved not to be serious, and he was enjoying coffee and a second piece of pie. Katie was scolding him and fussing over Found while Carrie refilled everyone's coffee cup.

"After today I should think you would be ready to move to Denver," Sam said to Carrie. "Things have been a mite busy around here, even for a regular little spitfire like you."

Lucas struggled hard to throttle the jealousy and angry words that threatened to rise out of his throat. For the last thirty minutes he had been forced to sit by and watch Sam stare at Carrie in open-mouthed admiration, showering her with extravagant compliments all the while, and he didn't know how much more he could stand. He had never thought of himself as a jealous man, but after the way he reacted to Duncan's compliments and now Sam, he knew he had misjudged himself. Where Carrie was concerned, he was wildly jealous and unlikely to be able to do anything about it.

"Don't say that," Lucas said, attempting to achieve a light tone. "She's liable to take it as a challenge, and I'll never get her to agree to move to Denver. I'd have to sell my company and be her wrangler for the rest of my life."

"Would you do that for me?" Carrie asked, then cursed herself for asking Lucas such an impossible question in front of all these people.

"Yes, I think I would," he said reluctantly. "I would hate it, and I'd cuss your stubbornness every day of my life, but I'd rather do that than live without you."

"Then it's a good thing I'm planning to go with you to Denver," she said self-consciously, trying to cover her emotion at his answer. "I couldn't have the children growing up listening to all that profanity. The girls would never be taken for ladies."

"Ma'am, any daughter of yours couldn't be anything but

379

a lady," Sam said reverently.

"Damnit, that's enough," Lucas swore, bringing his palm down on the table and turning wrathfully on Sam. "I can't have you, or any other man, giving my wife compliments faster than I can think of them myself."

"Mr. Barrow, I admire Mrs. Simpson more than I can say. She's the first woman I ever met who made me think marrying might not be a worse punishment than hellfire."

"I agree with every word you've said," Lucas said, keeping a tight rein on his temper, "but I'm the only one who can say it. You just get to *think* it."

"That don't hardly seem fair," Sam said, beginning to scowl himself.

"If you was engaged to a woman as good-looking as Mrs. Simpson, would you want some scurvy rascal to come oiling up to her, mouthing pretty phrases and generally making a pest of himself?" Jake asked before Lucas could think of a diplomatic way to say the same thing.

"Hell no," Sam said, bringing *his* hand down on the table. "I'd fill his hide so full of holes they could use it for a sieve."

"There you have it," Jake said, settling back with satisfaction.

"We've got to decide what to do about Found," Carrie said, glad to have a reason to interrupt this conversation.

"His name's Jonathan Blake, the second," Lucas said. "He told me that McCoy was only his stepfather."

"All the same, I think we should adopt him. Would you like to go with us to Denver, Found, I mean Jonathan?" Carrie corrected herself. She was a little disappointed when he didn't immediately accept her offer with enthusiasm. "Don't you want to live with me any longer?"

"It's not that, ma'am," Found muttered, staring at the floor and trying to find words. "It's just, well, you see, I'm . . ."

"I think he's trying to say he'd be more comfortable staying here with us," Katie said.

"Us?" Carrie echoed, turning her startled gaze on a blushing Katie.

380

"Jake and me. He's asked me to marry him."

"Couldn't do much else after she sewed me up twice," Jake said, turning almost as red as Katie. "This gal can be right handy."

"You two wouldn't be wanting to take over Carrie's contract, would you?" Lucas asked, and the guilty looks in their faces caused Lucas and Carrie to go off into shouts of laughter.

"You'll have to talk it over with Duncan, but if my recommendation will help, you've got it."

"And mine, too," added Carrie. "I can't think of anybody I'd rather turn it over to."

"And Found?"

"You can stay here if you like," Carrie said, turning back to the boy. "But we'd be proud to have you come live with us."

"If it won't hurt your feelings, ma'am, I think I'd like to stay here. You've been nicer to me than my own ma," Found hurried on, upset by the injured look in Carrie's eyes, "but I'm not like you. Mr. Lucas made me see that after I ran away." Carrie threw a startled and inquiring look at Lucas. "I know I'm saying it all wrong, ma'am, but I like it here in the mountains, and I like it around horses."

"You don't have to apologize anymore," Carrie said, giving him a big hug. "I understand, and my feelings aren't hurt. But you will come visit us sometime, won't you? I'd like to see you once in a while before you grow to be as tall as Lucas." Found fidgeted and shifted his weight from foot to foot at the thought of anything as wonderful as growing up to be like Lucas.

"Seems to me you have an opening for a wrangler around here," Sam said. "Mind if I try my hand at it for a while?"

"You!" Katie exclaimed.

"Yes, me. Even *scurvy rascals* get the urge to settle down once in a while. I thought I might try something like wrangling. I can still take off after horses, but it'd give me enough sitting time to find out if I like it."

"I'll leave you four to work things out among you," Lucas

said, rising to his feet. "Carrie and I have a lot to talk about, and I don't want any of you rushing out to ask me foolish questions," he said unashamedly pulling Carrie along with him. "I plan to be busy for quite some time."

"Lucas Barrow, how dare you say a thing like that," Carrie demanded as they walked arm and arm toward his cabin. "You practically told them you were taking me to your cabin and didn't want to be disturbed."

"Well, do you want to be disturbed?"

"Of course not, but —"

"No buts. I've had enough of kindhearted outlaws, adorable orphan boys, and dewy-eyed lovers. I want to go someplace where there's nobody but you and me, and I want to hold you in my arms and kiss you until you forget there's anyone else in the whole world."

"What a terribly selfish attitude."

"Isn't it though, and I'm not the least bit ashamed. Now tell me, do you want to spend the rest of the evening listening to Katie and Jake decide what they're going to do with *your* station, or would you rather spend it with me?"

"Do I have to answer that question?"

"Yes, and you have to answer it with a yes," Lucas said, dropping a kiss on the end of her nose. Carrie sighed contentedly and leaned against his strong body as they climbed through the trees to the cabin.

"Would you really have sold your company for me?" she asked, wondering if his answer would change now that they were alone.

"I would have if it were the absolute only way I could get you, but I would have hated it. After having a taste of running the whole company, it would be difficult to work for the manager of a single station."

"How fortunate these last days of posses and outlaws and stage robberies have convinced me I wasn't meant for frontier living."

"Is that the only reason?" Lucas asked.

"No. I decided a while back I would be willing to give up everything here for you. It wasn't worth what I would lose in you. Besides, there must be something I can do in Denver."

Lucas gave a shout of laughter. "Poor Denver, you'll never know what might have been. From now on you'll simply be told what will be."

They stopped along the path where they could see Lucas's cabin and look back at the station below. "No regrets?" Lucas asked.

"Oh no," Carrie answered quickly. "No matter what, I'll never regret choosing you."

Lucas dropped his head toward her upturned face until their lips just touched and they exchanged several feather-light kisses. Then locking their arms about each other's waist, they turned and walked toward the cabin.